Barristers & Bones

Las Vegas House of Spades, Book 1

J. L. Brannick

Trigger Warnings

Welcome to Las Vegas!

Always imbibe responsibly, whether you visit this fictional world or in person. *Barristers & Bones: Las Vegas House of Spades* is a dark romance with black comedy and elements of torture set in Las Vegas and a sprawling family mortuary compound. Please heed the trigger warnings. If you have questions, contact me at author@jlbrannick .com. Happy reading!

Trigger Content:

- Descriptions of embalming and body preparation

- Improper use of embalming instruments

- Body preparation on live people

- Torture, including but not limited to:

  - BTK, i.e., bind, torture, kill

  - Cosmeticizing a live person

  - Direct disposition

  - Live entombment (referenced)

  - Tongue removal

  - Improper use of a trocar

  - Improper use of a nailgun

- Child abuse (referenced)

- Attempted filicide (referenced)

- Murder (it's warranted)

- Suicide (referenced)

- Depression (referenced)

- Marijuana use

- BDSM elements

- Bullying and coercion

- Collaring and trackers

- A gross overabundance of attorneys

Chapter 1

Luna

My birthday—and too much tequila—triggered the nightmare. I could usually yank myself awake when the demons stirred, but tonight my guard was down, and my mind threw me back to that dark room where I swam in pain, blood, and thirst.

"Luna, wake up!" Sylvie yelled, shaking my shoulders.

I gasped like a drowning victim coming back to life. "I'm okay, I'm okay."

Sylvie Spade had saved my life that day, and her peculiar, slightly scary family gave me safety and security while I healed. She looked so pretty and sweet, with her wavy blond hair and dimpled smile, but it was complete bullshit. She could be as mean and lethal as any of her cousins.

"Goddamn it," she breathed, "I *hate* when you do that. It freaks me the fuck out."

It freaked me out too. I lay there panting and sweating for a few moments while she muttered next to me. Our apartment sat on the second floor, behind the iconic Palm Desert Oasis Mortuary, a sprawling funeral home compound with its own private cemetery in the center of sunny Las Vegas.

"How come I'm the only one who gets a hangover?" The watery, early-morning light made me squint, and my tongue felt like I'd eaten roadkill and washed it down with battery acid.

"Because you're a wussy lightweight. Come on, you're probably dehydrated too." She patted my leg, then pinched my butt to get me moving. I was too tired to retaliate.

We headed to the kitchen for water and aspirin, and I started digging through the freezer. "How about ice cream for breakfast?" I held up a container. I still felt shaky from the nightmare, and my body craved sugar.

She smirked and grabbed two spoons. "What's one more bad decision?" So we ate pistachio ice cream from the carton that tasted faintly of freezer burn while watching two *South Park* episodes.

Then Sylvie started her workday. "Come on. I already embalmed and bathed Ms. Elwood yesterday. We can do her face and hair." She dragged me down to the cosmetic preparation room on the other side of the quiet, dim mortuary.

The prep rooms and garage where the bodies were dropped off sat tucked away on the other end of the mortuary. As we walked through the quiet space, the smell of lemon furniture wax and vanilla air freshener filled the air. Filtered, colored light came in through the stained-glass windows and lit the pews.

The Spade family owned the mortuary complex, which Sylvie and her grandfather, Ezra Spade, ran. The House of Spades also owned several other, more questionable businesses around town.

Sylvie was the mortician, and Ezra ran the funeral home. Our other roommate, Alexa, and I sometimes moonlighted as "assistants." We were both poor law students, and Ezra discounted our rent in return for helping with the larger funerals. I sometimes assisted Sylvie with preparing the bodies, and it was a great setup—except for my occasional queasiness.

She had a separate cosmetic prep room where she kept all her flesh-colored fillers, cosmetics, hair products, and other items lined up on the shelves along the walls used to repair and beautify the bodies. A tray full of surgery-type tools for a little "under the hood" work also sat on her prep table.

At six in the morning, the day after my birthday, I helped Sylvie prepare the embalmed corpse of Ms. Elwood who'd died on the toilet.

"Why do so many people pass away in the bathroom?" I asked as we wheeled her body out of the walk-in refrigerator.

She shrugged. "A postmortem examiner told me when a person has a heart attack or a blood clot, it might feel like a bowel movement. Or the actual bowel movement itself could cause so much pressure, it triggers one."

We wheeled the gurney to the cosmetic prep room. "What was her cause of death?" I asked.

"The postmortem report stated her heart looked oversized and heavy, so probably a heart attack and age. We're all going to die somewhere. If I can't die asleep in my bed, the bathroom isn't a bad second choice—as long as it's clean." The Spade family had a straightforward, pragmatic approach to death.

I turned on the overhead light, chasing away the shadows. "That's probably why Ezra drinks a glass of prune juice with his breakfast." Along with being Sylvie's grandfather, Ezra was also my former legal guardian. He got custody of Sylvie and me a few months after I was taken out of my parents' house, half-dead on a stretcher.

"Yep. Ms. Elwood's daughter didn't find her for a few days."

"What shape was she in?" I murmured as we fastened flesh-colored caps over the eyes.

"Her organs had just started to break down, but it wasn't bad. Putrefaction hadn't set in, and besides the usual urine and bowel release, the smells were manageable." Sylvie kept a container of menthol ointment in her work area, which she wiped under her nose when an overly ripe corpse came in.

I surveyed the face and thought this one might take a little extra work. Ms. Elwood died in her late eighties, and her nose had somehow gotten smashed. She also looked a little sunken and concave, but I knew Sylvie could fix it. She and Ezra were the best at what they did.

The Spade family purchased the property in the early 1960s. First, they built a cemetery and then a sprawling funeral home, which they renovated and upgraded over the years. The Spades and the mortuary had become my home, and I loved my adopted family fiercely even though their level of morbidity and strangeness sometimes rivaled that of the Addams Family.

"Are you ready to do her mouth?" I asked, pulling out cotton gauze, a plastic mouth former, and forceps from a drawer.

"Almost. Thanks." She snipped the simple suture holding Ms. Elmwood's mouth together, then pried her jaw apart by placing the heel of her hand on the forehead and pushing down on the chin.

"Give me some gauze, will you?"

I handed her a wad, and she used forceps to work it into the throat to absorb any lingering moisture or gas. Then, she worked some into the nostril cavities and massaged the nose back into shape. Next, Sylvie added filler inside the cheeks and formed the mouth into a soft smile.

"How does that look?" she asked.

I leaned over and studied the less-wrinkled face. "A little more on the right."

She nodded and stuffed a bit more filler into the right upper cheek area. "How about now?"

"It looks good." I handed her the needle injector with a small nail and nylon wire already loaded.

She leaned in and punched the nail into the lower jawbone just below the gums. It hit the bone and held. Then she loaded it again and punched another one into the upper jaw. Drawing the wire together, she closed Ms. Elwood's mouth, tied off the wire, and tucked the small ends inside the lips.

Peering around her, I inspected the face. "Nice work. Now for the burial clothes and cosmetics."

Sylvie glanced at me. "You look like you're doing better."

I smiled as I watched her work. "Yeah, there's nothing like preparing a dead body in a dark mortuary to get my mind off my nightmares."

I thought the nightmare would be the worst part of that Monday, but after reading the email from my law school counselor later that morning, I realized I'd grossly underestimated the amount of feculence one day could hold. The glass doors of Fowler, Underwood, Carter, and Knox, Legal whooshed open with a surge of artificial chill that did nothing to cool my boiling temper. I marched up to the front desk and made eye contact with the receptionist.

"Hello. I need to speak with Roman Fowler. I'm Luna Cross, and he should be expecting me."

My irritation and resentment might have leaked through because the woman at the desk raised her eyebrow. Her nameplate read *Brenna Wilson*. The woman's blond, highlighted hair framed a pretty, made-up face, and her tailored dress fit well. But her expression made me want to check myself for food in my teeth or nasty stains.

"Are you a client?" she asked.

"No, I'm a law student. Roman Fowler has just been assigned as my mentor, and I'm supposed to complete my internship here. But I need to talk with him about–"

"A law student?" She interrupted, her painted lips twisting into the faintest sneer. "Do you have an appointment?"

"Klim Hudson from the law school sent me over. Roman should know I'm coming."

Brenna's fingers danced mockingly over her keyboard. "It's *Mr. Fowler*, and I don't see your appointment. You'll have to wait."

"If you could just tell him I'm here–"

Her smile sharpened. "Take a seat, Ms. Cross. I'll let you know when he's free."

"It will take maybe two minutes–"

"Have a seat," Brenna repeated, emphasizing each syllable.

I sighed, turned to the plush leather couch, and slid my backpack off. Pulling my laptop out, I decided to use my forced time with "bitchy Brenna" to do some reading. I figured I'd give her a few minutes, then start pushing back if she didn't get me in to see Fowler soon. Just over forty minutes later, I slid my laptop back into my backpack and stood up.

"It's been forty-two minutes. You haven't gotten up from your desk or picked up the phone to let Mr. Fowler know I'm here."

"Your observations are noted," she replied with glacial efficiency. "But Mr. Fowler is extremely busy. When he has a moment, I'll let him know you're here."

I had to hand it to F.U.C.K. Legal. The acronym of their names and their sleek, cold law office gave off a straightforward message. Their frigid receptionist was the perfect complement.

"Bullshit."

"Did you say something?" She rolled her eyes but didn't look up from her screen.

"You can keep rolling your eyes, but I doubt you'll find much back there."

Her fingers paused mid-air, then resumed typing at double speed.

"Do your employers know you treat visitors like this?"

"Ms. Cross, I assure you I treat everyone who comes to our offices with the respect they deserve," she retorted.

"I'm sure you do." I started walking around her desk toward the frosted glass doors behind her.

"Mr. Fowler will see you when he's ready," Brenna said loudly, standing up and trying to block me.

"That's a little hard to do when he doesn't know I'm here." I breezed past her and pushed into the law offices. I could move faster in my loafers than she could in her heels.

A large desk sat in the inner foyer, and a lean, middle-aged man in an immaculate black suit worked behind it. His desk faced an impressive conference room, and several luxurious offices lined the walls. And, of course, they had a view of the Strip.

"I'm looking for Roman Fowler," I told the man as I approached his desk.

Brenna trailed behind me. "You can't just barge in here–"

I cut her off like she'd done to me. "I've been sitting in the lobby area for the past forty-five minutes with your useless receptionist, who never buzzed Mr. Fowler to let him know I was here."

"That's not true!" Brenna insisted, with obvious forced indignation. "And I'm deeply offended by your accusation."

"I didn't intend to offend you, that's just a bonus." I spared her a glance and turned to the lean, middle-aged man in the crisp black suit. "Are you Roman Fowler?"

The man stood and turned to Brenna. "Ms. Wilson, we'll discuss this when our visitor is gone. Go back to your desk."

"Yes, Mr. Anderson," she murmured, glaring at me before she turned and walked back outside.

Damn it, this guy wasn't Fowler either. He reminded me a little of Mr. Anderson from *The Matrix*, with his slim build and formal manner. Minus the sunglasses.

I held out my hand. "Hello, Mr. Anderson. There's been a misunderstanding, but one I hope we can clear up quickly. Is Roman Fowler available?"

"Call me Gideon. He's on the phone but should be available shortly. Can I get you a coffee or cappuccino?"

"No, thank you."

He tilted his head. "May I ask why you need to speak with Roman? I'm the office administrator. Maybe I can help." Gideon sat on the edge of his desk.

Hope rose in my chest. Maybe I didn't even need to talk with Fowler if Gideon would dismiss me. Then I could be on my way.

"That would be spectacular. My name is Luna Cross, and I'm a law student. You're probably aware that we're required to have a mentor and complete an internship with an attorney."

Gideon nodded, but his demeanor cooled almost imperceptibly. "Where did you say you're from, Ms. Cross?"

It was a strange question. "Arizona, but I moved to Las Vegas in my early teens."

"I'm aware of the law school requirements. So Roman has been assigned as your mentor, and you plan to intern here?"

"No!" I winced and lowered my voice. "Not if he'll agree to release me. I had another attorney already lined up since I plan to go into water law. But Klim Hudson, my law school counselor, emailed this morning and told me he'd assigned me to this law firm and Roman Fowler instead."

Gideon studied me for several seconds, as if weighing my words. He didn't say anything for so long that I worried I'd angered him.

"No offense to any of you. Well, maybe Brenna."

Gideon's head cocked. "Klim assigned you to Roman?"

"Yes. And when I told him I already had an internship lined up, Klim said it was either Roman or I didn't graduate."

"And what was your response to that?"

I shifted uncomfortably, and my eyes slid to the side. "I'd rather not tell you."

Gideon's lips twitched. "That's alright. I'll call Klim and ask him myself." He reached over to pick up his phone.

I sighed loudly. "I called him the male version of a period cramp. See? You don't want me as an intern here. I've been told I have no filter and ask way too many questions."

"Noted. Why do you think Roman can get you out of the internship?"

"After twenty minutes of... discussing the issue, Klim promised that if Mr. Fowler would agree to release me, I could go back to my original mentor."

"And this was after you called him a period cramp. Anything else that might be pertinent to this issue?"

I rocked on my heels and looked around. "I may have said a few other things, but I don't recall."

"That's a typical attorney evasion."

I shrugged sheepishly. "Anyway. I'm sure you have other law students interested in interning at your firm. Students who'd be a much better fit here."

"We always have requests, but I'm not sure they'd be a better fit."

I ignored that last part. "So, will you call Klim and let him know your firm will release me?"

He smiled benignly. "As much as I'd like to help, you need to speak directly with Roman. I'm also curious what you'll call him if he tells you no."

Before I could answer, the door to the office behind me opened, and a tall, coldly handsome man in an expensive, custom-made suit strode out. His charcoal-brown eyes landed on me and his black eyebrow lifted. He had a lean, fit build, and a wicked scar running along his neck.

My back went up, and my palms got sweaty. I didn't like or trust attractive, well-groomed men; they tended to be self-centered pricks.

Gideon nodded to the man coming toward us. "You'll have to put your case to Roman himself, Ms. Cross. But if it were up to me, I'd say you'd fit in well here."

"I'm Roman Fowler, and you're Ms. Cross, I assume?" A frigid, amused smirk tugged the corners of the man's mouth.

"Yes." I held out my hand, and when we shook, a zing raced up my arm. His large, calloused palm felt solid and cool as he squeezed my hand and then let go. I wondered where the callouses came from.

"Klim Hudson contacted me and told me you'd be coming." His deep voice was flat.

My stomach dropped because I wanted to get to Fowler before Klim did. Stupid, bitchy Brenna.

Plastering on a benign, pleasant smile, I met his gaze. "It's nice to meet you, Mr. Fowler. I assume you have several law students who'd love to have you as their mentor."

"Probably."

"I've already lined up a mentorship with another attorney, so if you could tell Klim Hudson you're alright with having another student assigned to you, I'll leave you to your billable hours."

"No."

"No?" My voice had gone up a few octaves.

"That's right. No."

"Does that no mean you don't want me to take up any more of your time, or no, you won't release me?"

His lip curled. "I'm not releasing you."

"Why? I don't want to be here, and you can easily find someone who does."

"Because if I have to mentor someone, it might as well be you. Now tell me exactly why you don't want to be here."

The fake smile slid off my face. "Look, Mr. Fowler, I want out of this internship."

He studied me. "You've made that clear. Why, Ms. Cross?"

I unclenched my hands and tried to reel in my frustration. "I'm not interested in the areas of law you practice, and until Mr. Hudson informed me of the change, I'd never heard of you or your firm. Your offices are beautiful–if a little cold–and I'm sure your firm's acronym doesn't reflect your legal philosophy. Anyway, I have other plans."

Gideon covered up a laugh with a cough, but we both ignored him.

"And what are your plans?" Roman asked mildly.

"I want to go into water law. It's fairly specialized, and your firm doesn't practice it. So I'd appreciate it if you'd let Klim Hudson know."

"Your candor is refreshing. Still, no."

The bastard was playing with me now. "Okay, how about this for candor? I'd rather eat glass than intern with your firm where I'd have to deal with bitchy Brenna–and you–all day. Mr. Anderson seems decent, so I won't include him." I put my hands on my hips and leaned forward. "I plan to practice in another area of law, and we've got nothing to offer each other. Why are you forcing this?"

He smirked and took me in. "Ms. Cross, let's cut to the chase."

"Let's," I muttered.

"Despite your clear annoyance and disappointment about the last-minute change, I am not releasing you."

My eyes narrowed to slits. "Why?"

"Because I don't have to, and you won't bore me. Instead, we'll start with you shadowing me over fall break."

"Shadowing you?" I repeated, my words coated in annoyed disbelief. "As in, spend my fall break following you around?"

His cold eyes locked onto me. "Exactly. Make the most of this opportunity."

The room seemed to shrink, and his resolve crumbled my hopes. Pressing my lips together, I contemplated my next move. Silence stretched between us before I exhaled slowly.

"Fine. But don't expect me to be agreeable or pleasant about it." This arrogant mother fucker wasn't going to break me.

"I wouldn't dream of it." The scar on his neck stretched as he tilted his head, assessing me. "I'll pick you up at eight on Monday to start our week together."

I blinked at him. This just kept getting worse. "You're picking me up? *Why?*"

"Did I not just make that clear?" Amusement laced his tone.

Deciding on a different tack, I loosened my shoulders. "Listen, I'll meet you here. You don't need to chauffeur me around."

"Consider it a perk of the mentorship, and I'll let Klim know you're staying. See you Monday, Ms. Cross." He turned and walked back into his office. Somehow, my last name sounded like a swear word when he said it.

Dismissed, I turned to Gideon and blew out a breath. "Well, it looks like I'll see you next week. You appear to be the only sane one in this circus."

He smiled and patted my shoulder. "Hang in there. He's a decent man, he's just good at hiding it."

"You work with attorneys, Gideon. I think your opinion of what constitutes 'decent' is probably low."

"Fair point, Ms. Cross."

Chapter 2

Luna

I stomped into the apartment and slammed the door, muttering a few particularly ripe curses I'd learned from the Spade cousins over the years. Carl, our three-legged black and white short-haired cat, greeted me with an aggressive meow. He tolerated a little kissing and cuddling, but he wasn't above giving us a good swipe if we got too greedy. Scooping him up, I breathed in, letting his soft body soothe my raw nerves.

My phone buzzed, and I saw a text from Alexa pop up. She was a year behind me in law school, and I'd be graduating in the spring.

The thought of my graduation sent bitter frustration through me. I'd planned to leverage my internship with the water law attorney into a job before Klim *Fucking* Hudson and Roman *Fucking* Fowler decided to royally screw up my life.

Alexa: Want to split a pizza while we bitch about our day?

I needed to vent like a junkie needing their next fix.

Sylvie: Yes, with a pitcher of beer

Me: I'm in. I need a tequila shot too

Alexa: Luigi's in an hour. First one there orders

"How was your day, huh?" I scratched behind his ears, and he purred loudly. It sounded like screeching metal, but it always made me smile. "Better than mine, I bet."

After cleaning up and giving Carl his dinner, I walked the few blocks to Luigi's. The little Italian restaurant in our neighborhood had been around almost as long as the mortuary.

When I walked in, the scent of garlic and pizza crust greeted me. The restaurant had a scarred wood floor, tables covered in red-checked tablecloths, and dark red jar candles next to the parmesan shakers. Café lights and ancient Italian opera posters hung on the walls.

Alexa Torres waved me over to our usual booth. She rarely smiled and was the more thoughtful, quiet one of the three of us.

Except for our skin tone, we could have passed for sisters. I also had brown hair, but my eyes were green, and I'd inherited my mother's average build and perky nose.

"What happened?" she asked, pushing a pink-striped birthday bag over to me. She knew I hated my birthday. It was like torture every year when it came around, which explained the tequila shots last night and the hangover this morning.

"You shouldn't have."

She smirked at my sincere tone. "It's nothing big. Open it."

I pulled out the tissue paper and looked inside. The bag was stuffed full of cinnamon-flavored candies. When I was younger, Ezra worried my craving for cinnamon candy signaled a magnesium or calcium deficiency in my diet.

Grinning, I pulled out a cinnamon sucker, unwrapped it, and shoved it in my mouth. "Thanks. This is a perfect gift."

"So? How'd it go with your internship?"

A pitcher of beer and a few tequila shots sat at our table. I pulled out the sucker and picked up a shot, throwing it back without glancing at the lime wedges or salt shaker.

Grimacing, I wiped my lips with the back of my hand and stuck the sucker back in. "So much worse than I expected."

She leaned forward. "Tell me."

"I only want to repeat my sad, sorry tale once. When Sylvie gets here, I'll tell you everything."

Alexa poured us beers and sat back. "You look frustrated. Is it that bad?"

"Yeah, it is. I want to rip Klim Hudson's head off, then Roman Fowler's dick."

Sylvie walked in and slid into the seat next to Alexa. Sophia, our usual server, followed behind her, bringing out the loaded pizza. "Hey, ladies. Is funeral parlor poker brunch still on for Sunday?"

Sylvie grabbed a slice and bypassed her plate for her mouth. "Absolutely. If you get a break, come sit with us." Sophia nodded and strode off. The hot, steamy sixteen-inch half-vegetarian, half-meat lover's pizza smelled divine. Sylvie liked meat, Alexa was a vegetarian, and I didn't care, so I took the two pieces that touched both sides.

"I forgot to give you this yesterday–that's what half a bottle of tequila will do. Pretend I'm the Mad Hatter wishing you a merry unbirthday." Sylvie slid a card over to me.

"Thanks." I picked up the card and opened it–then snorted. It read "Happy Kindergarten Graduation to my Sweet Nephew" in big, colorful block letters. The Spade family had an odd tradition of giving each other the strangest, least appropriate cards for each other's birthdays. Fennick Spade, my foster cousin, gave me a Happy Talk Like a Pirate Day card a few years ago for my birthday. I'd looked it up and found out it was a real day.

Sylvie had included a gift card to my favorite bookstore in town. I sighed and leaned over the table to hug them both. "Thanks. You guys know me well. Now, let's eat."

Taking a big bite, Alexa nudged my foot under the table. "She's here. Spill."

So I told them, and when I finished, I pointed at another shot of tequila. "Can I have that?"

Both women nodded as they eyed me sympathetically.

"Can they do that?" Sylvie asked as she picked up another slice.

I let out a bitter laugh. "Who's going to stop them? For some reason, Klim thinks I'll have an 'invaluable experience' with Fowler and the partners at The Firm. That's what they call it–The Firm. That or FUCK, Legal." I rolled my eyes. "I need to research them and figure out what I'm really getting into." I threw back the shot, and this time I used a lime wedge.

Alexa leaned forward. "Something feels off about this. I have a little time, especially with fall break coming next week. I'll help you research them."

We ate in silence for a few minutes, and Sylvie finally leaned back, patting her stomach like she had a food baby in there. "Ezra asked if you two could help with the funeral tomorrow afternoon. It should only take a couple of hours, and he said he'd forego rent this month if you assist with this one and the Bertrand service next week."

Alexa raised her hand. "Count me in."

"Me too." I sometimes wondered if Ezra asked us to work the funerals to give him an excuse to waive our rent.

Sylvie shook her head. "Roman Fowler is really going to pick you up on Monday morning? Las Vegas reminds me of the Wild West, but people with money instead of guns make the rules here."

Alexa started typing on her phone. "If I'm around Monday morning, I want to meet him."

"He's an arrogant prick. I don't know how we're going to survive an entire week without killing each other."

Holding up her phone to Sylvie, Alexa pointed to a photo. "I think what Luna meant to say is he's a *hot,* arrogant prick... and so are his partners."

Sylvie's eyes went wide, and she grabbed Alexa's phone. "Who's with him?" she asked.

Alexa tilted her head. "His law partners. Why?"

"I know one of them." She shook her head and handed the phone back. "The internship is only for six months, right? You can make it six months."

"I'd rather stick needles through my nipples and just be done with the torture."

"Holy fuck, girl. Why would you put that image in our heads?" Sylvie shuddered and cupped her breasts protectively. "We're here anytime you need to vent."

"Thanks. What would I do without you guys?"

Sylvie picked up her beer. "Well, you wouldn't live above a mortuary or work funerals on the weekend."

I raised my beer in return. "Exactly."

The next afternoon, we dressed in black and manned our usual spots around the funeral chapel. Our job was to direct mourners and family members where to go in hushed, appropriate tones and ensure everything ran smoothly. We wore discreet gold nametags to let people know we were there to help.

Ezra stood next to the bereaved widower in a custom-tailored charcoal suit with subtle pinstripes. He was a tall, trim silver fox. Besides his full head of white hair, he reminded me of Gonzo Addams. He often wore pinstripe suits, owned a funeral home, and had a peculiar family.

As the mourners started trickling in, we answered questions and handed out funeral service programs. I wore stylish black boots instead of heels, since we often needed to move around large flower arrangements, furniture, and caskets. When the funeral began, we waited in the office until the services finished, and Ezra would let us know when he needed our help again.

"Let's pull up Roman Fowler and his law firm and do some cyberstalking while we're waiting," Alexa suggested.

"Great idea." I ran and got our laptops from the apartment, and we spent the next hour trying to find the dirt on Fowler, Underwood, Carter, and Knox, Legal.

"You weren't kidding. Their acronym is literally F.U.C.K. As in, the actual word fuck," Alexa realized as she typed on her laptop.

Sylvie raised her eyebrow. "Couldn't they have rearranged their last names?"

"After meeting Roman, I think it's intentional. Their firm is also referred to as 'The Firm.' It's so... egotistical."

Alexa sat up straight and pointed to a website that analyzed Las Vegas businesses and listed their net worth. "Their combined business interests are estimated in... the *billions*. Shit," she breathed. "Maybe their name isn't that pretentious."

Sylvie stopped typing and leaned back. "Jesus, these guys are trouble. And not just Roman and Drakos."

I glanced at her computer. "Who's Drakos, and what're you looking at?"

"Social media." She ignored my first question. "I figured Alexa would check their financials, go for their website, and maybe hack their client database–because she can't help herself."

"I plead the Fifth," Alexa mumbled as she typed away. She was our tech genius.

Sylvie nodded her head toward me. "You probably got distracted trying to learn about what types of law they practice."

"I don't know what you're talking about."

Alexa leaned over and looked at my screen. "You're reading about commercial real estate legal terms."

Sylvie flipped her computer around. "So I took the fun route, trolling through the local gossip and social sites. Here's a blogger who posted about the 'hottest attorneys' in Las Vegas, and every partner in that firm is listed. Look at the photos she included." The blogger wasn't wrong, and I inwardly sighed.

Except for the Spade cousins, it seemed like good-looking men were usually colossal assholes. So far, Roman had proven my theory correct. "This isn't making me feel any better about the internship."

Sylvie kept scrolling through the site. "It says they're well known in the legal community and give to charities. It also looks like some of them are serial daters."

I looked over her shoulder at the collage of photos the author had included and snorted. "That's one way to put it."

We continued digging for a few minutes when Alexa hummed. "They're from all over the United States, which made me wonder how they met. At least two—and probably all of them—were sent to that horrific boys' ranch in Arizona as teenagers." She glanced at me. "Your home state. Do you remember that news story?"

My stomach dropped. "The one that made national news about fifteen years ago?"

Alexa pointed to her screen. "Yes. Bitter Creek Ranch Academy. There were serious allegations of abuse and torture, and several boys went missing and were never found." She raised her eyebrows as her fingers flew over her keyboard. "Someone has worked hard to bury the fact that those men were there as teenagers. They did a decent job."

My heart squeezed with unwanted sympathy. "I was just a kid, but I remember it well. That place was evil. God, those news stories gave me nightmares."

Sylvie sat back. "The Vegas Legal blog has an extensive article about the partners. Several of them still practice law, but their business interests are where most of the money comes from. That, and family inheritances."

Her phone buzzed, and she read the text. "That's Ezra. They're wrapping up."

We shut down our computers and got back to work. As we helped Ezra carefully load the casket into the back of the sleek gray Cadillac mortuary hearse, I brooded about what Monday would bring. The thought of spending a week under Roman Fowler's thumb made the hairs on my arms rise.

Chapter 3

Luna

On Monday morning at two minutes to eight, the apartment doorbell buzzed, the flat sound vibrating through me. I checked the peephole and stared at Roman Fowler in another expensive suit, standing on the front stoop.

Alexa sat at the kitchen bar, eyeing me carefully. "Are you going to be okay with him?"

"Yes. Somehow, I convinced myself he wouldn't show up, and have been holding out a vain hope that he changed his mind or would get too busy." No such luck. I opened the door and stared up at him. He stood there, tall and domineering, then stepped around me and strode into the living room.

"Good morning." His voice was a low rumble as his dark eyes swept over me and the apartment. He took in the scattered law books on the coffee table and Alexa sitting at the kitchen counter. Carl eyed him warily from the back of the couch, his tail twitching.

"How do you know where I live?" I asked.

"Gideon must have gotten your address from the law school. Imagine my surprise when I pulled up to the Spade family mortuary."

"You're lying. Even the school doesn't have my physical address."

His lip twitched, but he didn't elaborate.

"You know what? It doesn't matter." I turned to Alexa. "This is Roman Fowler. My roommate, Alexa Torres. Sylvie Spade is our other roommate. She's at the mortuary already."

Roman nodded to her. "Alexa, nice to meet you."

I grabbed my backpack, which held essentials in case I got stuck with him all day. That thought had me pausing, and I turned around and dug through a kitchen cupboard, pulling out a box of Red Hot cinnamon candy and a bag of cinnamon bears.

Alexa stared at him, unblinking. "Hello." Then she noticed what I was double-fisting. "Do you think it's going to be that bad?"

I glanced at Roman and nodded.

"Are you ready?" he asked, checking his expensive watch.

"As I'll ever be. What are we doing this morning?" My insatiable curiosity got the better of me. I loved to learn new things, and my mind never rested. That flaw had almost cost me my life.

"Breakfast and business," he answered.

"That really narrows it down, thank you."

He glanced down at our coffee table stacked with an array of law books, nonfiction books, novels, and even an embalmer trade magazine. He picked up a true crime novel and thumbed through it.

"Most of the books in this house are Luna's," Alexa murmured from behind her computer screen.

His lip tipped up. "Good to know."

"She's smart. Don't underestimate her."

"Also good to know." He glanced at Alexa, then turned to me. "Shall we?"

He owned an expensive, sleek black Mercedes, which didn't surprise me at all. We drove in silence to a private golf course so exclusive that the air reeked of money and privilege. My father and grandfather belonged to a similar country club in Phoenix. A host ushered us to a quiet restaurant overlooking manicured greens, the sunlight glinting off distant ponds.

"Where the entitled, rich male class goes to do business," I muttered, observing the crystal chandeliers and servers in vests and ties.

Roman checked his watch. "Mr. Hutton should be here shortly."

He called a server over to order scrambled eggs, toast, and fruit for the table, asked for three plates, and then poured coffee. "This way we don't have to wait for Mr. Hutton to order." He leaned back. "He's known for two things—being drunk and being late."

I poured a splash of cream into my coffee. "Who's Mr. Hutton and what's your role here?"

"Todd Hutton is a commercial real estate developer. His father is the brains behind their company, and they're known for greasing palms and twisting arms to close deals. He's interested in selling my client some very expensive commercial land in south Las Vegas."

"Are you on a fact-finding mission, writing up the contract, or reviewing an existing contract?"

He'd picked up his coffee to take a sip but paused and glanced at me. "Due diligence. We're looking for any legal or development issues, then we'll draft a contract if our client is still interested."

Todd Hutton arrived ten minutes later. He wore an expensive golf shirt stretched over a big beer belly. Standing next to Roman, Todd appeared bloated and soft.

"This is Luna Cross, my intern."

I reached over and held out my hand. "Hello. It's nice to meet you."

Todd's smile turned to a subtle leer, and his handshake was weak and soggy. "You're the hottest law student I've ever met." He glanced at Roman and grinned knowingly. "I ordered a whiskey neat. Do you want anything?"

I mentally winced–it wasn't even nine in the morning. Roman shook his head and gestured to a seat at the table.

Tom sat, got his drink, and they exchanged pleasantries before discussing the property. I sipped coffee, dished up some fruit and toast, and listened as the two men talked about acres, zoning, and potential profits.

Then I heard Todd mutter something about utility hookups and water, and I sat up straight. "Mr. Hutton, how many water shares does the property have? Is there water already available at the site?" I'd caught both men off guard, but I knew enough about water and water law, and we lived in a desert.

Roman shot me a sharp look, the edge of his mouth quirking in what could either be amusement or annoyance. I didn't know him well enough yet to tell.

Todd Hutton faltered for a fraction of a second, a crack in his overly confident, swaggering veneer. "I'm sure there's water available."

"Ms. Cross brings up a good point. We need that information on all the utilities, and already requested that information."

"Of course," Hutton muttered, glaring at me.

His upper lip broke out in a sweat, which was never a good sign. At that point, Roman smoothly cut the rest of the meeting short, paid the check, and stood. The restaurant had filled up since we walked in, and Roman paused slightly and glanced at a few men sitting nearby. He placed his hand on the small of my back as we walked out.

I didn't like men touching me in public when they had no right to. But I paused before stepping away from his touch. "Is there a reason you're suddenly crowding me?" I murmured in a low voice.

"The three men sitting at the table we just passed are vicious, degenerate assholes, and I wanted them to know that you're with me. They sometimes target women."

Looking around, I noticed for the first time there weren't any women eating in the posh restaurant.

I sidestepped his hand once we were in the parking lot. "It worries me that being with you could put a target on my back. It's not too late, you can still get another intern. A rich, well-connected male law student would probably be more your type."

He beeped the locks on his car. "Your reticence makes me more determined to keep you."

I gritted my teeth and slid into the passenger seat. When he climbed in, I turned to him. "Are we done for today? I have some studying to do."

"No, we have one more stop. I'll let you know when we're done, and from now on, bring whatever you need to study and plan on spending your days at the office."

My temper snapped. "No way. Look, I'm not your employee, little sister, or… whatever. I have class and school obligations. I can't just blow it all off because you're a controlling asshole."

He gave me a hard look. "I know you're not my little sister since I'm an only child, and it would do you good to see how the law actually functions here in Las Vegas."

I scowled back. "I get the feeling your law firm runs less by the book and more in that grayish-black area."

Roman's head swiveled slowly to me, and he raised an eyebrow. "You live and work with the Spades. Don't you think that's a little hypocritical? We make sure we have enough power, money, and leverage so we don't get fucked over by the law again. The legal system won't keep you safe, even from me. Never make that mistake."

His cold eyes were shadowed. Our conversation had gotten intense fast, so I let it go, but he was in for a rude surprise if he thought I'd be held hostage in his office all day. The mentorship rules required me to complete a certain number of hours and have so many law-related experiences, and I was keeping track.

Studying him thoughtfully, I wondered what he was like in a courtroom. "Where are we going now?"

"To see one of my clients." A few minutes later, we pulled into the parking lot of Euphoria. Even I had heard of this place, it was one of the most notorious and popular strip clubs in Vegas, and excited nervous energy rolled through me.

"You think a trip to a strip club is part of my necessary hands-on legal experience?" My curiosity won out, and I got out of the car and tilted my head back to look up at the large, ostentatious white building.

"It's a *gentlemen's* club, and absolutely. This is another one of those places where 'entitled males' go to do business.'"

Faux Greek marble statues of naked women lined the walkway to the front doors.

"I've always wanted to go inside," I admitted, staring up at the building. "What are you doing here?"

His brow creased as he studied me. "The managing partner needs some legal advice about a VIP client."

"Okay. Can I talk to a few employees if there's time?'"

He shrugged. "It's up to them. But stay out of trouble and don't wander off. Their doors open at noon."

A bouncer answered the doorbell and buzzed us inside the thick double doors. Coming in from the bright Las Vegas sunshine, the dimly lit club temporarily blinded me. Even with the houselights up, the club looked like an exclusive salon or the lobby of a five-star hotel. The walls were covered in a deep plush shade of blue, accented with gold and crystal. Velvet sofas and armchairs were artfully arranged around marble coffee tables. Large chandeliers hung from the ceiling, glowing warmly over the space. A main stage sat at the back, and two smaller stages with sturdy poles were placed equidistant from each other further into the club.

A couple of cleaners worked in the bar area, and the subtle aroma of lemon solution mixed with perfumes and colognes lingered in the air.

"Roman Fowler," a husky female voice murmured as a striking woman approached us from the shadows. "Who did you bring with you today?"

"Fiona Parker, this is Luna Cross."

Fiona was probably in her early forties. She had short platinum blond hair cut into a sharp bob, tasteful makeup, and wore a feminine lavender-colored business suit.

"Nice to meet you." I held out my hand, and she gave me a firm handshake. "I've always been curious about your club. One of my classmates had her bachelorette party here, and now that I know a female owns it, I'm even more intrigued."

Fiona glanced at Roman. "I have a couple of other partners. So you're looking for employment? You're not dressed for an audition, but I'm sure there's something in back that would work." Fiona reached around and grabbed the back of my white button-down shirt, pulling it tight so she could see my figure. Then she walked around me and palmed my butt cheeks. I grunted in surprise and moved out of her reach. Roman didn't say a word, and I could tell he was trying not to laugh. Asshole.

"You've got nice breasts and a good, tight ass, and your innocent face and those big, green eyes with all that thick, dark hair would be a hit with the clientele. I'll need to see how you dance and move, though."

I choked and my cheeks flushed hot. Turning to face her, I held up my hands. "Thank you? But I'm already employed as a mortuary assistant, and today I'm just shadowing Mr. Fowler as his law student intern."

Fiona chuckled, unfazed by her mistake. "Aw, that's why you're blushing like a nun in a brothel. But seriously, if you can dance and you don't have any serious blemishes or scars, you could make a lot of money working here."

"I don't know how to dance, and I have no rhythm or coordination. My dance teacher kicked me out of her studio when I was six, so I think I'm better off getting a degree."

She chuckled. "We all have our strengths. What do you want to know about the club?"

"Well, I was going to ask how you find dancers, but I think you just answered that one. What's it like owning a gentleman's club, especially as a woman? What are your biggest headaches? And how do you manage clients and keep them in line?"

Holding up a hand, she grinned. "Let me answer those questions before you fire off more. It's lucrative, and I haven't run into too many problems as a woman. I've got competent help. The biggest issues are employee retention, local regulations, and partners." She gave Roman a pointed look. "I maintain order because my security guards are more than just bodies, and I have cameras everywhere. Now I have a question for you. How'd you end up with Roman as your mentor? You two seem... ill-paired."

"Right?! But Klim Hudson thought we'd be a 'good match' for some ungodly reason. I'm still trying to dissuade them."

Fiona's eyes sharpened. "Roman is an exceptional attorney and an astute businessman. But, listen carefully. Don't let your guard down." Roman grunted next to her, we both ignored him.

"I won't." If his client and probable business partner felt compelled to warn me, I needed to be careful.

They talked about a VIP client who'd racked up a substantial bill, and a few other minor legal issues before Fiona turned to me. "You're welcome to wander around and talk to the dancers while we finish our discussion."

Roman pointed at me. "Stay out of trouble."

"Absolutely." I rolled my eyes behind his back and rubbed my hands together as I turned to the dressing rooms.

Chapter 4

Curiosity tugged me into the bowels of the club. I weaved through the velvet sofas and coffee tables until I made it to the "employees only" hallway, turned the corner, and ran into a big, solid chest.

"What are you doing back here?" a deep baritone voice asked.

I looked up into the large, square face of a man with a shaved head and tattooed tree trunks for arms.

"I'm Mr. Fowler's intern. I wanted to look around and talk with a few dancers."

"Is this your first time in a gentleman's club?"

"Is it that obvious?"

He smiled and looked down at my pants and simple white dress shirt. "Yes."

I stuck out my hand. "I'm Luna."

He engulfed my hand in his huge one. "Tiny."

I stared up at him. The name didn't fit him at all. "Is that what you prefer to be called?"

He studied me. "No. My name is Samuel."

"Alright, Samuel. It's nice to meet you. Can I ask you a few questions, and will you introduce me to the performers?"

Samuel shrugged his large shoulder. "Sure. What would you like to know?"

I asked him about security, whether weapons were allowed inside, and the security-to-patron ratio. He patiently answered my questions, and as we talked, he walked me to the large dressing room area. A beautiful woman in ruby red pigtails and sweats walked by, and Samuel lifted his hand.

"Hey, Misty." He pointed at me. "This is Luna, Roman's employee." I didn't correct him. "Boss said she could wander around and ask a few questions."

Misty grinned. "Alright. I think it's just me and Sasha opening, but a few others should be here soon."

"Hello." I stuck out my hand, and she looked down at it like she didn't know exactly what to do. Then she transferred her insulated thermos to her left hand and shook.

"You good?" Samuel asked me.

"Yes. Thanks, Samuel." He nodded and walked back down the hall.

Misty turned to me. "His name is Tiny."

"His real name is Samuel. He said he prefers it."

Misty glanced back down the hall. "I didn't know that. You're here with Roman Fowler?"

"Yes. He's my law mentor, unfortunately. It's complicated."

"If there's a man involved, it's usually complicated," she mused. "What can we help you with?"

"I'm curious about how it all works." Misty led me into the dressing room as we talked. Another woman in shorts, a tank top, and no bra stood in front of a rack of what looked like sparkly strings and minuscule strips of cloth.

"Working in a strip club is like any other job, except the dress code is a bit different," Misty grinned and slipped her flip-flops off. "It really is just a job. Fiona treats us well, and a few girls do some escort work on the side, but they can't do it here. You learn the moves and tricks to make the most money with the least risk and effort. And then we go home, live our lives, and return for our next shift."

Sasha, the other girl, walked over and looked me up and down. She was taller than Misty and had a tight, tan body and violet-colored hair. "Hey, I'm Sasha. You looking for a job? You could work the dirty fairy angle if you know how to dance."

I mentally sighed. I'd been told I looked like a fairy most of my life. "I can't dance—at all. I'm also going to school full-time."

"Yeah? What're you studying?" Misty asked.

"Law."

Sasha casually peeled off her clothes as a few other dancers walked in. "It sounds boring." She pulled a purple thong off the rack and got dressed. It took about two seconds, and her outfit matched her hair perfectly.

"What else do you want to know?" she asked.

"Do you earn a living wage here?"

One of the girls who'd just come in walked over. "Honey, we make bank. But only if we're good."

"Do you get benefits too?"

"A free gym membership and discounts on food and drinks," her friend chimed in. "And the occasional life lesson."

"Life lesson?" I echoed. So, it sounded like no medical or dental benefits.

"Yeah, like never walk out to your car alone at night, and don't trust a man who says he's just here for the atmosphere." The girls laughed. They answered a few more questions while they put on makeup and body glitter. Then Sasha and Misty walked out to the floor to start their shift. I followed them out a few minutes later.

"Did you get your questions answered?" Samuel asked over the music.

"Yes, and I think you guys need to ask for health care and dental benefits."

He grinned and shook his head. "You're a strange one. Come back anytime." I waved at him and headed toward the bar to find Roman.

"Are you lost, little girl? You looking to give a little VIP service?" The slightly slurred voice came from behind me. I turned to find a pudgy, balding middle-aged man in a golf shirt and shorts leering at me, his smile wide and his gaze hazy. It wasn't even one in the afternoon, and this guy was way past buzzed.

"No, I'm not an employee." I tried to sidestep him, but he moved closer.

"Come on, give me a lap dance," he urged, reaching toward me with grabby hands. I'd already been mauled by Fiona, but this guy was another story.

I backed up. "Do I look like a dancer?"

He studied me with one eye closed. "Yeah, 'cause you're pretty, but you need to lose the clothes. What do you look like in a g-string?" His hands went to my shirt, moving fast for being so inebriated.

I deftly blocked him and stepped out of his reach when someone yanked his collar from behind.

"Back the fuck off," Roman clipped as he dragged the man away. "She's obviously not a dancer, you stupid asshole ." Roman shook him a few times then let go, and the man scurried away like a rat.

"Are you done talking to Fiona?" I asked.

Roman narrowed his eyes and took my arm. "Yes. We'll talk in the car." He pulled me through the exit, and the cacophony of sound faded as we walked outside into the bright light. I shook off his hold and looked around.

"Wow, it's so weird." I turned back to the club. "It's like a different world in there. The girls were nice about answering my questions."

"Do you go *looking* for trouble, or do you just naturally attract it?" Roman's voice was a mix of irritation and exasperation.

"Neither. He thought I was a dancer, that's all."

He put his hands on his hips. "You have to be more aware of your surroundings. This isn't the law school or a library."

"Thanks for the safety briefing, Dad."

His eyes flashed, and he suddenly backed me into his car. "If you value your next breath, you will *never* call me your father again."

My heart pounded. "Alright. But you need to back up because I *will* knee you in the groin if you ever do that again."

He slowly backed up, and I shook my head as I opened the passenger door. "You don't know this, but my father is pretty much Satan incarnate, so I won't call you that again."

Roman stared at me like he loathed me. "You need to do what I say and stay out of trouble."

"I'm fine. I can handle myself, and I know the *perfect* solution if you want to get me out of your life. Let me out of this internship." I slammed the car door before he could reply.

He walked around to his side and slid in. "That's still a no. Did you learn anything worthwhile about strip clubs, then?"

"They're called *gentlemen's* clubs," I intoned patiently, throwing his words back at him. "And I did."

"Like what?"

"That it's like any other job in some ways. Fiona doesn't allow the girls to act as escorts on-site. They also need health and dental benefits, and a retirement plan wouldn't be amiss."

His brows furrowed, and he stared at me. "Really? That's what you got out of it?"

"I formed a few tentative opinions, but my data is incomplete. Did you get done what you needed to?" I asked.

"Yes." Roman navigated the car out of the parking lot. "I'm hungry, and we're not far from the Lamb and Wolf Café. Call them and let them know I'm coming. I want the grain salad with salmon. Look up their menu and give them your order too."

"So you want takeout?"

He glanced at me. "No. I want the food ready to come out to the table when we get there. Tell them my name and that our ETA is about fifteen minutes."

Roman liked things a certain way, and I was quickly learning he got what he wanted. Pulling up their menu, I winced at the prices. "This is a lunch place? Their average plate is at least fifty dollars."

"Pick something and get our order in. I don't want to be there all afternoon."

I shook my head and decided on the shrimp scampi, then called and ordered, dropping Roman's name. The hostess suddenly perked up. "He's eating in then?" She sounded a little breathless.

"Uh, yes. He said we'll be there in about fifteen minutes."

"Perfect. We'll have Mr. Fowler's lunch ready to be served when he walks in. Tell him we look forward to seeing him." I hung up and stared at my phone. "You must tip really well because I can't imagine anyone being happy to see you otherwise."

He smirked. "We have a stake in the restaurant, so I go there a few times a month."

"Do you have a stake in Euphoria too?"

"Yes. It's one of our more... interesting businesses."

"It was likely a savvy move since you're probably one of its best customers. With your prickly personality, I don't know how else you'd get close to women."

He gazed at me. "You're certainly curious and have a lot of opinions about my interactions with women. Are you interested, Ms. Cross?"

I sputtered and my face went red. "No! I'm just teasing you. Geez."

He smirked, and I felt like Little Red Riding Hood staring up at a hungry, amused wolf. The posh restaurant sat outside the Rampart shopping mall, and I arched my eyebrow at Roman when the gushing host fawned all over him and rushed us to a premium corner booth.

Our meal came out less than two minutes later, and I didn't bother to daintily pick at my food because it was *good*. I ate steadily until it was gone, and when I looked up, Roman sat watching me with a strange expression.

"What? That was delicious. I'm going to drag the Sylvie and Alexa here one of these days."

He seemed to remember himself and broke eye contact to take a bite of salmon.

As we walked out of the restaurant, I turned to him. "Thanks for lunch. It was wonderful, despite the company."

He shook his head, and when we climbed into his car, I lay my head back against the headrest, absently gazing out the passenger window. I'd stayed up late the night before watching an Audrey Hepburn movie with Ezra, and I'd just eaten more carbs and food than I usually did in two days. I was sleepy.

"Take a nap. I'll wake you up when we get there." His car hummed beneath us as the cityscape swallowed us whole.

"Naps are for old people–like you."

He grunted, and the road's rhythm lulled me into reluctant drowsiness.

"Then consider it a tactical recharge."

"Okay." I slid my eyelids closed and dozed, not comprehending the danger that surrounded me.

Chapter 5

Roman

I studied Luna as she slumbered beside me in the car, her long, graceful neck stretched to the side and her thick, dark hair spread out on the headrest. Fiona was right, she did have nice breasts and a firm ass. When she'd come to the office demanding I let her out of the internship, I entertained myself fantasizing about what I wanted to do with her if I ever got her underneath me. I'd use and discard Luna like the unwitting pawn she was, but I could enjoy myself in the meantime.

She didn't care about our law firm's reputation, financial net worth, or that our corporation was staggeringly successful, thanks to all the businesses and start-ups we'd bought into over the years. Most people in the legal and business community knew who we were, but she hadn't. I also found it invigorating to spar with her. Luna had a quick wit and a wicked tongue, but she wasn't cynical or jaded. That would likely change by the time I got done with her.

She'd schooled that drunk asshole, Hutton, at breakfast and quickly picked up on me guiding her out of the country club restaurant. The men sitting at that table were dangerous, and I didn't want Luna to become a target because she was with me and looked like a wet dream wrapped in a cheap little suit. I'd be the one to ruin her, not anyone else.

Her brow furrowed and she whimpered softly. I wondered what she dreamed about and shook my head at her naiveté. She finally woke and stretched when I pulled the car into the parking garage, her lace bra and the faint shadow of her pink nipples pressing against her thin white dress shirt for a split second. I didn't feel any guilt for appreciating the view.

When we walked past the reception desk, Brenna glared at Luna like she wanted to rip her hair out. Luna simply smiled at her.

I pointed to the office door next to mine. "It's empty. You can use it while you're here." The smaller office was meant for a personal secretary or paralegal, but I hadn't bothered to hire another one when the last one quit. Gideon took care of most of that, and the last paralegal I had said I was too "abrupt and rude."

Luna still looked groggy and sleepy from her nap, and it made me want to slide my hand behind her neck, fist her hair, and pull her in for a soul-sucking kiss.

She perked up when she saw Gideon. "We visited Euphoria today. Have you been there?"

He smiled at her enthusiasm. "No, but I've heard about it from the partners."

Luna glanced back at me and snickered. "I bet they spend a lot of time there, and probably write it off too, huh?"

"I wouldn't venture to guess." Gideon's lip twitched because we'd had a similar conversation not long ago.

She grinned. "I bet it's a *big* write-off. To compensate for other things."

Gideon laughed, but I lifted an eyebrow. "I believe that was a sexual innuendo."

Sighing, she schooled her features and tried to look contrite. "That was inappropriate, I apologize."

I waved my hand. "It's good to know you're comfortable with them. Come on, you need to study, and I'll take you home in a couple of hours."

When I showed Luna the small office, I left the connecting door open while we worked that afternoon. Glancing in a few times, I noticed Luna wore noise-canceling headphones and spread highlighters out in a neat row on her desk while she studied. But she never seemed to use them. When I knocked on the dividing door a few hours later, she jumped. The room smelled like cinnamon, and I spotted a small sack on the corner of her desk. She frequently nibbled on it, and she even smelled like cinnamon sometimes.

"You ready to go home?"

She pulled the headphones off. "Pardon?"

"Are you ready to go?" I asked again slowly.

"Yes." She looked down at whatever she'd been reading, then back at me, as if she needed a minute to shift gears. I wondered idly if Luna had sensory overload issues or tunnel concentration, like my law partner Xander did. She packed her things, and I took her back to the mortuary.

She turned to me. "I'll see you at the office tomorrow. What time do you want me to be there?"

I smirked. "Nice try. I'm picking you up at eight again."

We got out, and Luna sighed loudly. "You don't need to pick me up or walk me to the apartment."

"But I want to." I followed Luna to her door, and she turned to me.

"Bye."

"May I use your bathroom?"

She studied me. "Are you messing with me right now?"

"A little." I waited her out.

She narrowed her eyes and put her code in. When we walked inside, she bent down and scooped up her three-legged cat, who waited at the door and meowed impatiently. "Hello, Carl. Did you miss me?" The cat had an unpleasant, grinding purr and seemed to barely tolerate her. And who named a cat *Carl*, for fuck's sake?

"What happened to his leg?"

"We don't know. He kind of adopted us. Ezra thinks he followed his late owner to the mortuary, and when the man was cremated Carl decided we'd have to do. The bathroom is down the hall." She put Carl down, and he looked up at me suspiciously, then started licking himself.

Luna smirked. "See? He likes you."

I raised an eyebrow. "And that's how he shows it, by licking his nonexistent balls? Why is he named Carl?"

"I named him after a character from the book series *Dungeon Crawler Carl*. You probably wouldn't like it, you're too pretentious and stuck up."

I arched an eyebrow and made a mental note to look up the series as she pointed down the hall. She'd thrown a good dozen insults at me today, but I didn't mind. If she knew what I planned to do with her, she'd do more than just insult me.

"The bathroom is the second door on the left."

As I walked down the hall, I studied the apartment. The first door I passed was closed, but the next one stood open. The room was neat, and an overstuffed bookshelf stood against one wall, crammed with books and a few personal items. Based on all the books, this was probably Luna's room.

It wasn't like most women's bedrooms I'd seen. There weren't feminine knickknacks or clothes strewn around, or an overpowering smell of perfumes and lotions. It was all about comfort and books. I tried to see if they had any security as I walked back into the kitchen, where a tall blond woman stood next to Alexa at the bar. All three of them were beautiful, but Luna was the one I wanted to fuck.

She pointed to her friend. "This is Sylvie Spade. Her family owns the mortuary."

Sylvie quirked her mouth. "Roman Fowler, of FUCK, Legal. So you're the jackass who ruined Luna's internship plans and our fall vacation. I know one of your partners. Are you as big of an asshole as he is?"

Luna didn't try to shut Sylvie up. Her friend didn't mince words, and she was protective of Luna. Good to know. "A pleasure to meet you, Ms. Spade. Tell your grandfather and cousins I said hello." I nodded at Alexa and turned to Luna. "I'll see you tomorrow at eight sharp. Don't stay up so late tonight."

Walking out, I cracked my knuckles as I strode to my car. Ever since I'd glimpsed Luna's flushed, animated face as she talked with Gideon last Friday, I'd been obsessed with her. She disliked the country club, ate without embarrassment when she was hungry, and had been fascinated by Euphoria. It would be a pleasure to spar and debate with her before I eventually had to break her.

When I walked into the office twenty minutes later, the partners were gathered around my oversized desk, already drinking my liquor and playing with my coin collection. We met like this at least once a week after hours to decompress and catch up. Sometimes we sparred at the boxing gym a few blocks away, or met up on the weekends to watch a game or shoot the shit.

Drakos glanced up when I strode in, still wearing his suit jacket and silk tie. "How's the new intern, mentee, whatever-the-fuck she is?"

"Better than expected. I think you've heard that she's Montgomery Cross's daughter. Klim changed her mentorship at the last minute and sent her to me." I smirked evilly and poured myself a drink. "Then she tried to weasel her way out of it."

Ivan shook his head and folded his muscled, tattooed arms. "So, of course, you didn't let her, being the contrary jackass you are. That would've been like waving a fucking red cape at you. I still need to do a background check on her." He wore faded jeans and black biker boots and was our expert hacker. Ivan had his law degree, but he hated being an attorney and was a savant with computers, so he did whatever the hell he wanted to, including our security and investigations.

I nodded absently. "I want you to dig up everything. Her grades, her finances, what type of birth control she's on, and what her weaknesses are. I want to know if she has a boyfriend, even her tampon brand if she uses them."

Drakos shook his head and took a drink. "Her birth control, boyfriend, and tampon brand? Are you planning to fuck her before or after you fuck her over? You're an evil bastard." He looked like a successful Wall Street broker in his silk ties, cuff links, and excessively expensive suits–until he opened his foul mouth and biting sarcasm spilled out.

I raised an eyebrow and took another sip. "Both."

Ivan studied me. "So you want the full monty on her. She's what, twenty-four? That'll take a day, maybe two."

Xander lounged against my bookcase, rolling one of my rare, ancient Roman coins between his fingers. He was the silent one. His long, dark blond hair hung around his shoulders, and he'd untucked his shirt and rolled up his shirt sleeves.

"You're obsessing again," he warned me.

Xander was the philosophical, introspective one. Sometimes he wore suits, but when he got to the office, he always shed his jacket and lost his tie. He also looked like a California surfer.

"It's not a fucking obsession."

"Uh-huh," Drakos needled. "That's why you want the 'full monty' on a young law student."

Unlike Xander, Drakos liked to stir up shit. We were tight like family, but black and white in temperament sometimes.

I stared them down. "Klim sent Ms. Cross to me to do with as I please. And since she's a Cross, I'll reel her in and ruin her slowly and methodically. But no one gets close to us unless they've been vetted. We protect our family."

We all fell silent, and the mood went dark. After the nightmarish way we met and became brothers, we'd adopted that motto so we all knew we'd have each other's backs. *Protegat Familia*: Protect Family. It meant protecting each other because our biological families sure as fuck hadn't. The air in the office thickened as memories tried to claw their way to the surface. The past was a shadow we lived under and never quite escaped.

I sighed and faced the elephant in the room. "That fucking hellhole has a way of grabbing us by the throat, even now."

Xander rolled the coin again and studied the movement. "It made us who we are, for better or worse."

"Ruthless, soulless bastards who have no problem using daughters as pawns and skirting the law?" Ivan mused.

Drakos grinned. "We don't *skirt* the law, we fucking break the law most of the time." His remark seemed to ease the tension.

Running my hand through my hair, I glanced over at Ivan. "She's just a girl I need to use and inconveniently want to fuck. She looks like a wet dream even in mediocre clothes, asks a thousand questions, and is too smart for her own good. But we vet her."

Ivan sipped his whiskey and studied me. "Then I'll get you her tampon brand."

When everyone was gone, I sat and studied the coin Xander had set on the corner of my desk. Luna didn't want to be interning at

The Firm or with me, but she'd made the most of it. She was unique, smart, and curious. I frowned.

The office had gone quiet, with only Ivan clattering on his keyboards a couple of offices down. Swirling the whiskey, I watched the liquid catch the light from the dim lamp on my desk and thought of Luna's incessant questions and probing green eyes that didn't miss much.

The scar on my neck twinged, and I absently ran a finger over it, feeling the raised skin. I'd gotten it years ago when a guard threw me into the side of an old outbuilding. I'd been centimeters away from being impaled through my throat on that long, rusty nail. Instead, the guards kicked the shit out of me as my neck bled all over, threw me into a cell, and left me for days. The wound had healed badly.

"Hey." Ivan's voice cut through the silence, snapping me back to the present as he studied me from the doorway. "Anything specific you're looking for?"

"Everything, every skeleton in her closet. I may or may not read it all, but I want it just in case."

He rubbed the back of his neck. "She's young, and she's probably squeaky fucking clean. Are you sure you want to drag her into our shit?"

"Yes," I replied with cold finality.

Ivan looked down at the coin. "You and your fucking obsessions. Alright, I'll send you what I find." When Ivan left, I drained the last of my whiskey and went home.

The gleaming glass panes of the cold, modern house reflected my headlights back to me as I turned into the driveway. The sleek modern structure, with a facade of concrete, steel, and glass, sat nestled in the foothills above Las Vegas. Intermittent greenery defied the desert, softening the house a little. The underground irrigation systems in almost every yard in the West still mystified me.

I left my Mercedes in the circular driveway and used my thumbprint to unlock the massive glass front door, shed my jacket, and threw it over the entryway table. Then I paused and studied the interior as if from Luna's eyes. It unfolded like a gallery of shadows and sharp angles.

I absently wondered what she'd think of this house. It was so different from her odd, vibrant apartment. She lived above a sprawling mortuary in the middle of a cemetery, for fuck's sake, but her apartment had more life and vitality than my cutting-edge, multi-million-dollar home. It looked like Ezra had renovated the space over the last ten years or so, but he kept the same 1960s vintage feel to match the mid-century modern mortuary it was attached to.

Looking around at my house with its natural stone floors, sleek furniture, and abstract art pieces, I still couldn't decide whether I liked the space or not. The back of the residence had floor-to-ceiling windows that offered an unobstructed view of Sin City's skyline and the infinity pool outside. I couldn't recall the last time I'd used the pool.

After shedding the rest of my clothes, I slipped into compression shorts and headed to the gym. My mind wouldn't rest as thoughts about what I wanted to do to Luna Cross kept intruding, which only angered me more. Over the years, I'd found the best way to quiet my brain was to work through one of the brutal sparring routines Gideon had taught us after we'd been liberated from Bitter Creek. It seemed to be a cross between Brazilian Jui-Jitsu and Krav Maga. I sparred with the punching bag, and as sweat dripped from my body, my thoughts eventually quieted.

When I finished, I toweled off and headed to the kitchen for some water and protein. As I stood at the kitchen sink drinking a foul protein shake, the pool spread out like a dark inky mirror, reflecting the glowing skyline. I finished my shake and stared out at the night, eventually walking out onto the back patio into the cool fall desert night. I stripped off my shorts and dove into the warm, black water, leisurely swimming laps as I continued to obsess about Luna.

Chapter 6

Luna

This was the third morning Roman showed up at eight sharp. My roommates had left this morning to go on vacation without me, and my mood was foul.

I swung the door open with an irritated growl. "I keep telling you, I have my own car. You don't need to pick me up." Not waiting for him to follow, I returned to the kitchen bar and started stuffing a few things into my backpack.

"And miss your sparkly charm and sunny personality on the drive over?" He glanced at my cat. "Hello, Carl. You little demon from hell." Roman tried to pet him yesterday, but Carl swiped his hand and spit at him. I'd called Carl a "good little kitty."

Strolling into the kitchen with his hands in his pockets, Roman wore yet another expensive suit and Italian leather shoes. He'd forgone the tie today, and looked like a sleek magazine advertisement for an expensive watch. The man annoyed me *so much*. I wore off-the-rack black, gray, and navy blue clothes. They were within my budget, easy to match, and helped me blend in.

"Did you take such a hands-on approach with other law students you've mentored?" I groused as I grabbed my generic black suit jacket.

"No. But you've already proven useful, and Klim wants you with me. He has good instincts." He was mocking me.

"Great, I feel so special. I'm ready, let's go." I stopped short. "Wait, I need one more thing." Digging through the kitchen drawer, I found a pack of Red Hots.

"You eat a lot of candy. It's bad for your teeth."

When he got into the car, I raised an eyebrow at him and bit into a Red Hot. Roman got a call on the way over, so I checked my emails while he talked to someone about zoning codes and multimillion-dollar returns. Yesterday, Roman had tucked me into the small, unused office next to his, and kept me there for half the day. He'd ordered lunch, then left me alone to study in the afternoon before driving me home. I had a feeling this would become our routine if I didn't do something.

When we walked in together again today, the look on Bitchy Brenna's face warmed my frosty heart. After she got over her initial annoyance, she couldn't decide if she wanted to smile at Roman or glare at me.

"Good morning, Mr. Fowler," she purred. "You have a few messages I emailed you."

"Thanks." He turned to me. "Find Gideon and have him show you the Garrison Development file. We'll discuss it over lunch." I could almost hear Brenna grinding her teeth.

I knocked on Roman's door a couple of hours later. I didn't ask him if he was busy. "Today is Wednesday and I've gotten my mentorship hours in for the week. It's also my fall break."

He didn't look up. "No."

"Are you saying it's not my fall break, or no, you're not going to be a decent person and let me go?"

"The second." His lip curled, but he kept typing on his expensive, sleek laptop.

"How about if I come in tomorrow and get Friday off?" I tried.

"No."

"Come on, man! Most attorneys don't even work on Fridays."

"How about you come in on Saturday too? I'll be here, so I might as well have some company," he countered, still not looking up.

I slumped against the door, annoyance sharpening my voice. "Fine, I'll come on Friday. But only because Sylvie and Alexa are out of town."

"Excellent." He finally looked up. "I have an afternoon appointment at a motorcycle restoration shop. Do you want to come?"

"Yes." My mind jumped ahead. "Can I ask a few questions?"

He shook his head. "You and your questions. You can ask *if* they have the time and you don't annoy them. We'll meet with the president at noon and grab lunch after that."

I left his office and headed toward the break room to grab another cup of coffee. At least they had excellent free coffee here.

"Hello, Luna," Gideon greeted me as I neared his desk. "I'm thrilled you came back."

"You make it sound like I had a choice. He's been picking me up every morning this week," I whined.

Gideon chuckled and kept typing. "Has he now? That's delightful."

"No, Gideon, it's really not. This is my fall break, and he's making me come in and be with him all week. For the whole day. What mentor does that?"

Gideon's phone rang. He patted my hand sympathetically and turned to answer it.

A man I'd seen a couple of times walked out of his office with an empty coffee cup in hand too. He was tall and muscular, had a nice, full beard and slicked-back hair, and wore a black pearl snap shirt with black motorcycle boots. I got the impression he didn't go to court much.

He smirked when he saw me. "Hello, Luna the intern. I'm Ivan Knox, one of Roman's partners."

"Hello, Ivan. I'd say it's nice to meet you, but after spending time with Roman, I'll reserve judgment about the rest of you."

Ivan chuckled. "That's smart. Has it been that bad working under Roman?"

I raised an eyebrow. "*Under* Roman? That's a funny way of putting it." I pointed to Ivan's office. "What is it you do exactly? You've got more monitors and computer equipment than any attorney I've ever seen. How many single-board computers do you have, and what are you doing with all of them?"

"How do you know about SBE's?"

Shrugging, I snuck another peek inside his office. "I have a friend who knows computers. Are you an attorney? What's your specialty?"

"My specialty is finding things out about people they don't want me to know."

I blinked at him. "You're an interesting foursome. Xander wears business attire, but it seems like an afterthought. He reminds me more of a skateboarder."

Ivan smirked. "He snowboards and surfs."

I nodded. "That fits. Drakos dresses so sharply, he gives me paper cuts. Where'd you all meet?"

Ivan's eyes went cool. So he wasn't going to tell me how they met. Waving my hand, I moved on. "I don't understand your firm's structure. You seem more like brothers than partners. What is it *you* do again?"

Ivan studied me. "I gather and analyze data."

I studied him back. "Hm. I wonder why a law firm would need someone who does that full-time."

"Is that a rhetorical question?"

"No. I'm actually curious."

His eyebrow went up. "We have other business interests, and I do background checks and vet companies and individuals."

My eyes narrowed. "Did you 'vet' me?"

"Of course."

I wasn't surprised. "What other business interests do you have? Blackmail? Money laundering? Pest control? What?"

Someone chuckled behind me, and I startled. Turning around, I saw Drakos sitting on the corner of Gideon's desk.

"Hello, little Luna. It's not even lunchtime, and you've already asked sixty-nine questions." He wore a sleek designer navy blue suit, a crisp white dress shirt, and an azure–blue silk tie and matching pocket square.

"Is that a sexual innuendo or did you actually count?" I asked, then turned to Ivan. "See? A paper cut."

Ivan chuckled. "Point taken."

"You don't have to drill us with questions like we're in a police interrogation. You could just enjoy our company." Drakos's grin was too wide to be sincere.

"What classes are you taking this semester?" Ivan asked, obviously changing the subject.

"Mediation, federal income tax, legal writing, and corporations."

Ivan nodded. "That's a challenging schedule. What's your favorite class?"

"Mediation."

Drakos laughed outright, and Ivan snorted and patted my arm.

"Get your hand off her, Knox. Mediation is overrated," Roman stated as he walked out of his office. "Why mediate and compromise when you can dominate and win?"

I turned to Roman and wondered why he'd told Ivan to get his hand off me. The man confused me. "I'm not surprised that's your stance. Not everyone enjoys litigation and confrontation, though."

He shrugged. "Mediation is a good way to glean information, I'll give you that. But you should never purposefully put yourself into a weaker position."

The men at this law firm—if one could call it that—were enigmas, and these three had sharp edges. I wondered how their experiences in Arizona had altered them because I knew firsthand a person couldn't go through something like that and not be changed in deep and significant ways.

That afternoon, Roman took me to Sin City Motorheads. From the outside, the business looked more like a motorcycle club that was maybe two shades away from being a motorcycle gang. It was located in a gritty industrial area in North Las Vegas, but the interior was a surprise. The showroom had a sleek, industrial edge to it with neon signage, a full bar on one side, and a few vintage motorcycles on display. There were also glossy, artistic photos of women straddling bikes wearing nothing but thongs.

As we walked in, I looked around with my mouth open. "Wow, this place is amazing."

A younger man with long, stringy hair and an easy smile sat behind the raised chrome counter, and he stood when we walked in. "Hey Roman, I'll tell Diego you're here. He's on a phone call."

"Thanks, Brodie."

"Who's Diego?" I asked.

"Diego Rodriguez—the president and part-owner of the Area Fifty-Three motorcycle club and biker bar where they meet. He also owns a stake in this shop. He's a likable, crass, mouthy asshole."

I smiled brightly. "It sounds like you're describing yourself—except the likable part."

Roman shook his head as his phone rang. Looking down at the screen, he stepped outside to take the call, and I wandered over to the Harley Strap Tank model on display and walked around it with my hands behind my back.

"Do you like it?" Brodie asked. The bike looked like a cross between an old moped and a vintage motorcycle.

"I've read about this motorcycle. It's one of the oldest and most rare models available. Isn't it named after those straps holding the gas tank on?"

"You know about motorcycles?" a gruff voice behind me asked. I turned and saw a tall, striking man with sarcastic eyes and a strong jaw standing behind me wearing a black leather vest with patches on it. He wore motorcycle boots similar to Ivan's, and his white smile stood out against his tan complexion.

I looked back at the vintage bike. "Not really, I've just read a few books about them. I ran across an interesting biography about some of the last vintage motorcycles and the history of Harley-Davidson in high school, though."

He stuck a toothpick in his mouth. "Yeah? What'd you learn?"

"That Harley-Davidson is named after four men, three of whom were Davidsons, and the business started in Milwaukee, Wisconsin in..." I closed one eye and tried to remember. "1905? Maybe a little earlier. Anyway, their continued success seems to be a testament to America's love affair with motorcycles and transportation."

"Huh." The man looked surprised.

I turned to him in earnest. "What's the oldest motorcycle you've worked on, and where do you find the parts? Are you working on any right now?" I looked down at his vest and pointed. "Hey, I read an article about the motorcycle gangs around here last year after the latest shooting in Laughlin. I have a few questions. What do the patches mean on your vest?"

The man tilted his head and removed the toothpick. "Who the fuck are you?"

"Oh, I'm sorry. I'm Luna Cross." I held out my hand. "Roman Fowler is my attorney mentor. Unfortunately, they didn't allow me to pick my own."

The man blinked, then grinned wide as he shook my hand. "He's your mentor, huh? What's he teaching you?"

I tilted my head, wondering if there was a double meaning in there somewhere. "Mostly how pigheaded and annoying he can be."

The man laughed as Roman walked back inside. "Diego, I see you've met Luna."

Diego eyed me again, then turned to Roman. "You have a claim on her? She's not your usual type, and–"

Roman cut in, his voice flat. "She's not available. I think it's fine if she sits in on most of our meeting, but there are a few... issues we need to discuss privately. Will she be safe if she wanders around? I'm warning you, she asks a fuck-ton of questions."

He grinned. "Yeah, I got that. Let's discuss the legal business first, then I'll go back and talk to the guys." We went to Diego's office, and he and Roman discussed a restoration contract and some indemnification issues. Then Diego walked us back to the garage area.

I touched Roman's arm as we walked, and he glanced down at me. "What did he mean by a claim on me?"

His jaw clenched. "Later."

Two fully tattooed men were working on a machine in the shop area, and three other vintage motorcycles lined the back wall in various stages of disrepair.

I slowly approached the motorcycle they were currently working on and stared. "Oh, my God. Is that a Knucklehead?" I whispered reverently.

Diego turned to Roman. "Are you sure she's not available?"

"No," Roman snarled.

The man on the floor looked up from my legs to my face and grinned. "Yeah, honey. How'd you know that?"

Diego stepped forward. "Luna, this is Rick." Then he pointed to the man in greasy blue coveralls hanging from his waist and a black wife beater, who stood in front of a computer monitor. "And that's Roy. This is Roman's law student, so hands off. But can you answer her questions and keep her company while Roman and I talk for a few minutes?"

Roy looked me up and down, then grinned. They both looked to be in their late thirties and had full tattoo sleeves. I couldn't wait to talk to them.

An hour later, Roman and Diego returned to the shop area and stopped dead. I straddled the Knucklehead, and Rick and Roy stood on either side of me, pointing out the different features and quirks. I'd hiked my pencil skirt up to my thighs so I could climb on.

"What the fuck, Luna?" Roman growled. Diego folded his arms, rocked on his heels, and grinned.

I smiled happily at Roman. "Okay, I'm not gonna lie. I may not like you dragging me to your office every day, but I fucking *love* these field trips. This place is amazing!"

Rick and Roy grinned, and Rick patted my bare thigh. "I think he wants you to climb off, honey. You're welcome back anytime, and we'll answer the rest of your questions."

Roman's eyes narrowed, and he flicked his fingers to me in a "come here" gesture.

"But they were going to start it for me," I protested.

His eyes narrowed dangerously, and I sighed. "Fine." I'd taken off my shoes, so I swung my bare foot over the bike and slid off, adjusting my skirt back down.

Turning to Rick and Roy, I patted them both on the arms. "Thanks, guys. That was fun."

Roy grinned a shit-eating grin. "Next time you want to straddle one of our bikes, we'll take it outside and take you for a ride."

"Luna. Now." Roman barked.

I turned around and faced him. "What's your problem, grumpy pants? They've been nothing but polite, and very patient with all my questions." I bent down, grabbing my shoes.

"Get your eyes off her ass. Right. Fucking. Now." Roman growled low. I straightened and turned around to see who he was talking to.

Roy ignored Roman and grabbed a few wipes from a container. "You've got a grease mark across your cheek, sweetheart."

Roman stalked over and grabbed the wipes out of Roy's hand, then held my chin between his thumb and forefinger. He studied my happy smile, then cleaned off my face. "You're a damn menace."

"No, I'm just inquisitive."

"I've heard of that," Rick offered. "Isn't an inquisitor one of the death squad from *Star Wars*?"

Diego smirked. "Pretty sure that's not what she meant." He turned to Roman. "Bring her back anytime."

Rick and Roy both nodded, and I smiled at them.

Roman grabbed my hand and started walking toward the door. "Fuck, no. I'll be in touch." He didn't turn around as we walked out.

Roman clenched the steering wheel and locked his jaw as he pulled out of Diego's parking lot.

I studied his face curiously. "Are you mad at me?"

"Yes."

"Why?"

"Because when we walked out to the garage, you had your skirt hiked up to your goddamn waist with your crotch pressed to that bike, and those two men were eye-fucking you."

I gasped and narrowed my eyes. "You did *not* just say that to me."

"Yes, I believe I did."

"You're wrong. They were perfectly appropriate, and they answered my questions. It was a great afternoon, so don't ruin it." I folded my arms and looked out the window. "And they were not staring at my ass," I mumbled.

"They were *absolutely* staring at your ass. You bent over right in front of them, and they didn't have a fucking choice. It's like throwing bacon in front of untrained dogs and telling them not to go after it. That doesn't mean they'd touch you unless you signaled you were up for it, but they sure as fuck will look."

My cheeks heated, and I changed the subject. "What did Diego mean about you having a claim on me?"

"They're part of a motorcycle club, and Diego has a few members he thought might be interested in you."

"Oh, that's nice I guess. I don't date, though. Law school is more than enough." I stared out the window.

"That's *nice*? Do you know what it would be like to be owned by a member?"

I turned to him. "I've read books, but maybe I missed something, so why don't you tell me?" He ground his teeth but didn't speak, and I thought it was better not to push him.

"Where are we going now?"

"To lunch, back to the office, and then I'll take you home."

"I have food at home. You can just drop me off there."

"No."

I glared at him. "You need to learn some new words. Every time I ask for anything, you say no."

He didn't answer, and I sat silently sulking. A few moments later, he glanced over and his lips twitched. "Do you hear that?"

"Hear what?" I asked suspiciously.

"Exactly. Blessed silence. Not a God damned thing—no questions, no snarky remarks, no arguments."

I rolled my eyes. "You're so funny. Seriously, why do you have to drive me around everywhere? Especially if you don't even like me?"

"Because I want to. What are you hungry for?"

Shrugging, I looked out the window. "I usually eat a cheese stick and an apple for lunch. I'm not picky."

"Okay. How about La Fontaine?"

"Too fancy."

He glance at me. "Chubbs?"

"Too greasy."

"Ruby's Diner."

"Sounds delicious, but it'll take us an hour to even get a seat."

"I thought you said you aren't picky? By all means, you throw out a few ideas."

"How about Luna's kitchen at the lovely Palm Desert Oasis Mortuary, and we eat chicken curry and sautéed veggies?"

He glanced at me and shrugged. "Sounds good. Your apartment it is."

"You told Sylvie you know her grandfather."

"I do."

"Can I invite him to lunch? Sylvie is out of town, and he's probably lonely."

Roman eyed me carefully. "You want to invite Ezra Spade to lunch with us because you think he's lonely."

"Yeah."

He wiped his hand down his face and sighed. "Luna, how well do you know Ezra?"

From Roman's tone, I knew what he was asking. "I know him, and the rest of the family, well."

"How well?"

"They're my foster family, and if you say anything bad about them. I'll make sure you regret it."

Roman's eye seemed to twitch. "Alright. Let's go eat lunch with Ezra Spade."

A half-hour later, Ezra buzzed the doorbell and walked in. "I brought homemade lemon bars. It's quiet at the mortuary without Sylvie and Alexa around, so thank you for the lunch invite." Holding up the plate of goodies, he smiled then stopped short when he saw Roman. I'd just laid out the food on the small kitchen table.

Ezra's eyes narrowed. "Hello, Roman. I didn't know you knew our sweet Luna."

"Nice to see you, Ezra. She's doing her law school internship with me. I haven't talked to you in a while. How's business?"

Ezra's eyes flickered, and I saw protectiveness and a warning in them. Then he smiled faintly. "We own a funeral home, so my business is guaranteed. You know what they say about death and taxes."

"The mortuary is just one of your family businesses, and enough people cheat on their taxes, so I'm not sure how accurate the second part of that statement is," Roman murmured.

Ezra inclined his head, and we sat down to eat.

"This is delicious, Luna." Ezra smiled at me then turned to Roman, his smile sliding off. "How's your law practice doing? Are you still buying up business interests?"

"Yes. And you? Have you had any of your business accounts trigger AML lately?"

Ezra's hand tightened on his fork. "Nothing like you dealt with a couple of years ago, from what I hear."

Sighing, I put my water glass down and pinched the bridge of my nose. "Are you two done slinging white-collar crime accusations at each other? You're giving me heartburn."

Roman leaned back. "I have no idea what you're talking about."

I rolled my eyes and ate a bite of chicken. "I'm taking federal tax law right now. And AML stands for anti-money laundering. Just stop."

Ezra cleared his throat and straightened. "I apologize. Why didn't you go with Sylvie and Alexa to Oceanside for your fall break?"

Glaring at Roman, I answered Ezra's question. "Because my mentor decided I needed to shadow him all week and had no problem ruining my vacation." I shoved a piece of carrot in my mouth and continued to glare.

Ezra picked up his fork again and studied Roman carefully. "Let's just hope that's all he plans to ruin."

Chapter 7

Luna

On Friday morning, Roman knocked on the apartment door fifteen minutes before eight.

Swinging the door open, I glared up at him. "You're early, and you *still* don't need to pick me up. In fact, you go on. I'll drive today, then I can leave early. It's Friday after all."

He grinned and walked inside. "Good morning to you too, Sunshine. It's refreshing that you're always pugnacious and always on time."

I gave him a flat stare. "I know what pugnacious means, and my name is Luna, so Sunshine doesn't really fit."

"Then Moonshine will work."

"Never mind. Sunshine is fine."

"I like Moonshine. And no."

I sighed. "There's that word again. I just need to put on my shoes and get my bag."

He walked over to the couch where one of my books lay on the arm and picked it up. "You're reading a how-to book about building a raised garden."

"It relaxes me."

"Have you ever had a garden?"

I searched around for my phone. "No, but I'd like to someday. I've never done or seen most of the things I read about–that's why I read."

He stared at me. "Does your brain ever shut down?"

"Maybe when I'm sleeping."

Shaking his head, he studied me as if searching for something. "Probably not even then."

Roman spent most of the morning on his phone, so I pulled out my never-ending homework, put on my noise-canceling headphones, spread out my highlighters, and studied. A few hours later, Ivan tapped my shoulder. I squeaked loudly, sending a few highlighters skidding off the desk.

"Holy shit! Don't sneak up on me like that."

He folded his arms and grinned. "I said your name–twice. I've been watching you for a few minutes."

I pulled my headphones off. "That's not creepy at all. What's going on?"

"Lunch is on its way. We bring it in on Fridays."

"Okay. Sounds good." I picked the highlighters up and straightened them.

"Your concentration is a bit scary. Why do you have so many markers you never use?"

My shoulders hunched. "I don't know."

"You have a near photographic memory."

"How do you... Oh, the background check. I don't have a photographic memory. My reading comprehension is just high, that's all." The background check annoyed me, but I knew they were fairly common. "What else did you learn about me?" I grabbed a cinnamon bear from the open package on my desk and chomped its head off.

Ivan smirked as he watched me chew. "You grew up in the Phoenix area, and your father is a federal judge there. You have stellar grades, a partial scholarship, and no criminal background."

"Pretty boring stuff." But my stomach tightened, and I chewed slowly. His smirk had a mean glint.

"Yep. Except you accused your father of taking bribes when you were younger, and your parents disowned you."

"I'm not sure how that's relevant to anything." A wave of anxiety hit me, thinking about that time in my life.

"You were twelve years old, and you've been living with the Spades ever since."

I stared at him as my mind violently jerked me back. My father had never laid a hand on me until that day, but he'd come home so full of rage.

"You know what? You had no right to dig into my background–"

"Background checks are standard–"

I held up my finger. "Shut up, I'm not done talking. And then walk in here and throw the most hurtful parts in my face just to see my reaction. And I was fucking *right* about my father. The law shouldn't be applied differently for rich, degenerate assholes." If Ivan knew, then Roman knew, and he hadn't said a word.

Ivan's eyebrow winged up mockingly. "I'm sure you believe that."

"I said it shouldn't. I never said it doesn't. Why are you trying to run me off? You know I don't have a choice about being here, right?"

He gazed at me for a few seconds, and he almost seemed... worried. Then the look vanished and his sneer returned. "No one's forcing you to be here. You could tell Klim to fuck off."

"Yeah, and lose my scholarship and maybe not graduate." Gazing around the office, I stood up. "Fuck this," I muttered as I shoved books, highlighters, and candy into my backpack. I couldn't be here anymore, at least not today.

"Aren't you going to stay and eat lunch?" he asked mockingly.

"Go fuck yourself. Roman may hate my guts, but at least he's not purposefully cruel."

Swinging my backpack over my shoulder, I shoved past him.

"Luna," he called. "Don't kid yourself about Roman. He's just better at hiding his cruelty."

I threw him the middle finger over my shoulder and strode out of the law offices, ignoring Brenna's little grin when she saw the tear running down my cheek.

When the rideshare dropped me off at home, I turned off my phone, changed into jeans and a sweatshirt, and headed over to the law school. The heavy door of the law library groaned as I shouldered my way inside, and the scent of old books and low-grade anxiety greeted me. I dumped my backpack on a table in the back corner of my favorite floor.

Muttering under my breath, I pulled out my headphones. "My whole vacation shot in the ass."

"Who got shot in the ass?"

I jumped at the sound of Jared Gardner's loud voice. He leaned against a bookshelf, staring down at me. Jared was probably the most handsome law student in our class, but he talked way too much about himself and had a grating, self-centered personality.

He'd asked me out a few times, and whenever we had a class together, he tried to sit next to me. The fact that I wasn't interested probably made him that much more determined; I just wanted him to leave me alone.

"Hello, Jared. How was your fall break?" I muttered as I put my headphones around my neck.

Jared raised an eyebrow. "Good, how's yours been? I thought you were going out of town with your roommates."

He seemed to know a lot about my life. "Change of plans."

"I hear you're interning at The Firm with Roman Fowler." He looked envious.

"I didn't even know who they were until a week ago."

Jared shook his head. "They're only the wealthiest, most prestigious law firm in Las Vegas. Is it true? Are you actually interning there?"

I sighed and rubbed my eyes. "Probably not anymore. I told one of the partners to go fuck himself this afternoon."

Jared's eyes bugged out and he sat down. "Are you nuts? Do you know the rumors about those guys?"

"This is Las Vegas. What successful business around here doesn't have rumors and gossip swirling around it? That doesn't mean they're true." The irony wasn't lost on me. An hour ago I'd stormed out of there with my middle finger in the air, and now I was defending them.

"It doesn't mean they're not. They're richer than Croesus, and they've got their fingers in a lot of pies."

"Rumors are like pigeons," I replied, flipping open a textbook. "They fly around and make a mess, but don't amount to much."

"How'd you get an internship with them, anyway? I thought you had something lined up with a water law attorney."

"I did, but Klim Hudson assigned me to Fowler instead. I'm there under protest."

He shook his head. "You need to be careful. I've heard Fowler and his partners are basically a crime syndicate, and they don't mind getting their hands dirty."

"It sounds like someone's been watching too much late-night reality TV." I'd grown up with the Spade family, so I wasn't as freaked out as I probably should have been, and neither The Firm nor the

House of Spades seemed to leave a trail of broken victims like my father did.

Jared leaned forward. "Around Vegas, there really are dead bodies buried out in the desert–or dumped in Lake Mead. Just be careful."

"It's good then that I'm just a lowly law student intern. What are the rumors anyway?" I broke down and asked.

"Besides the legal but morally gray shit? Bribery, blackmail, greasing palms." He ticked them off on his fingers. "Probably money laundering too."

I scoffed. "You're describing half the successful white-collar businesses around here."

"Look, Luna." His voice dropped. "I'm not saying Roman's firm is the mob, but they've got that same untouchable vibe. People get in the way or mess with their interests, and they end up like Schrödinger's cat—neither alive nor dead until someone opens the box."

"Except nobody wants to open the box," I concluded, my skepticism showing.

"Exactly." Jared nodded, as if pleased I was following along.

He might be a shmuck, but he wasn't stupid. Too bad he had such a shitty personality. "I'll avoid poking around. And like I said, I don't plan to go back, anyway." Even as I said it, I wondered if I had a choice.

"That'd be smart." He pushed away from the table and stood, his chair scraping against the floor.

I put my headphones on and turned back to my homework. Jared was a bit of a conspiracy theorist, and he hadn't told me anything I didn't already suspect. Shaking off his warnings, I got to work.

Hours later, my mind felt tired, and my eyes stung. It was time to quit. When I snapped my book shut, the thud echoed in the near-empty library.

Turning my phone on, I winced as notifications started pinging.

Roman: Ivan said you stormed out of the office. Don't leave again without checking in

He could go screw himself if he thought I'd be checking in with him when his partners were being pricks.

Roman: Are you returning today, or will you continue sulking for the rest of the afternoon?

Roman: It's after five. You owe me hours. I'll pick you up at eight tomorrow morning

"Un-fucking-believable," I muttered under my breath. My fingers flew across the screen as I typed out a response.

Luna: Can't. Tomorrow's Saturday

He texted back almost immediately.

Roman: Non-negotiable

Me: Fill in the acronym to your law firm here, and add a "YOU" at the end

He didn't respond. I shoved my things into my bag with less care than usual. Carl would be waiting for dinner, and Ezra had texted about binge-watching some TV together. Both seemed like heaven compared to the hell of dealing with Roman Fowler and his stupid partners.

Dusk had fallen, and I wondered if I could make it to my car before it got too dark. I pulled my car keys out and muttered to myself as I walked out of the library. "Stubborn, pushy asshole."

"Talking to yourself now?" a voice murmured to my right.

Jumping, I yelped and held up the keys I'd laced between my fingers. Roman leaned against a pillar outside the law library with his arms crossed.

"What in God's name are you doing, lurking outside the library? Jesus Christ, man. You scared the hell out of me."

"Where did you go this afternoon?"

Ivan's words came back, and I straightened. "I've had enough, I want out."

"Why?" His tone was cool, detached.

I turned and started walking down the steps. "Because you detest me and your partners hate me."

"Luna, stop."

"No. I'm not available whenever you snap your fingers. You don't own me."

He pushed off the pillar and closed the distance between us, stepping in front of me, his dark eyes unreadable.

"What happened at the office today?"

"Nothing I want to talk about. And this?" I wagged my finger between us. "Will not work. I have classes and responsibilities, and I need to study. You can't just—"

"Control your life?" He finished my sentence. "I wouldn't dream of it."

"Good, because you can't." I turned and started walking again.

"Luna, talk to me." His low, serious tone stopped me.

I hung my head, then turned around and faced him. "I know you did a background check on me. And today Ivan threw some painful memories in my face for no good reason." I stepped closer to him. "Well, guess what? My roommates and I did a background check on you guys. And we know about Arizona. We've also heard rumors about questionable legal activities and deviant sexual tastes."

His face went blank. "You can't believe everything you read."

"Trust me, I know. The point is, I don't throw it in your faces just to get a rise out of you or hurt you. And I didn't use it to try and get out of this internship."

He nodded carefully. "Understood. I want you to stay."

"This isn't a good idea." I stared up into his fathomless dark eyes. "Please, you need to let me go."

"I can't."

He sounded almost... sorry. Closing my eyes, I exhaled slowly. Why did I think I could persuade him?

I opened my eyes and met his gaze. "Then we need some boundaries."

"Boundaries?" he repeated, the word rolling off his tongue like a funny joke.

A few students came out of the library and glanced at us curiously before heading down the steps.

"Boundaries."

"Alright. I haven't eaten, so let's grab dinner and talk. There's a little Italian place near the mortuary. How does that sound?"

The idea of eating at Luigi's deflated my knee-jerk refusal. "Damn it, I love Luigi's."

Roman smiled, and it was the first time I didn't see mockery, scorn, or faint derision in his eyes. His smile charmed me, and I wondered what he would've turned out to be like if he hadn't been sent to that hellscape in Arizona.

"Then let's go eat and discuss boundaries." The faint mockery was back, only a little more muted this time.

"Alright. I'll meet you there in twenty minutes."

He folded his arms and looked down at the keys still threaded between my knuckles. "I'll walk you to your car and meet you at the apartment."

When I opened my mouth, he held up his hand. "I have another word for you. Yes. Yes, I'm walking you to your car."

My shoulders loosened and I glanced around. "I was about to say thank you. How'd you find me, anyway?"

"I had Ivan track your cell phone."

Stopping short, I turned to him incredulously. "Oh, my God. See, this is what I'm talking about. Boundaries."

He held up his hands. "I was worried. Come on, let's go."

Roman followed me home, and I ran up to my apartment to feed Carl. Then we walked over to Luigi's.

Sophia smiled and hugged me at the host desk. "I think your favorite table is open. You okay to seat yourselves?"

"Absolutely." I led him to our favorite booth, tucked away in the corner. I didn't bother with a menu, and a few minutes later, a server came over and took our order.

Roman eyed me. "How often do you come here?"

"Two, maybe three times a week. When Sophia sprained her ankle last year, I helped them over the holiday break and got to know everyone pretty well."

Roman leaned back and put his arm up. "Ezra mentioned you work funerals sometimes too. That's a strange part-time job."

The server brought us the house wine. "It's not that strange. Okay, there have been a few odd moments, but if the funeral is over thirty people, then Alexa and I dress in black, slap on discreet gold name tags, and help out wherever Sylvie and Ezra need us."

"I bet you asked Ezra endless questions about the whole process."

I smiled and took a sip of wine. "One of my favorite memories is when I first moved here, and I took a tour through the whole facility with him."

"Did he answer all your questions?"

"He did. I have my mortician apprentice license too."

"I did not know that." He studied me. "What's your proposal regarding these boundaries?"

The way he abruptly changed the subject was a typical attorney technique to catch witnesses off guard. "The other student interns say they put in five to ten hours a week. None of them are required to study at their respective firms, and *no one* carpools with their mentor. It's overkill."

I paused as the server dropped off our meals. I'd ordered chicken parmesan and Roman got the boneless pork in red sauce.

Roman's pork smelled so good that I leaned over, stabbed a piece with my fork, and stuck it in my mouth. My eyes rolled back and I moaned. "That's delicious. How'd you know to order it?"

Then I realized what I'd done. "Oh, shit. Sorry. I usually come here with Sylvie or Alexa, and we always share whatever we get. Here." Slicing off a piece of chicken, I swirled it into their world-famous marinara sauce and slid it onto his plate.

"Thanks. And there's no way I'm agreeing to just five hours a week. I like picking you up, we can work on weekends, and you study just fine in my office. Text me your class times, and I'll give you a schedule."

I wasn't going to let this asshole get to me. I stuck a piece of broccoli in my mouth and growled at him.

Chapter 8

Roman

Ivan could be a fucking prick sometimes, and Luna admitted he'd said something to set her off on Friday, but she wouldn't tell me what. I just hoped he hadn't scared her away for good.

The partners came over to the house on Sunday evening to grill, watch some football, and discuss a new business we were considering buying. Now, we sat in my oversized spa, sipping bourbon, enjoying the mild evening, and gazing out at the Las Vegas skyline. Xander was in the pool, swimming laps. He spent a lot of time moving and playing sports to try and keep his demons at bay. Dusk fell early now, and the blinking neon casinos and hotels glittered in the distance.

"What did you say to her?" I asked Ivan quietly.

He didn't pretend to misunderstand. "The truth."

"Which was?"

He shrugged and sipped his whiskey. "That she's smart as fuck, has a mostly boring background, but at twelve she accused her father of taking bribes, which you're well aware of, and she got... disowned for it."

"Why'd you throw that at her?"

Ivan set his drink down. "You're lucky I didn't tell her everything. I think your plan is shit, and I'm starting to like her–she's got spunk. Have you even read my report?"

"I read enough. And I don't feel lucky, I feel like breaking your fucking nose." I pointed at him. "Don't interfere again."

Drakos leaned back and spread his arms against the spa ledge. "You're barely pretending to keep it professional with her. Don't get me wrong, it's entertaining to see you two square off at each other like cats in heat. But I'm going to throw this out there. Things could get messy, and she's not her father."

Xander pulled himself up out of the pool and sat. "It's already messy. Be careful with her, she's better than any of us."

Truer words were never spoken, but I still didn't give a fuck. Klim had sent her to me, and she was *mine*.

Ivan leaned back and put his hands behind his head. "I feel like kicking the shit out of you. How about a sparring match at the gym tomorrow morning? Unless you aren't up for it." I knew he was trying to goad me.

"You deserve a good beating for interfering."

He grinned. "You're a mean, cold fucker but I do get a good workout with you. Fine. How about seven?"

Ivan and I met at the No Name Boxing Gym a few blocks from our office the next morning before work. We represented No Name's owner, Ryder Colton, but he ran a tight ship and we never had to come here for more than a good workout or a sparring match.

We'd both been trained by Gideon. Ivan had a few pounds of muscle on me and I was a hair faster. After a few rounds of intense sparring with a few good hits, we'd both worked through our aggression. Ryder stood on the sidelines, his arms crossed, watching us.

"Only a little blood and a dislocated shoulder. It's been worse," Ryder muttered as he snapped Ivan's shoulder back into place.

I showered and cleaned up in the gym, then headed to the office. My phone buzzed early that afternoon, and when I looked down and saw who was texting me, my mouth curled into a cruel smile.

Luna: I want to negotiate my schedule

I decided to let her stew for a while and I waited until after work to get back with her. When I got home, I changed my clothes, grabbed some food, then walked out to the back patio before responding.

Roman: Send me your class times and I'll give you your schedule

Luna: That's not negotiating. That's dictating, and we live in a democracy

I grinned down at my phone as I responded.

Roman: If you want to negotiate, we do it face to face. And who said your internship is a democracy?

Luna

On Monday morning before my first class, I'd gone to plead my case with Klim.

He peered at me from over the rim of his glasses. "Ms. Cross, to what do I owe the pleasure?"

"Roman Fowler," I ground out, the name tasting like sour milk on my tongue.

Klim leaned back in his chair and considered me. "I had lunch with him on Sunday."

"Are you two *friends*?"

Klim closed one eye. "In a manner of speaking."

If Klim and Roman were friends, I was screwed.

I started pacing. "We have the most unorthodox mentor-intern relationship in history. He can barely tolerate me, yet he wants to pick me up every morning." Whatever was going on between Roman and me seemed personal somehow.

Klim watched me pace. "Do you have a credible complaint? Has he acted inappropriately?"

Damn it, he was calling me out. "He's overbearing and condescending, and sometimes he looks at me like he wants to peel the skin off my bones. Then he demands I shadow him wherever he goes. It's too much."

Klim stared, giving me no sympathy. "I know you can both negotiate and work out a mutually beneficial schedule. There's a reason I paired you two, he's got a few things to learn from you."

I threw up my hands. "Klim, why is that my job? And I don't even know what that means!" Frustration boiled, and I wanted to reach over his desk and yank on his stupid bowtie. I didn't care what Roman could learn from me, and I was in no mood. I needed to get through law school, find a job, and start tackling my student loans.

Klim raised his eyebrow. "Do what good lawyers do. Compromise, find common ground, and be flexible."

"It's hard to be flexible when I just want to punch him in the throat."

Klim took off his glasses and gazed at me carefully. "I'll end this mentorship and reinstate your original choice if you give me a valid reason to do so. Frankly, I think you working with Arthur Thorgeson is a waste of your time and potential. He's well over seventy and he works *maybe* three full days a week. But if you can show me that interning at Roman's firm somehow harms you, or he's done something to offend you, I'll make the change."

I groaned and sank into the chair in front of his desk. "You know I don't have anything like that. He's the quintessential attorney who knows how to skate the line but not step across it."

Klim put his glasses back on. "Then negotiate with him. You may even find you don't loathe him."

"I never said I loathed him."

He gave me a small, pleased grin. "Good. You may not want to admit it, but you two are well-paired."

"How do you know him?"

"I know his family." He studied me and leaned forward. "Let me tell you something about Roman that he would hate for you to know. He's a brilliant strategist, and he did very well in school. His father wanted to send him to an expensive, exclusive boarding school as a teenager, but Roman wanted to attend his regular high school and play lacrosse with his friends, so he dug in. His father then wanted to send him off to England, and things escalated. When his father took Roman's dog and had her put down, Roman went a little crazy. His mother didn't intervene."

"Was the dog sick?"

Klim shuffled some papers on his desk. "No. She was a sweet, beautiful, perfectly healthy four-year-old chocolate lab who adored Roman."

"Oh, God." I felt sick to my stomach.

"And then his father had Roman shipped off the Hell."

"I've heard about that ranch in Arizona," I replied softly.

He stared at me with a haunted look in his eyes. "You two have more in common than you know. *Please* help him."

Chapter 9

Luna

On Tuesday morning, I walked into the reception area alone, and Brenna looked up from her desk.

"Oh, you didn't drive with Roman? Is he getting bored already? And what a perfectly basic Walmart outfit you have on." Her smile was as fake as her eyelashes.

Shaking my head, I glanced at her as I strode by. "I don't mind sparring with you, but you need to up your game. And your nose is shiny." Her hand automatically went for her purse before she could stop herself.

I walked through the doors to the offices and headed for Gideon's desk. He looked up and smiled. "Good morning, Ms. Cross, I'm glad you came back."

"Hello, Gideon, I wish I could say the same." I winced at how rude that sounded. "But it's always nice to see you."

I walked into Roman's office. "Take a seat," he said without looking up.

"No, I think I'll stand. So this is what it feels like to be summoned. I never got in trouble in school, so I never experienced the dreaded trip to the principal's office."

"That's a little dramatic." Roman finally gave me his attention, dark eyes appraising.

Despite knowing better, I opened our negotiations. "Look, I'm grateful for the learning curve here, and as much as it pains me to admit, I like the field trips. Your clients are varied and interesting, and you attempt to put up with my questions, my 'restless mind syndrome' as it's been labeled by my roommates. But I need to keep my grades up, which means I need to study and spend time at school."

His lips quirked. "Is that like restless leg syndrome?"

"Pretty much."

Roman leaned back and steepled his fingers. "How about Tuesdays and Thursdays until class and all day Friday? You'll still ride with me, and weekends and functions as needed. If you're studying for longer than three hours, you come here to do it."

He knew my schedule, damn Klim and his big mouth. Weekends, and I come here to study? The man was fucking insane. The rest didn't sound too crazy.

"Tuesday and Friday mornings, and I drive myself, plus I'll meet you at your out-of-office appointments if I'm able. That's a perfectly reasonable schedule."

He raised an eyebrow. "A minimum of Tuesdays and Thursdays until class, and half-day Friday. Occasional functions, and I drive."

"Oh, come on! You barely moved off your first offer. And when exactly am I supposed to study and have a life?"

"You'll have most of the weekend and evenings to study, and access to several top-notch legal minds. It's not like you go out much in the evenings or on weekends anyway. You and your friends are either at school, work, or holed up in your apartment."

My eyes narrowed. "How do you know that?"

"It's not rocket science—two of you are law students."

The man made me paranoid. "That's so generous," I replied sarcastically. "But, *again*, you don't need to drive me." I tried to calculate how many hours that would be as I felt this traitorous pull of excitement at spending more time with Roman. This was not good.

"Driving will be my pleasure. And weekends–"

"What if I have plans?" My voice raised to a high pitch.

"We'll negotiate those as they come along, but don't push me." The muscles in his jaw flexed. Roman stood, the move calculated to hurry this along.

I needed to get control of this negotiation. "So my personal life just evaporates? My study time—"

"I'll make sure you have plenty of time to study too," Roman interjected, his dark brown eyes sparkling. The bastard was enjoying this.

"Klim is a traitor. He's supposed to be my guidance counselor, yet somehow you know my school schedule, and he's on your side."

He didn't deny it. "Klim sees your potential," Roman replied smoothly, a little quirk playing on his lips. "As do I. Imagine the connections and doors we could open for you."

"I don't care about doors, or connections, or schmoozing."

He studied me and I swear I could see his mind plotting. "Then I'll make sure you have new experiences, learn new things, help assuage your insatiable curiosity."

Oh, he was *good*. "That is something."

He inclined his head. "High praise. You have to intern with someone; it's a law school and scholarship requirement. You can't graduate without it." The timbre of his voice wrapped around me like velvet. "So why not make the most of it? I can teach you so many things."

Why did that sound sensual? "I'm aware of that, and not all of them are probably legal."

Roman gave me a full-fledged grin. "Let's talk logistics."

Logistics. That was legalese for Roman getting his way. Rolling my shoulders back, I met his gaze squarely. "Right. Tuesdays and Thursdays until noon. Every other Friday for half the day, and one weekend event a month. You drive when it's convenient for both of us. I still want to go on the field trips when I can."

He stared at me for a few seconds as he mentally reviewed my counteroffer, then he shrugged. "Agreed. That was invigorating," Roman smirked and held out his hand.

I reached out and shook it, my small hand dwarfed by his. The brief contact sent an electric shock up my arm, and he chuckled when I jumped.

Pulling my hand back, I put it behind my back protectively. "I'm putting this in writing, and we're both signing it."

"I'd expect nothing less. Look at us, negotiating schedules like reasonable people," he mockingly marveled.

When I left for class later that day, I couldn't shake the feeling that I'd walked into some kind of trap.

Over the next few weeks, I prepared for mid-terms and settled into a routine at the law offices. Roman continued to drive on the days I came in, and when I looked back, I couldn't figure out exactly how that had happened. We sometimes ate lunch together before he dropped me off. We'd also gotten into the habit of discussing interesting legal concepts, or what we'd read or watched on TV.

"You read quite a bit, especially for a law student," he said one day as we discussed a sci-fi series we both loved.

It was true. Most law students read their homework, and that was all they could stomach.

"I'm a fast reader. And my mind would probably seize up if I didn't feed it something else occasionally. Or maybe start cannibalizing itself." I turned to him. "Did you know numerous animal species sometimes eat their own? Like chimpanzees, hippos, and polar bears. My friend had a cute little hamster who had babies–"

Roman cut in. "Thank you for that stomach-churning fact right before lunch." I smiled contentedly and leaned back.

That Friday, I prowled the offices to see who looked the least busy. Xander walked into the break room with a coffee mug, and I followed him. He was the quietest of the bunch and listened silently when the others got into discussions or arguments. Xander had said maybe five sentences in front of me since we met.

I put my hands together in a pleading gesture. "I need help with an income tax law question that may or may not be on the midterm. Do you have a minute?"

He gazed down at me. "Yes." He got coffee then turned and walked to his office. I assumed Xander meant for me to follow him.

His quiet demeanor didn't bother me. I'd never detected that undercurrent of animosity from him that I sometimes felt from the other partners.

Sitting in one of the uncomfortable chairs in front of his desk, I wiggled my butt. "This chair is horrible. It feels like I'm being pitched forward, and the cushion is as hard as cement."

"I know."

His chairs were a brilliant idea if you didn't like talking to people, and wanted to keep office visits to a minimum. "Huh. So they're uncomfortable on purpose, got it. Is depletion always a cause for depreciation? I understand depletion refers to irreplaceable resources, but does it then trigger depreciation?"

Xander tilted his head and studied me for a few seconds, and I wondered if he hadn't understood my question. Then he started explaining. "You'd need to distinguish and show the extent of depletion and depreciation." Then he took a legal pad and thoroughly illustrated the concept for me.

When he finished, I pulled the pad to me, reviewed his notes carefully, and ripped off the page so I could keep it. I beamed at him. "You'd make a great law professor. I've got it, thank you."

Roman didn't give me any assignments over midterms, and to my annoyance, I tended to study the best in the small office next to his. My noise-canceling headphones and highlighters became a joke around the office, and the day before my tax law midterm, I found a pack of highlighters sitting on my chair with a note scrawled on the packaging that read *"Good luck, X."*

Later that afternoon as I took the test, my lip twitched while reading through a question about depletion and depreciation. I mentally brought up Xander's diagram and answered the question.

After the test, Jared Gardner stood in the hallway waiting for me. "I haven't seen you at the library. How's the internship from hell going?"

"I'm fine, and the internship has gotten better. They let me study there when I'm not shadowing anyone. How are midterms going for you?"

"Good. How about dinner?"

I shifted uncomfortably. "I'm working at the funeral home this evening."

Disappointment flitted across his face, and he shook his head. "I've never met anyone who lives and works above a funeral home next to a cemetery."

"Well, the neighbors always mind their own business."

He squinted his eyes. "Was that a joke? How about tomorrow, then?"

Sliding my backpack on, I started walking backward toward the door. "I've got to go. See you later."

When my last mid-term in corporations rolled around, I knocked on Roman's door. He looked up, dark eyes fixing on mine with a now familiar intensity.

"Do you have a minute?" He motioned to one of the chairs in front of his desk. "Corporate mergers... how do they affect share-holder rights?"

He leaned back. "Still taking advantage of our 'great legal minds'?"

"Sure. If it makes you feel better to call yourselves that."

Smirking, he looked back at his laptop. "Let me finish this email and we'll go to lunch and discuss it."

I watched him work. His hair had gotten a little longer, and a dark strand fell across his forehead. He was so compelling and charismatic, with his razor-sharp mind behind that chiseled, striking face. He still didn't seem to like me, and sometimes he stared at me with frigid, flat eyes, but since I'd walked out that Friday after my altercation with Ivan, he'd been less cold.

We walked past Brenna, who smiled at Roman and stared through me. She had a faint line of lip gloss across her incisors. "You've got lipstick on your teeth," I informed her, pointing to her mouth.

"I'm not falling for that again," she bit out. I shrugged, knowing she'd check as soon as the door closed behind us.

We went to a little lunch spot just off Fremont Street and ate at an outside table, enjoying the fall sunshine while we discussed my corporation question.

"It's all about leverage and who's in control," he explained as we dug into our food.

"Sounds like a normal day dealing with you," I needled him. He raised an eyebrow and then explained the intricacies of corporate mergers while I listened and tried to absorb his explanation.

"Okay, I think I understand it enough to fumble my way through." I wiped my hands on my napkin as we finished up.

"Anything else, Ms. Cross?"

"No, Mr. Fowler. That was informative, thank you. You're sarcastic and abrupt, but you don't dumb things down or try to mansplain to me."

Roman searched my face, his eyes settling on my lips. "You're certainly not dumb, and only an idiot would talk down to you." He seemed to shake himself. "You've wasted enough of my day, let's get back."

Shaking my head, I chuckled humorlessly as I started to stand. "I should know a compliment from you will also come with a verbal slap."

Just then, a man walked up to us. "Roman, nice to see you. This is one of my favorite lunch spots too."

Roman straightened. "Hello, Cameron." They shook hands, and the man took a seat at our table, but after an awkward pause, it appeared Roman didn't plan to introduce me. He could be such a prick sometimes. I tried not to let the slight hurt me, and took matters into my own hands, sticking my palm out across the table. "Hello. I'm Luna Cross, Roman's law student intern."

"Luna, it's a pleasure to meet you. Cameron Wilder." He grinned and shook my hand.

Cameron wore expensive, business-casual clothes, and had thick brown hair with gray at his temples. He was probably in his late thirties and extremely attractive. His name also sounded familiar. "Oh, I know where I've heard your name," I exclaimed.

Roman stiffened next to me, but I pressed on. "You own Wilder Technologies and there's a scholarship in your company's name at the law school. One of my best friends won it last year. It made a huge difference–you have no idea. So thank you." I'd heard Cameron's tech company had created several legal research programs, and he'd gifted millions to the law school.

He grasped my arm and squeezed. "I'm glad. What's your friend's name?"

"Alexa Torres. She's also my roommate."

"I remember reviewing her application. What year are you?" Before I could answer, Roman's phone rang, and he looked down at it.

"I need to take this." His blank face didn't give me any clues, so I shrugged and pointed to the restaurant.

"I'm going to use the restroom then." I turned to Cameron as Roman answered the call. "It was nice to meet you."

Cameron stood as I got up. "You too, Luna. I hope we meet again." He'd been charming and polite, and I wondered why Roman seemed so annoyed.

When I exited the restaurant and started toward our outdoor table, I felt a hand on my arm. Cameron stood in the doorway as if he'd been waiting for me.

"I'll keep you company while Roman finishes his call if that's alright."

I glanced at Roman, who was still talking on his phone, but he watched us with a clenched jaw. Turning to Cameron, I smiled. "Sounds good to me."

He took my elbow and led us to an empty bench. "Do you plan to work with Roman when you graduate?" Cameron asked.

I chuckled, then realized Cameron was serious. "Uh, no. He has no interest in hiring me as an attorney, and I plan to practice water law."

A confused look crossed his face, and he glanced over at Roman. "I don't know a lot about that area of law, but I know water is vital to Las Vegas. Isn't training and then hiring an intern the major reason firms take them on?"

Cameron had zeroed in on the troubling enigma that still plagued me about Roman and this situation. I turned to him and sighed.

"I'm more confused than you are. To be honest, he doesn't like me, and I've asked countless times to be released from this internship."

A shadow fell over my lap, and I looked up to see Roman standing over me with his arms folded. He reached down and took my hand, pulling me up. "Let's go. I have work to do."

Cameron stood too. "Luna, come to lunch with me next week. I want to continue our conversation."

My body locked, and I didn't know how to respond. "I'll, uh, check my schedule. That sounds nice, though." As soon as the words were out, I wanted to smack my forehead. Dating was typically awkward and painful for me, and this exchange with Cameron was a perfect example.

His gaze softened at my discomfort. "You have to eat, right?" He turned to Roman. "I'll call you tomorrow. I'd like to discuss a few things."

"Cameron, she's my intern, and during that time, she's not going on dates, having lunch with, or *fucking* anyone I introduce her to. I'd say it was good to see you, but that would be a lie. If you'll excuse us."

I took in a sharp breath. "You did *not* just say that."

Roman glanced at me and grinned wickedly. "Yes, I believe I did."

Cameron shrugged, not intimidated by Roman's cold bluntness. "That's not up to you, is it? Luna, it was a pleasure to meet you. I'll be in touch."

"You too, Cameron." I smiled at him and waved with my free hand as Roman growled and started dragging me away.

When we were out of earshot, he leaned down and murmured in my ear. "For the love of God, stop being so provocative or I might have to hurt someone. Cameron came close, and I usually like the fucker."

I stopped dead on the sidewalk, violently yanked my hand out of his grip, and glared up at him. "Stop being such a mean asshole. It wasn't my fault, and if you ever say something like that again, I might have to hurt *you*."

He closed his eyes and took a deep breath, then let it out through his nose. "Come on, let's get back to the office." We sat in loud silence on the drive back.

I had another nightmare that night, only this time it varied from the usual horrific flashbacks, and it made the dream more terrifying.

Alexa was the one who shook me awake this time. "Luna, wake up. You're scaring me. Luna!" I gasped, and my eyes flew open. My body was clammy, but I felt sweaty and sick. Rolling off my bed, I stumbled to the bathroom and threw up what remained of my dinner, barely making it to the toilet.

My head hung over the bowl as I waited for the heaving to stop. Alexa ran hot water over a washcloth and when my stomach settled, she handed it to me.

She looked worried and rubbed my back soothingly. "It must've been a doozy. I don't remember you throwing up before."

My hands shook, and sweat and tears bathed my face. "It was different this time. Oh, God, what if they're getting worse instead of better?"

"Didn't your therapist encourage you to talk about them? I'll listen."

After washing my face, rinsing my mouth a few times, and brushing my teeth, we walked out to the kitchen. It was just after five in the morning, and we gave up trying to go back to bed.

"Where's Sylvie?" I asked her.

Alexa turned to me with the tea kettle in her hand. "She got up a few minutes before your nightmare started. I think she went down to the mortuary. They had a suicide come in yesterday."

We shared a look, and I thought of Sylvie down in the embalming room by herself. "What was the cause of death?"

"Intentional overdose."

I sighed in quiet relief. It was still horrible, but at least it wasn't by hanging. The three of us had suffered childhood trauma, and we all knew each other's triggers. No wonder we got along so well. "Let's keep an eye on her over the next few days."

Alexa nodded. "Tell me about your dream. How was it different this time?"

Speaking about that night always left me feeling gutted and hollow. I rubbed my hand over my face and sighed. "It was bad."

She grabbed two mugs and pulled a packet of tea down from the cupboard. "How bad? Worse than your usual dream?"

"Yes. I think I was an adult this time, and... Roman Fowler stood in the closet doorway."

"Well, fuck," Alexa exhaled.

"Yeah." I didn't tell her about me pleading with him to help me wake up, to stop my father, to not blame me—for what I didn't know. But in the dream, Roman stared at me with his cold, flat eyes as I lay there panting in pain, my arm at an odd angle, blood coating my face and chest. Then he stepped back and shut the closet door.

Chapter 10

Luna

The dream faded, and Thanksgiving came. I didn't ask Roman about his plans because I was afraid he'd demand I go into the office. After spending my entire October fall break with him, I thought it was a reasonable fear.

Sylvie needed assistance embalming a large corpse that had come in a few days ago, so we planned to do it on Thanksgiving morning. Before heading to the embalming room, I ate a fast breakfast and changed into leggings and a long-sleeve t-shirt so I'd be comfortable under the protective equipment.

As I walked through the funeral parlor, I veered to Ezra's office when I saw his light on.

"Hey. What are you doing here on Thanksgiving morning?" I asked.

He looked up at me from his desk and smiled. "Good morning. I wanted to catch up on a few things, and I already have the turkey in the oven. How's your internship going?"

I shrugged and leaned against the doorframe. "It's frustrating and strange. But I like the field trips."

He frowned thoughtfully. "Fenn wonders why you're interning there, especially since you already set things up with Artie. Kilian seems to think the partners are alright."

Fennick and Kilian Spade were Sylvie's cousins, along with the twins Callum and Declan. They oversaw the House of Spades' other holdings, and I loved them all like brothers, but I had no illusions.

"The partners have a successful law firm, but they have a lot of other business interests. It reminds me of the House of Spades." I knew not all the Spade businesses were entirely legal, but I didn't care. These people had become my family when my own threw me away like garbage.

Ezra studied me. "Most people seem to grudgingly respect them, but be careful, Luna. Roman is ruthless."

My lips turned down. Cameron Wilder had voiced the same concerns. "I will. When should we come over today?"

"At noon, and we'll eat around one, or when the turkey gets done."

"Sounds good. We're bringing three pies, brownies, and ice cream." I smiled as I left his office. Thanksgiving always got a little rowdy at Ezra's house, but I soaked up the craziness like a sponge.

It was quiet today in the mortuary's work area. I donned a plastic apron, face visor, and the rest of my protection equipment, and found Sylvie in the embalming room. The concrete floor had a drain in the center, and a steel sink and countertop sat on the opposite wall. It reminded me vaguely of a school cafeteria.

Sylvie had already wheeled the body in and was in the process of washing and disinfecting him. "Hey. Good timing. Get your rubber boots on and come help me spread his thighs."

She used to wear runners with shoe covers until she'd splashed bodily fluid from a particularly ripe corpse onto her leg one day, and the viscous liquid had seeped down into her shoe.

We'd both promptly switched to rubber boots. Mine were a bright sunshine yellow with white polka dots, and hers were a shimmery, sparkly pink.

After we finished cleaning him, she cut the carotid artery so she could drain the body. I looked down at the massive man on the table while she made the cut and hooked him up to the drain tube.

I glanced over at Sylvie. "He's a big one. I'll get the spreader so we can reach his femoral artery."

"Thanks. I'll man the trocar, and we'll get him drained first."

Sylvie usually injected the embalming fluid through an artery at the thigh, but the tissue spreader sometimes had to be used if the body was too thick. I'd never "manned the trocar," which was a long, sharp hollow instrument used to suction fluids and gases out of the body. Sylvie also used an arterial tube to inject the embalming fluid after draining the corpse.

That's why she got paid the big bucks. Getting the fluid pressure just right was important so the face and body didn't appear too emaciated or bloated. I sometimes got a little squeamish when she made those cuts or used the machine, and the occasional hissing or slurping sounds didn't help.

She set the body into position beforehand since it was difficult to re-set after embalming. It took some time to replace the natural fluids with the embalming solution. Sylvie had chosen a color with a nice, rosy tint. After she finished, we thoroughly washed and sponged the body down, massaging and disseminating the new fluid throughout the limbs.

When we were done, we both stepped back and inspected our work. The corpse had smelled faintly of human waste and sweet rotten flesh before it went bad. Now it just smelled faintly of chemicals, and he was ready for his burial clothes, eye caps, a little makeup, and then the casket.

"Promise me you won't try to casket him yourself," I grunted as we wheeled him back into the refrigerator.

She shut the door and turned to me. "Don't worry, I'll use the lift and get one of the cousins to assist me. Happy Thanksgiving. I hope this won't put you off your turkey."

"Maybe just the cranberry sauce," I teased.

When I first moved in with Sylvie and her mother, I was a silent, broken shell, and that first holiday season had been dark and bleak. But Sylvie's mother took her own life a few months later, and it was my turn to be the strong one for her.

Then Ezra and the rest of the Las Vegas Spade family took us both in and showed us nothing but unconditional love and patience. And now, I looked forward to the holidays.

My life had gone in a direction I'd never imagined, but with time and perspective, I realized that I'd been lucky to get out from under my parents' sphere and influence. They were incapable of healthy, parental nurturing or love, but Ezra and the cousins had given us that in spades.

I remembered the day we toured his sprawling mortuary and its adjoining cemetery. He'd told us the local stories about haunted graves and ghost sightings, and showed us all the strange nooks and crannies in the sprawling estate. It was like finding the secret garden, only this one was filled with a mortuary, a graveyard, and dead bodies that came and went.

We peeled off our protective gear, washed up, and headed back through the funeral home. I heard Ezra talking to someone in his office, and I recognized Roman's voice. What in the world was he doing here? My jaw clenched and adrenaline hit my system. He was in for an earful if he thought he could drag me into work with him today.

When I walked in, Roman sat in one of the client chairs in casual clothing. I paused and stared—I'd never seen him in anything but a suit.

He looked up when we walked in. "I couldn't get you on the phone this morning, so I stopped by."

"Look, it's Thanksgiving—"

"I'm calling on a client and thought you might like to come along."

Temptation and curiosity got the better of me. "Which client? And why do they want to meet on Thanksgiving morning?"

Ezra chuckled, but Sylvie shook her head and pointed to me. "One question at a time, then you wait for an answer. We've discussed this. I'm going to grab a shower and start on the brownies."

Ezra studied Roman, then sighed. "We're eating at one this afternoon at my house. You're welcome to join us."

Sylvie cut in before I could protest. "You have to refrain from being your usual asshole self, and fair warning, the cousins are going to be there."

My lips tightened, and I glared at Ezra and Sylvie. "What are you doing?" I whisper-hissed out of the corner of my mouth.

Sylvie quirked an eyebrow. "What? It's just a meal."

Roman smirked, then stood and inclined his head to Ezra. "I'd love to join you, mainly because Luna is so keen on the idea." He turned to me. "I'm meeting the owner of the Wild West Wedding Chapel."

My eyes went wide and I clapped my hands together, Thanksgiving dinner forgotten. The famous barn wedding chapel was one of those few remaining iconic places in Las Vegas that never seemed to change, and I'd always wanted to go inside.

"Yes. I want to go," I answered quickly before he could change his mind. "Let me take a shower, and I'll be ready in twenty minutes."

He leaned forward and sniffed me. "That might be a good idea. You smell like formaldehyde."

I shrugged. "It's embalming fluid."

His nose wrinkled. "It reminds me of my college biology class. And my great aunt's house."

I patted his arms a few times, purposefully rubbing my hands on his nice shirt, even though I'd just thoroughly washed them.

He grabbed my forearms and stepped away. "Enough. Go shower."

I grinned and quit teasing him. "You can wait in the apartment."

Ezra stood. "I just invited him to the break room for coffee. He'll be here in the office when you're ready." I got the impression Ezra didn't like Roman in our apartment. At first, I didn't like it either, but I'd gotten used to him coming inside when he picked me up and dropped me off. He hadn't given me a choice.

A half-hour later, we were headed to the Wild West Wedding Chapel. My hair was still damp, but I'd gotten ready in record time. Roman turned to me and raised his eyebrow. "Did you just help Sylvie embalm a body?"

"Yes. I told you I'm a registered apprentice embalmer, and I got my license a few years ago."

He studied me. "Why?"

"They needed reliable help, and I was curious about what went on in the embalming room, but you have to be properly licensed. I'm happy to assist, but I don't have Sylvie's skill or finesse."

"What's your relationship with them?"

I shifted in my seat. "I already told you this too. Ezra was my guardian, Sylvie is my foster sister, and they're my family now."

He glanced at me. "What about Ezra's nephews?"

By the tone of his voice, I thought I knew what he was asking. "The cousins? They're family too. It's like having four annoying, overbearing, obnoxious brothers."

We sat in silence for a few minutes, both of us lost in our thoughts. "You're not what I expected," he murmured, almost to himself.

"Thank you? You're worse than I expected, but you're growing on me—like foot fungus."

He rolled his eyes. "You're the most mouthy, disrespectful intern I've ever met."

"When you wouldn't release me from this internship, I tried to warn you."

We reached the chapel just off Las Vegas Boulevard and Clark Avenue. Its rustic wood barn exterior, with the old wagon and ancient hitching post out front, clashed spectacularly with the sleek commercial buildings around it.

I turned to Roman. "How do you know the owner?"

"Heath Cassidy is a friend of Gideon's. Heath worked with him at the FBI for a few years before Gideon quit."

"Gideon worked for the FBI? That explains a lot about him. Do you want me to sit in on the meeting or make myself scarce?" I really just wanted to wander around and find an employee or two to question.

"It's likely you can sit in. But if you do wander around, don't let me find you with your skirt hiked around your waist this time."

I shook my head. "That's not going to happen, I'm wearing pants today."

He grunted skeptically. The building was just as rustic and western on the inside, with scarred wood floors and wooden beams. Western memorabilia hung along the walls, and I noticed an extensive collection of antiques from various saloons and brothel houses. I stood entranced as I took in the exhibit.

It was like a miniature Old West museum crossed with a Las Vegas wedding chapel. The back half of the building had been split into two chapel halls, but the walls looked retractable, probably to accommodate larger events. I could hear muffled voices and wedding music coming from one of the chapels.

A broad-shouldered man with an impressive dark blond handlebar mustache came out of the front office to greet us. He wore a black cowboy hat, jeans, and a gray tweed vest. He even smelled like leather and cigar smoke.

"Roman," he grunted. "You sumbitch. Thanks for coming out this morning. Who's this with you?"

Sumbitch? I mouthed to Roman.

Roman's lip quirked and he introduced us. "She's my law student intern. Luna, this is Heath Cassidy."

Heath turned to get another look at me. "Aw, honey. Why do you want to be a lawyer?"

"So I can protect myself." I hadn't meant to blurt that out, but Heath just nodded sagely and patted my shoulder with his big, scarred hand. Roman tilted his head as if my answer had surprised him. It had surprised me too.

He turned to Roman. "I have a wedding to officiate soon, so let's talk. Luna, come with us." I looked back longingly at the brothel antiques along the back wall, but walked into his office behind Roman.

"What can I help you with that couldn't wait until Monday?" Roman asked.

Heath smirked. "You're a damn workaholic, Fowler. I knew you'd be working today, so don't give me your shit. I've got two issues. I need your investigation team to do a background check on my accountant. I think he's embezzling, but I'd like to know for certain. The other is a nuisance lawsuit a man filed who got married at my chapel a few months ago."

"What's the lawsuit about?" Roman asked.

Heath rolled his eyes. "He's sayin' he didn't know the marriage would be legally binding."

Roman scoffed. "That's definitely a nuisance lawsuit, and the man is an idiot. No judge in Clark County will rule in favor of a case like that. Las Vegas makes too much money on those quick, 'drive-thru' weddings to jeopardize that cash cow. We'll counter-sue and request attorney fees. Email Gideon the Petition, and I'll get someone on it next week. I'll also have Ivan look into your accountant."

Heath grimaced. "That saying 'what happens in Vegas stays in Vegas' is complete horseshit, pardon my French. Marriages, gambling debts, sexually transmitted diseases, and a bucket load of bad decisions follow people home. I love Sin City, but you can't leave your common sense at the State line when you come here and expect not to have a few rattlesnake bites when you get home."

Roman nodded. "Half the attorneys in town make a living off those bad decisions. Anything else?"

When Heath shook his head, I leaned forward. "If you're done discussing legal issues, can I ask you a few questions?"

"Sure thing. Shoot." Heath smiled, and I realized how handsome he was. The man even had dimples.

Roman bumped my leg, and I shook myself, then remembered my questions. "Where did you get your amazing brothel house memorabilia, and has anyone cataloged it? Who are the most interesting people that have been married here? You have more of a southwestern accent, where'd you grow up?"

Heath leaned forward, grinned, and fired answers back at me. "The collection is mostly from my great-great-grandmammy. She was a working girl and then a madam in a brothel in Virginia City. I've added to it over the years, and it's only been partially cataloged."

"Wow. That's fascinating family history."

He absently twirled his handlebar mustache between his thumb and forefinger. "Yep, it is. The most interesting person who's been married here was one of the Rat Pack in the 1970s. The marriage lasted three months, it was before my time, and my uncle performed the ceremony. I grew up in Whetstone, Arizona, just outside of Tombstone."

I asked a few more questions, and he readily answered them all. The man had a quick mind, and I enjoyed talking with him. When we wound down, he leaned back and sighed. "I feel like I need a cigarette, darlin'."

I blushed and Roman growled beside me, but Heath just grinned. Before he took off to officiate the wedding, he offered to teach me how to shoot.

"You said you want to become an attorney to protect yourself. If you ever want to learn to shoot or handle a gun, I also own a shooting range off Decatur Boulevard in south Las Vegas, and I'd be happy to teach you. Give me a call and we can set it up."

I smiled as I shook his big, callused hand. "I already know how to shoot, but thank you for the kind offer, and the tour." I sighed and looked around. "I love this place."

When we left the chapel, I turned to Roman as we walked to his car. "That was amazing! Okay, I won't complain anymore about you crashing my Thanksgiving."

Roman didn't talk during the car ride to Ezra's house, but I shrugged it off as him being his usual rude self. I texted Sylvie to see if she needed help with the food, but she told me she was fine and she'd meet us there.

When we walked into Ezra's house, Kilian and Sylvie were opening champagne and setting out appetizers. He looked up and stared at Roman. "What're you doing here?"

Kilian looked a lot like Fenn, only he didn't have that crazy gleam in his eyes. Kilian was very literal, extremely blunt, and had no filter. If you gained weight, had an ugly shirt on, or he was about to shoot you in the head, he'd calmly inform you.

Fenn walked into the dining room with plates, silverware, and napkins. "Hey, Lulu." He stopped when he spotted Roman. "Why the fuck would you bring Roman Fowler to Thanksgiving dinner? You're not *that* hard-up, are you?"

He looked like Charlie Hunnam from *Breaking Bad*. There were a few scars on his cheek, and his thick blond hair usually needed a trim. He also wore a perpetual grin, like he was either laughing at something or looking for trouble.

Roman raised his eyebrow. "Hello Fennick. Happy Thanksgiving."

Fenn set the plates down and handed me the silverware. "It was until about ten seconds ago."

Sylvie popped a cork and poured champagne into flutes. "Ezra invited him, and we're all going to get along." She stared us down.

Fenn smirked as he set the table. "Syl, that's funny coming from you, since you're the one who usually starts the arguments."

I looked around. "Where's Declan and Callum?"

She handed us each a champagne flute and nodded behind me. I turned to see the twins walk in. They were fraternal, but they both looked vaguely like the late actor Paul Walker from *Fast and Furious*. Declan held a twelve-pack of beer and Callum carried a bottle of whiskey. Declan spotted Roman, turned to Ezra who was walking in behind him, and held up the beer. "We're gonna need a lot more of this if you invited the partners to Thanksgiving."

Ezra smiled. "It's just Roman, we'll be fine."

Sylvie turned to me. "What'd you think of the Wild West Wedding Chapel?"

"It's freaking amazing. The inside is just as over-the-top as the outside, and the proprietor looks like a younger Rooster Cogburn from *True Grit*." I told them about Heath and the brothel collection.

Ezra set cranberry sauce and a green bean casserole on the table. "I'm sure we have a few women of ill repute in our family line somewhere too."

Callum nodded and set the whiskey down. "Probably, and that's an accurate description of Heath." He turned to me and grinned. "Did Heath flash his dimples at you, and offer to teach you how to shoot?"

I stared at him in surprise. "Yes. How'd you know?"

Callum glanced at Roman and smirked. "Because he only does that if he *really* likes someone."

Roman turned and glared at me.

Chapter 11

Luna

Setting his glass down on the table, Roman folded his arms. "Speaking of Heath, I meant what I said about not getting involved with someone while you're interning with me."

I pointed my finger at him. "You had to bring that up again, didn't you? I've *never* done that."

He scoffed. "What about Ray and Rick at Diego's garage? And there was Cameron, and now Heath."

Everyone stood in the dining room, watching us with wide eyes, Fenn grinning like he enjoyed the drama. This was not the time or place for this, so I sucked in a breath and let it out slowly. I reminded myself that I was *not* going to let this fucker get to me. "You're wrong. Trying to be a decent, reasonable person isn't flirting. It also beats the hell out of being paranoid and rude."

I gave him the silent treatment during dinner. We spent the rest of the afternoon watching football and then played a few hands of poker. I'd said less than five words to him since he'd accused me of flirting.

Roman glanced at me a few times, then finally sighed and put his cards down. "It's Thanksgiving. Let's call a truce and enjoy what's left of the day."

Ezra nudged my foot under the table, so I set my own cards down and turned to him. "Alright. But if you blame me for something like that again, I swear to you that by the time my internship ends, you'll think I've gone mute."

He studied my face, his lip tipping up. "Understood."

Fenn sighed long and loud. "Now that you've kissed and made up, can we finish the game?"

When we walked into the offices together the following week, I realized with a start I actually *enjoyed* coming to work here. Roman still acted like a prick most days, but I liked discussing odd topics with the partners around Gideon's desk, and they were entertaining, enlightening, and fun to tease. Sometimes I fired off a million random questions just to irritate them. Ivan was still on my shit list, though.

One afternoon, he cornered me by the coffee machine. "Roman mentioned you're interested in water law. Why?"

I stared at him. "Why do you want to know?"

"I'm curious, which is something you should understand."

Nodding, I leaned against the break room counter. "My uncle Alistair on my father's side owns a national wastewater management company. Unfortunately, he has the morals of a snake, just like the rest of his family."

His gaze went sharp. "What do you mean?"

There was no need to share my father's sordid past, but I could tell him about my uncle. "Alistair's company dumped millions of gallons of chromium-tainted wastewater into unlined ponds, and his company was fined a *fraction* of their net revenue. That's just one example."

"What about your dad?"

The same old shame and anger slid through me, and I turned to the coffee pot. "My father has been taking bribes most of his career. God and the devil only know what else he's been involved in."

Ivan leaned against the counter and crossed his arms. "Luna, what happened when you were young?"

"You already know," I answered quietly.

"Not from your perspective."

Turning around, I faced him. "I was too young and naive to be careful. He'd sometimes leave screens up on his computer showing vast sums of money in various accounts. I was curious about how a judge could have accumulated that much money, and eventually I cross-hatched the dates to a few key rulings in his court."

"Well, shit."

"You could say that."

"What happened?" he asked.

"I didn't understand the ramifications of confronting him. I figured the facts out, but the nuances escaped me." I glanced at him. "You have an idea of what happened. You already threw it in my face. Anyway." I turned to leave.

"Why is water law so fascinating to you?"

He seemed sincere, so I stopped and turned. "The economic value of water in the United States alone is around sixty *trillion* dollars. People kill for it, steal it, and die without it. Water rights in the Western States are especially critical, but water law is beyond complicated."

Glancing over, I noticed Roman standing in the doorway. I wondered how long he'd been there.

Ivan blew out a breath. "Fuck. That's about six times the annual federal U.S. budget."

I nodded. "And think about it. Whoever controls water also controls agriculture, industry, and development. And there are futures, trading, investments—even water banks."

"Water banks?" Ivan asked.

"Yes. You've heard of oil reserves. They do it with water too. Anyway, I think that answers your question."

Ivan straightened and glanced at Roman. "She's teaching *us* now." He walked past me and patted my shoulder.

My conversation with Ivan had torn open old wounds, and on the drive home, I sat quietly, looking out the window. Slipping a package of Hot Tamales out of my backpack, I ate a couple and turned to Roman. "You want any?"

He shook his head. "I like the smell, but cinnamon candy is for people who hate their tastebuds." He glanced at me. "What's your problem? You haven't asked me a single question, and usually you're about ten questions in before we leave the parking garage."

"You're hilarious." I sighed. "Ivan brought up a few ghosts."

"What do you mean?"

"My biological family is... a bad topic for me."

He glanced at my profile. "And?" He prodded.

I didn't trust Roman not to throw in my face whatever he learned about me, and it'd be a cold day in hell before I told him what my father had done, so I changed the subject. "In case anything comes up last-minute this weekend, I'm working a funeral tomorrow, and we have funeral parlor brunch poker on Sunday morning."

"What's funeral parlor brunch poker?"

"Once a month on a Sunday, Ezra holds an unofficial poker tournament at Palm Desert, and we have a potluck brunch to go along with it. It's a great marketing tool, and it's usually a lot of fun."

"Who comes?" he asked.

"Mostly our friends and neighbors, and a few people from the community."

We pulled up to my apartment, and Roman turned to me. "Sounds interesting."

I smirked at his dry tone. "See you on Tuesday. I'd tell you to have a good weekend, but your weekends probably involve drinking blood and animal sacrifices." He shook his head as I got out. At least he hadn't come up to "use the bathroom" this time.

At the funeral on Saturday morning, I did a double take when I noticed Sasha and Misty from Euphoria walking into the funeral home together. They were both fully clothed and didn't have as much makeup on, but Misty still wore a sparkly dress. Breaking from my usual position at the chapel door, I went over to say hello. Misty spotted me first and elbowed Sasha.

"Hi," I said in a hushed voice. "I don't know if you remember me. I'm so sorry for your loss and I wanted to–"

Misty leaned in and hugged me, and Sasha followed suit. My parents never hugged or touched me, and I didn't know exactly where to put my hands, or how long to hug. It always felt painfully awkward unless it was one of the Spades or Alexa.

"We remember you. You're Luna, Roman Fowler's intern." Misty pointed to the front of the funeral chapel where an older deceased woman had been laid out in a pink pearlescent casket. "Ms. Maybell is my aunt."

Sasha looked at my gold nametag. "Do you work here?"

"Sometimes. I live here too."

They both stared at me, then Sasha started grinning. "You're messing with us, right?"

"No." Turning, I pointed to Sylvie and Alexa, both standing by the chapel doors, dressed in black with the same gold nametags. "Those are my roommates, and we live in the apartment above the mortuary."

"Girl, that's creepy-cool," Sasha whisper-hissed with a big grin.

I made a split-second decision. "Listen, tomorrow we're having our monthly poker brunch at the funeral home here. It starts at eleven and it's pretty laid-back. If you want to come, just let me know. We do a potluck brunch with mimosas, then have a poker tournament. It only lasts a couple of hours, but it's a lot of fun and the food is always good."

They stared at each other for a second, then grinned. "Fuck, yes," Misty squealed.

An older man shushed us, and I motioned to my spot by the chapel door. "I need to get back, but I'll see you tomorrow then."

On Sunday morning, Sylvie and I set up the tables and chairs and laid out the tablecloths, face cards, and poker chips. Ezra had baked a large cheesy breakfast casserole, and Sylvie and I whipped up a big green salad and thick brownies.

Then we pulled out the champagne and orange juice and mixed up a few mimosas. When Sasha and Misty arrived, the party was in full swing with a mixture of people from the neighborhood, including Sophia and the cooks from Luigi's.

Sasha looked around. "It seems so cheerful and bright in here today."

I grinned. "Not having a dead body, sad mourners, and heavy organ music helps. Come meet everyone, and let's get a mimosa."

A few hours later, Sylvie and I waved as Misty and Sasha stumbled into a ride share, drunk and giggling. We looked at each other and started laughing.

"Damn, their stripper stories are funny as shit," Sylvie muttered.

"Did we really agree to take pole dancing lessons?" I asked.

"Yep, I think we did. You wouldn't shut up with the questions, and we might still be a little buzzed." She wasn't wrong.

Ezra invited us to dinner on Monday night, and all the cousins were there. I sighed when Fenn and Declan started in about Roman before we'd even dished up our plates.

"You seem to spend a lot of time with your mentor. Is there something you want to tell us?" Declan asked mildly while he dished up several helpings of lasagna.

Sylvie pointed her fork at him. "Hey, Porky Pig. Save some for us."

"Here, have some garlic bread." Fenn tossed a piece of bread on her plate. "Yeah, Lou. What the fuck's going on, and why'd he sound like a jealous boyfriend at Thanksgiving?"

My back went up. "He didn't sound like a jealous boyfriend, and it's not like I *wanted* to do my internship with him, okay?"

Declan finally passed the lasagna. "I've never heard of an attorney picking up their intern and driving them to work. You sure nothing's going on?"

Kilian dished himself some salad and shook his head. "Leave her alone, it's none of our business."

My heart warmed at him defending me. "Thank you, Kilian."

He kept going. "If she wants to get involved with her mentor, she's old enough to clean up her own fuckups now."

I sighed and took the salad bowl from him. Protesting my innocence wouldn't do any good; I just needed to ride it out and wait until they changed the subject.

Fenn nodded. "Why is it you and Sylvie are always up to your eyeballs in trouble, and it always turns into a big fucking mess?"

"We are not, asshole. You're the one sitting there with a black eye and a split lip," Sylvie retorted.

"Yeah, but my messes usually don't require a full clean-up crew and new paint and carpet."

Callum winced. "That was disgusting, I didn't know a head could explode that way."

I set my fork down and sighed. "I was only fourteen, okay? It's been over ten years, and you guys *still* throw that in my face."

Sylvie nodded. "It's not like we ask for it, and you can't blame us since you're the ones who taught us how to shoot."

Fenn grimaced. "Yeah, but I didn't know you were going to shoot a man in the gut and splatter his head against your bedroom wall. It was a fucking mess–no drop sheet, no clean kill, no exit strategy."

Alexa set her fork down and pushed her plate back. "Maybe you could wait until *after* we eat our lasagna to take this trip down memory lane."

Ezra reached over and patted her hand. "Unfortunately, they have the manners of troglodytes."

Sylvie glared at Fenn. "Well, she didn't know how to make a clean kill back then, and I didn't have access to a cremator."

"True. That has come in handy a few times," he admitted.

My father sent a hitman to kill me when I was fourteen years old. I should have seen it coming, and I didn't know for certain, but I thought it was my mother who'd warned me. An envelope with no return address showed up one day containing a scribbled note on the back of a business card for an exclusive hair salon in Phoenix. The note said *He took a K out on you.* I'd had to google what "K" stood for–it was short for a contract.

Three days later, a man entered my bedroom window at Ezra's house. When he straightened, I shot him. I'd meant to shoot him in the chest, but hit his groin instead. He'd stumbled and howled in pain before coming after me again. Even though my breath was coming in short gasps, I steadied myself and remembered what Kilian had drilled into me. *If you want to incapacitate or kill someone quickly, aim for their head.*

The second shot hit true. Blood, bone, and brain matter splatted across the wall behind the dead man. Sylvie ran into my room when she heard the shots, and I clearly remembered the *Bart Simpson* t-shirt she had on that night. Without his hearing aids in, Ezra had slept through the whole thing so we called Fenn to help us.

When he walked into my room that night and saw the carnage, Fenn had exhaled slowly and put his hands on his hips. "We're done fucking around here. I don't care how young you two are, you're officially part of the House of Spades. Now quit bawling and pull yourselves together, we need to get a cleanup crew in here."

The hitman had an *Assassin's Creed* tattoo on his forearm, which I thought was unoriginal. Fenn casually cut off the man's arm and prepared a package for my father. He sent the arm and paper copies of bank account statements I'd stolen and delivered them to my parents' doorstep in Phoenix. My father had apparently gotten the message because he hadn't tried anything since.

Sylvie and I stared at each other now as we relived that horrible night. "That was..."

"Nothing I ever want to repeat," I finished. She nodded solemnly.

The only good thing that came from them bringing up that bloody night was the cousins not giving me any more grief about Roman Fowler.

On Tuesday morning, I knocked on Drakos's open door. When I walked in, he sat with his suit jacket and tie on, staring at his computer screen. His silk tie was a deep lilac today and looked nice against his charcoal suit and light gray dress shirt.

"I have a few questions about tax law." He might be the smartass of the group, but the man wore his expensive designer suits well. Without waiting for an invitation, I sat.

"Hello, Luminous Luna. Please, come in. Have a seat." He enjoyed tacking on obnoxious adjectives to my name.

I was already sitting. "Thanks. I will."

He leaned back. "Tax law is like playing chess with a dull-witted but tenacious opponent."

"That's so helpful. I'm ready for my exam now."

Rolling his eyes, he leaned back. "Hit me. Then I have a few questions of my own."

"How would you determine the yearly valuation of a privately held family company?"

He didn't miss a beat. "There's either an asset-based or income approach, and you need to take into account devaluation." Drakos launched into an explanation that made surprising sense, gave me a few examples, and answered a couple of follow-up questions. I sometimes forgot how smart Drakos was under all his cutting, cynical commentary.

"Now, my question for you." He steepled his fingers. "Sylvie Spade."

My back shot straight. "What about her?"

"She's your roommate and best friend. I've run into her a few times."

His mild comment made me think he'd met Sylvie more than just a time or two, and then I remembered Sylvie's reaction when she'd seen that photo of Roman and his partners. Groaning, I fisted my hands in my hair. "No. No way. You stay away from her."

"Why?" he snapped, glaring at me. "We just spent the last twenty minutes of my billable time discussing tax law. I'm good enough to get my brain picked but not good enough for your roommate?"

I held my hands up placatingly. "No offense, okay? I'm sure you're a great guy, if a little sarcastic, rude, and offensive at times. But Sylvie is... singular, and she's had trauma in her past."

Drakos's gaze sharpened. "What kind of trauma?"

Ignoring his question, I rolled my shoulders. "She might also be a little crazy. Ezra finished raising her with the Spade cousins."

"Do you think you're scaring me?" His smile worried me.

"Her dad–how do I explain this? He's evil. Like Hitler or Caligula evil, and she *enjoys* taunting him."

He leaned forward and palmed his desk. "All that makes me want her even more. Tell me about her, you owe me."

I sighed and threw up my hands. "She's viciously street-smart and has this wicked humor that can gut you while she's making you laugh. She's also a chess player."

His eyes went sharp. "She plays chess?"

"Do you not know *anything* about her? She's won chess tournaments, and she's *good*. See? You don't even know her. You need to–"

"No, and thank you for the information. You can leave now." He turned back to his computer.

"You should do the right thing and change your mind." He wasn't going to change his mind, I knew this when he pointed to his door.

"Fine, asshole. But I'm warning her about you."

A slow smile spread across his face as he started typing on his laptop. "Good. She'll know I'm coming."

"Your firm is aptly named. You're all fuckers, and we're not done with this conversation." I stalked out of his office and ran straight into Roman.

Chapter 12

Roman

I grabbed Luna as she bounced off my chest. "What conversation aren't you done with?"

She stared up at me and her gaze slid back to Drakos's office. "He asked about Sylvie."

"Ah." She appeared rattled, so I took advantage and held her against me for a few more seconds. Her forearms were slim and supple under my hands, and her firm breasts pressed against my chest. She also smelled like cinnamon candy and something citrusy. She was becoming more comfortable around me and didn't seem to realize it. Good.

"Why does that make you crazy?" I asked mildly.

"Because he's *Drakos.* He'd try to eat her for lunch, she'd kick him in the balls, and the chaos theory would unleash." Luna lowered her voice as if telling me a secret. "Stability to instability, order to disorder. And we'd all get sucked in, just like a black hole."

I heard a low chuckle behind me and turned to see Ivan leaning against his doorframe. "I did an abbreviated background check on Sylvie Spade, and Luna's not wrong."

Luna pointed at Ivan. "When she hears about that, I'd advise you not to be in the same room. Her temper is fierce." Then she turned to me, her bottle-green eyes wide. "You and your partners are trouble, I have a moral obligation to warn her."

"What do you mean, we're trouble?" Annoyance flared in my chest, and I didn't care how hypocritical that made me.

"Just what I said. Alexa also did background checks on you, and except for Xander, you seem to go through women like kids and their Halloween candy."

"That's asinine. You're a woman and I think I've been a calming, stabilizing influence on you."

Her mouth dropped. "No, you haven't."

Ivan chuckled. "And with that, I'm going back to work."

"I need to go too." She started backing up.

I followed her. "You don't think I'm calming or stabilizing?"

Alarm and annoyance flitted across her face. "No."

"I'll have to work on that then."

She stopped and sighed. "That's not completely true. You've helped me study, and I like when we discuss books or ideas. When you're not a mean, grumpy asshole I like talking with you." Her eyebrows crinkled as if she just realized that.

Her admission warmed and chilled me all at once. I relished being around her too, and enjoyed her quips, opinions, and even the incessant questions. She wasn't judgmental, didn't gossip, and had an insatiable curiosity. I still planned to ruin her, I just might take a little longer doing it.

Patting her on the shoulder, I grinned. "That didn't hurt too much, did it?"

"Your smug expression ruins your handsomeness sometimes."

"You think I'm handsome?"

Her face went from pink to a nice shade of red. "You know you're handsome—until you open your mouth."

Luna turned and strode back to her office, and I watched her pert ass as she walked away. She was beautiful, naturally sensual, and her mind hummed with energy. Somehow, my plans weren't so black and white anymore.

Drakos stepped out of his office and watched her walk away. "Should I be offended that she doesn't want me anywhere near Sylvie?"

I shrugged. "No. She's not dumb."

Drakos eyed me. "If she knew the truth, you'd lose her." I didn't deny it.

Ivan came back out of his office. "They did a background check on *us*?" He sounded offended.

Straightening my cuffs, I glanced at them. "They know about Bitter Creek."

Ivan's eyes narrowed to slits. "I'm sure it was her little hacker roommate who researched us. I take it Luna still doesn't know about her father's involvement."

I shook my head.

"Are you going to tell her?" Drakos asked.

"No."

We all stood silently for a moment, and then Drakos sighed. "I hate being reminded of that vile shithole. It was the endless days in solitary for me, staring at that cracked ceiling. I see those mother fucking cracks in my sleep sometimes."

"Plotting revenge is the only good memory I have," Ivan sighed. He gazed at me. "Are you still going through with your fucked up plan?"

"Probably." That was the best answer I could give him.

"You're a bastard, and I need to let off a little steam. You up for me punching you in the face this afternoon, or are you too afraid to get your ass kicked?"

It was a good idea. "I'll meet you at the gym after I drop Luna off at school. I've got some aggression to burn off too."

"Good. See you around two."

My feelings for Luna had run the gambit since she'd walked into our offices. When Klim told me who she was, I'd reveled in the irony and started mapping out my revenge. But then I'd gotten to know Luna, and the irony had taken on a whole new meaning. Because I was starting to like that evil snake's daughter.

Chapter 13

Luna

The tax law quiz had been a beast, and I mentally thanked Drakos for going through valuation with me. That test question had been a convoluted, nasty word problem that I'd relished solving. It had been similar to my conflicted feelings about Roman.

Over the past month, I'd started to thaw toward him. Thinking of Roman made me check my phone. He'd gotten into the habit of texting me after an exam or presentation to see how it went. I pulled out a cinnamon bear from my pocket and brushed off a little lint, then bit it in half and read his text.

Roman: How'd your tax law quiz go?

Luna: It was taxing. I just walked out.

Roman: A tax pun, huh? I don't have a good return.

Luna: Was that a tax joke? I can't tell.

Roman: You give me too much credit.

Luna: Was that a tax joke too?

Roman: Let's stop there. Fiona asked me to meet her at Euphoria. I'll pick you up.

I stopped and the two students walking behind me had to split up to avoid plowing into me.

"Sorry," I mumbled as I looked down at my phone. I typed out a reply, slightly annoyed he'd just demanded and didn't ask. But the field trips were always interesting, so I let it go.

Luna: Sure, I'll come. Meet me at home in fifteen minutes.

Roman refused to call or text me when he got to my apartment, instead he always came inside. This time, I waited for him on the stoop as I watched dusk fall over the cemetery surrounding the funeral home.

He grinned when he saw me. "Are you that excited to see me?"

"No, I'm that excited to see Euphoria on a Thursday night. It's probably different than a weekday at noon."

Roman inclined his head. "True."

He wore black pants and a black shirt with the sleeves rolled up. He looked like he was picking me up for a date. That stray thought sent my pulse pounding, but ideas like that were dangerous.

I looked down at my drab clothes. "Should I change?"

He shrugged. "Maybe. You'll probably be mistaken for law enforcement or a social worker. Do you have anything sparkly?"

I laughed, then realized he was serious. "Hm, no."

"Anything more celebratory or girls' night out'?"

"You mean slutty and short?" I asked, trying to get under his skin.

He pinched the bridge of his nose. "Never mind. Let's go."

Grinning, I smacked his shoulder. "I'm teasing you, and I have a dress that might work. Come in while I change."

He seemed resigned as he walked up the steps. "Alright. I'll text Fiona and tell her it'll be another hour."

Why would it take an hour to change? "No, it won't." I could feel disbelief rolling off him.

Sylvie and I bought consignment designer dresses for a friend's wedding last fall, and I hoped the silky, bronze slip dress would work. I changed into the dress, put on some makeup, and let down my hair.

When I walked out fifteen minutes later, Roman sat on the couch thumbing through my collection of books. He looked up, his body stilled, and his eyes traveled my length. "That will work." I blushed and heat bloomed in my stomach.

He held up two books. "*The Complete Works of Edgar Allen Poe* and *The Joys of Tantric Sex*? Interesting mix."

"How do you know those are mine?"

He raised his eyebrow, and my face flushed when he held up the tantric sex book. "What have you learned?"

I shrugged and tried to grab the book out of his hands. "It has some ideas I'd like to try sometime." I pointed to the Poe book. "And he's still one of my favorite horror authors."

"What specifically would you like to try?"

The flush on my face spread down my chest and settled in my belly, making my insides pulse. "There's no way I'm discussing that with you."

His eyes traveled over my face. "We discuss everything else, and we're both adults. I think we can handle it."

He was so wrong. Instead, we talked about Poe during the drive to Euphoria. "'The Tell-Tale Heart' is his creepiest work," I insisted, patting his thigh. "The man is slowly going mad, and the description of the beating heart in the floor balances horror and irony perfectly."

He shook his head. "It might be in the top five, but 'The Cask of Amontillado' is more chilling. Being unable to stop someone from burying you alive is the worst form of psychological torture." The tone in his voice made me wonder what he'd been thinking about.

When we walked into Euphoria, pulsing music hit us. Even with the elevated noise level, the low lights and plush furniture gave off a sensual, intimate quality, and dancers moved across the stages in undulating moves that blatantly simulated sex. When Roman put his hand on my back, goosebumps erupted across my skin.

He leaned in so I could hear him over the noise. "Come sit for a minute, and I'll let Fiona know we're here." His breath brushed across my bare shoulder, and I tried to hide a shiver. Roman smelled faintly of cedar and spice, and the warmth from his hand seeped into me. He'd been an asshole when we first met, but the more time I spent with Roman, the more I grudgingly liked the man. He didn't seem to like me, though. I needed to keep my head firmly in place and not do anything stupid.

Misty danced on one of the stages, winding herself around a pole, wearing an aqua-colored thong and nothing else. The first time I met her, she explained that the dancers couldn't be completely naked if the club served alcohol, hence the thong. Her firm, high breasts had likely been augmented, but they weren't overly large.

Roman led us over to an intimate two-top a couple of rows back from where Misty danced. There were chairs around the edge of the stage, and a few men sat there, empty glasses and detritus strewn on the bar ledge in front of them.

A pretty server in skintight boy shorts and a small off-the-shoulder blouse came over. "Welcome to Euphoria. My name's Candy. What can I get you to drink?"

Roman bent his head near the girl's ear. "Let Fiona know Roman is here. And I'll have a whiskey neat." He turned to me.

"A perfect vodka martini with a twist, straight up, please." I raised my voice above the music.

Candy turned and blatantly scanned Roman. "One whiskey neat, and one perfect vodka martini, lemon twist, straight up." She smiled and walked off, her ass and hips swaying provocatively.

Roman kept his eyes on me. "A vodka martini?"

"You seem surprised."

"You're a young woman. That demographic usually likes sweet, fruity drinks."

"And your demographic likes whiskey, so you didn't surprise me at all."

He smirked. "I'll have to work on that."

Were we... flirting? I couldn't shake the feeling this was more than just Roman visiting one of his clients. His head suddenly jerked up, and he stood. I turned and saw a man take Misty by her neck and cock his fist back.

"No!" I screamed. Misty jerked back, but the man caught her on the side of her mouth. He then tried to slam her head into the stage, but she jabbed his crotch with her long fingernails and squeezed. The man grunted in pain but didn't let go of her.

I started toward Misty, not understanding what was happening. Why would a patron attack one of the dancers? The squat, rotund man moved fast for someone his size. His dirty-blond hair was slicked back into a ratty ponytail, and he had gaudy gold rings on his fingers.

Another man stood in front of the attacker, and when he saw Roman bearing down, his hand slid behind his back, probably reaching for a gun. In a flash, Roman picked up a highball glass off a table and threw it at the second man's head. He ducked and stumbled, and Roman lunged forward, kicking him in the thigh, then followed up with a quick punch to his neck. The man fell to his knees and started choking.

Scooting around them, I dove toward Misty. The ponytail guy still had ahold of her neck, and I grabbed his hair and tugged on it as hard as I could. "Let go of her!"

He yelled, released Misty, and turned on me. I tried to back up and give myself room to dodge him, but a chair got in my way. Grabbing my wrist, he tried to yank me to him, but Roman wrapped his arm around the attacker's throat from behind and stuck a gun to his temple. "Let her go, or I'll put a bullet through your walnut-sized brain, Strack."

The man let go of my wrist and put his hands up. "Okay. Okay, man. It was just a misunderstanding. The bitches are fine."

"If you touch either one of them again, I will end you. Tell me you understand." Roman's arm tightened around his neck.

"I understand," the man choked out. But he stared at me with mean, dead eyes while he answered Roman. Samuel and another bouncer appeared and subdued the two men, and I turned to Misty, who stood holding her face.

A half-hour later, we sat in Fiona's office. She leaned against the corner of her antique desk, scowling at everyone in the room. Misty sat huddled on the couch next to me, wearing a robe and holding an ice pack to her mouth.

I put my arm around her and patted her shoulder. "That was a nice jab to his crotch."

Misty pulled an icepack off her swollen mouth and winced as her split lip started bleeding. "Don't make me smile. It's been a shit night."

Fiona cocked her head at me. "Will you help Tiny get Misty cleaned up? Roman and I need to talk."

Misty grabbed my hand and squeezed. "No. I want her to sit in on your conversation and tell me exactly what you plan to do." She looked up at Samuel and her face flushed. "And his name is Samuel, not Tiny. He'll help me get cleaned up."

Fiona stared at Misty for a few seconds, then turned to Samuel. "Do you prefer Samuel?"

"Yes. Or Sam is fine." He hadn't taken his eyes off Misty.

"Alright." Fiona pointed to me. Do you know this woman?"

"Yeah. I first met her when she came here with Roman. She's the one who gave us the idea to ask for benefits, and she helped me from getting beaten up even worse tonight." Her eyes filled with tears.

Fiona turned to Roman. "Thank you for getting Lionel off her, and fuck your intern for putting the idea of benefits in their heads.

Do you have any idea how much that cost us?" Roman's eyebrow went up, and he turned to me.

Misty kept going. "We've also hung out. Luna works at the mortuary where my aunt's funeral was held, and she invited us to Sunday poker brunch there. It was pretty fly. I mean, have you ever been to a party at a funeral home? We plan to go next month too. So yeah, I know her. We're friends."

Roman stared at me. "You invited Fiona's dancers to poker brunch?"

"Well, not all of them. But they're welcome if they want to come."

"And you're just telling me this now?"

"No."

"No?" he asked slowly.

"I didn't tell you. Misty did." I turned to her. "Do you need us to take you to the hospital? You have health insurance now." Fiona rolled her eyes, but I saw her lips twitch.

Misty smiled and winced again. "No. They won't tell me anything I don't already know. But I do want to get cleaned up." She stood and walked over to Samuel, then took his hand. "We'll be in the dressing room if you need us."

They walked out together, and Fiona turned to Roman. "One of Strack's sons got past our new bouncer."

"Who are they?" I asked.

Roman's jaw clenched. "Lionel Strack. His brother is Jerome, and their father's name is Silas Strack. They're all psychotic and dangerous, with different but equally repugnant reputations. Do you remember the men at the country club I warned you about?" I nodded. It had been my first day interning with him.

"They're part of a larger drug syndicate here in Vegas, and they own several shell companies and businesses."

"What types of businesses?" I asked.

"Those that take cash and are less mainstream, like massage parlors, strip clubs, pawn shops, or nightclubs."

I turned to Fiona. "Why did he attack Misty?"

"Intimidation. They want to launder money through Euphoria," Fiona answered. She gazed at Roman. "Your firm is a silent partner, but I think it's time to make it public. We also need to discuss additional protection–I expect a partner discount." She gave him a knowing look, then stood and started pacing, her hands on her hips. "I detest those lowlife bastards. They're like cockroaches. They always come back, and they never seem to die. Lionel attacked one of my girls out in the open and on stage. I know they did it to spook my dancers. This needs to stop."

On the way home, I stared out the window. Roman seemed lost in thought, and I mulled over what I'd learned. "All these field trips we go on, you're checking in with your business interests, aren't you?"

Roman didn't speak.

"What about Sin City Motorheads? And that sprawling pawn shop we went to a few weeks ago?" He didn't answer, which was answer enough. "Is that why Ivan sometimes does background checks on your clients? Because you're vetting them as potential business partners?"

He stirred. "It's legal to have clients as business partners in Nevada, as long as the arrangement is fair and reasonable, they consent in writing–"

I waved my hand. "I know all that. How many of these businesses that we've been visiting does your firm have a stake in?"

He studied me. "Most of them."

"Even the Wild West Chapel?"

"Not that one."

I stared ahead, trying to grasp the implications of how deeply they'd enmeshed themselves into the Las Vegas business sector. "I make a good cover, don't I? You dragging your intern around to the businesses you supposedly do legal work for. But the reality is, you own or have a partnership in most of them. Do you know how they all run?"

"Mostly. Ivan knows more about the two tech companies than I do."

Two tech companies. Jesus, no wonder these guys were loaded. "What do the Stracks want?"

Roman sighed. "Access to businesses to help them launder money. They've been successful with several establishments they don't own but just have an... arrangement with, but Silas is a greedy fucker."

He walked me up to my apartment. "We need to talk. Invite me inside."

I unlocked the door and hesitated, but he quirked an eyebrow. "Come in," I sighed, too tired to fight.

Kicking off my shoes, I pulled out the filtered water pitcher and poured us both a glass, downing mine.

He took a sip and watched me over the rim. "I need you to accompany me to a black-tie event on Saturday night. If you recall, our deal includes occasional weekend events."

"I don't have enough time or money to find anything to wear." The thought of him taking one of those women I'd seen him with online tightened my stomach, but I shoved it aside. "You should find someone else."

"No, and I'll send something over."

I huffed out a breath. "I *really* hate that word."

Chapter 14

Roman

On Friday at noon, I drove Luna home. "Have you heard any-thing about Misty?" she asked.

"Fiona said she's going to be fine."

"Did that Strack guy get arrested?"

I glanced at her. "Yes."

"I bet you can still find someone else to go–"

"No."

She sighed and sat back in her seat. "You're being a grumpy dick today."

"And your mouth is going to get you in trouble," I returned as I pulled into the funeral home.

"It already has. I'd say thanks for the ride, but I didn't want it to start with. Bye." She got out and slammed the door. I watched her walk to her apartment with narrowed eyes. She'd wormed her way under my defenses, and I knew my plans were in jeopardy. Her father didn't care about her, and she detested him–a feeling we both shared.

Whatever I did to ruin her life wouldn't enrage him or get under his skin. The bastard would probably gloat. I should have figured it out when Klim seemed so eager to throw her to the wolves. He hadn't meant to throw her to the wolves at all, he just wanted me to get over my searing hatred.

Fucking Klim. What he didn't foresee was that I'd become obsessed with her. Luna was pure, wicked sunshine, and she was mine. Time for a new plan.

When I got back to the offices, the partners were in the conference room eating takeout from an expensive as fuck Michelin star restaurant that didn't officially offer takeout.

Ivan pointed his fork at me. "I want to talk about Luna."

I shook my head and leaned forward to grab a plate. "Too bad, I don't."

Ivan wasn't deterred. "Luna's father doesn't give a rat's ass about her, and she hates his guts."

"I'm aware. I still plan to fuck her."

Drakos laced his hands behind his head. "So, what? Now you're thinking that maybe instead of ruining her law career before it starts, you'll just destroy her life by fucking her while she's your intern?" He looked disgusted.

Xander leaned back and studied me. "She doesn't deserve to have her life wrecked so you can get your revenge."

I glared at Xander. "Thank you for stating the obvious, but I'm not sure that's how revenge works."

Gideon stood. "I agree with Xander. You framing her for stealing from this firm and cheating on a law school exam is juvenile and asinine. Her father may have been a major shareholder in Bitter Creek Ranch, but Luna wasn't. And now that you all know her, destroying her will make you feel exponentially worse." He turned to me. "You need to fix this."

I gazed at my partners. "I still plan to have her."

Ivan sighed. "You and your fucking obsessions."

We resumed eating, and a few moments later Brenna knocked on the conference door. "Hello, gentlemen. I saw lunch arrived, and Gideon invited me today. Oh, this looks good." I glared at Gideon. There was a reason the reception desk was out front, away from the rest of us. I didn't like her lurking around and using that fake, friendly voice, and I detested how she treated Luna. I needed to get rid of her.

Chapter 15

Luna

Alexa eyed the expensive-looking zipper bag and shoe box that had just shown up on the doorstep, then turned to me. "Well? Aren't you going to open them?"

"I'm not wearing the dress, so it's better to not even look."

She rolled her eyes. "You and I both know your curiosity is going to make you pull everything out and try it all on, even if you don't wear it tonight."

I was already unzipping the garment bag. "Okay. I guess it won't hurt to look."

The creamy white couture dress and strappy sandals were exquisite. My breath caught as I held the dress up and turned it over to see the back. Then I saw the price tag, still attached to the inside label.

"Holy shit," I whispered.

"It's beautiful. The color reminds me of a pearlescent full moon." Alexa stared at the gorgeous dress, looking a little stunned by its elegance. Then she studied my face and sighed. "You're really not going to wear it?"

"He's my mentor, it wouldn't be right. There's also this." I held up the price tag so she could see it.

She choked. "This dress is more expensive than my car."

I nodded and turned to her. "Why is he doing this? Most of the time, he's cold and mean. He can't stand me."

Alexa shook her head. "I'm not sure who picked it out, but that dress doesn't say *I can't stand you.*"

Later that evening, the doorbell let out its annoying flat buzz as I finished putting a few things in my jacket pocket.

I huffed out a nervous breath and turned to my tripod feline companion. "You going to miss me, Carl?" He yawned and went back to licking himself.

My stomach clenched, and I wondered how Roman would react. When I swung open the door, he stood in the doorway in an expensive, well-cut black suit, black shirt, and tie. He looked so good that I straightened and stared for a few seconds.

As he walked in, his eyes flicked past me, pausing on the couture dress and strappy shoes lying across the back of the couch. The man knew my sizes; I tried not to think about that.

He eyed me up and down and raised his eyebrow. "Why aren't you wearing the dress?"

My back went up. "Did you decide to go with the funeral home aesthetic tonight? I bet Ezra would be happy to hire you."

He arched an eyebrow as he took in my simple black pencil skirt and jacket. It was similar to what I usually wore at the office. "And you decided to go with the insurance office manager look."

His comment stung, but I raised my chin. "A simple, off-the-rack suit works fine for an intern."

He waved his hand. "Suit yourself. Are you ready?"

"Was that a pun? I can never tell. You're not mad?"

He seemed to rein in his retort. "I did look forward to seeing you in that dress, but it appears you're done throwing a tantrum about coming, so there's that, at least."

I rolled my eyes. "I never 'threw a temper tantrum.' Let me put it back in the garment bag, and you can return it."

"Keep it, now let's go." He took my arm and started walking toward the door.

I tugged out of his grip. "There's no way I'm keeping that dress."

"Why?"

"The price tag is still on it, and I can't take something like that from my mentor. It's exquisite, but this isn't a date and I'm not Cinderella. I don't feel right keeping it."

He shook his head and strode to the door. "We'll argue about it later. I never understood the draw of that story when Cinderella would have been better off suing her stepmother for breach of fiduciary duties instead of getting tied up with Prince Charming."

I followed him. "You're kind of a legal nerd. You know that, right?"

"That's an interesting observation, coming from you. Gideon is driving us tonight." A sleek black suburban with tinted windows sat in the mortuary's circular driveway.

Gideon hopped out and opened the door for us, smiling at me. "Good evening, Luna. You look lovely, and I like the shoes."

I smiled. My one concession had been a stylish pair of black pumps with ankle straps, and Gideon had noticed.

"Hi, Gideon. Thank you, and thanks for driving tonight." I patted his arm and slid into the spacious backseat, the leather cool beneath my hands.

Gideon shut the door, and Roman's cedar and spice scent filled the space, along with a momentary sense of intimacy, as he slid in after me. Tourists and locals walked along the Strip, dressed in everything from shorts and sandals to tuxedos and dresses, as they took in the bright lights and glitter. The venue for the charity event was one of the newer casino hotels on the Strip, built when an older one had been imploded several years ago. Gideon drove us around to the opulent front entrance, and my stomach knotted in excited dread as the vehicle stopped.

Roman turned to him. "I'll text you about ten minutes before we need you to pick us up."

"Very good. Ivan requested I stay close this evening."

Roman nodded, looking grim. "Thank you. I'll be on alert." He studied me, then reached behind my head and removed my hair clip.

"Hey! What are you doing?" I tried to grab the clip as my hair unraveled well past my shoulders.

"You might be taken for one of the servers with your hair up. I want people to be able to tell the difference so everyone behaves themselves."

I hurriedly ran my fingers through my long, dark, curly hair, hoping it looked elegantly tousled instead of just messy. The valet opened the door, and Roman slid out and extended his hand back to me. I took it and squeezed until he stopped scanning and turned to me with his eyebrow raised.

"Why does Gideon need to stay close? Who's here tonight that Ivan is worried about?"

He shook his head and wrapped his hand around my fore-arm, guiding me inside the lobby. Turning left, we headed down a red-carpeted corridor where several well-heeled couples were gath-ered. "I forget how observant you are sometimes. It's a precaution."

A precaution, my ass. Something was happening, but I didn't know what. Roman and his partners were sometimes careful and taciturn when I asked certain questions, and they were as adept as any politician at giving non-answer responses. Like right now.

"Why aren't the other law partners attending tonight?"

"We take turns since none of us like these events. It was my turn."

Sucking in a deep breath, I let it out slowly. "Alright. Let's go do some schmoozing." He squeezed my arm gently and guided me forward.

Outwardly, Roman fit in with these people. He moved with confidence and control and wore designer, custom-tailored clothes. As we approached the ballroom, I started seeing them—the Las Vegas ultra-rich, and those who'd probably flown in on private jets from the East and West coasts just for the evening. Several reporters and camera people hovered at the entrance as we walked in.

"My advice is to smile and nod politely, then excuse yourself if you get cornered or don't want to speak with someone," Roman murmured.

"Smile, nod, and try to look pretty?" I arched an eyebrow. "Arm candy–I've got it. The first two shouldn't be hard."

"Looking lovely won't be a stretch for you either, it's not asking countless questions that'll be the issue."

"Hmm, another backhanded compliment."

He inclined his head, and we stepped into the carnivalesque atmosphere. A few reporters headed Roman's way, and when they glimpsed me on his arm, they hesitated.

"Who's the girl in the cheap suit?" I heard someone whisper.

"Anyone know her? Is she one of his subs?" someone else asked. "She doesn't look like it," a man with an expensive camera answered. My simple attire seemed to confuse them.

Roman leaned in close, his breath warm against my ear. "Well, this is interesting. Maybe you'll be a new trendsetter."

"God help me," I muttered back. "What does he mean by sub?"

He shook his head slightly and didn't stop to answer questions. Guiding me forward with a hand at the small of my back, we walked into the event.

"Let me introduce you to a few people." As we circulated through the ballroom, I began to realize Roman was skilled at making people feel singled out and important, and women followed him with their eyes.

A server approached us, and Roman took a whiskey and handed me a glass of champagne. I sipped the drink and looked around the room. Rich, well-heeled people mingled together, talking in small groups as they sipped their drinks.

As we stood there, a man and woman approached us. The man was unremarkable, but the woman looked like a blond version of Jessica Rabbit. "Hello, Roman darling. It's wonderful to see you tonight. I've missed you," the woman murmured in a soft, cultured voice. She wore a gold gown with a significant slit up her thigh and a deep neckline.

"Hello, Marla." Roman flicked his gaze to the man. "Tucker. Meet Luna Cross."

Marla turned to me, her smile going flat. "Is she your secretary or administrative assistant?" Her lipstick looked wet, and her long red fingernails glistened as she took hold of his arm.

Roman shook his head. "Neither."

"Your new submissive?" her voice sounded incredulous.

"No, and you know better than to ask," Roman murmured dangerously. He stepped away and palmed my back.

Marla blanched but tried again. "Your paralegal then? She doesn't look old enough."

I glanced at her with a confused look. "I wasn't aware there's an age requirement to be a paralegal."

She ignored me. "Isn't Gideon still with you?"

I put the woman out of her misery. "I'm Mr. Fowler's legal intern."

The woman's posture relaxed, and she turned to me. "So Roman is mentoring you. That's odd. He told me he usually prefers male law students since there's less chance they'll develop a crush on him." I tried not to wince, wondering if I might fit into that category.

"Not this time," Roman answered.

Her wet lips turned down. "Your choice of attire is... interesting. Are you making some kind of statement?" Her date sipped champagne behind her with a bored expression.

"No."

Roman took my arm and turned. "If you'll excuse us, there are a few people I need to speak with."

She looked at him hungrily. "It's lovely to see you again. Call me if you ever need... anything. Enjoy your evening." Her message was clear.

A trail of whispers followed as we walked away, and I turned to Roman. "Let me guess, ex-wife?"

"No ex-wives."

"Ex-girlfriend then, or ex-submissive?" He was silent, and I knew I was right. "Huh, I learn something new every day. You're into submission and dominance. I'll have to ask Declan about–"

He stopped abruptly and faced me. "If you have questions about it, you will ask *me*. Do you understand?"

In hindsight, I should have guessed months ago. His dominance wasn't an affectation, it was something deeply engrained in his DNA.

"Luna, answer me." He didn't sound angry or annoyed, just determined.

"Alright. If I have questions, I'll ask you."

He relaxed, and we started walking again. "You survived your first shark encounter."

"Sharks would be easier—at least they don't pretend they aren't dangerous," I murmured, thinking more of him than Marla.

As we moved through the crowd together, Roman would sometimes whisper facts about people before they came within earshot. We had a system down, and I began to think I'd make it through the night unscathed when a man I recognized stepped in front of me.

"Good evening, Luna." Cameron Wilder gazed down at me, looking handsome in a charcoal suit and red silk tie.

I smiled up at him. "Hello, Cameron. It's nice to see someone I recognize here tonight."

"Are you up for lunch or coffee next week? I've called the office a few times, but you're never available."

I glanced over at Roman, but his face was blank. "Do you have your phone on you?" I asked.

He grinned, pulled it out, and unlocked it. "Here, you can type your number in."

Suddenly, Roman stepped behind me and slid his arm around my waist as if he were claiming or marking me. "She's with me tonight, Wilder. You need to back the fuck off."

My body stiffened, and I froze in place. Cameron glanced down at his arm, then looked up to study my shocked face. "She doesn't seem to be aware of that. And wouldn't it be a serious faux pas to be romantically involved with your law school intern?"

Roman swore viciously but didn't step back.

Cameron looked down at me and smiled. "If you want to do lunch or coffee, call my office and have them put you through to Marcus, my assistant. Leave your number with him. I *will* call you back, Luna. Have a good evening." He glanced up at Roman, and for the first time, I saw ice in his eyes.

Roman's arm spasmed around my waist, but he let me go and stepped back as Cameron walked off. I slowly turned and stared up at him. "What–" my voice croaked, so I tried again. "What in *the fuck* was that?"

He studied me with hooded eyes. "He is not as friendly or safe as he seems."

"Neither are you, and that's saying something because you aren't safe or friendly at all."

Roman leaned down and got in my face. "Cameron likes floggers, handcuffs, and a little pain when he fucks. Maybe he just wants to do lunch, but I highly doubt it, and his preferences don't seem to be your cup of tea."

My eyes went wide and my breathing sped up. For once, I couldn't get any questions out. He studied my face carefully. "Or is it?"

I swallowed. "Well, maybe not... all of that."

He growled low in his throat, and I grew damp. Our conversation had gone off the rails fast, and I needed to get myself together. Turning my head to avoid his gaze, I noticed another woman approaching us, her eyes on Roman. I tried to turn away, but Roman slid his hand around my back and held me to his side.

The slender, dark-haired woman wore a well-cut black dress that was more subdued than Marla's, but somehow more sensual. She wore a thick gold collar around her throat, and the man standing beside her eyed Roman with intense dislike.

"Good evening, Madison. Charles," Roman greeted them. "This is Luna Cross."

I noticed the woman couldn't quite meet Roman's eyes, and Charles grunted a hello. Then Madison focused on me. "Hello, I'm Madison Carlisle." She seemed to expect me to know who she was.

Roman hadn't given me any information about this couple. "I'm Luna Cross, Mr. Fowler's law student intern and reticent partner for the evening. It's nice to meet you."

Her lips curled up in surprise. "Oh. So you're not his next... companion."

I cocked my head. "Truthfully, we can barely tolerate each other, and you're the second woman to approach us who's probably a former submissive. You can just tell me whatever it is you want to say."

The woman's face flushed and she snuck a peek at Roman, then she took my arm and pulled me out of earshot. "Has he asked you to sign a nondisclosure agreement yet?"

My head jerked back. "No, and I'd tell him to go screw himself if he did."

She looked almost relieved and then despondent. The woman was beautiful and seemed sincere, but she was also a little broken.

Madison glanced over at the men staring at us. "Be careful with him. He's mesmerizing and addictive, but also cold and closed off. Don't think you're special to him, no matter how mind-blowing the sex and submission are."

I blinked. "Our relationship isn't like that."

She gazed at me, then turned to Roman. "From the way he stares at you, he wants it to be. Just... be careful." She looked over her shoulder and stepped back. "It was nice to meet you, Luna."

Roman took my hand and pulled me back toward him, away from Madison.

"It was nice to meet you too. Thank you for the salon recommendation."

Madison smiled a little as Charles led her away. I turned to Roman and gently tugged at my hand. He let go but stepped closer, looking around as if assessing for other threats.

"Why are your former subs warning me about you? And why do you have them sign NDAs? Is it really necessary? I bet that's an interesting legal document."

He raised an eyebrow. "You couldn't even wait for the night to be over before you start in with the questions."

"I have *so* many questions, but since I can't ask Declan, you did this to yourself. How long do we have to stay?"

Roman shrugged. "I tend to give it an hour or two, and by that time I'm ready to punch someone. It's been long enough, let's go."

As we headed toward the exit, I sighed inwardly when a short, barrel-chested, middle-aged man stepped in front of Roman. I just wanted to go home. The man's custom-tailored suit did little to disguise the extra weight or his double chin that seemed to disappear into the collar of his shirt. Two hard-looking men stood a few feet behind him.

"Roman Fowler," the man sneered. He had watery eyes and a bulbous nose. "Who's your pretty little date?"

"Hello, Silas," Roman greeted him with an icy smile. "This is Ms. Cross, as you're well aware."

He eyed my suit with something akin to amusement. "She's a pretty thing even in ugly clothes, Fowler, I'll give you that. Does she like it rough? My boys are looking forward to accommodating her when you get tired of her holes." My stomach tightened at his disgusting words.

"You and your 'boys' stay the fuck away from her if you value your balls, Strack. I hear Lionel is still in jail."

So this was Lionel Strack's father, Silas Strack. The man's eyes turned cold. "He'll be out soon. And then I'll properly introduce him to Ms. Cross." This man gave off serious serial killer vibes.

"Over my dead body," Roman said pleasantly.

Silas's lips twisted, and he winked conspiratorially. His breath reeked of alcohol and cigarettes, even from ten feet away. "We shouldn't be at odds. If you want to make some real money, we have a business model that'd make you a very rich man."

"I'm already a very rich man, and there's no fucking way we'd use our firm or our business interests to launder money for you. We aren't stupid enough to get into bed with either you or the drug syndicate." Roman leaned in. "And if you don't stay clear of us, I'll make sure you live to deeply regret it. Or die regretting it. Either works for me."

Silas studied Roman with bloodshot eyes, then pulled a cigar out of his pocket and sniffed it. "Don't be offended, Mr. Fowler. We respect your reputation." His eyes went hard, and he nodded to me. "But Lionel wants the girl. I'll see Ms. Cross again soon." My stomach cramped and my knees started shaking as Silas waddled off with his two men in tow.

Roman took my arm. "Let's go."

He pulled his phone out and called Gideon as we walked. "We're ready." He hung up, and we walked swiftly toward the pickup area. When we hit the front entrance of the massive hotel, Roman gently herded me back against a pillar. "I came to an unpleasant realization tonight."

"That Silas Strack is creepy as hell?"

"That I need to hand your mentorship off to Ivan."

Adrenaline hit my system, and my body stilled. If he'd let me out of this situation months ago, I would have been ecstatic, but now I felt hurt and betrayed. "Why?"

"I trust Ivan." He cupped my cheek, and my breath whooshed out. "I also don't like watching other men circle around you without being able to do anything about it. Even you wearing that god-damned suit couldn't keep men from eye fucking you tonight."

"What?" I choked out.

"I want more from you, Luna, so it's time to hand off your internship."

My heart sped up, and anger surged through me. "You are such an *asshole*. First, for not letting me out of this internship to begin with, and then for making me actually like you after the way you've treated me–for months!"

A sly grin spread across his face, making my ovaries clench. I stuck my finger in his face and whispered hoarsely, "Get that smile off your face right now." I pulled away from him and started pacing, my hands gesturing wildly as I ranted. "I'll admit, I tried on that dress and those shoes. Because I'm curious to a fault, and the dress is gorgeous." I turned and marched back to him. "But I'm done letting you jerk me around. You want to hand me off? Fine, but don't try to cock block me, or act jealous, or... buy me clothes ever again!"

"You're a woman, so technically I can't cock block you."

"You know what I mean. Are we clear?"

"No."

"No?" I sounded strangled.

He reached up and brushed a strand of hair off my face. "From now on, I'll buy you whatever the fuck I want."

This was a game to him, but he could really hurt me. Hell, he'd already done that by treating me so contemptuously for months and then coldly dumping me on Ivan. And now the demented Strack family was after me. "If I've become such a problem and you plan to pawn me off anyway, then I'll go back to my original internship. On Monday, I'll call Klim and let him know."

As Gideon pulled up, Roman leaned over and murmured in my ear, "The fuck you will."

Chapter 16

Roman

My patience was long gone. We didn't say a word during the ride to her apartment, and she unlocked her door and turned. "Tell the partners goodbye for me. I hope you won't be a moody prick if we happen to see each other again."

I caught the door before she could close it and tsked. "Gideon will be here on Tuesday morning to pick you up." I leaned in as her beautiful green eyes flared. "Don't stand him up." I gently pushed her inside her apartment and closed the door so I wouldn't be tempted to follow her in and fuck her on the living room floor.

"Everything alright?" Gideon asked mildly as I slid into the passenger seat a moment later. He'd experienced the tense, silent ride from the casino too.

"No. Xander was right, this is a fucking mess."

Gideon hummed. "Lionel Strack is a misogynistic psychopath. When he gets out, he'll come after her."

"Ivan is putting a tail on him." I sighed. "We met Silas and his bodyguards as we were walking out. She's on his radar too, and he confirmed Lionel wants her."

Gideon's mouth went tight. "She needs protection."

"I know. She yanked the shit out of Lionel's ridiculous little ponytail, and it probably took him three or four years to grow that thing." I smirked, despite the deep frustration roiling through me.

"How'd the evening go other than Silas? Did it fluster her to be so underdressed?"

"No. She didn't seem to care, and she *still* ended up causing a stir." I told him about Cameron Wilder.

Gideon nodded, unsurprised. "Her beauty and curiosity pull people in, and her intelligence and humor don't hurt either."

"Everywhere we go, she draws attention. I don't like it."

He grinned but didn't respond. A few minutes later, he pulled into my driveway. "You need to figure out what you want. I rather like her, despite who her father is, and I don't want to see her get hurt–by the Stracks *or* by you. If you don't claim her, maybe one of the partners will. Or you could hand her over to Cameron. He seems enamored by her, and he could keep her safe. Of course, he does have a penchant for rough sex. But then again, so do you."

"You know goddamn good and well none of the partners will step on my toes. *Fuck*, I'm not talking with you about this." As I got out, he chuckled at my frustration. Gideon liked to get under my skin sometimes.

Shedding my suitcoat as I walked into the kitchen, I headed to the liquor cabinet. The cool, still evening greeted me as I sat by the pool and nursed a bourbon while staring out at the Vegas skyline, brooding and planning.

There was no way I'd step aside and let one of my partners, or fucking Cameron Wilder, have Luna. Maybe that made me a prick, but the added bonus would be getting under her corrupt father's skin, because Montgomery Cross may not care if she lost her scholarship or couldn't take the bar. But I'd bet he would completely lose his shit if he knew his daughter was fucking one of the delinquent teenagers from Bitter Creek Ranch. The demons inside my head quieted for the first time in months, and I picked up my phone and started typing out a text to Klim.

Roman: As of right now, I'm no longer Luna's mentor.

Klim: What the hell am I supposed to do with that on a Saturday night at midnight? What happened? Is Luna alright?

Roman: Ivan is her mentor now

Klim: Goddamn it, Roman. Did you fuck her?

Roman: Not yet.

Klim: Does she know about her father?

Everyone kept asking me that. Luna had been mine to torture and ruin before I met her, and now she was just *mine*. I didn't care anymore about her fucking father.

Klim: You have to tell her

I didn't respond, smiling grimly as I set my phone down and picked up my bourbon, taking a sip. A few minutes later, another text came in.

Klim: Goddamn it, Roman. You and I are going to have words

I wanted Luna, no I *craved* her, my obsession finally reaching a flash point. Setting my drink down, my mind buzzed with restless energy as my feet took me to the gym. I stripped naked and shadow-sparred with the punching bag for a good half hour. Then I showered and called Ivan.

"What?" he growled, sleep in his voice.

"What'd you learn about Luna's childhood when you did her background check?"

Ivan was silent for several seconds, then he let out a long, mournful sigh. "You fucking asshole. You didn't read my report, did you? Don't ask me for the 'full monty' and then not read the whole goddamned report, you motherfucker."

"What are you talking about?"

"Pull it up and read the *entire fucking thing*." He punctuated the last three words. "I wondered how you could still hurt her after reading about... Fuck! I should have made sure you knew."

My heart started pounding. "Ivan, what did I miss?"

"Just read it." Then he hung up.

Cold dread seeped through me as I searched for Ivan's email with the report attached. Walking to my bedroom, I propped myself in bed and read the entire report this time, starting at the beginning instead of just focusing on her last few years.

I read about a fairly typical childhood for a kid with narcissistic parents. Then I came across the section where the report outlined how Luna had been severely beaten by her father one night. The paragraph discussed "extensive contusions on the face, lacerations, broken ribs, and eyes swollen shut." The report also outlined her broken arm and Luna being left for dead in the bottom of her parents' clothes closet. She'd been eleven fucking years old at the time, and she'd spent her twelfth birthday lying there, waiting to die. I owed Sylvie Spade more than I could repay.

Montgomery had probably planned to send in a clean-up crew while he was out of town to get rid of the body, but Sylvie had found her first. Sylvie and her mother lived with husband number three on the same street as Luna in an upscale Phoenix suburb, and they'd become fast friends. When Luna went missing, Sylvie had gone looking for her, breaking in through Luna's bedroom window and cutting her arms in the process.

My breath sawed in and out as I fought for control. Luna had been lying half-dead in her own blood and filth, locked in a closet while her parents went out of town so they wouldn't have to deal with the mess.

Then her father had done to her what he'd done to us, and used his extensive reach and legal influence to lie, bribe, and cover up his crimes. He'd blamed the attack on a random break-in, and threatened Sylvie's mother to keep the girls quiet. Frustration, bitter regret, and pure rage flowed through me. And hate. So much hate for Luna's father.

"Fuck. FUCK!" I bellowed. I got out of bed and paced my room, but I couldn't contain my anger. Stalking out to the back patio, I stared out into the night.

Luna had experienced her own hell at the hands of her father, and I wanted to soothe her hurts, protect her, and then fuck her senseless. Throwing my phone on the lounger, I stripped and dove into the pool, then slowly swam laps while the contents of that report rattled through my mind as my tired arms and brain slowly went numb. Now that I wasn't her mentor, all bets were off.

Chapter 17

A few seconds after Roman pushed me into my apartment and closed the door, Sylvie walked out of her room.

She studied my face, then hissed, "What did that fucker do to you?"

The adrenaline had dissipated, and I felt numb and tired. "Nothing."

"I hung the fairy princess gown in your closet so Carl wouldn't destroy it. Now talk to me. What happened?" She watched me carefully.

I pulled off my jacket and threw it on the couch, knowing I'd regret not hanging it up tomorrow when I had to pick cat hair off it. I trudged into the kitchen and started rummaging through the cupboards, looking for candy.

"Roman dumped me as his intern." I found a half-empty box of Red Hots behind the oatmeal and threw a few in my mouth.

Sylvie followed me into the kitchen and stared at me. "What? That makes no sense whatsoever." She held up a finger. "Wait. This calls for cheap wine. It'll pair nicely with your cinnamon candy." She poured two glasses, and we plopped onto the couch. "Okay. Start from the beginning."

So I told her everything–about the internship and the partners, Lionel and Silas Strack, and Roman telling me he couldn't be my mentor anymore. When I finished talking, my wine glass and the candy box sat empty.

Sylvie poured us more wine and sighed. "Well, I wasn't wrong. This internship is a lot more exciting than one with Artie would have been. Do you like him?"

"Of course I like Arthur." I knew she wasn't talking about Artie.

"No, dumbass, Roman. Do you like him?"

"Sometimes. And other times, I wish I was an octopus so I had eight hands to smack his smug face with."

"Don't play dumb, you suck at it. Do you *like* him?"

I worried if I admitted it out loud, things would go from bad to worse. So I settled for something in between. "I refuse to like him. It's an unethical, horrible idea. The man is my mentor, and I'm his intern. Or was. He may be hot, but he's also moody, domineering, into BDSM–which I found out about tonight–and has more baggage than the lost-and-found at JFK."

Sylvie laid her head on the back of the couch. "Denial is just a lie you tell yourself. You like him."

"I *can't* like him." My voice sounded almost pleading. Carl must have felt my anxiety because he padded over and hopped on my lap, kneading my skirt with his one front paw. I scratched behind his ears as he purred loudly.

Sylvie stared down at him. "That cat is weird. I swear he barely tolerates us until we're depressed or anxious, and then he's right there. What're you going to do?"

"What any smart woman would do. Stay far away from him and pretend he has the plague."

On Monday, as I walked to Klim's office before my first class, a sense of déjà vu floated through me. I'd come to Klim a few months ago for the same reason. Back then, I was angry and annoyed. Now I felt conflicted and sad. His door stood open and he sat at his desk, drinking coffee and studying his computer screen.

"Hello, Klim."

He looked up and pulled his glasses off. "Luna. I thought I'd see you today. What's going on with you and Roman?"

"We're ending our internship."

"Tell me the truth. Did something happen?"

"No, and don't make it weird. I swear the man hates me and barely tolerates having me around. It's just... time."

Klim set his coffee down. "He said Ivan is taking over."

I rolled my eyes. "Klim, I like you. In fact, you've done more for me than my own parents ever did. If you hadn't reached out about that scholarship, I don't know what I would've done." I looked at my feet and blinked a few times. "Anyway, thank you. But let's get real here. Ivan isn't even a practicing attorney. He's more like their NSA, or central intelligence."

Klim smiled briefly. "That's an interesting analogy and more on-point than you know. I'll make a deal with you. Let's give it a week with Ivan, and if you still can't stomach interning there, I'll give you credit for the time you've spent there and call Arthur myself to help smooth your way. Alright?"

The man was trying to drag it out, and I didn't know why. "You don't need to smooth anything over with Arthur. Why are you stalling?"

"I'll help you in one week, but not before then. And I don't know what you mean."

I narrowed my eyes. "Sure you don't. One week, but you call Gideon and tell him I drive myself from now on."

Mondays were always busy, and they seemed to go by quickly. But not today. By the time I walked out of the law school, I had a pounding stress headache I'd barely been able to touch with two ibuprofen and an energy drink.

On Tuesday morning, I got to the offices just before eight.

Gideon sat at his desk, and he looked up when I walked in. "Good morning. How was your weekend?"

"I think you already know. I've been dumped onto Ivan, so where do you want me? It'll only be for a few days, then Klim promised I could mentor with Arthur Thorgeson starting next week."

Gideon pointed to the small office I'd already been using. "The same spot. I don't think much has changed." He studied me for a few seconds. "May I give you some advice?"

"Please."

He looked at me placidly. "Don't poke the bear today." I opened my mouth to ask him what he meant, but his phone rang.

I'd beat the partners to work this morning. Roman's office was still dark, so I shut the connecting door, put on my noise-canceling headphones, and worked on a few motions. When I looked up again, the connecting door was open and Roman stood in the doorway, watching me. "Hello, Luna. Are you done pouting?"

I pulled off my headphones, sucked in a breath, and exhaled on the count of five. "My weekend was fine and no, I'm not done pouting. Are you done being an asshole?"

His eyes lit and he straightened. "I told you that mouth would get you in trouble one day."

I stood. "But not today. Oh, look at the time. I need to get to class." I drank him in as he stood there with that strand of hair hanging over his forehead and his dark, piercing gaze. Why was I so drawn to *him* of all people? I shoved my computer and pens into my backpack.

"Your class doesn't start for almost two hours, and we want to discuss our latest project with you."

My head came up. "What latest project?" My stupid curiosity.

"Come find out." He nodded his head toward his office.

Ivan sat in one of Roman's client chairs, and he gave me an obnoxious finger wave. I slowly put my backpack and phone back down on my desk and entered his office. Roman shut the connecting door behind me.

Ivan studied me, and this time his face remained serious. No smirks, annoying grins, or little digs. "I hear you met Silas Strack the other night. Be careful, the Stracks aren't playing with a full deck."

Roman leaned against his desk. "He's right. Don't go anywhere alone, and if you see anything out of the ordinary or something doesn't feel right, get out."

"I don't know why they'd come after me, but I'll be careful." I squinted at them. "What do you know that I don't?"

Ivan's lip tipped up. "A lot of things, and most of them would make you blush." Strangely, his comment made me relax a little. This was the Ivan I knew and mostly disliked.

Roman gazed at me, his eyes drifting down to my clenched hands. Then he held out a bowl of... cinnamon bears?

I automatically took one and bit its legs off. "Why do you have cinnamon bears on your desk?"

Ivan chuckled and Roman shrugged. "Let's discuss our latest development. Ivan is your official interim mentor, but you'll be assigned another one shortly. We'll also be expanding our legal practice over the next month to include another area of law."

My mind started sifting through the possibilities. "Criminal law? You could represent each other that way. It would save you a lot of money." I popped the rest of the candy in my mouth.

Ivan stared at me. "That's not a bad idea."

I'd been kidding. "It doesn't matter. Klim said he'd move me next week. If you prefer, we could call this my last day."

Ivan grinned. "Nice try."

"If you're still holding out for Arthur Thorgeson, he's coming here." Roman informed me, watching my face carefully. "After listening to you discuss water law issues and the amount of money involved, we decided to bring him on board to mentor another attorney before he retires."

"The Firm is buying Artie's practice out, and you're branching into water law?" I asked slowly.

Roman nodded. "We researched it, and you're right—it's important, and there's a fuck-ton of money involved."

"Why?"

"I just explained it to you."

My mind took a few seconds to process what he was telling me, and then anger started to bubble in my chest as I stood. "On Saturday night, you told me you didn't want to be my mentor anymore. And when I informed you I'd finish my internship with Thorgeson, you decided to buy him out. Why are you doing this? What do you want from me?"

"Ivan, give us a minute." Ivan stood and headed to the door, shaking his head as he walked out.

I folded my arms. "I'm done playing your games. Why are you trying to ruin my life? What do you want from me?"

Roman straightened and stood in front of me. "I want everything," he murmured.

The intent in his gaze was clear this time, and naked, predatory lust stared back at me. I slowly licked my lips, as if trying to taste his phantom touch. Why did I have to be attracted to *this fucking man*? He insulted me, ran roughshod over my wishes, and seemed to enjoy frustrating and mocking me. But he also stimulated my mind and answered my questions, and the sparks between us burned white hot. Roman reached out and grasped my suit jacket, gently pulling me closer. My breath quickened and my pulse hiccupped.

Gazing up at him, I carefully rested my hands on his arms. "What does that mean?" I whispered.

His sculpted biceps felt hard and warm through the fabric of his dress shirt, and his heady scent surrounded me. He leaned in. "I want you, and I plan to have you. But I don't want guilt, repercussions, or consequences to cloud this, so you're no longer my intern, and I'm not your official mentor anymore."

"But... you hate me."

He shook his head and pulled me closer, pressing my breasts against him. "I tried to, but I don't. We'll spend time together outside work. We're also going to fuck, Luna, many times, in every position, and on every feasible surface."

"You give me whiplash," I whispered. "You don't like me, but you still want to have sex with me?"

I pulled back and searched his eyes. He grasped my face, running his thumbs across my cheeks. "I don't hate you, Sweetness. And yes, I absolutely want to fuck you."

Roman leaned in slowly and ran his mouth along my jaw, causing goosebumps to erupt across my skin and making my nipples go stiff.

"Oh, God," I whispered.

I felt him smile as he ran his lips across mine, and then he kissed me. Soft and probing at first, but when I opened my mouth to him, he surged inside. I whimpered as his tongue breached my lips.

Roman tilted my chin up and devoured my mouth, our tongues tangling as heat slashed through my core. He pulled back but kept his mouth on mine, then dragged my jacket halfway down, trapping my arms. His hands slid up and cupped my breasts, palming and squeezing them just enough to ache. I moaned into his mouth at the contact as I arched into his touch. The feeling of being bound while he plundered my mouth made my heart race, and when his fingers brushed across my nipples, sharp need and hot lust sliced through me. He worked his mouth down my neck and ran his tongue along the hollow of my throat as he expertly undid the buttons on my shirt.

When he peeled it back, uncovering my flesh-colored lace bra beneath, he looked down and groaned low. "Jesus Christ, you're magnificent."

He licked across my hard nipples through the lace, then bit down. My hips bucked against him as his cell phone rang on his desk. I crashed back to reality, remembering where we were.

As if sensing the change, his head came up and he studied my face. Slowly, he buttoned my shirt up and pulled my jacket back in place, freeing my arms.

"This is happening," he murmured, ignoring his phone.

My heart pounded so hard in my chest it almost hurt. "You think so?" His arrogance pricked me, but my raspy voice took the bite out of my words.

His lips pressed together as if trying to suppress a smile, and he reached over to adjust my collar. "Yes, Sweetness, I do."

Chapter 18

Luna

When Roman took a phone call a few minutes later, I quickly gathered my things and escaped the building. When he called me that evening, I didn't answer.

My mind was in a daze, and I felt distracted and torn. Roman's kisses and dirty promises ran through my head, and my breasts throbbed with need when I thought of him licking my nipples through the lace of my bra.

I couldn't sleep, and I lay there aroused and conflicted as thoughts raced through my mind. Even in daylight, my brain wouldn't shut down or stop replaying what happened in his office. Finally, I grabbed my trusty Cherry Box vibrator from my nightstand to try and get some relief, but afterward, I still felt edgy and needy.

On Wednesday afternoon, I almost wept in relief when the professor ended my last class early. Ten minutes later, when I walked into the parking garage alone and distracted, I didn't register the two men who came up from behind to flank me until it was too late. One of them grabbed my forearm and the other yanked viciously on my hair.

Pain radiated through my skull, and I cried out. Then I let out a long, loud scream. "Help me!" I turned my head and recognized Lionel Strack. His taller, muscular accomplice wrapped his arms around me from behind and lifted me up, then started walking toward a van.

They were *not* going to take me. I knew the statistics of survival if they got me into their vehicle, so I screamed and thrashed, throwing my head back and clipping the man on his chin. Then I kicked with all my might, aiming for his groin. He cursed and dropped me, but before I could run, Lionel grabbed my arm and wrenched it hard. I screamed out in pain as he punched me in the stomach, and when I doubled over, he grabbed my hair again and held up my head.

"You're gonna love what we have planned for you, little cunt-bitch. There are a lot of men who want a piece of you before we finish you off," he sneered in my face, spittle hitting my cheek. I jabbed him in the neck as Kilian had taught me, but my strength was waning. He gasped and gurgled, his grip loosening.

"Get the fuck away from her!" someone yelled. Footsteps pounded toward us. "Call the police!" a man shouted. The voice sounded familiar, and other voices yelled back. I knew then we'd been spotted. My body was yanked forward, so I stood facing Lionel Strack's ugly, blotchy face. Before I could put my arm up or get another hit in, he slammed his fist into my jaw, causing everything to go black.

The next thing I knew, I lay on my back, surrounded by two EMTs and Jared Gardner, his pinched face staring down at me.

"What happened?" I mumbled. An EMT held a cold gel pack to the side of my jaw and several people milled around, but a campus security guard held them back.

Jared knelt beside me. "Two men tried to kidnap you in the parking garage, I was trying to catch up with you when I saw them grab you."

My whole body ached, and a few tears leaked out. "Thank you. Thank you so much." My jaw hurt to talk, and I wanted to break down, but I needed to keep it together. "Will you find my backpack?" I didn't like Jared Gardner much, but right then I was so glad to see him.

"Yeah. What's going on, Luna? I know that Fowler asshole has something to do with this."

I shook my head, and pain radiated from my face so I stopped. "I got myself into this mess, Jared," I murmured. Roman may have put me in Lionel Strack's path, but I'd attacked him and grabbed his stupid ponytail.

Gazing around, I looked for my backpack but jostled my elbow and cried out in pain. One of the EMTs found it and sat it beside me. Laying back on the stretcher, I tried to gather my thoughts, but my mind felt unfocused and fuzzy from the hit to my head. I gazed up into the brilliant blue Las Vegas sky, and tears started coming.

Several hours later, I lay in a hospital bed surrounded by Sylvie, Alexa, and Ezra while a second doctor examined me. The nurse had wrapped and elevated my elbow, then instructed me to keep an icepack on it, along with my jaw. They couldn't do much about the big bruise on my stomach. I was hooked up to an IV and several monitors, and they'd tried to give me a catheter, but I'd declined.

After a police officer took my statement, I was tired, high on pain medication, and could hardly hold my eyes open. Why would I need two doctors? This second one seemed callous and rough as he moved my elbow around and probed my jaw too hard. I groaned in pain, even with the medication in my system.

He pushed his glasses up on his head. "You've got a sprained elbow, a severely bruised jaw, and probably a concussion from the blow. I can't say you're lucky, but it could have been much worse."

Ezra muttered under his breath, and Sylvie smirked. "Nothing like stating the obvious. Why are you here, again? Dr. Penrod already came in and gave Luna the same diagnosis."

Alexa watched the man suspiciously.

He glanced at Sylvie. "We just want to be thorough. Speaking of which, only two people are allowed at a time in a patient's room, and visiting hours end soon."

Ezra stood, bent over, and kissed my forehead. "I need to go anyway, let me know when you're discharged. I think it's a good idea for you to stay at Fenn's compound for now."

"I'll think about it," I croaked.

The doctor stood as well. "We're keeping her overnight for observation. She'll probably be discharged tomorrow morning."

When he walked out, I was glad to see him go. Before leaving, Ezra turned to Sylvie and Alexa. "One of you needs to stay with her tonight."

Sylvie nodded. "I'll take the first shift."

Alexa stood. "There are a few things I want to look into. Call me if you two need anything."

My mind drifted in and out as they talked around me, the painkillers swimming through my system, making me groggy and high.

The next time I woke, Roman stood next to my bed, leaning over me and examining my face. When he saw I was awake, he ran his fingers along my uninjured jaw.

"You look like you went through a meat grinder. You'll do anything to avoid coming into the office, won't you?"

Sylvie huffed from the visitor chair.

I grinned, then groaned in pain. "Don't make me laugh or smile."

"Does it hurt to talk?"

"Not too much."

He pushed loose strands of hair behind my ears. "Tell me what happened."

So I told him. "One of my classmates saved me. Jared yelled for help and chased them off."

Roman sat on the side of my bed and trailed his fingers along my forearm. "I owe him, whoever he is. I'm sorry. We had a man on you, but he didn't know your last class of the day had been cut short. Lionel got out early this afternoon, and he lost our tail. We underestimated his eagerness to get to you."

"You had a man on me? What does that mean? Where's Lionel now?" I wouldn't admit it out loud, but I was scared.

"He's in the wind, but we're looking for him." He took my hand without the IV line and rubbed his thumb across my wrist. "You walked into the parking garage alone. We discussed this." He turned to Sylvie. "Will you get her a fresh ice pack and some water?"

Sylvie ignored him. "Do you want fresh water?" she asked me.

"Ice chips sound better. My tongue feels like it's been freeze-dried."

Roman glanced at Sylvie. "I need to talk to her alone. Don't worry, I'll keep her safe."

She glared back. "You've done a shit job so far. Do better or we're taking over." Then she turned and strode out.

Roman took my face in his hands. "Luna, I need to keep you safe. Will you let me do that?" He seemed so intent, and the usual coldness in his eyes was gone.

"How?"

"Any way I can, and you may not like it." He let go of my face and seconds later, the same doctor who'd examined me the second time stepped in.

"What is he doing here?" I asked, trying to sit up. "I don't want this doctor."

He didn't look at me. "I've got her dose." Then he pulled out a syringe and quickly plunged its contents into my IV line.

"What are you doing?" My voice rose and I turned to Roman in panic. "What did he just give me?"

"It's alright. He's with me."

That didn't make me feel better, and I started pulling the tape off the back of my hand to remove the IV tube, but Roman stood.

"I'm sorry." He held my hands immobile while the drug worked. The sudden appearance of that doctor threw me so much that I didn't start struggling until I felt the contents of that syringe hit my system. Roman slipped something on my finger as I tried to get my hands out from under his.

"Roman, what are you doing? Don't let him... Please help me." My mind started to lose focus and my eyelids drooped.

"Shh. I've got you." The door opened again, and I expected to see Sylvie with ice chips, but Ivan and Xander strode in as the doctor left.

Ivan looked at my bruised face and grimaced. "Looks like you've had a rough day. We're going to find Lionel."

My tongue felt heavy, and I couldn't lift my arms for some reason. "Wha... wha's happening?"

Xander frowned at Roman. "For fuck's sake. You know she has to voluntarily say yes."

"Yes?" I asked slowly.

Roman took my left hand and held it up. "Look, she's wearing an engagement ring, isn't she?"

Ivan smirked. "You had that in your pocket thirty seconds ago."

Roman scowled at Ivan. "Shut up, you aren't helping me convince him."

Studying my left hand, I wondered where the thick gold band had come from.

Xander wiped his hand down his face, then pointed to Roman. "If I could think of a better way to protect her, I'd kick your ass."

I slumped over on my side and started sliding off the bed like an overcooked noodle.

Roman lunged for me, grabbing my hospital gown and pulling me back into the bed. "We don't have long, let's get started."

Xander sighed, then straightened and started reciting words. "Do you, Roman Fowler, take Luna Cross as your wife, and solemnly pledge–"

My heavy eyes flared, and I tugged drunkenly on Roman's sleeve. "Your *wife*?" I slurred.

"Yes, love."

"Why's he...?"

"Because we're getting married. Xander, keep going."

"Do you, Roman Fowler, solemnly pledge to love and care for Luna, in sickness and health, to take her for your lawfully wedded wife?"

"Yes," Roman clipped. I started struggling weakly, my brain screaming at me through whatever drug Dr. Douchebag had pumped into my IV.

Ivan sighed loudly next to Xander. "I can't lie and say I don't appreciate the titillating view, but your bride's hospital gown is wide open, and she's flashing us her tits. It's distracting. You're a lucky man, by the way."

Xander nodded and looked up at the ceiling.

"For fuck's sake, *don't look*," Roman growled. He pulled the ends of my hospital gown closed, then sat me on his lap and wrapped his palm around my chin to keep my head from flopping over.

"We're trying not to," Ivan shot back.

Xander kept doggedly going. "Do you, Luna Cross, solemnly pledge to love and care–"

"Skip to the yes part," Roman urged.

"Do you take Roman as your lawfully wedded husband?"

I stared at Xander, trying to figure out what he was blathering on about and why he asked me about.... I didn't know. My eyes drifted shut.

Roman nibbled on my neck, whispering in my ear. "Do you remember what we did in my office yesterday?" I nodded. "Did you like it? Say yes, Sweetness."

I sighed. "Yes."

Xander's voice rose. "I now pronounce you man and wife."

My eyes flared open, and I tried to get my brain to understand what was happening.

Ivan stepped forward and laid... something on the bedside table. "You need to have her sign this."

Roman sat behind me, cradling my body between his legs. "I'll help you. Just sign right here." He put the pen in my hand and wrapped his own around it.

"I... read..." I slurred, then trailed off, closing my eyes and forgetting what I wanted to say. "So tired."

"You can sleep after you sign it. You can shut your eyes then," Roman murmured.

I rested my heavy head back against Roman's chest and felt him move my hand with his own, signing the paper with me. Their voices sounded far away, and I couldn't think anymore.

Roman gently picked me up and laid me in the bed as he spoke to his men. "Ivan, see if you can get this filed tonight. The marriage license office in Downtown Vegas closes at midnight. Can you get there in twenty minutes?"

I opened my eyes to see Ivan nod and grin down at me. "That was the strangest wedding ceremony I've ever witnessed. Enjoy your honeymoon, Mrs. Fowler." He strode out as Roman told him to fuck off.

I could still hear Roman talking, but my brain couldn't process their words anymore, and I slipped into unconsciousness.

When I woke the next morning, weak sunlight crept through the blinds. Someone warm and solid lay behind me, and an arm draped over my waist—an arm with an expensive-looking cufflink and a sleek watch. Sylvie slept on a chair in the corner of the hospital room, and I relaxed when I saw her. My dreams had been hazy and strange, and I felt hungover and groggy.

A dull ache throbbed in my elbow and stomach, my jaw hurt, and I needed to use the bathroom. Then I remembered the strange second doctor coming in last night when Roman had been here, and I froze. Did I dream that? I slowly looked over my shoulder and noticed Roman staring down at me. He had a five o'clock shadow, and he looked bleary-eyed and rumpled. Had he slept here last night?

"What are you doing here?" My voice sounded raspy and weak.

His eyebrow raised. "Do you need to use the bathroom?"

I nodded when my bladder reminded me why I'd woken up.

"Do you need help?"

"No." I regretted not agreeing to the catheter when I thought of him having to help me in the bathroom. That got me moving, and I carefully sat up and steadied myself. When the room stopped spinning, I stood as Roman put his arm around my waist and gathered my IV cart. Then he helped me shuffle into the small restroom.

I held my gown closed in front and stared up at him. "I can manage from here."

His eyes swept over me, zeroing in on my jaw, and his eyebrows narrowed. "Leave the door unlocked, just in case."

"Okay." I shut the door in his face but didn't lock it. The overnight backpack Alexa had brought me yesterday sat on the counter, and I used the bathroom, cleaned up, and brushed my teeth. Then I tackled my hair, pulling a brush through my tangled strands–until I noticed something glittery on my left hand. I held it out and saw a thick gold band with a large square-cut emerald winking back at me. It looked like a gorgeous, expensive-as-hell wedding ring.

My brush clattered to the counter, and I brought the back of my hand closer to my face. Roman pushed the door open and quickly scanned the bathroom. "Are you alright?"

"What's on my hand?" I asked hoarsely.

He gazed at me staring at my finger. "A wedding ring. We got married last night."

"What?" Foggy bits and pieces of the night before had been floating in the back of my brain, even while I slept. My mind seemed clearer now, but I was still confused.

"Why? I don't understand. Why would you do that?"

He stepped inside and closed the door. "Because it's the best way to protect you."

I stared at him. "There have to be other ways."

His eyes narrowed and he folded his arms. "Look at your face, and you're lucky Lionel didn't break your fucking arm, or your jaw." His eyes narrowed dangerously. "You've been beaten and had your arm broken before, and I let you get hurt again. No more." His hand slashed through the air.

"It's not your job, or your responsibility." I looked back at the ring and noticed my shaking hand.

"Yes, it is. If Lionel had kidnapped you, he and his men would've taken turns raping and cutting you up." He stalked closer to me. "Then he probably would have sliced your throat open or cut your veins and watched you bleed out. By then, you would've begged for death."

"Okay, that got dark fast," I mumbled, holding my stomach.

"Your *life* just got dark. And like it or not, you're my responsibility for the foreseeable future."

Adrenaline hit my system, and an ache built in my chest when I absorbed my situation. I used to imagine what my husband would be like. When I was younger–before my father sold his soul and my parents threw me away like trash–I wondered if he'd be funny and kind, tall or short, blond or dark-haired. I also imagined how we'd meet, what our wedding would be like, and where we'd have it. A generic hospital room in Las Vegas had never been one of my wedding venue choices though.

My body ached, but my mind was now clear of the painkillers, so I tried to reason with Roman.

"There have to be other alternatives, another way. We're both intelligent people, we can figure out something besides this." I held up my hand with the ring on it. "You had no right. I never planned to get married, I... I don't want to end up like her." My voice broke, and I turned and braced my hands against the sink, my head hanging. The flash of anger had drained me, and I felt shaky and unsteady.

As I got older and started to understand the dynamics of my parents' marriage, I doubted I'd ever get married. My mother was a selfish, cruel doormat. Had she always been like that, or had it happened over time as my father slowly chipped away at her independence and self-worth? By the time my father left me in that closet to die, my mother did nothing. She hadn't been home when he'd raged and beaten me, but she never came after me. So I vowed I'd never be like her, even if that meant living and dying alone.

Roman turned me around and gathered me in his arms, tucking my head under his chin. "If we're married, the Stracks can't risk the exposure, or bringing the wrath of The Firm down on them, and even that's not guaranteed since they're unhinged and psychotic. To work with a drug syndicate, they'd have to be crazy. This is the best protection I've got to offer you."

"You should have talked to me." My voice was muffled against his shirt.

"We heard from an informant they were already planning another kidnapping attempt, and you're putting your friends and Ezra in danger by going back to the mortuary and dragging them into this."

A long sigh escaped me. Roman knew what angle to argue to get his way since he'd had a lot of practice, and he was a cut-throat attorney.

I pushed out of his arms and looked up at him. "Alright, I get it. I don't agree with how you went about it, but I understand your reasoning. I'm still so fucking mad at you." My voice broke a little.

His lip tipped up. "I'll have to work on helping you get over your anger then."

I glared at him. "When this is all over, we'll get the marriage annulled."

His grin died a fast death, and his voice was quiet and final. "There won't be an annulment."

"What?" I expected him to agree immediately and then we'd discuss a possible time frame and parameters. I even had an outside hope that if Lionel got caught right away, I could be back at the mortuary in a week, maybe less.

"We'll talk about it when I get you safely home. Not in a hospital bathroom with your friend asleep in the other room."

"We need to talk–"

A knock sounded, and Sylvie spoke through the door. "Luna, are you okay in there?"

"No. I mean, yes. God, I don't know. Physically, I'm okay."

Sylvie opened the door and peered inside. I leaned heavily on the bathroom counter and raised my left hand. "It appears Roman and I got married last night."

Chapter 19

Roman

Sylvie pushed the bathroom door open, and her head slowly swiveled toward me like a goddamn doll in a horror movie. "What the fuck did you do, Fowler?" Then she started yelling.

Sylvie's temper was a sight, and I mentally wished Drakos good luck if he planned to take on this hellion. We also needed to be gone before Fennick Spade showed up. The man was a loose cannon. I realized as Sylvie continued to rail at me that when I married Luna, I'd also married into the Spade family. Holidays and special occasions were going to be interesting.

I let Sylvie vent for a moment, then pointed to Luna. She stood slumped against the bathroom sink with dark circles under her piercing green eyes. "You can rail at me all you want, but look at her. She needs me, and the Stracks won't stop coming after her if they think she's vulnerable. Use your brain instead of your temper."

Sylvie glared at me with deep loathing. "We could have protected her, and if you think I'm bad, Fenn is going to go bat-shit crazy. You're a snake, Roman Fowler, and Drakos even more so for dragging me away last night so you could marry her in a fucking *hospital room*."

"You and Fennick may rage at me, but you both know what she's up against."

"I'm not stupid–I get that you're her best chance." She walked up to me so we stood toe to toe. "But if you hurt her, I'll come after you and I'm crazy enough not to give a shit about what you or your fucking firm would do in retaliation."

This woman was a little crazy, but she also knew the score. I detested the Spade men being part of Luna's life, and I hoped for everyone's sake it was all strictly familial.

"Understood. I'm taking her home so she can recover in a safe place, and we can talk privately when she's ready. I live in a gated community with guards, and my house has additional security."

"She doesn't need–"

I cut her off. "She puts you, Alexa, and Ezra in danger if she goes back to the mortuary."

She ground her molars. "Goddamn it to fucking hell. Alright! But don't try to keep her from us."

Luna cleared her throat weakly. "Don't talk about me when I'm standing right here, but I may not be standing for much longer. I need help getting back to the bed."

I strode over to her and scooped her up in my arms, then nodded to Sylvie. "Grab her IV. She can rest a little while we get her checked out. I have an off-duty police officer outside guarding the door, but there are too many variables here I can't control. She's not safe."

When Alexa walked into the hospital room an hour later, she stared at me with death in her eyes. Sylvie had texted her, giving her an earful about what I'd done last night.

I finally turned to her. "What? Sylvie had her say. You might as well get yours out now."

"You're on my shit list until further notice. You and your partners used every marriage license loophole there is."

"What do you mean?" But I knew exactly what she meant.

Alexa's eyebrow went up. "I hacked the system, Fowler. I know you waived her presence at the marriage license division by getting that subpar doctor of yours to give you a hospital exception. That's why he was here examining her yesterday. And who married you? Ivan, that wannabe hacker, motorcycle gang-banger?"

Her description of Ivan made me grin because I knew his head would explode when I told him. "No, Xander married us, and before you look it up, he's legally licensed to perform marriages. But Ivan was a witness and ensured the signed marriage certificate was filed before midnight."

"Then they're on my shitlist too. For now, let's get her safe."

Later that morning, I carried Luna into my house. Sylvie and Alexa followed us inside, bringing in suitcases and bags with Luna's belongings they'd picked up from the mortuary apartment. I suspected half the bags held books.

Sylvie whistled mockingly as she walked into the foyer, then the vast living room. "This place is like a modern art museum. Do you even live here?" she asked.

I kept walking. "You can set her things down in the foyer and leave. She needs sleep now." Luna had gone silent and drowsy, and I wanted to take care of her without her friends looking over my shoulder.

"Listen, dickhead. We discussed this," Sylvie growled, following me down the hall to my room where I laid Luna on my massive four-poster bed and slipped off her shoes.

Alexa touched Sylvie's arm. "As much as it pains me to admit, he's right. We'll come back tomorrow afternoon. Let the guard at the gate know who we are, and text us the gate code." She gazed at me challengingly.

"I will, but she needs sleep."

"You don't have to go," Luna murmured weakly from the bed, her eyelids drooping. It was clear the painkillers they'd given her before she left the hospital had kicked in.

Sylvie walked over to her. "It's okay, you need sleep. At least one of us will be back tomorrow afternoon to check on you."

When I locked the front door behind them, a wave of brutal satisfaction rolled through me. Luna was alone with me in my house. I returned to the bedroom and gazed down at her, snuggled under my bedcovers. She looked drained, and the angry purple bruise on her jaw stood against her pale skin, but she was still beautiful. This wasn't how I'd pictured her first time in my bed, but I wasn't complaining. Even with her immobile arm and bruised face, lust rose in my gut. She didn't know it yet, but she wouldn't be sleeping in another bed.

"Get some sleep. I'm going to take a shower and get cleaned up. I'll bring you some water and leave it on the nightstand first."

She sighed heavily. "Okay. Even though you did it in the most underhanded, asshole-ish way, thank you for keeping me safe. We can get it annulled when the Stracks lose interest in me," she murmured as her voice faded. She was asleep seconds later. My gut tightened in anger and annoyance at her bringing up a fucking annulment a second time. We needed to reach an understanding when she woke up.

While I showered, my mind replayed what Lionel and his man had done to her in that parking garage, and what they probably would have done to her if they'd taken her. I braced my hands against the tile wall while the hot water sluiced down my body.

My mind went back to Bitter Creek Ranch. I knew what it was like to be beaten and to choke on unrelenting helplessness. Xander had been there the longest, and his friends, Peter and Jonas, never made it out. He told us Luna's father visited there at least once, but he wouldn't talk about it.

I'd wondered so many times while I was there if my own father knew what he'd sent me to. By the time we got out, I didn't care. After learning how to amass power and wealth, I set about ruining him. My mother had divorced him seven years ago when he lost his fortune, and she caught him cheating with his twenty-year-old assistant. My partners and Gideon were my family. And now Luna. How had that happened? I finished my shower, toweled off, and got dressed.

As she slept, I brought Luna's bags in and put her clothes away in my oversized closet. She'd be annoyed at me for going through her things, but I didn't care. The sooner she got used to the living arrangements, the better. I shook my head when I studied her clothes hanging next to mine. Almost everything she owned, including her underwear, seemed to be black, navy, or gray. I'd have to get my personal shopper to order some lingerie. Luna's eyes would glow in an emerald-green corset. And her breasts... fuck. Shaking off the thoughts, I headed to my office.

That afternoon, I spoke with Ivan and Drakos on a video conference call. "How'd she take being suddenly married?" Ivan asked.

"She raged, called me an asshole, and told me she never planned to marry. Then she grudgingly thanked me for keeping her safe."

Drakos smiled fondly. "Lovely Luna. She's something else, isn't she? Did she throw anything at your head or demand an annulment?"

"She was too weak to throw anything, but she did say we'd be getting an annulment. I told her it wasn't going to happen."

"You don't plan to annul the marriage?" Ivan asked carefully.

"Fuck, no. I want her, and I plan to keep her. Don't start with your bullshit about her being just an obsession. Despite her parents, she's somehow still idealistic, kind, and so fucking sweet. So, no, there isn't going to be an annulment."

Drakos cleared his throat. "And how'd she take *that* bit of news? Or does she even know yet?"

"She heard me, but I don't think she believes me. We got interrupted, and we'll finish that conversation when she wakes up."

Ivan sighed. "She can hold a mean grudge. I like it better when she's teasing us and asking annoying questions."

I nodded. "We're on her friends' shitlists too. Drakos, Sylvie knows you were at the hospital last night to get her out of the way. I'd sleep with one eye open for the foreseeable future."

Drakos grinned, and his eyes almost glowed. "Yes, she kept throwing out the term 'unlawful detention' and talked about medical castration when I held her down in that empty hospital room."

Ivan winced. "And she's a Spade. Good luck with her."

Drakos rubbed his hands together. "I know. She's fucking perfect, isn't she? My sources tell me Lionel didn't have his daddy's permission to try and take Luna yesterday."

I shook my head. "The police caught his accomplice, but Lionel is still at large. Lionel's a fucking idiot, so I'm sure he's getting help."

Ivan leaned forward. "If the drug syndicate thinks the Stracks could mess with their business by going after your wife, they may take them out for us."

My head came up when I heard the shower in my bedroom turn on. "Luna's awake. I've got to go. Let me know if you hear anything about Lionel."

I hung up and went to the kitchen to make some food. A few minutes later, Luna walked in, dressed in a black robe and no bra. I tried not to stare at her unfettered breasts and creamy skin under the silk. She looked a little less pale, and the bruise on her jaw wasn't quite as vivid in the evening light.

"How're you feeling? Do you need more pain medication?"

She looked around the kitchen. "No. Can I have some water?"

I got her a glass and set it on the kitchen table. "Sit. Let me feed you."

Luna was too quiet. She probably struggled trying to dress, but didn't want to admit she needed help. Usually by now, she would have asked me a half-dozen questions about things that caught her eye as she wandered around my house in curiosity. Her silence concerned me.

I set two plates of pasta down and ate while she pushed her food around. Luna finally sat back and sighed. "This is... I should be raging at you for what you did. But my body still hurts and I just feel numb."

Setting my fork down, I studied her. "We can skip the yelling and raging, I don't mind. How about this? For the next two days, I'll take care of you, and you work on healing. After that, you can yell all you want. You need a quiet place to rest and recuperate."

Her intelligent green eyes probed me carefully, but I kept my face neutral. She sighed and picked up her water glass. "Forty-eight hours, and you tell me if you hear anything about Lionel Strack."

"I will. Now eat."

She took a bite and turned to me. "This is homemade. Do you cook?"

I shrugged. "I can prepare the basics, and I thought pasta would be easier with your sore jaw. My housekeeper picks up my groceries and usually leaves a few home-cooked meals in the freezer. This is her doing. I'll introduce you tomorrow."

We ate silently for a few moments but after a couple of bites, she set her fork down. "This is delicious, but I'm not hungry and I don't want to make myself sick."

"Then let me show you the house." I stood and cleaned up.

Except for her uncharacteristic silence, having her here seemed to soothe the beast that usually prowled inside me. When I wanted to fuck and dominate a woman, we went to her place or I got an expensive hotel room. Having people here who weren't my partners or employees sometimes irritated me, and it was more difficult to control the situation when I wanted them gone. But with Luna, the house seemed less cold and quiet.

"Come on. After you look around, we can sit out on the back patio. It's quiet out there, and you can ask me all those questions I see percolating in your head."

She rolled her water glass between her palms and watched me. "Alright. And you can show me which bedroom I'll be staying in."

I stilled at her comment. "Your things are already in it."

She looked confused. "But that's your room."

"Yes."

Emotions flickered across her face. Confusion, anger, and annoyance at first. And then I saw it, lust and heat. She could try to deny it, but her pupils had dilated and her nipples were hard. I knew she wanted me—our first kiss in my office had been explosive.

She carefully set her glass to the side. "Why? If you married me just to keep me safe from the Stracks, why do we need to share a bedroom?"

"Because I want you, and this needs to appear real."

She stood and put her uninjured hand on her hip. The front of her robe gaped, showing me her flushed chest and the swell of her beautiful breasts. I wanted to pull the tie on her robe, slide my hands up her thighs, and finger her wet cunt. I fought down a groan and adjusted my length under the table.

"If it's just us here, no one will know where I sleep."

My temper and need crackled. "*I'll* know where you sleep, and it's going to be with me." I stood and leaned over her. "I know you want me. You dry-humped my leg in my office and your nipples could cut glass right now. And we're *married*."

Her cheeks turned pink, and she clenched her robe shut. "You don't need to be crude. And finding you attractive versus having sex as a fake married couple are two completely different things."

She was lucky she hadn't denied wanting me, but I knew I'd have better luck if I eased her into this and didn't push too hard. So I breathed through my nose and stepped back.

"We have a forty-eight-hour truce, so for now, you need to heal and I need to find Lionel Strack. Do you want a house tour, or would you like to look around yourself while I make some phone calls?"

My mind was torn. I wanted to soak her up and take her long and hard, but I might alienate her before I could reel her in, and having this fight while she was recovering might slow down her healing. The angry contusion on her chin had gone from a vivid red color to a sickly shade of purple, and it made me want to castrate Lionel before I skinned him alive.

Her shoulders straightened. "I want you to give me the grand tour so I can annoy and pester you with all my questions."

Good. She seemed to be bouncing back a little. Luna gazed around the gleaming white kitchen with its sleek, industrial appliances. I grabbed a fresh ice pack and made her hold it to her jaw and elbow as we wandered through the house. She asked questions and made several biting observations about some of my designer's more severe choices.

When we got back to my bedroom, she stopped short and stared at my massive bed, then looked up at me and licked her lips nervously. "I haven't seen your patio yet."

I smiled at her agitation.

Chapter 20

Luna

His house could have been featured in an architectural magazine—for all I knew, it probably was. But it was also austere and had a strange, quiet quality to it, almost like it was in stasis. His full gym with the black punching bag in the corner felt like the only room that reflected his personality.

The apartment over Ezra's funeral home was nowhere near as luxurious or impressive, but the space had a flamboyant, whimsy feel to it, like it was actually lived in. Roman's house felt like a museum.

On the surface, with his money and sophistication, it seemed like a house Roman would choose. But sometimes I caught glimpses of him that weren't polished, biting, or cynical. He'd smile at a question I asked, or we'd get lost in discussing a book, a current event, or a place we wanted to visit. I realized with a jolt that I liked being with him when he forgot he hated me, like when we ate meals together and just sat and talked. He seemed the most relaxed then. I wondered how our new marital status was going to play out.

Staying with him in his large, masculine bedroom filled me with warm anxiety. At the end of his tour, I followed him to the back patio area. Roman led me past the kitchen to his backyard, where an infinity pool stretched out before the bright Las Vegas skyline. Plush outdoor furniture had been placed invitingly around the patio, and lush planters with a mixture of herbs and desert flowers dotted the space. A massive stone firepit had been constructed close to the spa, and the entire area felt like an exclusive, five-star resort.

A sigh escaped me. I gazed around, then sat in one of the oversized loungers. "Alright, now I understand why you live here. How do you keep your beautiful pots alive in this desert climate? And are those table herbs growing in there? I can't even keep a cactus alive."

He sat on the edge of my lounger and studied me. "Drip lines and a gardener. How're you feeling?"

"Fine."

His eyebrow went up. "Don't lie."

"I feel *so* good."

His lips twitched, and he grasped my thigh. "Maybe we do need to discuss one thing during our forty-eight-hour truce. I like to play when I fuck, and I particularly enjoy giving well-deserved spankings. Now, I'll ask you again. How are you feeling?"

He'd delivered his little bomb in a pleasant tone, which made it even more effective. I shivered as reluctant lust, irritation, and something darker slithered through me.

"I'm not sure if I like to play during sex, and I feel a spanking isn't warranted at this point."

A full-on grin spread over his face. "Noted, and we'll have to find out what you do like, won't we? Now tell me how you're really doing."

My breathing sped up and my nipples pebbled at his words, but I mentally shook myself. "My arm feels like someone tried to snap it like a green bean, my face aches, and my ribs are bruised. Oh, and I woke up married to you. Other than that, I'm peachy."

Roman brushed my hair over my shoulder. "Alright, I can work with that. I'm going to grab a couple of painkillers–you won't be able to sleep without them. Do you want the prescribed meds or the over-the-counter ones?"

I started to get up. "Just over-the-counter stuff. It's okay, I'll get them."

"No, I've got it." He stood and headed inside. I watched him, his pants molding to his tight ass, and the muscles rippling across his back as he opened the door. When he returned, he held two pills in his palm and handed me a glass of water.

The pills looked benign enough, but I hesitated. "It's not that I don't trust you." I stopped short and leaned back in the chair, folding my arms. "Yes, it is. It's exactly that. You had that beady-eyed doctor drug me last night."

He gazed down at me. "I'm sorry I had to drug you."

"Would you do it again?"

"Yes."

I glared at him. As apologies went, it was a shitty one. "Then you're not really sorry, are you?"

"I know you're in pain and won't be able to sleep without pain meds. You can trust me to take care of you."

I held up my ring finger with the wedding band. "I have excellent reasons to worry."

He sighed, as if trying to reign in some patience. "Do you want me to bring the entire bottle out here so you can see it? Either way, you need something."

He was right. My arm hurt, my jaw ached, and my stomach suddenly felt queasy. I just wanted to curl up somewhere, feel sorry for myself and maybe cry and sniffle a little, then sleep. "Fine. I'll take them." My eyes suddenly filled with tears, and an overwhelming sense of hopelessness flooded me. Turning my head away, I held out my hand for the pills.

Roman set the water down. "Fuck. Come here." He picked me up, then turned us around so we sat in the lounger with me in his lap.

The bottom of my robe slid open up to my panties, but I didn't care. I gulped on a sob but got myself under control. "Damn it, I hate crying. It never makes anything better."

Living with my parents had conditioned me to keep my emotions locked down or they could be used against me, and breaking down in front of Roman, of all people, made me feel vulnerable and weak.

I started to slide off his lap, but he squeezed me to him. "Please stay. I just want to talk." Sitting there, tense and unyielding, I thought through his request and then carefully relaxed against him.

He set his chin next to my cheek. "I've heard crying lowers stress and releases chemicals, so maybe it does help to cry. Here." Uncurling his hand, he held out the two small white pills. "They're just an over-the-counter pain medication with a sleep aid, I promise."

Sighing, I picked them up. He reached over and grabbed the water, and I put the pills on my tongue and drank. His masculine scent enveloped me as I sat in his lap, mingling with the rosemary coming from one of the flowerpots nearby. As the blue hour approached, the Vegas skyline started to sparkle. We watched together for a few minutes as his warmth seeped into me.

"Can I ask you something?" I murmured.

His body tensed a little under me. "Yes."

"What does Gideon really do for FUCK, Legal?"

He chuckled. "Your brain is fascinating. Gideon makes everything run and basically does whatever needs doing. He used to work for the FBI, but after a couple of unfortunate incidents, he resigned and we formed our firm."

"You mentioned Heath worked with him. What did he do for the FBI?"

"He was an area assistant director."

I shifted and looked up at him. "Wow, that's pretty high up. Where'd you meet?"

His face went blank, and the peaceful feeling between us evaporated. "In Arizona."

"What happened there? I'm from Arizona and know about that ranch facility where your parents sent you. I was only in elementary school at the time, but everyone heard about it." I reached out and laid my hand on his chest, instinctively searching for his heartbeat.

The story dominated the news cycle, and the haunting photos that had leaked to the media after the FBI raid still gripped me.

He stared out into the dark. "Tonight isn't the night to dredge up those memories."

Roman's mind seemed far away. He might be sitting here with me on his lap, but he'd been dragged back to the past, and I didn't know how to bring him back.

"How'd you keep Sylvie away long enough to sneak your doctor into my room last night? And what did that slimy bastard give me?"

His arm tightened around my waist. "Drakos ran interference, and it was a liquid anesthesia."

I waited for a few seconds, then poked him. "How did Drakos keep her away?"

"He pulled her into an empty hospital room, distracted her, and apparently warned her again he's coming for her."

No wonder Sylvie was so agitated. "What does that even mean?"

Roman shrugged underneath me. "It means he wants to date her."

I rolled my eyes. "I'm not an idiot, it means more than that. You guys seem a little... Neanderthal sometimes." The medication he gave me started kicking in, and as drowsiness hit me, I laid my head on his shoulder. "She told me they've met before, but there's more to it than that."

"What makes you think so?" He settled me into him and softly ran his fingers along my thigh. I could feel his hard length beneath my butt cheeks, but I was too tired and comfortable to get worked up about it.

I let out a big yawn and snuggled into his warmth. "She dislikes him too much, and he's extremely focused on her."

He continued to run his palm up and down my leg, sending tingles through me. "Hm," he murmured noncommittally. Roman knew something he wasn't telling me.

The pain in my body quieted to a dull throbbing, and my eyes drifted closed. "Knowing Sylvie, it was something traumatic—that's what bonded us. She hates her father as much as I hate mine, and they've both tried to kill us. Funny thing to have in common, isn't it?" I mumbled.

A quiet breath dragged out of him as I drifted off to sleep in his lap. A little while later, he carried me to his bedroom. I was too tired to argue as he laid me down in the bed, and I rolled over and fell asleep again seconds later.

In the middle of the night, I woke up with a gasp after bumping my injured elbow. Roman forced two more pills down me as I grumbled at him, but I quickly fell back to sleep.

The next morning, I woke up on my uninjured side with my good arm curled in front of me and my face burrowed into Roman's chest. Our legs were tangled together. My phone buzzed on the nightstand, and I groaned softly.

It stopped, and I started drifting off. But the buzzing started up again, jerking me back to consciousness. I slowly rolled onto my back and thought about the best way to get vertical without hurting myself too much. Roman sat up and leaned over me, picking my phone up off the nightstand. He looked at my screen, then answered.

"Whoever the fuck you are, why are you calling her at six in the goddamned morning? She was fast asleep and getting some much-needed rest."

When I heard Jared Gardner's loud voice asking who the fuck Roman was, I sat up and groaned as aches and pains rolled through me.

Roman cut him off. "She's not in the hospital anymore. She's here at my house, sleeping in my bed." His eyes slid to me, then trailed down my body where my robe had parted, giving him a front-row view of my breasts.

I awkwardly gathered my robe and sat in a tired daze. Roman paused, then let out a mean chuckle. "You don't want to go there, little boy. Luna's my *wife* now and if you insinuate something like that again, I'll make sure they never find your body."

For once, Jared didn't seem to have anything to say. Roman turned and stared at me. "Lose her number and don't call her again." He turned my phone off and threw it on the bed beside me.

"Why is that snot-nosed kid calling you?" he growled.

I didn't let his irritation bother me because Jared probably annoyed his own mother. Moaning softly, I lay back in the warm bed, then turned and snuggled into the covers. "I don't know. He's like a nasty rash that won't go away no matter what I try. I'm cold."

He sighed and gathered me close, giving me his body heat.

Chapter 21

Luna

We slept for another hour, and my bladder finally woke me again. Gingerly, I tried to roll out of his arms, but they tightened around me. "I need to pee," I mumbled into his chest. He slowly let me go, and I shuffled into the bathroom. After my brain started working a little, my face flushed when I thought about how easily I'd fallen into his bed and slept in his arms.

It took a while to shower and clean up, but on the bright side, I did feel a little better. Roman sat on the bed looking at his phone when I came out of the bathroom in my robe. Suddenly, awkward tension bloomed in my stomach and I pointed to the closet.

"I'm, uh, just going to get dressed."

He set his phone down and watched me. "Gideon is coming over. Do you need anything?"

"If he's coming from the office, I left a textbook on my desk. Can he pick it up?"

"Yes. Do you need anything else? Any clothes, toiletries, feminine hygiene products?"

My face flamed red. "Mm. No, thank you." I hurried to his large walk-in closet and shut the door.

After wrestling on a thong and a pair of drawstring shorts with one hand, I tried to put on a bra. After several frustrating minutes, I gave up and tried a shirt next. By the time I gave that up too, I was tired, frustrated, and a little sweaty. If I extended my arm too much, my elbow barked in pain. I stood with my head hanging down when Roman walked in, freshly showered with a towel wrapped around his waist.

I held the shirt up in front of my breasts, and he paused when he saw me. "Do you need some help? All you have to do is ask."

My eyes snagged on his lean, cut torso. Roman had delicious, defined abdominals that led down to a perfect V. A tattoo curved around his side and twisted up to just below his nipple. The tattoo read *veritas odium parit,* and a snake wound around the words. I wondered what the Latin saying meant.

His cock bulged under the towel, but he stood, uncaring, as his gaze traveled over my exposed skin. I realized I stood in front of him partially naked too.

"I can't put on a bra or a shirt with one hand."

He smiled, then dropped his towel and walked over to me.

I couldn't help myself—I glanced down, then my wide eyes bounced back up. "Is that all for me?" I half-joked.

His thick, long length jutted out from between his hard thighs and seemed to point straight at me. Cupping my chin in his hands, he leaned down and skimmed his lips across my uninjured cheek. "It is. And by the time I sink my cock into your wet, needy pussy, you'll be begging me for it. But we'll work up to that."

My body tingled with sharp awareness as his shaft brushed against my stomach. From the first time Roman and I squared off in front of Gideon's desk, I'd felt this pull to him. It had been juxtaposed with his dislike toward me, and I'd buried my feelings deep. It made no sense, but sometimes I thought he hated me even while the sparks ignited between us. I'd ignored it for months, but now I didn't know what to do with this heat between us.

I swallowed and straightened. "You have a high opinion of yourself. It'd take a miracle to make me beg you for anything."

He reached over and gently pulled the shirt out of my fingers. Then he wrapped his large, calloused hands around my forearms and pulled me into him. "A miracle?" He grinned softly and leaned in. "Or my mouth buried between your thighs, biting and sucking on your sensitive little clit while I lick up your juices?" He slid his hand behind my neck and massaged my scalp. "Are you brave enough to see if I can make you beg?"

The challenge in his eyes snared me, and I stared at him, wrestling with my need. I licked my lips, and he growled softly. Leaning in, he nipped at my lower lip, then slanted my head to fit against his mouth. As he probed, Roman walked me backward until I felt the dressing table at my back.

"Does it hurt?" he murmured, stroking my cheek.

"A little." My jaw twinged, but his soft lips felt so good on mine.

"Then I'll have to kiss other places."

He lifted me onto the table and spread my legs, then cupped my ass cheeks and pulled me into his hips so I was flush with his cock. My body shivered at the intimate contact, even through my shorts. His hands felt so good, and when he touched me like this—as if he had every right to stroke, nip, and bite on my pale skin—heat flooded me, and my thoughts scattered.

As he kissed me, he rubbed his chest against mine, running his pecs across my bare nipples. Roman nibbled on my lower lip, then grazed his teeth down my neck and bit hard enough to cause a small sting. I moaned, need rolling through me.

Running his hands up my sides, he slid his thumbs across my nipples. I gasped at the contact and arched into him. He nuzzled the crook of my neck, then kissed his way down my chest. When he leaned over and sucked a peak deep into his mouth, I arched in pleasure and felt a twinge of pain from my bruised ribs.

"Your sweet tits are so lush and ripe. Do you like to feel teeth on your nipples while your pussy gets stroked?" He bent and took a breast in his mouth.

"I don't know, I–ah!" Gasping, my back bowed in pain and pleasure when he started nipping and tugging on my nipple.

He fisted my hair and pulled my head back until my neck arched. Then he ran his teeth across my shoulder blade and bit down hard enough to make my blood race.

"You'll learn to take what I give you, and I'll teach you to crave it. Have you been spanked and fucked before?" His thumb rubbed against my sore breast, and I couldn't put words together. "Answer me, my little cock teaser."

"No," I gasped. "Have you?"

He smiled against my neck. "I like to *give* the spankings."

I reached down, wrapping my hand around his shaft and squeezing. "And I want my own library, but we can't always have what we want."

Chuckling, he moved his hand up the inside of my thigh, running his fingers underneath my shorts. Then he slid a finger inside my panties and trailed it across my slit. "So fucking wet for me. Will you give me a taste?"

My head rolled to the side, and I started panting. "We shouldn't do this."

"Yes, we should. Or are you afraid I'll get you addicted to my tongue and cock?"

His words sent deep desire and alarm pulsing through me, and I wondered if he could really do that. But I wanted him, and my pussy wept on his finger. "No, I'm afraid you'll disappoint me–like most men do."

He stilled at the words I hadn't meant to say and grinned. "Challenge accepted. Let's find out then, shall we?"

Roman nudged my shorts and thong aside, then rubbed the head of his cock along my opening, making sure to hit my clit. My hips moved restlessly to meet him, and he chuckled darkly. Stepping back, he stripped off my shorts and panties, then parted my legs and stroked my center.

I grabbed onto his shoulders. "Sweet Jesus, that feels so good."

He pulled my legs apart, pushed me back on the counter, and leaned in to lick and suck on my clit. I let out a low wail as he worked me with his tongue. Then he slid two fingers deep inside me. The man knew what to do with a woman's clit, and he hit nerve endings I didn't know I had. No fumbling, no impatience. He feasted like he relished my taste, making me writhe and twist in mindless pleasure underneath him.

Replacing his fingers, he thrust his tongue inside me and rubbed the pad of his thumb against my center.

My thighs clamped around his head. "How do you know *exactly* where to touch?" My heart pounded and my toes curled as an orgasm built.

"That's it," he murmured as he raised his head and shoved his fingers back inside me. The stretch made me cry out, and a climax crawled up my body. When he leaned over and flicked his tongue relentlessly against me, I orgasmed long and hard.

He grinned against my thigh. When I finished twitching underneath him, he kissed and bit me there, then climbed onto the dressing table to straddle my hips. Leaning over me, he palmed and stroked his cock. Then he took my good hand and held it in front of my face. "Lick."

I stared at him, not fully understanding what he wanted. "Lick your palm and wrap your wet little hand around me. Your jaw is too sore for me to use your mouth."

Heat flushed across my cheeks at his crass, blunt words. He had a dirty mouth and a creative mind, and I wondered if he planned to keep me in a perpetual state of wet embarrassment. I needed to fight back, or I knew he'd completely overwhelm me. Keeping eye contact, I slowly brought my palm to my mouth and leisurely licked across it several times before wrapping it around his cock. Then I started pumping him.

His eyes slid closed, and his head fell back. "If your slick palm feels this good, your sweet little pussy is going to be heaven." Bringing his head forward, he opened his eyes and watched me work him.

I started bringing my other hand up to touch him, but he grasped my wrist and held my arm in place. "Don't jar your elbow. It will hurt, and I'll lose you." He palmed my breasts and rolled my nipples between his fingers, pinching and pulling on them. My hips arched up, and I squeezed his cock harder. His rhythm broke and he wrapped a hand around mine, pumping his length several times. Then he threw his head back, groaned, and came all over my chest and neck.

He slowly opened his eyes and bent over me. "The next time I come, it'll be balls deep inside you. Are you on birth control?"

My eyes flared, and reality smashed into me. "That's none of your–"

He growled dangerously. "Don't finish that sentence. My tongue was just inside your soaked cunt and you're wearing my pearl necklace. Now answer the question."

"Yes," I bit out.

"Good. I'm clean and I know you are too."

"How do you know that?" I tried to prop myself up on my elbows and instantly regretted it. "Ouch! Fuck!" I quickly lay back down.

He shook his head. "Ivan did your background check."

He confirmed my suspicions as he climbed off me and grabbed his still-wet towel off the floor, then wiped it across my chest. Pausing, he ran his thumb through the semen on my neck and brought it to my mouth.

"Suck," he commanded.

Again, I stared up at him. But this time, I knew exactly what he wanted. My nipples puckered, and he watched my face carefully.

"Take it," he murmured as he pressed his thumb against my lips. "Your pupils are blown and your chest is flushed. Your body wants this."

I slowly opened my mouth and took his thumb inside, swirling my tongue around it and tasting his salty, musky essence.

After a few seconds, he pulled out and brushed my cheek. "Such a good, sweet girl. Soon, you're going to take me deep in your throat, and even deeper in your pussy."

His calling me a good, sweet girl made me want to punch him in the face and crawl up his beautiful body all at once. "You think so?" I taunted.

His lips tipped up, and his eyes took on a dangerous glow. Leaning over me, he kissed and licked my nipple, then softly blew on it. The traitorous bitch puckered and went rock hard.

"That, and *so* much more." His hand carefully wrapped around my throat, and he squeezed gently, not caring about the sticky semen still coating me there. My pussy contracted hard, and I began to worry that Roman really could make me addicted to his touch.

Chapter 22

Luna

After I cleaned up a second time, Roman helped me put on a bra and shirt. Then he wrapped his hands around my covered breasts from behind and softly kissed my shoulder.

"It's a sad shame to cover these," he lamented. Then he turned me around and kissed and nuzzled my neck and the side of my face that wasn't covered by a fist-sized bruise. His mouth sent lust coursing through my system again. I felt a little less tired and sore this morning, but my mind churned with confusion. Since he'd handed my internship off to Ivan, Roman had come after me with a single-minded focus, and now we were married.

When Gideon arrived later that morning, he brought Roman's laptop, my textbook, and some shopping bags with him. He also brought a bodyguard. Milo was middle-aged, had a shaved head and a serious expression, and he also wore a suit. He looked like a retired FBI agent.

Gideon placed my textbook on the counter and patted my shoulder. "I'm sorry to hear you were injured, but congratulations on your marriage."

I wasn't sure what to say. "Thanks?" Roman shook his head at my half-assed response, but Gideon just smiled.

I made coffee and toast while Roman introduced me to my bodyguard. "Luna, this is Milo Carlson. When you leave the property, you go with him. He'll be living in the apartment above the garage."

When Roman gave me the tour yesterday, I'd glimpsed the massive, four-car garage at the far side of his house, but he hadn't shown me the apartment above it.

"Hello, Ms. Fowler. I've got your phone number programed in my phone." Milo pulled his phone out, and a few seconds later mine vibrated. "I just forwarded you my information."

His calling me Ms. Fowler sent a shot of adrenaline through me, and I cleared my throat. "Just Sylvie."

He nodded. "And I'm Milo. If you need to leave the house for any reason, contact me and I'll escort you. If Mr. Fowler leaves the house, you need to let me know, and I'll come stay in the main house until he gets home. Finally, if you plan to have guests, let me know so there aren't any misunderstandings."

"Got it. I feel like a grown woman who's been assigned a babysitter, but if that keeps Lionel from punching me in the face again, I'll play along."

Milo smiled. "It would make my job easier."

We talked for a few more minutes, and I found out Milo was indeed a retired FBI agent who now worked for The Firm. I wondered what else he did for them.

"I'll get settled in." After Milo left, Roman and Gideon holed themselves up in Roman's office for an hour. I was still reading at the kitchen bar when they came out.

Roman walked over to the coffeepot and poured himself another cup. "I want you to wear a tracking device."

My head snapped up, and I stared at him. "Why?"

"Because I could find you faster if you get taken."

"But you'd also know where I am, all the time."

His lip quirked. "Exactly."

I narrowed my eyes. "What kind of tracking device? How would I wear it, and what's its range?"

Gideon chuckled. "I'm glad to hear you rapidly firing off questions again. It means you're feeling better."

Roman reached into his pocket and pulled out an exquisite, expensive-looking, crafted metal necklace with an O-ring. Attached to the ring was a round, coin-like object dangling from it, and the band was held together with an intricate lock.

"It's GPS so we can find you anywhere," Roman murmured as he studied me.

I stared up at him, then glanced at the necklace. "Why is there a lock on it?"

"So it can't be easily removed."

My eyes narrowed. "What type of metal is it?"

His grinned this time. "Tungsten."

"What if I want to take it off?"

Roman shrugged. "We can't always have what we want." The cheeky bastard had thrown my words back in my face.

I turned to Gideon and changed the subject. "Roman said you do more for The Firm than just administrative work. Can I ask you some questions?"

Gideon smiled and straightened his cuffs. "You can, but I may not answer."

"That's fair. Do you know what's happening with the Stracks?"

"I have a good idea."

"Are the partners going to take him out when they find him?"

He glanced at Roman with a raised eyebrow. "Your assessment is reasonable, but I can't give you a definitive answer."

I took his nonresponse as a yes. "Does anyone know where Lionel is?"

"Not specifically right now, but we're narrowing his location down."

"Do you know why Klim paired Roman and me together?"

Gideon's expression didn't change, but I sensed a shift in the room. "I wouldn't venture to speculate. You and Roman make a good pair, you know. I'll help you plan a wedding celebration when things quiet down and we neutralize the threat."

I shook my head. "You don't need to do that, but thank you for the offer. When the police find Lionel, we're getting the marriage annulled."

Roman carefully set his coffee down. "Gideon, I'll see you later at the office. My *wife* and I need to come to an understanding."

Gideon raised an eyebrow, and his lip quirked. "Luna, I hope you feel better. Good luck."

When he walked out, I turned to Roman. "Is the forty-eight-hour truce over, then?"

He pushed off the counter and came to me. Swiveling my stool to face him, he leaned in. "Not if you don't want it to be." He held up the band and studied me. "You have two choices. You can allow me to put it on, or force me to find another way. But you're wearing it."

Goose bumps broke out on my arms from the heat of his stare. "I don't want to wear it all the time."

He reached up and ran his fingers down my cheek to my injured jaw, then glided them over my throbbing elbow. "And I don't want you to wind up in Strack's hands."

Cupping the back of my neck, he leaned in and brushed his lips across mine. Then he ran his tongue over my mouth, and I opened for him.

He groaned low in his throat and gave me a long, wet, open-mouthed kiss. When he pulled back, I panted and held onto him.

"Let me keep you safe. Wear the necklace for me," he whispered softly in my ear.

His breath sent a ripple of lust through me. "Why does it have to lock? I don't like... being locked in." My breath hitched.

Until the words came out, I hadn't realized it wasn't the tracking device that sent dread through me, it was the lock. He didn't know about the nightmares or my trauma. Maybe if he knew how scarred I really was, he'd be the one pushing for an annulment.

He stilled for a moment and sucked in a breath, then gathered me into his arms. "Wrap your legs around me."

My thighs curled around his waist before I registered what I'd done. He pulled me to him and walked us to his bedroom, cradling me to his chest. My heart thudded, and untethered, random thoughts flitted through my mind.

Laying me across his bed, he leaned over and brushed my hair back. Then he ran his hands up my waist, pushing my shirt up to my neck. His fingers brushed lightly across my skin, leaving a trail of goosebumps. When he reached around and unhooked my bra, then leaned over and took a nipple in his mouth, my back arched and my breath stuttered.

He diligently worked me, and when my breast was swollen and throbbing in his mouth, he gave the nipple a firm suck, then went to work on the other. My clit swelled and throbbed, greedy for his attention. I felt empty, so I reached in and unzipped his pants, then slid my hand in and palmed his thick, hard cock. His size gave me pause until he bit my nipple and then flicked it with his tongue.

This was a spectacularly bad idea, and I knew giving in to my lust for him would end in pain and heartbreak. But I'd never ached inside for a cock before. Never felt that emptiness in my pussy that I'd read about in novels or heard other women describe. But I understood it now.

Stroking my thumb across the tip of his shaft, I ran it through his pre-cum.

His hips bucked. "I need to fuck you like I need my next breath. Say yes."

I exhaled a long breath and admitted the truth. "Yes. I want you."

His mouth slanted over mine, and he devoured me in a hot, carnal kiss. Then he crawled off, pulled down my shorts and thong, yanked his own clothes off, and came over me. His hand cupped my slit, and he pushed a finger inside.

"You're soaked." My hips thrust up to meet his hand, and he smirked and worked another finger in. "Look at you, panting for my cock like my good, slutty girl."

My eyes rolled back and my neck arched when he called me that as he worked his fingers inside me. "Please, I need you."

"Say it. Tell me exactly what you want–exactly what you need."

"You, inside me. I need your hard–" I gasped as he replaced his fingers with his hot, solid length, and even though I was soaked, he had to work to get inside me.

"Fuuck me, your wet little pussy is choking my cock."

"It's too much," I wailed softly. My back bowed and I grabbed his hips as he worked himself into me. "Oh, God!" I gasped and held my breath as both pleasure and pain filled me while he reached in and expertly stroked my clit.

"Your dripping, swollen cunt disagrees. You need to breathe, love. Take a breath for me."

It took me a moment to register his words, but when my vision started to tunnel, I forced myself to gasp in air as he started moving rhythmically above me. My body loosened underneath him, and a climax built. He leaned over me and grasped my good hand above my head, then pounded into me. His stare was too intense, too knowing, and I turned my head to the side.

Roman grasped my chin and brought my face back to his. "No, Luna. Give me your eyes," he growled. "Watch while your sweet little pussy takes my cock."

The world slid away as we stared at each other while he pounded inside me. "You are my wife. Mine to protect, mine to ruin. *Mine.*" He punctuated his words with deep thrusts.

When he stroked and worked my clit, my orgasm built deep inside, then broke and rolled through me. I clamped down on him and came hard, gasping under the onslaught. My climax triggered his, and he pushed himself deep inside me. His hot come filled me as his fingers dug into my hips, holding me tight against him.

Time seemed to pause as we lay there, locked against each other, breathing heavily. Eventually, our heart rates regulated and Roman let go of my hips to prop himself on his elbows, his shaft still inside me. "I'll give you a key to the lock if you promise to tell me when you take off the tracker." His words caused my insides to clench, and I knew he felt it. He brushed a damp strand of hair off my cheek and held my stare. "Please. I need to keep you safe."

"Okay. While Lionel is still out there, I'll wear it."

He smiled and rubbed my cheek with his nose. "That wasn't so painful, was it?"

My eyes narrowed. "Don't be a sore winner, Fowler."

Grinning, he kissed me hard and pulled out, then sat me on the side of the bed and stood next to me, holding the band.

"Lift up your hair," he demanded softly.

With a nervous breath, I reached up and gathered my hair with one hand. He stared at my neck and cupped it, sliding his palm up and down its length. Then he watched my eyes as he put the band on me and clicked the lock into place. The tracker and lock clinked lightly against each other at the hollow of my throat when he let go. Then he leaned in and bit my collarbone, causing a shudder to ripple through me.

"I want to fuck you in this, and only this." He stared at it, then reached out and fingered the metal.

My phone vibrated on the nightstand, and he slowly pulled back and stood. I reached over and grabbed it, seeing Sylvie's name on the display.

I answered as I looked up at Roman. "Hey. Are you on your way over?"

"Alexa got called into work so she can't come. I have one more makeup consult, and then I'll head over. The Sawyer sisters are fighting over what shade of lipstick their mother would want to be buried in, and I'm ready to pull all their hair extensions out. Speaking of fake, how's the first day going with your new husband?"

Roman looked pained to hear Sylvie's voice, and I smiled. "We haven't killed each other yet, but it's still early."

He palmed the side of my face. "We could try fucking each other again. We've got the rest of the day," he murmured in a conversational voice.

My eyes went wide, and I smacked his stomach. "She can hear you!"

Sylvie gasped. "You guys fucked already? Goddamned it, he's slick. I'm rescheduling the consult, I'll be over in fifteen minutes."

I shook my head, even though she couldn't see me. "No, don't do that. You don't want the Sawyer sisters' wrath turned on you. Besides, coming earlier won't change anything."

"Fine," Sylvie huffed out. "But try to keep your barn door closed until you two figure a few things out."

"Did you just compare my vagina to a barn door?" I scowled at Roman as he grinned down at me.

"Relax. I'm sure Roman knows by now your barn door has rarely been used."

My face flushed. "You need to quit with that metaphor."

She chuckled. "He is kind of a stud, though."

I sighed and hung my head. "Stop already."

"Fine. Do you want me to bring anything else? More books, a bottle of wine, your trusty vibrator?" Roman's eyes narrowed when he heard Sylvie talk about my vibrator.

"All three would be appreciated, and I'll try to keep my barn door closed. See you in a few."

When I disconnected, his hand slid around me, and he grasped the hair at the base of my neck. "Keep provoking me. Give me a good reason to re-consummate our marriage and carve out time for an extended honeymoon."

My insides tingled, and visions of us tangled together in a hotel room bed somewhere swam through my mind. But I needed to step back and slow this down. We'd kissed for the first time a few days ago, and now we were married and sharing a room and a bed. I'd also just had the best sex of my life–by far–with no end in sight until we annulled the marriage.

Suddenly, nerves and uncertainty welled up inside me. I needed time and some distance to process what was happening between us.

I gazed at him cautiously. "Is there a quiet place somewhere I can use to study?"

He stared at me as if he knew what I was thinking. "The second guest bedroom has a desk by the window. It's all yours."

It was just what I needed–a place to escape, step back and process all these strange feelings before I got into this sham marriage too deep. Maybe I could sleep there. I looked down at my phone to escape his stare.

"Luna."

"Yes?" I didn't look up.

"You can use it as an office, but you're not sleeping there."

My shoulders tightened. "Fine." I hated that he read me so well.

He took my hand and pulled me to my feet. "Give me a kiss, wife." This time, his kiss was soft and probing, and my body loosened and melted into him.

When Roman left for the office, I cleaned up and dutifully texted Milo about Sylvie's visit. I didn't want him harassing her. He showed up less than two minutes later, walking in through the garage door.

"How do you know Ms. Spade?" Milo asked. By his tone, I could tell he believed all the rumors about the Spade family.

"She's my best friend."

"How long have you known her?" I could hear a hint of disapproval.

"Since elementary school. She and her grandfather took me in when I turned twelve, and I've lived with them since."

He stared at me. "You *lived* with the Spades?"

"Yes. Ezra was my guardian, and Sylvie's my foster sister. All of them are family in the ways that count. Don't make her uncomfortable."

Milo let Sylvie in a few minutes later, and she looked him up and down. "Who are you? Does Roman have a damned butler?"

Milo shook his head. "He doesn't need a butler, he has Gideon. My name is Milo Carlson, and I'll be Luna's bodyguard for the foreseeable future."

She nodded approvingly and turned to me. "I can tell you don't love the idea, but you need one."

I sighed. "Milo is retired FBI and Gideon vouched for him, so I think besides being a judgmental dick, he's safe."

Sylvie smirked. "You've heard of my family, I take it." Then she turned back to me and looked me up and down. "What's on your neck?" She marched over and glared at the necklace. "There's a fucking *lock* on it. Why?"

My face flushed, and I turned to Milo. "You've met Sylvie. If I go anywhere today, I'll let you know."

"If Roman isn't here, I stay in the house."

I folded my arms. "You don't need to stay in the same room with me."

He nodded. "I'll be in the kitchen if you need me. If someone comes to the door, let me answer it."

I took Sylvie to the guest bedroom I planned to turn into my office. It looked out onto the pool on the other side of the kitchen and had its own luxury bathroom with a steam shower and a soaker tub.

She wandered through the space. "His guest bedroom is bigger than our living room."

I sat on the bed and gazed around the room. "I know."

She nodded toward my neck. "Tell me about that."

My fingers went up to the band. "It has a tracker. Roman said he wanted to be able to find me quickly if the Stracks got ahold of me."

"Hmm. That's actually smart. Why the lock?"

"He said he wanted it to be harder to take off, but I told him I didn't want to be locked in." My gaze shifted away. Sylvie would understand, but shame still swam through me.

She straightened off the doorframe and sat next to me. "You have every right to feel however the fuck you want without worrying about anyone else. And think about it, Luna. If anyone could understand your feelings about being locked in, it would probably be him and his partners."

I gazed unseeing at the floor. It was true. Some of the leaked photos from the Ranch showed small, cramped cells with chains drilled into the walls where the boys had been kept. Thinking about those cells gave me a vicious case of claustrophobia.

I took her hand and turned her arm around, staring at the now-faint scars on her forearms she'd gotten when she climbed into my bedroom window to save me. "He gave me a key to the lock."

Sylvie nodded and studied me. "Did it help?"

"Yes." I let go of her hand.

"How was it?"

"How was what?"

She rolled her eyes. "The sex, dumbass."

A blush moved over my face and chest, but not all of it was from embarrassment. My eyelids fluttered just thinking about it. "It was... so good."

"Bitch," she chuckled.

"More like a bitch in heat," I mumbled.

She smacked my thigh and laughed. "If we can get you extracted from all this bullshit with the Stracks, I think you and Roman should give this marriage thing a good-faith effort."

I stared at her, wondering if I'd heard her right. "Are you serious right now?"

"I am. Give yourself a chance. I think Klim might be right, maybe you two could help each other heal."

I stared at Sylvie. "If we're delivering atrocious, unsolicited advice, I have some for you. I think you should give Drakos a chance too."

Her eyebrows went up, and an appalled look settled on her face. "Point taken, forget I said anything."

Chapter 23

Roman

When I got home that evening, Milo met me in the garage.

"How'd it go?" I asked.

"Fine."

I raised my eyebrow. "Why do you look exhausted then?"

He shrugged, then started chuckling. "She's an inquisitive little thing, isn't she? The first part of the day she was mad at me for questioning whether I should let a Spade into the house, and then after her friend left, she asked me endless questions about my job, the FBI, and what I do for The Firm. She's got a sharp mind."

"She does." I was used to her insatiable curiosity and endless questions, but it'd taken some adjusting. "The Spade family has an unusual reputation around town, but I trust them with her, and she won't stand for them to be kept away."

Milo nodded. "Got it. I'll apologize to her."

I was happy to be home and anxious to get inside and see Luna. It'd been a long time since I'd felt this sense of anticipation. "I'll be home for the rest of the evening, and we'll be using the pool tonight so don't wander around the grounds."

He grinned. "No problem. I'll make myself scarce and head over to Gideon's for poker night then. Have a good evening."

The house smelled like sauteed garlic and butter when I walked in. Following the sound of soft music, I found Luna in the kitchen where she'd hooked up a little speaker to her phone. Luna had been here one day, and the house already felt more like a home. As I watched her, she bent over and looked through a drawer, her shorts riding up her heart-shaped ass. My cock instantly hardened.

She straightened and smiled when she saw me. "Hey, good timing. If you're hungry, I just put chicken breasts and asparagus on the grill."

I didn't use my expensive as fuck, built-in grill and outdoor kitchen often, but it sounded perfect tonight. "Whatever you're cooking smells delicious. I'll change and come help."

She'd pulled her hair back into a high ponytail, and my collar around her neck gave me a dark satisfaction. It'd been a while since I came home and just relaxed. When I walked back to the kitchen, she stood out by the grill, so I grabbed a bottle of wine and two glasses and headed outside.

Luna held a pair of tongs, and she pointed them at me. "This grill and the entire outdoor kitchen area are amazing. You have a pizza oven, for heaven's sake. Ezra has a nice grill, but nothing like this. Do you even use it? It looks brand new."

I poured the wine and handed her a glass. "Not often. Do you want me to bring the plates out or grill the chicken?"

She took the glass and sipped. "Thank you. If you'll watch the grill, I'll bring the rest of the food out. Is that bar there a rotisserie?" She pointed inside the outdoor oven. "And can you cook with wood too?" She motioned to a few features I'd never used before. I told her what I knew and suggested she read the manual. She nodded as if she really planned to read the damn thing.

When the chicken was done, we ate at the outdoor dining table and she told me about Sylvie's makeup consultation with the Sawyer sisters.

"They got into a bitch-slapping fight in Sylvie's office over which shade of lipstick they thought their mother would prefer." She shook her head. "Everyone processes grief in a different way, I guess."

"Sylvie has a strange career, and you're her assistant. You and your friends are the most interesting women I've ever met."

"Not me. I'm about as vanilla as they come."

She didn't know how wrong she was. "When do finals start?"

"In a few weeks. They shouldn't be too bad this time, but I'll have to disappear for a while to study." As long as she crawled into my bed every night and let me have her sweet little pussy and lush body, I could live with that.

As we talked and ate, I stared at the collar around her neck and the ring on her finger. Lust and need swam through me, and I wanted to shove the plates aside and throw her onto the dining table before sinking my cock into her addictive heat. I knew Luna would never be a plaything I'd share with my partners. The thought made me see red, even though I'd never cared about sharing before.

"Are there any updates about Lionel Strack?" she asked.

Pulling myself out of my dark thoughts, I sipped the wine and sat back. "No. He's still missing, but we have half of Vegas looking for him." I started to refill her glass, but she held a hand up.

"Oh, that's enough for me. I want to study for a couple of hours tonight."

It was the start of the weekend, and I knew she really wanted to hide in the guest bedroom and avoid me to put some distance between us.

I smirked and set the bottle down. "Do you know what I want to do?"

She gazed at me warily. "No, what?"

"Go swimming with you."

"I don't think Alexa and Sylvie packed me a swimsuit."

Standing, I peeled off my shirt and threw it on the chair. Then I pulled down my shorts and stepped out. My semi-hard cock jutted in front of me, and I lazily stroked it while she watched helplessly.

"That's fine. Then I won't have to peel it off you. Would you like to swim with me?"

She stared down at my length and bit her lip. A flush crept up her chest and spread across her cheeks. I fucking loved her pale, soft skin and those sparkling green eyes.

"Yes," she whispered, gazing at my shaft.

Taking her hand, I wrapped it around my hard cock and squeezed. "You have too many clothes on." I let her hand go and grasped the hem of her shirt, then pulled it up over her head, careful of her elbow. Reaching around her, I unclasped her bra and removed it, then pulled her to standing and pushed her little shorts and thong down her legs.

"Step out." She kicked the shorts away and reached for my cock again. Her small, soft palm tortured me as she squeezed and stroked my length. She finally let me go when I turned her toward the pool steps.

I refilled her wine glass and followed behind her, watching her sweet ass move as she walked. She glanced around, as if afraid someone would see us, but my house sat on a large, sloping lot, and the backyard was completely private. I'd paid a fuck-ton of money to make it that way.

She dipped her toe in the water and looked over her shoulder at me, lips curling. "It's like bathwater." Luna walked in, sunk down into the pool, and sighed. "It feels... strange swimming naked, but I could get used to it."

"Good. And we'll be doing more than just swimming."

She smirked as she bobbed in the water. "I love your backyard. It's peaceful and quiet, and your flowerpots smell delicious."

This was also my favorite part of the house. Setting our wine glasses down, I waded over to her and thumbed her throat, playing with the lock on her collar. "Does this bother you?"

She laid her hands on my chest and tilted her head. "Not as much as I thought it would."

Satisfaction and lust slammed through me. "Have you ever fucked in a pool before?"

Her face turned bright red, but her nipples pebbled and she shifted restlessly against me. "No."

Grinning wickedly, I drew her against my hard cock. "Good."

Later that night, after I'd fucked Luna in the pool, against a pool jet, and on a pool lounger before coming deep inside her, I wrapped her in a towel and carried her to the shower, where I took her one more time, nice and slow. She'd tried to take me in her mouth, but her jaw was still too sore and I made her stop. She lay next to me, naked and fast asleep in my bed, her dark wet hair draped across my pillows.

I ran my eyes over the whisker burns and finger-sized bruises I'd left on her skin, knowing I should've been more careful. But I had no willpower or control when it came to her–she was an addictive drug in my system.

Leaving her to sleep peacefully, I carefully rolled out of bed, put on a pair of shorts, and cleaned up the dishes outside. When I picked up our discarded clothes, I grinned at her small damp thong. My phone buzzed as I was finishing up.

"Diego, isn't it past your bedtime?"

"You're fucking hilarious, asshole. How's the fine Mrs. Fowler doing? Rick and Roy have been dragging their asses all day when they heard you'd tied her down, and they had to give up their dream of a threesome with her on a motorcycle."

I smirked and rubbed the back of my neck. "And she swore they were perfect gentlemen."

He snorted. "Yeah, it's probably better she doesn't know they've been fucking their fists while thinking about her straddling that bike over the past month. How's it going?"

While we talked, I poured myself two fingers of whiskey and returned to the back patio. "Fucking good. She's a surprise."

He chuckled. "Yeah, she surprised me too. Where is she now?"

"Fast asleep in my bed."

"You wore her out. Good. Get her used to taking cock–hard and often–then you can keep her worn out and happy. Maybe she won't notice what a controlling, moody bastard you are. Does she know you like to tie your women up and cane them occasionally when the mood strikes? I also hear you share with your partners occasionally, and you're into extra-large anal plugs."

"Jesus, who's been talking?"

"Your last sub. She was pissed you dumped her ass, but I understand why."

I shook my head. "So much for the NDA she signed. I know you didn't call to insult me or talk about my wife taking my cock. What's going on?" Sin City Motorheads was a one-of-a-kind motorcycle restoration business Diego had started when he was in his early twenties, and he'd come to us to partner with him. Roy and Rick might be on my shitlist right now, but those perverted fuckers were geniuses when it came to restoring vintage motorcycles.

"It's fucking busy, and we have more business than we know what to do with." He sighed. "But I'm calling with bad news. Brodie, my front-end guy, heard a couple of bikers talking at Titties last night. They were running their mouths off about how the Stracks are pissing off the drug syndicate."

Titties was a sketchy biker bar not far from Motorheads in North Las Vegas. My chest tightened, thinking about Luna being on the drug syndicate's radar. "What's the bad news? If they take the Stracks out for us, all the better."

Diego grunted. "If only life were that easy. There's more. Rumor is that Lionel put a bounty on Luna's head, and he wants her alive."

I hung my head, and fury burned through my system. "Please tell me you're fucking with me. I hope the syndicate gets fed up with them, peels their faces off, then stuffs their balls down their throats before killing them."

"Remember, this is just what Brodie heard from two drunk bikers, but if Lionel keeps going this way, chances are he *will* end up with his balls stuffed down his throat."

"Do me a favor, will you? Spread the rumor that if anyone touches a hair on Luna's head, I will fucking bury them in the desert alive. I'm also putting a bounty on Lionel's head for twice what he's offering–and I want him preferably dead."

Chapter 24

Luna

Late Sunday morning, I groaned awake, rolled over, and noticed Roman's side of the bed was empty. I sat up, looking around. The air smelled faintly of sex and his cedar scent, but the house felt empty.

After cleaning up, I tugged on a loose sundress with a built-in shelf bra and walked out into the living room. I could hear someone in the kitchen and followed the noise.

Milo stood in the kitchen and held up his coffee cup when I walked in. "Good morning. Roman left early, but I made coffee cake and cut up some fruit if you're hungry."

The aroma of brewing coffee and warm vanilla made my stomach growl. "Thanks. Did Roman say where he was going?" I fingered the tracker at my neck.

"He's meeting with one of the partners. That's all I know."

"I'm going over to the Palm Desert Oasis Mortuary for our monthly Sunday poker brunch. I assume you're coming with me?"

"Where you go, I go." He tilted his head. "Did Roman okay it?"

Irritation blossomed in my chest, and I squared off with Milo. "Roman doesn't have to 'okay' where I go."

He held up his hands. "I think we got off on the wrong foot."

"Yes, I think we did. Because you keep putting yours in your mouth. I don't need to explain my family to you, and Roman already has a damn tracker on me, so you can both go fuck yourselves. I'm leaving in ten minutes. If you're coming, be ready."

I turned and strode to my makeshift study, not ready to smell Roman's scent or see his belongings mixed in with mine in the room we shared. My mind raced as I ran through the conversation with Milo. He'd been judgmental and then patronizing, but my emotions were all over the place, and I'd lost my temper.

When I returned to the living room, he was on the phone. "She's right here. Do you want to talk with her?"

"Really? You called him?" I knew he was talking to Roman.

Milo handed me his phone. "I'll be in the car when you're ready with the coffee cake."

He walked out to the garage, and I put his phone to my ear. "Hey."

"Hey." Roman waited for a few seconds. "Anything you want to talk about?"

"No."

"Are you angry?"

"More like frustrated, annoyed, and irritated."

He exhaled. "What happened?"

"He asked me if you gave me permission to go."

"Ah."

I stared down at my feet. "Yeah. Did he get the idea from you that I need to get approval every time I leave the house?"

"Maybe. I didn't tell him you couldn't leave without my permission, but he knows you're wearing my tracker."

My stomach tightened, and I walked over to the back windows to gaze out at his multimillion-dollar views of the Strip. It was overcast and a little smoggy today–the weather fit my mood perfectly. "Do you have any updates on the Stracks? How long do you think we'll need to do this?"

He paused and his voice went low. "What do you mean by 'this'?"

"You know, *this*. Me living at your house, us being married, me having to ask permission to go anywhere, and a judgmental bodyguard attached to my hip?"

"I don't have any news, but we have some leads. And Luna?"

"Yes?"

His voice went low. "My patience and our truce are officially done. If you refer to our marriage in that tone again, I'll take you over my knee and spank your sweet ass until you can't sit for a week. Are we clear?"

"Roman?"

"Yes, Sweetness?"

"Are all your dress shoes expensive?"

He paused. "Yes. Why?"

"If you ever spank me without my permission, I'll scratch a big penis on the right toe of every leather dress shoe you own. So every time you look down, it'll remind you of what a prick you can be."

Roman chuckled darkly. "*When* I spank you, I'll make sure you're panting and begging me for it first, and your juices are dripping on my thighs while I deliver it."

My insides clenched, and I cleared my throat. "Well then. If you can do that, I might not carve up your shoes."

"Count on it. I need to keep you safe, but when the threat ends things will go back to normal, I promise."

But what was "normal" for us? I laid my forehead against the window. "Okay, I'll try to be patient with Milo. And you."

"And I'll try not to be too overbearing."

My mouth tipped up in a wry smile. "I'll be sure to remind you of that promise."

"I would appreciate it because you make me lose my head sometimes. Enjoy your brunch. Drakos and I may swing by later if that's alright."

"You're always welcome. Sylvie will be there, so I can't vouch for Drakos."

When I walked out to Milo's SUV, climbed in, and handed him his phone back, I felt better. Roman didn't seem to hate me anymore, and against all odds, we enjoyed each other. The sex with him was also... addicting. Damn it, the bastard had been right.

When Milo and I walked into the funeral home, Ezra came over and hugged me. It was the first time I'd seen him since the hospital, and I hated that pinched, worried look on his face.

He pulled me away from Milo and studied me carefully. "Are you alright? Sylvie said Roman drugged you and then *married* you." His eyebrows furrowed and a dark scowl moved over his face. "Do you need us to take him out? We can make it look like an accident, just say the word."

"No! No, thank you. I'm... warming to the idea." Sometimes I forgot that for all his old-world charm and kindness, Ezra was a Spade, and the Spades' idea of familial loyalty sometimes included breaking kneecaps and burying bodies together. I'd have to be careful not to complain about Roman around them.

He studied my face carefully, then broke into a smile. "Ah, I see now. You're starting to like him, aren't you? He can be arrogant and cynical, but I do think he'll keep you safe, and as much as it pains me to admit, I respect the man."

I stared at Ezra with my mouth open as the truth hit me. I *did* like Roman. When did this happen? Glancing around, I found Sylvie and Alexa setting up the tables and pointed at them. "I'll go help set up. Love you." I awkwardly kissed his cheek, and his eyes twinkled at my discomfort.

Turning to them, I held up Milo's coffee cake. "We brought a baked good to contribute, and I think Misty and Sasha are coming again."

Alexa grinned. "This is going to be a strange crowd today."

Sylvie snickered as she laid out utensils and poker chips. "We've got geriatric folks from the neighborhood, the Spade cousins, and dancers from Euphoria." She turned to Milo and shook her head. "And now Ms. Fowler and her bodyguard."

My heart stuttered a little at the title. The ramifications of our marriage were just starting to sink in, and I didn't know what to do with my chaotic feelings.

Scowling, I picked up a deck of playing cards and started shuffling. "It's still Ms. Cross, thank you very much, and I've got another surprise for you. Roman and Drakos may be stopping by too."

Sylvie turned to me, and her eyes narrowed. "Did you invite Drakos?" She sounded like I'd betrayed her.

"Hmm, kind of?" She growled, and I winced.

"If Fenn shows up, today could turn into a shitshow," Alexa muttered.

She wasn't wrong. Fennick Spade was a charming lunatic, and we loved each other like cantankerous siblings. But I also knew never to get on his bad side.

Sylvie smirked at Alexa. "You're the best poker player I know, but I do enjoy watching Fenn give you a run for your money." Sylvie glanced at me and zeroed in on the necklace around my throat. "Fuck me. It's going to take a minute to get used to seeing you wearing an eternity collar."

My head jerked. "What? What is that?"

She and Alexa glanced at each other and she pointed to my neck. "It's basically a submissive collar."

My hand flew up to the band. "No. This is just a necklace."

Alexa shook her head. "I'm pretty sure she's right, especially with the lock."

"What does that mean?" My heart rate picked up, and I started hyperventilating a little. "How did I not realize it?"

She grabbed my hands and squeezed. "It's alright, Luna. Maybe it is just for the tracker."

Sylvie snorted. "Yeah, right. I don't think it's that innocent–this is Roman Fowler we're talking about. But I have to admit, it looks pretty badass–like a cross between a collar and an expensive necklace from Tiffany's."

Alexa pursed her lips. "The man does have good taste."

I sat in one of the folding chairs and held my head in my hands for a moment, realizing just how devious Roman had been. He'd scuttled my water law internship, manipulated my schedule, then drugged me and somehow talked me into marrying him–though the details of that night were fuzzy, and now he'd gotten a collar on me. He confused and infuriated me at turns and it was like working on an intricate, complicated puzzle but with a few vital pieces missing. Sylvie patted my shoulder, but she and Alexa gave me some space to brood.

Fenn and Kilian showed up as we started to eat. After greeting Ezra, Fenn walked over and put his arm around me, hugging me to his side a little too tight. I held my drink out so I wouldn't spill.

"I hear you've been busy, Lou. Why the hell didn't you call me? And what the fuck happened to your face?" There was a playful edge to his voice, but I could tell he was angry.

I took a sip of my drink. "Hello, Fenn. Thank you for the offer, but I'd rather not owe you my firstborn." Fenn's light blue eyes held a perpetual, half-smirk that varied in degrees of craziness depending on the situation.

He let go of me and patted my head, rattling my teeth a little. "You're such a joker, and if I really wanted your firstborn, I'd marry you off to one of my lieutenants and take *all* your kids instead of just one."

I patted his shoulder a little too hard. "And that's why I didn't call you."

He grinned down at me, but his smile faded as he eyed the bruise again. "Instead, you married one of the coldest, most calculating assholes in Vegas, and he's a fucking attorney to boot. No offense."

"None taken." He took potshots at attorneys every chance he got when he was around me.

"I try not to fuck with them, but if things go tits up, you call me. We're family."

I smiled genuinely this time. "I like him. He's protective, and he can be... nice sometimes."

Looking down at the collar and tracker around my neck, he shook his head. "With a father like yours, it explains why you think Roman Fowler can be *nice*. How's he treating you?" Fenn was the only person I knew who referred to my psychotic father in such an open, matter-of-fact way. It was kind of a relief.

"He's a manipulative asshole at times, but he doesn't get annoyed with all my questions, and he assigned a bodyguard to me."

Fenn smiled and kissed my cheek. "You might have just saved that fucker's life. Your mind is beautiful, Lou, don't let people tell you differently. I've got something for you." He pulled what looked like a black flashlight out of his pocket and handed it to me. "It's a flashlight taser. Be careful with it. Tasers are legal in Nevada, but this one might not be *entirely* legal."

I took the thing and studied it. Fenn and Kilian's presents were always unique and a little scary. "Thank you?"

"Such a smartass."

A few minutes later, Samuel, Misty, and Sasha walked in with Samuel holding Misty's hand. Misty had changed up her hair color a little and now sported white tips at the end of her red pigtails.

When she saw my jaw, her eyes widened. "The bruise on my face is almost gone, but yours is..." She didn't finish.

I knew it was now an ugly, almost florescent greenish-yellow color, and the concealer hadn't helped much. "Florescent green?"

She took my hand and squeezed. "I'm so sorry he came after you when you were only trying to help me. This is my fault."

"No, it's that asshole's fault who thinks it's okay to terrorize and beat up on women. I'd do it again." Samuel nodded at me in silent thanks and put his arm around Misty. She patted his shoulder and snuggled into him. They were both good people, and I was glad they'd gotten together.

We talked and ate while Milo stood by the door, carefully observing every person who came and went. We started playing poker, and Sasha came over to sit beside me, sipping her mimosa out of a plastic champagne flute. Her violet hair matched her sparkly eyeshadow today.

"There's a rumor you and Roman Fowler got married last week. Is it true?" Sasha was a straight shooter, and it didn't surprise me she'd poked the elephant in the room.

I fingered my wedding band. "Yes. Xander performed the ceremony. I know it's a little sudden, but we've been working together for a few months now..." I trailed off, unsure if I should try to sell the marriage or not. Roman and I hadn't talked about it. We hadn't talked about a lot of things.

Misty grinned happily. "Congratulations! That's so wonderful." She studied my face and her smile faded. "Right?"

Samuel took Misty's hand and kissed it. "It's smart, is what it is, he'll keep her safe. Let's go get some food."

Sasha studied the large ring on my finger. "My ex-boyfriend is a jeweler, and I picked up a few things. That ring is worth a fuck-ton. And that emerald? It's at least three karats, and it matches your eyes perfectly." She took another sip. "I don't think he's just keeping you safe. Did Roman also give you that collar, and what's that hanging next to the lock?"

I let out a long breath. "Yes, and it's a tracking device in case the Stracks come after me again."

She leaned forward and studied it. "Do you know what the collar means?"

"Kind of. Not really." Turning to her, I drained half my mimosa. "Honestly? I don't know what the hell is going on. He's been cold then hot, cruel, and then kind. He dumped me as his intern last Saturday, kissed me on Tuesday, married me the next day, and we had sex–" I stopped talking abruptly.

Sasha's eyes widened. She grabbed my hand and squeezed. "First, I have to know. How was it?"

My cheeks warmed so fast it felt like I had a second-degree sunburn. "So good," I whispered.

Her eyes glazed over. "I fucking *knew* it. With some men, you can just tell." She seemed to shake herself. "Look, my advice is from sad personal experience. You two need to communicate. Figure out what you want and what's best for you, then tell him and make sure he listens." She pointed to my neck. "And ask him exactly what that means."

Setting my cards down, I blew out a breath. "I'm so confused. Sometimes I'm so flaming mad at him I want to rage, and the next minute he's being thoughtful and sweet, and I want to crawl in his lap and wrap him around me."

Roman and Drakos walked in as if I'd somehow conjured up the devil himself just by thinking of him. Roman met Milo at the door and stopped to talk to him while Drakos looked around, found Sylvie, and strode over to her.

When Roman made it to our table, he leaned over and kissed the side of my neck. "Hello, Sweetness. What's the buy-in?"

Several hours and three mimosas later, we walked up to my apartment together. I felt fuzzy but content. The poker tournament had taken on a life of its own once Fenn and Roman won their tables and advanced to the next round. But Alexa had methodically and coldly beaten them both, been deemed this month's funeral parlor poker champ, and gone home with over a thousand dollars. Good for her. I knew she could use the money way more than either of those two.

Drakos and Sylvie disappeared not long after Drakos arrived, and I noticed Ezra's prized chess set sitting on the kitchen table. I'd have to ask her about that.

I wanted to grab a swimsuit and a few other things since half my belongings were still here. It felt strange being at the apartment but realizing I wasn't living here at the moment.

Carl meowed loudly, wound himself around my legs, and then jumped up on the bed next to Roman to watch me pack.

"He sounds like a muscle car without a muffler." Roman didn't try to pet him this time.

"It's part of his charm."

I pulled a couple of bikinis out of my drawer, but Roman shook his head. "You don't need those. I'll just peel them off right after you put them on."

A blush crawled up my neck, and I picked up a modest one-piece and put it in my bag while staring at him. Roman's lip twitched, and he raised an eyebrow. I also opened my nightstand drawer and pulled out the lotion and lip balm I kept there, but Roman leaned over and looked inside before I could close it. He pulled out my small vibrator and nipple clamps before I could slam the drawer on his hand.

"Hey! Get out of there."

"What are these?" he asked innocently as he held my little pink Cherry Box vibrator out of reach as I tried to grab it. Then he dangled the clamps.

"None of your business! Now give them here." My face flushed hot as we wrestled.

When he kept teasing me, I pushed him back on the bed and crawled over his body. He chuckled and wrapped an arm around my waist, then rolled me underneath him, shoving his hips between my thighs.

My knit dress rode up, and he dropped my toys on the bed and slipped a hand underneath, running it up my leg. I stilled and my thighs fell open as he reached my panties. He'd just slid a finger across my damp slit when the front door opened.

"Anyone home?" Alexa called.

"Fuck," Roman sighed as he pulled his hand out and rolled onto his back.

"We're in my room," I croaked out.

I pushed my dress back down and sat up seconds before Alexa came to the doorway. When she saw us, she smirked. "Sorry to interrupt. Sylvie has disappeared, but do you want to eat dinner with Ezra, Kilian, and me later?"

My knee-jerk reaction was to say yes, but I lived with Roman now. I gazed at him. "Are you okay with having them over for dinner? We can grab something to grill on the way home."

He searched my eyes and then shrugged. "Yes."

Smiling, I turned to Alexa. "Do you guys want to come over, maybe around seven? You can eat with us, and I'll try to track down Sylvie in the meantime."

Alexa picked up Carl and absently stroked him. She had to talk a little louder to be heard over his purr. "Seven is perfect. That'll give me a few hours to study and help Ezra unload a body that's coming in."

Roman shook his head. "You all have a strange familiarity with death, especially for being so young."

Alexa shrugged. "We live in a mortuary and our best friend is a mortician. Besides, a good portion of my family *is* dead. Death is as normal as breathing or drinking. It's part of the human experience." Carl started wiggling, and Alexa set him down. "I wish we could do funerals here like they do in New Orleans. Mixed in with the grief and mourning, they make it a celebration with live music and dancing."

I smiled. "And great food because–New Orleans. If you die before Sylvie and I do, we'll make sure you get that."

On the drive home, we grabbed some groceries for dinner and Roman looked around curiously. "When did grocery markets start putting coffee shops, banks, and dry cleaning into their stores?" he asked.

"It's been so long I can't remember. Who does your grocery shopping, anyway? It's obviously not you."

Roman shrugged. "My housekeeper."

I stared at him and shook my head. "It's like we don't even know each other."

Roman took my hand and ran his lips across my fingertips. "We'll have to change that then, won't we?"

We sat in silence on the rest of the drive home, each lost in our own thoughts. I remembered my conversation with Sylvie at brunch and I turned to Roman, touching my neck. "Sylvie and Alexa say this band is really an eternity collar. Is that true?"

He gazed over at me, and his expression didn't change. "Yes."

Chapter 25

Roman

When I confirmed the necklace around her neck was an eternity collar, I expected Luna to be angry or start yelling. Maybe cry or tell me to pull over so she could get out. Something.

But her silence was worse. She studied me for a few seconds, then stared back out the passenger window, and I didn't know what the fuck to do with that.

When we got home, she put her things away while I unloaded the groceries. It had been a while since I'd invited anyone to the house besides my partners and Gideon, and it amused me we were having the fucking Spade family over tonight.

Luna walked back in and paused at the entryway. I straightened and studied her. "Talk to me."

Her hands bunched, and she hesitated as if searching for the right words. Then she gestured between us. "What's happening here? I know I shouldn't, but I can't be with you, have sex the way we do, laugh and eat together, and talk like we do without developing... feelings. Please be honest. Why did you really marry me? And why are you saying this marriage won't be annulled when the threat is over?"

I leaned against the counter and crossed my arms. "What do you think is happening?"

Her chest heaved, and she started pacing. "I don't know! I've had enough people in my life lie and hurt me. Abandon me. If that's what you'll do, just be quick about it and let me go."

She looked lost and sad, her beautiful green eyes shining a little. A few months ago, I would have relished her pain and confusion, knowing whose daughter she was. Now, I just wanted to soothe her. I took her shoulders and slowly pulled her into me. I should've told her the truth before we got to this point, but I didn't want to lose her or open those wounds for either of us.

Sighing, I settled my chin on the crown of her head. "I married you to keep you safe and because I've wanted to fuck you since we first met, and you told me you'd rather eat glass than work with me. I'm also drawn to you, God help us both." I fingered the collar on her neck. "This *is* for the tracker, and I wanted something visible that couldn't be removed quickly. I'm also a dominant, possessive bastard who loves seeing you wear my collar and wedding ring while you scream my name and come underneath me."

Her body jerked and she let out a surprised snort, then melted against me. "I wish I didn't like that part so much. But here we are."

She had a knack for surprising me, and I grinned over her head. "The collar means what we say it means, and I don't want to annul this marriage even when Lionel is eliminated. We might have gotten married for unconventional reasons, but I'm a possessive asshole, and the thought of you being with anyone else makes me homicidal."

She sighed and stepped back, and I reluctantly let her go. "Why did you force the internship?"

I studied her carefully. "We knew your father in Arizona."

Her face blanched. "I thought so. How did you know him?"

I stayed silent.

Her eyes slid away from mine. "Do you know what... he did to me?"

"Yes, but I didn't find out until recently. Ivan knew before I did, and he didn't approve of my behavior. He tried to scare you away for your own good."

Her eyes looked haunted, and I knew that look because I'd seen it in the mirror after my time at the Ranch. It had slowly burned into hard resolve, an unhealthy hatred, and a driving need for revenge.

"He doesn't care about me. I'm not dead only because of the Spade name and the insurance I kept against him. That's it." Luna gazed up at me, searching my eyes. "Do you still want to hurt me?"

My lips quirked. "Not like that. I'm sorry, love. I never should've tried to take out my revenge on you, even if he hadn't done what he did to you. But I'm not sorry I have you now."

She gazed at me with soft, scared eyes. "Promise me you won't lie to me."

I took her hand and squeezed. "There are things you're better off not knowing."

Luna nodded. "I get it. After living with the Spades for half my life, I understand the gray areas a little better. But if it concerns me or my parents, you'll tell me."

Fuck. It was a trap of my own making. She still didn't know her father was a partner in Bitter Creek or had shielded certain people from prosecution after it had been closed down. And she couldn't know my own depravity. I took her shoulders and kissed her hard. "From now on, if it concerns you or your parents, I'll tell you."

Then I walked her backward until she hit the counter. "Now give me your mouth." She tipped her face up and I held her in place while I ravaged her, bending her back. I reached down and pulled off her little knit dress and saw she only had on black lace panties underneath. Her beautiful breasts and sweet body made my cock go rock hard.

I wanted to devour and fuck her into oblivion as I found dirty ways to turn her into a wet, juicy mess. Cupping her breasts, I plumped them tightly in my hands and licked and sucked on each one. When I bit down on a nipple, she jerked and arched into me. I reached down and tugged off her panties, then helped her step out. But instead of leaving them on the floor, I grabbed them up and placed her wrists behind her back, then used them to tie her hands. She stared up at me with hazy, half-lidded eyes.

"How's your elbow?" I asked, testing her bonds. The position made her breasts jut out at a tantalizing angle.

Her cheeks were flushed and her breath came in fast pants. "*Now* you ask. It's fine."

I smirked and palmed her pussy. Watching her face, I gathered some of her moisture onto my fingers and brought them to her mouth. "Taste yourself. Taste what a wild, little cock whore you are for me to get so wet when I tie you up and make you wear my collar."

Her eyes flared, but I saw a spasm run through her body. I slapped the side of her ass lightly when she kept her lips closed. "If I shove my fingers deep into your cunt right now, will you be soaked for me?"

Her cheeks went red, but she held my gaze. "Yes."

"Good girl. Now open."

She opened her mouth, and her eyes slid closed as she lapped her juices off my fingers. The feel of her mouth sucking on them sent sharp, hot lust shooting right to my cock. Pulling my fingers out slowly, a string of her saliva came with them. I ran my wet fingers down her cheek and wiped them off on her heaving chest.

"You suck so well. When your jaw is healed, I'm going to fuck your mouth until your spit, tears, and my semen cover your sweet face. Now let's see how much you want my cock."

I turned her around and laid her face down across the counter, spreading her thighs. Moisture glistened and my mouth watered at how pink and ready she was for me. Just like I promised, I shoved two fingers roughly inside her and worked her clit.

"Oh, God!" She bucked under me.

I slammed my fingers in and out of her, grinding my palm against her pelvic bone, hitting her just right. She rocked on the hard marble counter, whipping her head back.

Suddenly, I pulled my fingers out, undid my belt and zipper, and freed my hard, thick length. When she glanced back over her shoulder, her cheeks were flushed a beautiful pink.

"Please," she panted, "I want you inside me."

Shedding my clothes, I ran the head of my shaft against her slit, teasing her with it. "Even if you're still sore, and you know I'll have to rail your cunt to make my cock fit?"

Her head arched back at my words, and I grinned at seeing her body's reaction.

"Yes, I need you."

"Then beg me. Beg me to fuck you."

Her head snapped up, and her eyes lit with fire. Her hands may have been tied, but she pushed her ass back at me, searching for my shaft. I tsked, then pinched and rubbed her sensitive clit.

Her head whipped back and she groaned. "God, you're evil. Alright! Please fuck me. Shove your cock inside me and make–"

A soft wail escaped her as I slammed inside, holding her hips tight. I had to bend my knees a little to line us up, but it gave me momentum and I watched as she flailed underneath me.

Her pussy felt so wet and tight, just how I imagined it would be. Rolling my hips against her, I worked my thumb against her clit and watched her climax build. When she got close, I stopped and pulled out.

She cried out at the loss. "Why would you do that? I'm so close."

Leaning in, I murmured in her ear. "I know, but I'm not done with you yet." Sliding my arms underneath her, I pulled us off the counter and turned her around with her wrists still tied behind her back.

Then I grabbed her ass. "Wrap your leg around me." She obeyed, and I picked her up and strode out to the living room, setting her on the end of the couch. She put her legs down, and when she stood, I turned her around and bent her over the back of the couch, pushing her head down.

Her legs shook as I knelt and spread her thighs. I loved the feel of her soft, velvety skin, and the contrast of my darker hands around her pale globes. Her musky scent drifted up to me, and I breathed it in as I ran my hands up her thighs. Parting her cheeks, I knelt, lifted her up a bit, and licked her slit.

She cried out, the sound echoing in the room. "Holy shit, that feels so good," she groaned. "Please, I want to come."

After working her slit over, I ran my hand down her back. "If you let me spank you, I'll let you come." I'd teased and edged her until she was cursing and begging me nonstop. Then I bit one of her ass cheeks, carefully monitoring her reaction.

Her breathing sped up. "You son of a whore. If you don't let me come–" She choked when I rubbed her clit, then slowly pushed my thumb into her back hole. Tensing beneath me, I felt her pussy flutter. "What are you doing?" she whimpered.

"Fingering your ass." Luna gasped softly but didn't protest or tell me to stop. "Do you want me to fuck you until you make a filthy, wet mess of yourself and come all over me?"

"Yes," she gasped out.

"Then let me spank you. The first time is always the hardest, but don't you want to try something new? Isn't your curiosity pricked? Aren't you wondering if maybe you might... *like it*?" I whispered the last two words softly into her ear.

She was silent for a few seconds. "Yes," she finally whispered back.

"Then say, 'please spank me, sir,' and I'll give you what you need."

"Spank me, you jack–ah!" Her breath caught as my palm landed with a loud thwack on her backside. Then I methodically spanked her ass cheeks, pussy, and the insides of her thighs, letting the intensity and heat slowly build. She squirmed and cried out beneath me, but she didn't beg me to stop.

Eventually, I paused and ran my hands along her soft, hot skin, then pumped my fingers inside her sopping wet slit. She sobbed quietly and pushed back against my fingers. I palmed my hard cock, ran my length along her slit, then slowly pushed inside. If I still believed in heaven, this right here would have been it. Her surrender to me– her soft sobs and soaking pussy–fed my dark needs, and I wanted her to crave this as much as I did.

Luna's long wail as I worked inside her made my toes curl, and an orgasm threatened. I'd never hungered for anyone the way I did Luna. Over the last ten years, I'd fucked many beautiful women. My last one had been an experienced submissive, and she wanted to try almost everything, including threesomes, bondage, denial, and needle play.

But *nothing* had ever come close to the obsessive need boiling in my cock for the woman panting underneath me. I reached around and worked her clit while I pounded inside her, moving the heavy couch a few inches with my thrusts. I wouldn't be sharing Luna with anyone, but I would use bondage and denial with her.

Luna begged me to let her orgasm. "Please! I need to come. Don't stop this time. Please."

I palmed the front of her neck and leaned over, brushing my lips against her ear. "Your dripping wet cunt is like a goddamned vice, and your red ass cheeks feel so hot and perfect against me." I stroked her clit and shoved my thumb deep into her ass. "Come, Sweetness. Come all over me."

She gasped and panted as she processed all the stimuli, then her back bowed and she moaned out her orgasm as she clenched around me. I held back my own to let her experience her full climax, still working her with my fingers. When she finally wilted under me, I grabbed her hips, lifted her off the couch a few inches, and hammered her from behind, bracing my feet against the floor.

An intense orgasm rolled through my spine, and I slammed into her one last time, coming hard and long until I felt my cum spill out of her. When I finished, I wrapped my arms around her torso and pulled her up, hugging her from behind.

Then I wrapped my hand around her neck where my collar lay and kissed the side of her uninjured cheek. "You like being spanked and fucked, and told when to come. We'll have to explore that, won't we?"

I could feel the blush climb up her neck, and I grinned as I reached down and cupped her dripping pussy then swung her up to take her to the bathroom for some aftercare. "How do you feel about piercings?" She shivered and wound her arms around me.

Chapter 26

Luna

Roman stood at the closet door with his hands on his hips as I dressed. "It isn't safe for you to go to campus. You can get the lecture notes from a classmate."

We'd had a nice evening with Alexa, Ezra, and Kilian out on the back patio last night. We grilled, drank wine, and talked most of the evening. But I'd been tired and a little tipsy by the time our guests left, and Roman had tucked me in at ten last night. It had been a nice day yesterday, but I'd gotten behind with my homework, finals were coming up, and I felt the pressure this morning.

"I need to go to class. A couple of my professors count class participation as part of the grade, and I can't afford to let my scores drop."

He ran his hand through his hair. "Your professors can go fuck themselves."

My eyes narrowed and I folded my arms. "I'm going. Milo said he'd wait outside each class for me, and Klim let me know the campus police are on alert. It's stupid to think I'll stay here and hide. I can't afford not to graduate, and staying hidden would just be letting that bastard win."

Roman's jaw clenched, but I didn't back down. Law school was my ticket to gainful employment and financial freedom, and I craved the familiarity of it. It was also a variable I could control.

He scowled and pointed his finger. "You don't leave Milo's side except to sit in class. And if you need to pee, you do it with him standing outside the bathroom."

I nodded and unfolded my arms. "Okay. I'm not stupid, and I don't have a death wish. I just want to graduate."

"Fuuck me. And I just want to push you back onto the bed, pull your skirt up, and spank you until you're a drenched, crying mess again. Then shove my cock into your heat and stay there all day."

"You have a very sadistic and vivid imagination." My sore pussy clenched as if searching for his hard length, and my tender ass reminded me I was still recovering from one of Roman's enthusiastic spankings.

"With you, my sadistic, filthy mind has no bounds."

I stifled a moan and held up my hands as if warding him off. "I need some recovery time, and my bottom is already sore thanks to you."

He grinned and grabbed my arms, pulling me into him. Then he slid his hands down and grabbed my ass cheeks, squeezing hard enough for me to hiss out a breath.

"I have a meeting this morning, or I'd already be balls' deep inside you."

"Then lucky me," I deadpanned. He chuckled, kissed me again, and headed out the door. I had to change my panties before leaving for school.

Colleen, one of my classmates, heard what had happened in the parking garage and asked me about it after class. My elbow still felt tender, but I'd removed the wrap and used makeup to cover the bruise on my jaw. From her furtive looks, it hadn't been very effective.

"Holy shit!" Colleen gasped. She'd just glimpsed the ring on my finger. "Did you get *engaged* over the weekend too? You've been busy!"

A few other students heard her exclaim and came over, Jared among them. "She didn't just get engaged, she got fucking *married*," he snickered bitterly.

"What? Luna, I didn't even know you were dating anyone," Colleen exclaimed.

I stared at Jared coldly but answered her. "It was a little sudden, but I think my being attacked made him decide he couldn't live without me."

"More like his dick couldn't live without you," Jared muttered under his breath.

Someone sucked in a sharp breath, and I heard whispers around us. Before I could tell him to fuck right off, Colleen turned on him. "For once in your life, shut your trap and quit being such an asshole."

"Excellent advice. And if you don't, I'll do it for you." I heard a calm, deep voice say behind me. I turned and saw Roman standing next to Milo. "You must be Jared, the unpleasant rash Luna mentioned she couldn't get rid of. Although I do have to thank you for being there the other day."

Jared narrowed his eyes, then swallowed as Roman stared coldly back at him. Jared turned to me and shook his head. "Be careful, Luna."

As he walked off, the silence sat awkwardly for a moment, and a hint of guilt slid through me. I hadn't meant to hurt him, and he had saved me from Lionel. Shaking off the guilt, I introduced Colleen and a couple of other classmates to Roman. When they left a few minutes later, Milo took off as well.

Roman reached over to take my backpack and slid his other hand behind my neck, pulling me to him.

Having him here at the school felt almost surreal and a little jarring—like two distinctly separate parts of my world were colliding. His presence both soothed and agitated me.

He gave me a thorough kiss, then pulled back and brushed a strand of hair off my shoulder. "Hello, Sweetness. You ready to go?" He smirked as if knowing he'd thrown me off.

My eyebrow went up. "If you're done pissing on my leg and marking your territory." He barked out a laugh and leaned in to kiss me again. The man had very talented lips.

Roman drove me to the offices on Tuesday morning. As we walked past Brenna, she watched me without expression until she saw the collar on my neck and the ring on my finger. Then her eyes widened, and her face seemed to pale. I expected a snide remark or a jealous, hateful look, but she seemed anxious. I mentally shrugged. Maybe she didn't know how I really got the fist-sized bruise on my jaw and thought Roman had given it to me.

As finals approached, we fell into a routine. Milo took me to class and became my shadow around campus when I was there, and then Roman took me with him to the offices on the other weekdays. In the evenings, we'd usually cook and eat dinner together, then find a new room or surface in Roman's house to copulate on. He seemed to like his back patio the best, and he'd installed silk ties to one of the loungers.

Sometimes, we'd eat dinner with the Spades or have the partners over to the house. One evening when Roman had to work later than usual, I caught myself moping and realized with an unpleasant start that I liked having him here, and I missed him when he wasn't around.

I studied myself in the full-length mirror that morning as I got ready for the day, finding a few new bruises and bite marks on my body. Roman came up behind me and ran his hand down my waist over the smudges there.

"Do they hurt?"

"No. My pussy and nipples always seem to be tender though."

He grinned. "Good. That will remind you of me during the day." He cupped both my breasts and ran his thumbs across my peaks, and I arched into him. "I'm a deviant asshole because I love seeing my marks on you. Tell me if I do something that scares you or you don't like."

Worry and shadows clouded his eyes, but I slid my palms around his neck and pulled his face to mine. "I must be fucked up too, because I like seeing my marks on you." I let go and walked around to his back, studying the scratches I'd left there last night. "Do these hurt?" I asked softly, trailing my fingers over them.

He turned and gathered me in his arms. "No, and I love making you lose your shit enough that you mark me without realizing it." I rubbed against him, then pulled his face down to mine as he slid his hand down to test my wetness. We got a late start that morning.

Alexa and I studied for finals together on my favorite floor in the law library, and Milo sat at the table next to us. A few hours later, she sighed, stretched, and cracked her neck.

I pulled my headphones off. "Are you quitting for the day?"

"No, I just need a break. My brain stopped absorbing after reviewing my civil procedure notes."

I grimaced. "Is Garrick still teaching it?"

"Yeah, and his voice is so monotone, it's like he's trying to bore us to death. I'm going to stretch my legs and grab a smoothie at the student center. Do you want anything?"

"No, I'm good. I'll just have some of yours."

She grinned. "You can have as much as you want, but fair warning. I'm getting the green smoothie."

I grimaced. "Never mind, I think I still have some Red Hots in my backpack. Do you want me to go with you?"

Waving her hand, she stood. "No, I'll be fine."

She walked out, and I put my headphones back on. About twenty minutes later, my phone vibrated in my backpack. I was still working through a practice question and ignored it–until my phone buzzed a second time.

I pulled it out and saw a text from Alexa.

Alexa: Hello, Ms. Fowler, we have your friend. If you want to keep her alive, lose your bodyguard and go to the corner of Cottage Grove and Maryland Parkway. You have four minutes.

It took me a second to read and then re-read the text, and realize it had been sent from Alexa's phone, but it wasn't her. Primal fear and dread flooded me, and I blanked for a split second. But Alexa couldn't afford for me to lose my shit now. I texted back.

Luna: I need proof.

I didn't want to ask for proof of life. No need to give these fuckers any bad ideas. Less than ten seconds later, a photo of Alexa in the back seat of a vehicle came in. She had a bloody lip and looked furious, but she was alive and seemed relatively unharmed. If there was anyone who wouldn't lose their head even after getting kidnapped, it was Alexa.

I quickly dug through my backpack and pulled out a few things, stuffing my license and a credit card into my back pocket, and my flashlight into the back waistband of my jeans.

Then I stood and ran. It would take too long to persuade Milo, and I was pretty sure I could outrun him.

I heard Milo shout, his chair screeching as he stood. "What the fuck?" He yelled.

"They have Alexa! Corner of Cottage Grove and Maryland," I yelled over my shoulder.

"Luna! Stop right now!" he bellowed.

I plunged headfirst down the stairs, taking them two or three at a time. Milo pounded after me, but he was twice my age. "Luna, fucking stop! You're going to get yourself killed!"

My mind raced and my lungs burned as I dashed out of the library, barely missing a couple lingering in the doorway. People turned and stared at me running through the courtyard as Milo pursued me. So many thoughts and feelings raced through my mind, regret and self-disgust among them for not anticipating something like this. So stupid! I pumped my legs faster.

"Do you need help?" a tall woman standing with two others on the auditorium steps called after me.

"Yes! Call campus police!"

The lady tried running with me, but she wore high heels. "Where are you going?"

"Corner of Cottage Grove and Maryland. Tell them it's Luna Cross!"

She stopped, and I hoped like hell she'd make the call. I didn't take time to slow down or look back. My little ballet flats stayed on my feet, but I could feel every hard slap on the pavement as I sprinted down the wide sidewalk.

I slid my phone into my back pocket as I ran, and untucked my shirt. Scanning the area, I approached the arterial road going past the school. Maryland Parkway was a six-lane street that cut through the working part of downtown Las Vegas. It went through North Las Vegas, down past the University, and connected with the airport. I wondered what the kidnappers' plans were.

The metal tracker on my collar thumped rhythmically against the hollow of my throat as I ran, and my gasping breath seemed so loud.

I hoped Milo had notified Roman, but I knew the clock was ticking. I'd dragged Alexa into danger, and now time was running out.

The intersection came into view, and I slowed my pace, gazing around frantically as I drew near. Feet slapped on the pavement behind me, and I glanced back to see Milo maybe twenty-five or thirty feet behind me. Then I heard a series of short honks and turned to see an oversized black SUV pull up to the curb in front of me. I held up my hands to show they were empty, and the back door swung open.

"Luna, God damn it! Stop!" Milo yelled as I dove into the back seat. A large man with a ruddy complexion and bad teeth held the door open, and when my torso was inside, he tried to shut it but my legs were still in the way. I knelt on his lap, grinding my knee in his groin, and grabbed the back of the front driver's seat. Then I brought up the flashlight taser Fenn had given me and simultaneously pressed the switch, shoving the taser into the driver's neck.

The man underneath me punched my side and tried to shove me off, but the damage was done. The SUV had started to speed up when I tased the driver, but now the vehicle swerved toward the curb and jumped up onto the sidewalk, coming to a rolling stop.

Alexa sat in the back passenger seat behind the driver, and she pivoted around, brought her legs in front of her, and kicked the man underneath me in the face and chest. He wasn't buckled in, and he had to grab the door frame to keep from falling out. Milo came running up to the side of the vehicle, saw the man's hand holding onto the frame, and tried to drag him out. I heard faraway shouts and what sounded like sirens in the distance.

The man yelled, and another smaller man sitting in the front passenger seat pulled his gun up and swiveled toward Milo. Alexa screamed at Milo to duck as I moved my arm over and pushed the end of the flashlight taser into the other man's shoulder just as his gun went off. But I moved a fraction of a second too slow, and I watched in terror as blood blossomed on Milo's shirt.

Chapter 27

Luna

Pandemonium erupted when Milo went down. I tased the man underneath me almost as an afterthought and then tugged Alexa out of the vehicle. Our exit wasn't graceful, but I wanted her out of that SUV and away from those men.

Milo lay on the ground, groaning and clutching his right shoulder. A red stain quickly spread over his white shirt as I stared down at him.

Alexa knelt beside him, but her hands were still incapacitated. "Luna, stay with me. We have to stop the bleeding."

The buzzing in my ears lessened, and I came back to myself and dropped to my knees. "Yes. Okay, stop the bleeding," I chanted. Ripping off my shirt, I rolled it up and pressed it hard against his wound. Less than a minute later, the police found us and the EMTs arrived seconds behind them. Someone eventually freed Alexa from the zip ties on her wrists, and a bystander kindly handed me an extra-large blue t-shirt with Pescadero Pool Care scrawled across the front. It smelled a little like stale sweat, but I was glad to have it.

An hour later, I still wore the t-shirt as we sat in the hospital emergency room, waiting to hear any news about Milo's condition.

I looked down at my hands and vaguely realized I had blood under my fingernails. Alexa and I blearily watched the local news on the TV mounted to the wall as we waited. They mentioned the shooting but didn't have any relevant details.

A doctor walked out and looked around. "Milo Carlson's family?"

I raised my hand. "Here," I lied.

She walked over and stood in front of us. "He's out of surgery and we're monitoring him. He'll live, barring infection and complications, but it's going to be a long recovery. Mr. Carlson is lucky the bullet didn't nick his artery." I nodded and thanked her.

The doctor took off, and the emergency doors slid open. Fenn walked in and his lip quirked when he saw us, but I could see the worry in his eyes. "Lou, have I taught you nothing? You run *away* from the bad guys, not to them."

Roman and Gideon strode inside a few seconds later, and Roman stalked over and stood, looming over us. He stared down at me, the tips of his expensive Italian leather shoes almost touching my small black flats. "Milo called and said he was chasing you. That you ran away from him. Why?" His low voice didn't fool me when I could see the vein on the side of his neck pulsing angrily.

I felt emotions rise where minutes ago I'd been numb and heartsick. They'd tried to take Alexa, and she had the split lip, lacerations on her wrists, and bruises to show for it. She opened her mouth, but I squeezed her hand and slowly stood. He didn't move, so I carefully pushed him back a couple of feet.

Craning my neck, I gazed into his worried, angry face. "Milo is going to be okay. He'll need a lot of recovery time, and he... lost a lot of blood." I swallowed and Roman glanced down at the oversized, blood-stained t-shirt I wore.

"What happened?" he asked.

Gideon said nothing but watched Fenn carefully. Fenn folded his arms and kept an eye on Roman, but he didn't interfere.

"They grabbed Alexa." Tears filled my eyes. "We were studying together and she went to the student center for a smoothie. I shouldn't have let her go alone... no, I should have stayed away from her."

"It's not your fault," Alexa murmured beside me.

I tipped my head back and willed the tears away. Then I told them about getting the text and running. Gideon's phone rang, and he stepped away to take the call.

Roman's cold eyes scanned my face. "You ran away from your bodyguard and dove into their vehicle," he repeated.

His eerie calm worried me. "You said if they ever got their hands on me, they'd probably gang rape me and slice me up before they dumped my body. I couldn't let them do that to her."

Gideon walked back over, his phone to his ear. "We got the coordinates to Lionel's safe house, his men plugged it into the SUV's nav system." Gideon shook his head. "I'm sending a team in now. We need to go.""

Roman's jaw clenched, and he wrapped his arms around me. "Fenn is watching you tonight. But if you run from him, me, or one of my bodyguards again, I'll do more than just paddle your sweet ass. I'll tag your fucking ear if I have to. Now promise me you won't run again–and mean it."

I gazed up at him, tired, scared, and frustrated. Then I shook my head. "If they grab someone else I care about, I can't tell you I wouldn't do it again."

Fenn sighed behind Roman. "You should've just lied, Lou. Roman's an attorney, he lies all the time."

Roman ignored Fenn and took me by the shoulders as if he wanted to shake me. "You drive me fucking *insane*, and we're not done talking about you diving into that SUV. Stay safe." He kissed me hard and deep before pulling away and striding out with Gideon.

Fenn called one of his men to retrieve our belongings from the law library and then took us to Ezra's house, which sat right next to his. The large, older ranch-style adobe homes were located a few blocks from the mortuary, south of the airport between Paradise Valley and Green Valley North. All the properties in their neighborhood sat on acre lots, which was an anomaly in Las Vegas.

When we got to Ezra's home, we both cleaned up the best we could. Alexa slapped some ointment and a butterfly bandage on her lip and waited impatiently for Fenn's men to bring our belongings. When she got her laptop back, she cradled it like an infant.

"I need to look up a few things," she told me vaguely and disappeared.

I washed Milo's blood off the best I could, and Ezra loaned me another shirt. Then we sat in his kitchen, drinking whiskey and eating leftover apple crisp and ice cream as I told them what happened.

Ezra leaned back, his plate half empty. "It wasn't the smartest thing, Luna, diving into a moving vehicle full of degenerate criminals. But I can't say I'm sorry since both you and Alexa are safe. The Stracks wouldn't think twice about torturing and killing any of you."

Fenn pointed at Ezra's half-finished dessert. "You done with that?" Ezra nodded, and Fenn pulled the plate over and shoveled a bite into his mouth. Then he pointed his spoon at me. "What's going on with you and Fowler? I thought this was a marriage of convenience—meaning he'd keep you alive, and then you'd conveniently get the marriage annulled when the threat is neutralized. Watch yourself with him. He's a soulless bastard, and he and his partners are fucked up."

"What do you mean?" I asked.

He picked up his whiskey and took a sip. "It isn't fair, but something inside a person is damaged when you go through what they did. And if they ever do heal, it's usually messy."

Fenn could have been talking about me, and I looked down at my plate, feeling the sting in my chest as I stirred melted ice cream around. He knew what had happened to me. He and Kilian had been in their early twenties when Ezra brought Sylvie and me home.

He studied my face and realization dawned. "Shit, Luna. I didn't mean you."

My fingernails still had a few specks of blood underneath them, I noticed absently. When I got home, I planned to soak in Roman's tub and scrub myself clean. "We're all damaged in some way, aren't we?" I replied. "Every time I've brought up getting an annulment, Roman tells me it will never happen. I don't know if I want one now either."

Ezra and Fenn exchanged worried glances, and Ezra turned to me. "Luna, do you plan to stay with him when the Stracks are neutralized?"

"Maybe, but he might not want to when he gets to know me better."

Fenn studied the collar around my neck, then sighed. He leaned forward to catch my eye, then reached out and took my hand, turning it over so my wedding band was visible. "He married you and put a collar and tracker on you. A man doesn't do that with a woman he plans to cut loose. Fowler also had his tongue down your throat at the hospital today, and he looked almost feral."

I glanced at Ezra. "Shut up, Fenn."

He smirked and let go of my hand. "I've never seen him lose his shit like that before. The bastard is usually ice-cold."

Ezra studied the collar around my neck. "Is that a GPS tag?"

I blushed harder. "Yes. He said he wanted to be able to find me fast if I got taken, and he didn't want it to be easily removed."

Fenn grunted. "It'll be interesting to see what he does with the collar after the threat ends."

That thought had my insides tightening, and I took the whiskey in front of me and gulped it down, then grimaced at the burn in my throat. "God, that never gets better."

Ezra shook his head. "It's single malt whiskey. It's not meant to be slammed back like cheap tequila."

Alexa appeared in the kitchen doorway with her laptop in hand. She was biting her lip. "Luna, I need to show you something, and you won't like it."

Hours later, I lay in my old bed staring up at the ceiling, thinking about Alexa's bombshell. It took a long time to fall asleep, and early the next morning, someone brushed a strand of hair off my cheek. I felt the mattress depress beside me, and I opened my eyes and looked up.

Roman stared down at me in the darkness. "Let's go home."

Tears filled my eyes. "I didn't know," I whispered.

"What didn't you know, Sweetness?"

"I didn't know my father was a partner in Bitter Creek Ranch."

He was still in his clothes from yesterday. It didn't look like he'd been home yet, and there were bloodstains on his shirt.

His body locked, and he studied me carefully. "How did you find out?"

I sat up and scooted back, my heart sinking as I wrapped my arms around my knees. A small part of me had hoped he didn't know—that it had all been a crazy, cosmic coincidence I'd ended up as his intern. Would I ever get away from my father's reach and his ability to wound and damage me?

"Alexa figured it out. The internship, my being from Arizona, and the Ranch being located there didn't add up for her. So she dug around last night and found tax documents that linked him."

"Get your things, let's go." He turned and started walking out of the bedroom as if he expected me to follow him.

"Am I safe with you, Roman?" I asked quietly.

He stilled, his head down as he faced away from me. "No, and not for the reasons you think. But you're mine now, and I vow to keep you safe from everyone else."

He walked out, and I slowly got out of bed and dressed. The house was quiet and dark in the early morning, and when I entered the kitchen, he and Fenn stood glaring at each other. The silence felt deadly, and I almost wished they were yelling instead.

Shouldering my backpack, I cleared my throat. "I'm ready."

Fenn didn't break his stare. "You don't have to leave with him. You can stay here with Ezra or, better yet, move in with me again—just like old times."

Roman's eyes glittered dangerously, and Fenn was purposefully trying to bait him. Sylvie and I had sometimes stayed with him when Ezra went out of town before we moved into the mortuary apartment our senior year in high school.

"Thanks, Fenn. But I need to go home and figure a few things out." I turned to Roman. "Can we go through a drive-thru and pick up coffee on the way? I need caffeine badly."

Roman smirked at Fenn. "Yes. We'll hit a drive-thru on our way *home*."

Fenn shook his head. "She called your place 'home.' I get it, you fucking bastard. But if you still plan to use or hurt her to get to Montgomery Cross, know this. I will hunt you down personally and do my best to take you and your partners out. I've lost enough family, and I refuse to lose anyone else."

His words warmed and chilled me all at once. As I felt the animosity and anger swirling around these two men, I realized what a horrible idea it was to have them in the same space when emotions were running this high. They were both extremely alpha and used to controlling their environments and the people around them.

Even knowing all that, I walked over to Fenn and cupped his cheeks. "Thank you for loving me like your own sister and protecting me when I was so vulnerable and lost. You, Kilian, and the twins are my brothers, and I would die for you. But now I need to find out where I stand and see whether Roman and I can work through this, or part ways and call it a day. If that happens, I'll need your help again."

He kissed my forehead as Roman growled behind me. "Get your fucking lips off her."

We both ignored him, but I knew what Fenn was doing. "Stop flipping him off behind my back. Please keep Alexa and Sylvie safe, and tell Ezra I'll call him later today." Then I walked over to Roman, took his hand, and pulled him out of the house.

I sipped my large coffee and studied his profile on the way home. "What happened last night, why do you have blood on your shirt, and where's Lionel's safe house?"

His lip quirked at my questions. "Lionel got away, but he has a bullet in his thigh, and his soldiers are... incapacitated. You make me fucking daft. We're going to have a long talk about what will happen if you keep putting yourself in danger."

"You already mentioned that, several times."

"If you hadn't used that taser on the driver, we may not have gotten to you in time. Where the fuck did you get something like that, anyway?"

I decided not to tell him Fenn had given it to me. "Where's his safe house?"

Roman shook his head in disgust. "In a penthouse condo just off the Strip, if you can fucking believe it. The man's a moron."

Chapter 28

Luna

Despite knowing about my father's involvement, and understanding more about Roman's reasons for forcing the internship, I was still relieved to be home. Roman's house had grown on me, and having my things scattered around made it feel more like my home.

A stack of books littered his coffee table, and my hoodie hung on the ugly modern sculpture in the entryway. His house wasn't as pristine and lifeless as it had been the first time I saw it. But now, I needed to reassess whether I could stay here with him.

Roman threw his keys on the counter and turned to study me. "I'm going to get cleaned up."

While he showered, I snuck into our bedroom, grabbed some clothes, and went to the guest bedroom to shower. Laying my clothes on the bed, I showered quickly but stopped short when I walked back into the bedroom with a towel wrapped around me. Roman stood leaning against the door jamb. My heart thudded, and heat coursed through me as we stared at each other.

Clearing my throat, I tugged the towel around me and motioned to the pile of clothes on the bed. "Let me get dressed, and then we can talk."

He closed the door, walked over to me, and slowly backed me against the wall. Then he rested his hands on either side of my head, effectively blocking me in. Leaning down, he murmured against my neck, "I want to fuck you against this wall, then in our bed, and after we eat and sleep for a few hours, take you again on the kitchen table. *Then* we can talk."

"And I'd like to get paid to drink margaritas and read all day. We don't always get what we want." My voice grew soft. "You hate me because of my father, and you lied to me about why you wanted me as an intern."

He leaned in and ran his mouth against my jaw, nipping and licking as he went. "We *can* have what we want. I don't hate you, and I never lied to you, Ms. Fowler."

He bit my earlobe and gently kissed me, sliding his tongue across my lips. His touch sent lightning through my system, and my hand came up and wrapped around his neck before I knew what I'd done.

He groaned into my mouth and pushed me against the wall as he ground his length into my lower stomach. Then he slowly pulled back and laid his forehead on mine. "You still want to talk first?"

The bastard had gotten me hot and needy, then thought he could leave me like this. "No, damn you." I rolled up on my toes and crashed my mouth against his.

He chuckled darkly and jerked the edge of my towel, pulling it out of my fingers and dropping it to the floor. Then Roman found my hands, slid his fingers through mine, and brought them over my head.

"You could have died yesterday, or been shot. I need to be inside you."

My heart pounded, and heat rose in me. But doubt also crept in. Why would he care if I got hurt unless he wanted to be the one to inflict the pain? And why did I *still* crave him and think of his house as my home after knowing he wanted revenge against my father and planned to use me to get it?

"Stop thinking and worrying, Sweetness. We'll get there." He ripped his t-shirt off and rubbed his chest against mine, groaning as our skin connected. My nipples pebbled, and I broke out in goosebumps. He took my wrists in one hand and held them above my head, then palmed my pussy, working his fingers against my clit. When my hips started bucking against his hand, he shoved his fingers deep inside.

"Your cunt is soaking wet for me. Your body knows who you belong to, even if your brain hasn't figured it out yet."

My head arched back when he leaned down and sucked, then bit, on my nipples. "Oh, God. How can you do this to me, every single time?"

"You make me fucking crazy, so it's only fair." He let go of my wrists, then slid his gym shorts and briefs off, kicking them away and wrapping his hands around my waist. "Put your legs around me."

I stared up at him, frozen in indecision and lust.

"Or I can bend you over the bed and fuck you hard from behind, with your hair wrapped around my fist. Either way works for me."

My cheeks flushed with heat, and I moaned softly as I brought my leg up.

He palmed my ass, hoisted me up, then positioned his cock to my opening. "Open your eyes. Watch me take you against the wall."

When I opened my eyes, he shoved inside, hissing in pleasure as he worked his thick, hard length into me. "Good Christ. Your cunt feels like tight liquid heat. When I'm done drilling you here, I'll fuck you over the dresser next."

My neck arched, and a crushing orgasm started building inside me at his dirty, unfiltered words. When he brought his hand around to work my clit, I cried out his name and came, pinned against the wall.

Two hours, a hasty meal, and two orgasms later, I passed out in his bed with our limbs tangled together. When I woke, it was still dark outside. Roman wasn't in the bed, but he'd left a living room lamp on. I put on his dress shirt and found him out by the pool on a lounger, watching the Vegas skyline and smoking a joint.

Closing the patio door, I walked over as he held it up to me. "It's an Indica-dominant, organic strain. Good for PTSD and whatever ails you."

My heart squeezed when he mentioned PTSD–we both knew a little about that. Marijuana might be legal in Nevada, but my drug of choice was usually tequila shots or white wine. I extracted the joint from his fingers and took a hit, coughing a little. Without thinking, I sat on his oversized lounger and swung my legs up, curling into him. Handing the joint back, I put my head on his chest.

He wrapped an arm around me, and we lay there for a few minutes, listening to crickets chirping in the bushes and smelling the scent of sagebrush and marijuana drift on the breeze. I gazed up at the night sky, spotting the quarter moon and a few planets blinking brightly overhead.

He took a slow hit, then handed me the joint again. I took another hit, then gave it back to him. "Two is my limit. I don't have a tolerance, and we've postponed our talk long enough." I exhaled and gazed up at him. "I need to know why."

Melancholy and sorrow swirled through me. I tried to be angry at him for systematically shoving through my barriers and suspicions, and making me care for him when there were so many red flags that didn't make sense at the time. I could only blame myself for not heeding my own instincts.

Roman smashed the joint into an ashtray on the side table then wrapped his arms around me, drawing my body flush with his. "When my father sent me to the Ranch, I was grieving and angry, but what happened there made everything that came before seem small and insignificant. That place... It came straight from the darkest bowels of Hell. Most of the guards were sadists, and they'd beat one of us in front of the other boys and then throw us in solitary with just enough food and water–that was if we were lucky and they didn't get creative with their torture. Some boys tried to run, and a few disappeared."

He stopped talking and gazed out at the night. The two hits from his joint didn't lessen the impact of his words. "I'm sorry," I whispered.

"Ivan found out they'd told everyone those dead boys had run away. I knew we were fucked unless we got ourselves out."

"How'd you get away?"

He put his free hand behind his head and gazed up at the sky. "We smuggled a few messages out to Xander's little sister, but they caught him one day."

I didn't want to know, but I asked anyway. "What happened?"

"They mounted him on a doorframe by driving screwdrivers through his palms then whipped him until his back was a bloody mess. He still has nerve damage and nightmares."

"What did they do to you?" I whispered.

He smiled mirthlessly. "They knew how to beat us without causing lasting damage but inflicting maximum pain, and they used deprivation and exposure regularly." He gazed down at me. "I don't want to give you nightmares, love. That's all I'm going to tell you."

Nodding, I patted his stomach. "Okay, I've got enough of my own. How long were you there?"

His hand spasmed against my shoulder, and Roman let out a long breath. "One year, three months, and five days. It felt like twenty years. Gideon and his agents got us out. Xander and his sister had a secret code, and Gia is the one who contacted the FBI."

"How'd you find out who the owners were?"

"The same way Alexa did. Ivan is slowly digging them up, and we've methodically hunted them down over the years. They avoided prosecution because, like your father, they were in positions of power. Revenge is a dish best served cold, and we've taken our sweet time." He ran his nose along my hairline and inhaled. "Drakos started going after the guards too. His mouth earned him a lot of enemies, and they seemed to target him more than the rest of us."

"What does your tattoo mean? *Veritas odium parit?*" I asked as I trailed my fingers down its length.

"Truth breeds hatred."

His words chilled me, and I slid closer to him, seeking his warmth. No wonder Roman wanted to cause my father whatever pain and anguish he could inflict. I couldn't blame him.

"Where does Klim Hudson fit in?"

"His younger brother died there. He and Gideon helped us get some semblance of our lives back, and assisted us in getting into law school."

It all finally clicked into place. "Klim tracked me down and offered me a partial scholarship. Then sent me to you and your firm on purpose, knowing who my father was." He held me to him but didn't answer. "When I asked you to release me from the internship, you refused."

"Klim probably thought if we got to know you, it'd help us let go of our hate. But I want Montgomery Cross to pay."

"By punishing me." I pulled away from him and sat up.

He watched me carefully. "At first, before I knew you, and what he did to you."

"And now? Do you still want revenge?"

"Yes."

Pain coursed through me. His admission didn't surprise me because his animosity and hatred were there when we first met. My subconscious had tried to warn me, but I couldn't put the pieces together until Alexa unburied my father's involvement in the Ranch. There was no reasonable explanation for Roman's insistence on me being his intern—except this.

I sat up and slid off the lounger. He watched me with hooded eyes. "I'm sorry for what happened to all of you. You'll never know how sorry." I took a step back, despair rising in my throat. "But I won't be a punching bag for him. He... doesn't care about me, and I loathe him."

Roman sat up. "You're not leaving."

I backed up. "I can't be with you if you only want to hurt me. When you're at work on Monday, I'll come and get the rest of my things. Fenn and my cousins will watch over me until the situation with the Stracks settles down."

He stood, and before I could get away, he snaked his hand out and grabbed my arm, pulling me into him. "I don't want revenge from you, and Fenn won't protect you like I will. Lionel tried to kidnap you today, and he's desperate and wounded now."

I struggled in his arms for a few seconds, then went limp. "You need to let me go before we get in too deep and hurt each other more than we already have."

"No. I can't."

"I hate that word."

"But you don't hate me. I've lost enough in my life—I'm not fucking losing you too." He swept me up in his arms and carried me into the house, not stopping until we were back in his bedroom. Laying me down on the bed, he crawled over me, bracing himself on his elbows. "That hellhole broke something in me, and now I want to hurt everyone to some degree. When it comes to women, I've twisted it into dominance and submission. But you love what I give you, and we fit in our own dark, fucked up way."

I turned my head and stared at the wall as Fenn's words rang in my head. We were both so damaged, I wondered if we could ever be happy. "I've already been broken, now I just want to be left alone." Tears leaked out.

He leaned in and licked them up, kissing the corners of my mouth. "No, you don't, and neither do I. Ivan gave me the police report, and I know exactly what happened to you. Your parents should be rotting in prison."

"Ivan had no right," I whispered.

"He had every right after what those fuckers did to us. Knowing what happened to you, and why, makes you one of ours. It makes you *mine*." Leaning back on his heels, he studied me in the moonlight. "We don't have to pretend with each other, and I love having you in the house, puttering around and asking a million questions. Leaving books and candy wrappers around. I want us to fight for this, Sweetness. Don't let him win again."

My heart ached, and bone-deep sadness settled over me. I wrapped my arms around him and pulled his face beside mine. "I'm sorry, I'm so sorry. I hate him so much..." Burying my face in his neck, I struggled not to break down.

He kissed my hair and wrapped his arms tight around me. "I never should have blamed you. But it brought us here, and I'm fucking keeping you."

His declaration loosened something inside me, and I turned into him and let go. Roman held me while I cried against him. It had been years since I'd let myself break down like this, but I couldn't hold back anymore. My mind emptied and shut down for once, and he settled me into his arms as I wept–for both of us.

Chapter 29

Roman

Leaning against the wall, I scanned the people coming and going outside Luna's classroom as she finished her last final before winter break. Studying had kept her busy, and Gideon took over Milo's bodyguard duties while Luna finished her exams. There hadn't been any sightings of Lionel lately, but we knew the psychotic bastard was still out there.

A few students started trickling out of the classroom, and Luna emerged behind them. She glanced around and spotted me, giving me a tired, happy grin. I loved watching that smile spread across her face. Straightening, I held out my hand, and she took it without thinking.

"Are you done for the semester, then?" I asked, taking her backpack.

"Yes. Thank you, Jesus. Did you spell Gideon off?"

"I did. It's Friday, and lunch is being brought into the offices. Do you want to go there, or somewhere else to celebrate?" She'd stayed at the house studying since Milo had been shot, but I knew she needed to get out.

"The office sounds good."

When we walked into the reception area, Brenna watched us quietly. She seemed more subdued lately and didn't glare at Luna.

"Hi, Brenna. Do you have any good snarky insults for me today?" Luna asked.

Brenna raised her eyebrow. "No, because I haven't thought of you at all."

Luna smiled. "That wasn't bad, and your eyelashes don't look fake at all." Brenna smirked as we walked past her through the office door.

Gideon looked up and smiled when he saw us. "Good afternoon, Ms. Fowler. How'd your last final go?"

"I think it went well, but I'll find out next week. What's been happening around here? How's the water law acquisition going, and how's Arthur doing?"

"Fine, and Arthur fits in surprisingly well. He's even better connected and well-versed in the gray nuances of the law than most the partners are."

She grinned. "I take it you found out he's married to a Spade, and he's Fenn and Sylvie's uncle."

We hadn't discovered that little tidbit until right before we signed the contract to bring him and his portfolio on board. Neither Luna nor Ezra mentioned it, and I had to give them credit for that little surprise. No wonder she wanted to intern with him.

We walked into the conference room and saw Drakos and Ivan dishing food out of to-go boxes. "What'd you order this week?"

"Italian from Francesco's," Drakos answered. "Hello, Luscious Luna. I haven't seen you in ages. It was nice of Roman to finally let you out of his sex dungeon. Are you pregnant yet?"

She shook her head. "Drakos, I think you're the reason the middle finger was invented."

Drakos wasn't fazed. He wrapped his arm around her shoulder and kissed her noisily on the cheek.

"Hands off, asshole," I growled. He smirked and smacked his lips together.

Ivan grinned at Luna. "He wasn't joking about the sex dungeon. How're you doing?"

"I'm better now that the semester is officially over. Where's Arthur?"

Ivan rolled his eyes. "He takes Fridays off. When he found out we usually work a six-day workweek, he told me I needed to get a fucking life. How come you didn't tell us he's family?"

"I didn't know you planned to buy my exit strategy out from under me. He's not the staid, dry attorney you thought he was, is he?"

Ivan shook his head. "He has more connections than Al Capone."

Xander walked in, and Luna stilled. When she set her drink down and watched him pensively, I realized this was the first time she'd seen him since I told her what happened to him at the Ranch. She got up and walked over, touching his arm.

"I'm so sorry, Xander," she murmured. "I didn't know about my father's ownership in the Ranch."

He shook his head and patted her shoulder. "You were just a child, we don't blame you."

Luna glanced over at me, and shame settled in my stomach. "I don't think *you* blamed me. Thank you for that." Xander carefully wrapped his arms around her as he stared at me over the top of her head. I met his gaze and raised an eyebrow because the quiet motherfucker wasn't going to make me feel guilty. I didn't want to ruin her now, but I sure as fuck wanted to keep her, and maybe that was worse. Luna stepped back and smiled up at him.

I didn't like it. I stood behind her, palmed her stomach, and pulled her into me. Xander watched her face as I leaned in and kissed her neck softly. When she reached up and curled her arm around the back of my neck, he smiled and shook his head at me.

Ivan squeezed his shoulder. "Let's eat." The moment passed, and we filled our plates with chicken piccata and antipasto salad while we talked about the past week.

As we finished up, Gideon walked into the conference room with a grim expression. He motioned me with his head, and I followed him out.

He didn't waste any time. "Fiona called. One of her dancers was attacked in the parking lot of Euphoria about an hour ago. They have Lionel on video, looking right at the camera."

"Fuck. Do you know which dancer?"

Gideon cocked his head. "Why? Do you know any of them personally?"

"No, but Luna does."

"Ah. I'm not surprised."

I stepped into my office and called Fiona. "Talk to me."

"Lionel Strack and another man I didn't recognize cornered Misty in the parking lot." Fiona paused, and I could hear her breathing heavily. "Roman, they stabbed her in the stomach and chest, then kicked her in the face as she lay bleeding. She'd be dead if Samuel hadn't been watching the camera feed, waiting for her to arrive."

I palmed the back of my head. "*Fuck*. How bad is it?"

"Her lung collapsed, her intestines were probably nicked, and she lost a lot of blood. They likely fractured her cheekbone, and she's in surgery right now." Her voice went husky. "I need Lionel to *pay*."

Fiona never lost her composure, and she was the consummate business partner, but this had turned personal for both of us. I hung my head and leaned a hand on my desk. Misty was one of Luna's friends.

"Text me Samuel's contact information, I'm sure he's at the hospital. We'll send someone to help him guard Misty so he can focus on her. Don't let any of your employees be alone in the parking lot. If you plan to stay open, you need additional security. Let me know if you want our help with that."

"I called the police, and I plan to go to the media. That fucking drug syndicate needs to rein him in. If they won't, I'm going to smoke that bastard out."

I straightened and stared out at the brilliant blue sky. "If we don't give them the courtesy of informing them first, this could blow up in our faces."

"I don't give one flying fuck right now!"

"You need to keep the rest of your people safe. Think, Fiona. Be smart. Give me twenty-four hours and then you can go public."

"Fine," she bit out. "You have until tomorrow at three." She hung up.

I walked into the conference room and shut the door. Luna was the first to sense something was wrong.

She gazed at my face when I walked in and stood up. "What happened?"

Drakos and Ivan had been debating about something, but when Xander stood too, they shut up and turned to me.

"Misty was attacked outside Euphoria."

Luna clutched her stomach, and Ivan tilted his head. "Who's Misty?"

"A dancer there, and my friend. How bad?" Luna murmured.

I clenched my jaw, not wanting to cause her more pain.

"Roman, how bad is it? Is she..."

"She's alive, but it's bad."

She reached out and blindly grabbed Xander's arm. He held her while I told them about what had happened.

A half-hour later, Fenn and Sylvie came to pick Luna up and take her to Fenn's house for safekeeping. I was down a man, so I'd called in *another* fucking favor from Fennick Spade.

When Sylvie walked in, she went straight up to Drakos and pointed her finger in his face. "You've had more than enough time to take care of Lionel fucking Strack, Lucifer. Now it's our turn."

Drakos smirked and grabbed her finger, pulling her into him. "Hello, my sumptuous Sylvie. Have you missed me?"

"Yeah, like gonorrhea or syphilis. Let go of my hand, Satan, and walk away."

He leaned in. "You can't banish your demons if you still like playing with them."

She rolled her eyes and tugged her arm away. "Come on, Luna. Let's leave them to it."

Luna came to me and put her hands on my cheeks. "Please be careful. I... like having you around." The mild surprise in her voice made me grin.

Sliding my hands around her waist, I pulled her into me, kissing her hard and deep. "And I like being around. Stay with Fenn and Kilian. And Luna?"

"Yes?"

"If you put someone else's safety above your own again, you and I will have more than just words."

She smiled sweetly and patted my cheek. "We'll see about that."

Chapter 30

As we walked out of the law firm, I stopped at Brenna's desk, and my serious expression must have given her pause. "One of the dancers at Euphoria was stabbed and beaten in their parking lot today. Don't go to your car alone, and when you get to the office next week, call one of the partners or Gideon to walk you inside, okay?"

Her hands froze over her keyboard, and she stared back at me.

"Promise me," I urged.

She slowly nodded. "I promise." Brenna brought her hands down to her lap. "Luna, are *you* alright? Are you safe?" Her eyes flicked to the collar at my throat.

Her concern seemed genuine, but I didn't understand where it was coming from. "As safe as I can be with one of the Stracks after me."

"You be careful too." She searched my face. "Not that I care or anything." This time, there was no bite behind her words.

When we were safely in Fenn's vehicle, he turned to me. "What do you want to do, Lou?"

Fury and helplessness roiled through me. "I want to take Lionel Strack out in the most brutal, vicious way possible."

Fenn blew out a breath. "Kilian texted me on the way over. He knows where Lionel is."

"Where is that fucking bastard?" Sylvie growled.

"About five blocks away from Euphoria. What do you want to do?" he asked me again.

My mind raced as hatred and relief flooded through me. I didn't know if I could voice what I really wanted to do. "How'd you find him?"

"His father owns a nail salon and a 'massage' parlor between Flamingo and Spring Mountain Road–one of those 'happy endings' parlors with apartments on the second floor. They use it to launder money, and Kilian has one of their regular customers on his payroll. The guy saw one of Lionel's men there."

I wasn't surprised Kilian found him first. Information was his currency, and he'd told me once that certain information could be more valuable than any tangible good.

Ivan and Kilian were both geniuses at gathering secrets, but Ivan seemed to have one flaw. He relied heavily on technology, whereas Kilian didn't have a favored method. He was an equal-opportunity collector, and he had people all over Sin City on his payroll.

Fenn glanced at us. "I'll drop you two off at my house, then we'll pick him up."

I leaned forward. "Should we tell Roman and Drakos?"

He shrugged. "It's up to you. Maybe tell them after we have him."

Sylvie's eyes narrowed. "We might even want to wait until after we eliminate the fucker. And you're not dropping us off at your house."

We talked Fenn into taking us to the mortuary and bringing Lionel to us when they picked him up.

I called Samuel to check up on Misty while we waited. "She just got out of surgery." He sounded like he'd been crying.

"Tell me honestly, how bad is it?"

"She's still alive, and they say she'll recover, but it was close. Between her collapsed lung, perforated bowel, and blood loss, it was touch and go. She's going to be recovering for a while, and Strack kicked her in the fucking face."

"I want to kill him slowly, Samuel."

He exhaled and pulled himself together. "Me too. One good thing–her cheekbone isn't broken, but she'll need more surgeries and a lot of time off."

Angry tears filled my eyes. I hated Lionel Strack almost as much as I hated my father. "Tell her we'll come see her as soon as she's up for visitors."

"I will. Luna, thank you for telling the girls to demand health insurance. The doctor just came in–I need to go."

I hung up and stared at my phone for a few seconds, adrenaline and hatred boiling through me. When Fenn dropped us off at the mortuary, I turned to Sylvie. "Do you remember the *Tales from the Crypt* episode where that dead man's wife wished he were still alive, and he came back thrashing and screaming from the embalming fluid burning in his veins?"

"I remember. That was a good one."

"Lionel needs to suffer, and I want to *really* hurt him."

Sylvie nodded slowly. "I have a few ideas."

"Like what?"

She rubbed her hands together. "Like playing show-and-tell before we torture him. There's that wicked-looking aneurysm hook, and the artery forceps."

"Your big suction needle would work too."

She gave me a creepy, happy smile. "My trocar. We'll start there and see how it goes."

An hour later, Kilian honked twice at the mortuary garage door with an unconscious and slightly dented Lionel Strack in the back of his vehicle. Sylvie opened the garage, and Kilian pulled inside. Fenn and Kilian pulled Lionel out of the back cargo area by his duct-taped hands. He groaned a little and started coming around.

"How'd you get him?" Sylvie asked.

Kilian grunted under Lionel's weight. "I sent a man in pretending to be with Door Dash. He tasered Lionel, and then we drugged him. Where do you want the ugly asshole?"

Sylvie studied the man. He was rotund and probably weighed three hundred pounds. "Let me get a gurney and we can load him onto it and take him to the embalming room."

Fenn stared at my tear-stained face and determined look while Sylvie grabbed a gurney from against the garage wall. "What are you two planning?" he asked cautiously.

"Do you really want to know?" My conscience told me I should feel guilty about wanting to torture Lionel before we killed him, but the guilt wouldn't come. Lionel had attacked Misty and he probably would have kicked her to death if Samuel hadn't been watching for her.

The men hoisted Lionel onto the gurney, and Kilian pulled out a knife and expertly sliced off the duct tape and his shirt. Fenn pulled his shoes and pants off, and then Kilian cut off his boxers. They were suspiciously efficient at cutting off his clothes.

Lionel's thigh was bandaged where Roman had shot him, and when Kilian disturbed the area, the man groaned and started waking up.

"Do you have any handcuffs?" I asked.

Kilian walked over to the SUV and rummaged through the glove compartment. He pulled out two pairs and a pack of thick zip ties.

I looked at him when he handed the items to me. "Do I want to know what else you have in there?"

He shrugged. "It's better to be prepared. Why don't you let Fenn and me take care of him? We'd do a straightforward BTK. Cut off a few fingers, maybe an ear, then kill and cremate the fucker and be done with it."

I glared at him. "He stabbed Misty twice, then kicked her in the face while she bled on the ground."

Kilian held up a hand. "We could also cut off his testicles, pour alcohol over the wound, and *then* kill him if that makes you feel better."

Sylvie cuffed Lionel's wrists to the gurney. "Save that for his father. This one's personal."

I pulled a few zip ties out and tried to get one around an ankle to secure it to the gurney leg. But Lionel had swollen, thick cankles, and the lone zip tie wouldn't make it all the way around both the gurney and his leg.

Fenn watched me with a pained expression, then took the zip ties out of my hands. "Here. Combine two together like this, then make sure it's tight enough." He deftly added one zip tie to another and secured it around Lionel's ankle, then repeated the process so there were two zip ties holding his leg down, and motioned me to do the other leg.

I combined the ties and secured his other ankle just like he'd shown me. "Okay, I think we have him."

My heart rate spiked, and queasy determination coursed through me. Sylvie and I wheeled him into the embalming room, and the men followed.

"You aren't licensed, you two can't come in here," she protested.

Fenn smirked and ruffled her hair. "That's the least of our problems, Syl. Besides, I want to watch you two work. You coming or not?" He asked Kilian.

Kilian sighed. "Fine, but this better not put me off my dinner."

I shot Sylvie a furtive eye roll. Kilian had come to family dinners with bloody hands and gore on his clothes countless times. The Spade family had a DIY approach to crime and punishment, and after watching my father twist and corrupt the judicial system to suit his own needs, I didn't entirely disagree with their philosophy.

We pushed Lionel's gurney into the embalming room, and Kilian looked around, shaking his head. "This area of the mortuary gives me the creeps. Some people don't like abandoned houses, graveyards, or sewer grates with red balloons. Those places don't have anything on embalming rooms."

Sylvie looked around as if trying to see it through Kilian's eyes. "Huh. It's like a second home to me. Okay, let's get started." She sounded almost chipper.

Performance nerves crawled through me at having an audience. I'd never purposefully tortured or killed someone before when it wasn't in self-defense, and Fenn didn't look like he was going anywhere. Sylvie and I put on protective gear as Lionel started waking up. I was by his head, and he saw me first.

"Well, if it isn't Fowler's little whore, Luna Cross. You stupid bitch. How's your face, sweetheart? Did I break your jaw when I punched you? And how's that stripper friend of yours doing after our little visit this morning? My brother wanted to play with her first, and I should have listened to him. He likes to have his women gang-raped, then he shoves broken bottles up their cunts and asses and watches them bleed out. How'd you like that, huh?"

I pulled down my face shield as he spewed insults and turned to Sylvie. "New plan—let's get the largest scalpel blade you have and a couple of suture needles, then cut his tongue out, cauterize the wound, and stitch his mouth closed. I don't want to listen to his garbage while we work on him."

Sylvie leaned over the other side of Lionel and snapped one of her rubber gloves next to his ear. "I like the plan—cauterizing the stump so he doesn't bleed back into his throat and drown in his own blood before we're done. Smart"

Lionel's ruddy face went from red and splotchy to pale and bloodless when he finally noticed the three Spades standing in the room with me.

Fenn grinned and handed Sylvie a wicked-looking scalpel with her name engraved on it, then looked across the gurney to me. "Can I help? I know this is your kill, but this fucker really needs to feel pain before he dies."

Lionel started rocking on the gurney and tried to spit at me, but it dribbled down his chin. "You worthless fucking bitch! I'll torture and piss on you, then violate your corpse. Silas will hunt you down and–ah!" He screeched in pain as Sylvie slapped his bullet wound, then stabbed him with the scalpel in his other thigh.

I flinched at the shrill sound and turned to Fenn. "If you want. We need to secure his head and find a spreader to keep his teeth out of the way."

Sylvie motioned to the PPE closet. "We'll definitely need rubber boots today. I don't want his urine and blood getting into my shoes." We left Lionel screaming and rocking on the gurney as I switched out my shoes for my yellow polka dot rubber boots, and Sylvie put on her glittery pink ones.

Kilian shook his head as he watched. "For fuck's sake. You two look like you're getting ready to do a little gardening in those boots. It's disturbing."

Fenn put on a plastic apron and a face shield, then turned and grinned at us like we were getting ready to finger paint. Over the next hour, Fenn helped us work over Lionel Strack, and Kilian leaned against the wall and played a game on his phone while we worked.

Sylvie did the honors with Lionel's tongue, and the smell of burned flesh, blood, and urine saturated the air. I leaned over his bloated, red face and looked into his pain-filled wild eyes after Sylvie finished cauterizing the stump.

"Now I'm going to cap one of your eyes with this cement-based glue." I held up the glue and flesh-colored eye cap for him to see. "Do you know why we're only doing one eye? Oh, that's right. You can't talk and spew your filth anymore because you don't have a tongue. So I'll just tell you." I studied his snotty, tear-stained face. "We're only capping one eye because we want you to see the instruments we plan to use on you. You love to rape and cut women up, so it's ironic two women are the ones who are going to torture you to death."

Fenn held Lionel's head still while I carefully glued his eyelid shut and capped it. The glue must have stung because he screamed when I applied it, then quieted down to a blubbering whimper.

While Fenn continued to hold his head, Sylvie and I stitched his lips up with long, curved suture needles using thick black thread. We didn't worry about these stitches showing. Instead, we sewed big X's across his mouth. "This is for Misty, and all the other women you and your family have brutalized or killed," I whispered as we sewed.

The sounds coming from him now were ghoulish and disturbing, and Lionel seemed to break at some point. He started sobbing and choking through his nose.

We gave him a few minutes to calm down, and then Sylvie held up the trocar to Lionel's one good eye. "See this? Do you know what the open needle at the end of this aspirating tube is for? It's used to suck the liquids, blood, and organs out of a body. Once that's done, embalming fluid is pumped back inside, which is mostly formaldehyde."

I patted Lionel's shoulder. "To a living person, formaldehyde is like acid. It'll eat you from the inside, and I've read it's an excruciating way to die. Almost like getting your vagina and anus ripped open with broken glass."

The zip ties Fenn used to secure his head cut across Lionel's brow as he tried to shake his head, sending blood into his eyes. He looked pretty ghoulish at this point, with black X's across his lips, one eye capped, and the other wide and terrorized.

Sylvie turned the trocar on, holding it comfortably in her hand. "First, I'm going to use this on your minuscule little testicles. We'll puncture your scrotum first, then stick this inside, and suck out your balls. They're small enough, it shouldn't take long."

Lionel went still for a few seconds, then convulsed and retched. He tried to force his mouth open, ripping a few sutures across his lips and causing his skin to tear in places. But his mouth stayed shut. Blood, mucus, and tears covered his face as he aspirated vomit into his lungs. Some of it oozed out his nostrils, and I gagged a little just watching him.

Kilian pocketed his phone and walked over, studying Lionel's face clinically. "He's going to asphyxiate and die from his own vomit. Do you want me to rip his stitches out and revive him?"

I stared down at Lionel and contemplated our options. Maybe he'd suffered enough, and we should just let him die. His face looked almost purple under all the bodily fluids. But then I thought of Misty, laying in a hospital bed with stab wounds and a contusion on her face from being kicked by this man.

I shook my head. "Sylvie, if we create a space between his stitches, maybe you could suck out enough vomit."

"Good idea." Sylvie turned to Fenn. "Clip a couple of stitches on the left side of his lips, will you?" He grabbed a small pair of steel scissors and clipped the threads. Then Sylvie shoved the trocar into Lionel's mouth and turned it on just enough to get most of the liquid out. Lionel's breathing stabilized.

Sylvie leaned over the gurney enough so he could see her out of his uncapped eye. "You and your family are a scourge to women. You stabbed Misty and kicked her in the face, then bragged about raping and torturing women. And you've tried to kidnap Luna–twice. So we're going to enjoy this. There are countless nerve endings in the male testicles, so this is going to *hurt*."

I looked at Sylvie with wide eyes. "What do you want me to do?"

She nodded to her scalpel over on the counter. "Make an incision in his scrotum and I'll do the rest."

My lips curled up in disgust, but I grabbed the scalpel, and before I could think too much about it, I leaned over Lionel's sweaty, stinky body, grabbed his scrotum with my rubber-glove-covered hands, and made a cut. Lionel screeched in pain and rocked on the gurney. I stepped back to give Sylvie room to work and looked down in time to see blood dripping off the scalpel onto my cheery yellow polka-dot boots.

Sylvie grabbed Lionel's scrotum at the base with one gloved hand to keep his testicles from retracting, stuck her trocar into the incision, and turned it on.

His back bowed off the table, and a terrible muffled, high-pitched scream came from his mouth as his scrotum emptied with a sick, sucking sound. I glanced over at Kilian and Fenn who both had disgusted, pained expressions on their faces, and Fenn held his hands over his crotch.

Kilian shook his head. "This is going to put me off my dinner, *and* give me nightmares."

Sylvie stepped back and studied Lionel. He was sobbing and choking now, and a few seconds later, he started retching again.

Kilian pocketed his phone. "Do you want to revive him for another round?" he asked. "You still haven't injected him with embalming fluid."

Sighing, I stepped back. This was probably going to put me off my food, too. "No, let it happen. It's somehow fitting he chokes on his own vomit." Kilian nodded and put his arm around my shoulder, knowing somehow I needed a little comfort.

But Sylvie huffed. "Come on, don't be a quitter. I wanted to see his reaction to embalming fluid."

Fenn pointed to Lionel's purple face. "If we're going to revive him, you need to do it now."

Sylvie glanced at me, then sighed. "*Fine*. I guess we're done." She turned off her trocar.

Over the next few minutes, we stood back and watched Lionel die of pulmonary aspiration. When he stopped convulsing and thrashing, then lay still for several minutes, Sylvie stepped forward and placed her fingers on his neck. His body twitched a little, and gas bubbles foamed out of his nose. I started and drew back. Even with the Spade cousins standing around me, I felt a little jumpy.

Fenn gazed down at the corpse and smiled. "From now on, when I need information out of someone, I'm going to use this threat."

Kilian winced. "You people worry me sometimes."

We started cleaning up and stripping off our protective gear when Fenn's phone buzzed. He pulled it out of his pocket and glanced at me. "Roman's on his way here, and he's pissing mad."

My mind raced, and I wondered how Roman knew where we were. Then my hand drifted up to my tracker. "What'd he say?"

He handed me his phone.

Roman Fowler: Why is my fucking wife at the fucking mortuary?

I started handing the phone back to Fenn but decided to answer.

Luna: This is your fucking wife. You told me to stay with Fenn and Kilian, and I did.

Roman Fowler: Do not FUCK with me right now. I set up a fucking meeting with the fucking Vegas drug syndicate and was about to walk in when Ivan informed me Fennick and Kilian Spade took Lionel Strack out the back of a fucking massage parlor.

Luna: Oh

As soon as I sent that text, I winced. Roman's frustration and fury seemed to vibrate through Fenn's phone, and there were *a lot* of f-bombs in his texts.

Roman Fowler: Oh? That's all you have? I'll be there in five minutes. Don't fucking move from where you are standing right now.

I winced and handed Fenn's phone back. "He said he'll be here in five minutes. What should we do?"

Sylvie started forward. "Hide the body, lie while the cremator heats up, then burn the evidence. Let's get cleaned up and meet them in Ezra's office."

Fenn grinned and folded his arms. "Or just own up to the fact that you nice people tortured and killed someone."

I pointed at him. "You helped us."

"Yes, but I'm not a nice person."

Sylvie waved her hand. "He was a psychotic murderer who got off on torturing and killing women. We did the world a favor. We're wasting time, what do you want to do?"

Sighing, I started putting the surgical tools into the bin to be cleaned and disinfected. "I prefer option one–hide the evidence and lie."

Kilian folded his arms and gazed around the room. "It looks like a butcher shop in here with all the blood and sharp instruments, and he'll want to see Lionel's body. There's no way you can hide all this before he gets here."

Pulling off her face guard, Sylvie sighed. "Damn it, you're right. Let's clean up a little and make it look less like an episode from *Dexter* though. I'll turn on the cremator."

A few minutes later, we heard sharp, impatient raps at the back door while we worked. Kilian walked out and came back with Roman and Drakos. Roman's eyes narrowed on me and his lips were slashed into a narrow line.

His palpable fury riled me, and I smiled sweetly at him. "Hi, Honey. How was your day?"

Chapter 31

Roman

My eyes drilled into her. "Do you think it's a good idea to provoke me right now, Sweetness?"

"Why would now be any different?" she returned.

The room looked like something out of a horror movie, except Luna wore cheery, blood-splattered, yellow polka-dot rubber boots. "What in the *actual fuck* happened here?"

"You're going to be disappointed if you came to help. It ended kind of abruptly."

Her retorts made me want to fuck that little mouth of hers with my hand on her neck so I could feel my cock lodged deep in her throat. It had been a frustrating day. "Your ass is going to have a long talk with my palm when we get home if you keep throwing lip at me."

Fenn chuckled. "It usually makes me want to give her a wet willy." He turned to Luna. "You into kinky shit, Lou?"

Kilian winced. "Fowler, don't put images like that in my head. She's like our little sister." Their obvious familial banter eased something in my chest.

Luna picked up a scalpel in one hand and a long, wicked-looking tube with a sharp end in the other. "You can always try, husband." Some of my anger dissipated because I fucking loved her calling me "husband."

Sylvie glanced at Drakos and grimaced. "You had to bring Beelzebub with you."

Drakos didn't get in her face for once–he was too busy staring at the tortured, naked, dead body of Lionel Strack handcuffed and zip-tied to the gurney. It looked like they'd been straightening up the prep room when we walked in, but no one had bothered to clean him up.

"Fuuck me, Lollipop," Drakos grinned. "I think your cousins are a bad influence on you."

I glanced at Drakos. Why the fuck was he calling Sylvie Spade *Lollipop*? Luna was right, there was something going on between those two.

Kilian frowned. "This wasn't *our* idea. I just wanted a nice, clean BTK."

BTK–bind, torture, and kill. He said it so casually, like this was a typical conversation for them. I studied Lionel's bloody, mutilated face with the black stitches across his lips and one capped eye. He also had a few stab wounds on his legs, and blood and bodily fluid around his groin area.

"Who's idea was it to torture him?" I asked.

Luna stepped forward. "Mine."

Drakos snorted. "There are three Spades standing next to you. There's no fucking way this was your idea."

But I studied her, and she held my gaze without flinching. "He bragged about stabbing Misty, and kicking her in the face while she lay bleeding on the ground. Then he told us about some of the other... things they like to do to women. I would've done worse if he hadn't died on us." Her voice shook a little, and I realized Luna was agitated and likely coming down from an adrenaline high.

Fenn shook his head. "It's always the ones you suspect the most. He was an evil bastard who deserved a bad end."

"Is that true?" Drakos asked Sylvie.

She shrugged. "We were all willing to make the psychotic weasel suffer before we killed him. Fenn's right, some people should be allowed to die with dignity. He wasn't one of them."

Kilian winced. "They sucked his testicles out. Luna sliced his scrotum and Sylvie used her trocar."

Drakos whistled and turned to Sylvie. "That's just *evil*."

Luna absently played with her tracker as she watched me. If she thought it was coming off now that Lionel was dead, we were heading for a fight.

"I think people forget I'm a Spade in all but name," she murmured.

Seeing Lionel's brutalized, fleshy body on the gurney gave me grim pleasure, but I was still angry she'd put herself in danger by helping to take him out. I hoped to God Silas and Jerome Strack never found out.

My eyes traveled back down to her boots. "Come here." She hesitated for a moment, but finally walked over to me.

I kept my arms folded and looked down at her. "Good choice."

"What happened at your meeting?" she asked.

"We aborted it and blamed police presence in the area. I was five minutes away from selling my soul."

"I should have told you we had Lionel sooner, but we were a little preoccupied."

Reaching out, I tucked a few strands of dark hair behind her ear and traced my fingers along her cheek. "At least you don't smell like formaldehyde today."

Fenn rolled his eyes. "The selfish asshole died before they could use embalming fluid on him, but he suffocated in his own puke first. Luna, why is it every time you're involved in a kill, it turns into a clusterfuck?"

The asshole was trying to provoke me again. I tipped my head down. "How many kills have you been involved in?"

"I'd rather not say," she muttered.

"Not that many," Kilian answered for her. "Three, including this one. Her father took a hit out on her when she was fourteen. The second man was after Sylvie, and this is the third."

Drakos whistled. "You two have been busy."

But I was stuck back on the comment about her father. How had we not heard about this? I planned to give Ivan shit for missing it. "Your fucking father sent someone after you? What happened?"

"I took care of it."

"What happened?" I repeated.

She glanced at Fenn, who raised an eyebrow but kept his mouth shut. Fenn likely wanted me to know about the danger she'd been in, even before getting on Strack's' radar.

Luna sighed. "I was able to... get him first." She looked so lost and sad that I wanted to rip her father's spine out.

"Tell me."

"I shot him." She shifted, and I knew there was more. "It was a little messy."

Fenn shook his head. "A little?" He turned to me. "He had a torture kit on him."

Hate and loathing churned in my gut. If her father was capable of sending a hitman after his own child, he needed to be put down like a rabid dog.

Drakos eyed Sylvie. "What's *your* story?"

"You wouldn't understand. My story isn't a picture book." Sylvie turned and continued cleaning up her workspace. "Stop annoying me."

"Do I annoy you, or is it something else?" Drakos drawled.

I cut them off before they could start in on each other. "We have a dead body and a crime scene. Is there a plan, or should I call in my clean-up crew?"

Fenn scoffed. "Don't insult us. We have a better clean-up crew, and our own crematory. This isn't our first rodeo."

Kilian started making calls, and I turned to Luna. "You need to leave the killing to me from now on. I don't want you implicated."

"Well, I don't want you implicated either. How did Ivan figure out Fenn had him?"

"Cameras. Why didn't you call us?"

"Because I wanted to be involved and knew you wouldn't let me."

It was hard to argue with that. I turned to the Spades. "I'm leaving and taking Luna with me."

Kilian nodded. "Good. We've got this."

Luna removed her wellies, and while she changed and cleaned up, I sprayed off her ridiculous yellow boots in the big industrial steel sink, shaking my head at the absurdity of it all. Glancing around, I realized we were all a little fucking nuts.

Chapter 32

Luna

When we walked into the house, Roman pulled me into his bathroom, turned on his oversized shower, and stripped me down. Then he carefully cleaned me while methodically working over my body with his mouth and fingers, before leaning me over the tile bench and giving me a few solid smacks on my ass cheeks.

"You knew I was looking for Lionel, but you went radio silent when the Spades found him. By involving yourself in his death, you put yourself in danger, wife. We need honesty, and I need to know you're safe." He punctuated each word with a hard slap and ran his hands along my burning globes and thighs before dipping his fingers into my dripping pussy. Then he let loose with another volley of spankings, interspersed with a few well-placed strokes. My confused mind struggled to process the pain and pleasure as he heated up my bottom and thighs. I tried not to moan or cry out.

"Are you going to do it again?"

Panting heavily, I shifted under his hands but stayed silent.

"I can do this all night if I need to. You might not be able to sit, or sleep on your back for a week, but–"

"Maybe," I gasped out.

He paused. "Maybe? What the fuck does that mean?"

"I might do it again, under the right circumstances. He deserved to die and I wanted to see him suffer–so much. He hurt her, and then kicked her when she was on the ground, bleeding." I hiccupped and buried my face in my arms, trying to hide my emotions.

He stilled, then exhaled slowly. "Fuck me." Leaning over my back, he pushed my wet hair to the side and trailed his lips across my shoulders. Then Roman wrapped his arms around my torso and pulled me up. "Are you talking about Misty or yourself?" he asked quietly.

Suddenly, I couldn't breathe. Memories pounded at me while shudders wracked my body. The shower was warm and steamy, but I felt cold inside. My mind tried to suck me back to that dark place, but this time I took big, deep breaths and fought with everything I had to stay in the present.

Roman turned me around. "I've got you, love, you're safe here with me. Just breathe." We sat naked on the bench as he cradled me in his arms, whispering promises and stroking my damp skin. My panting subsided and the crushing darkness started to recede.

"I'm so tired of going back there."

"Misty's attack hit a little too close to home, didn't it?" he asked quietly.

I nodded against his hard chest as I tried to steady myself. Turning, I straddled him and wrapped my arms around his neck, laying my head on his shoulder. "It still hits me out of the blue and knocks me off my feet sometimes. Do you have flashbacks?"

He squeezed me, wrapping his arms tight around my waist, his erection rubbing against me. "Not in the same way. The memories come out when I'm not in control, or I can't dictate my surroundings." He rubbed his whiskers across my cheek and sighed into my hair. "It's why I need to be in charge. You might've noticed by now I like to hold you down or tie you up when we fuck."

I snorted against his neck. "I'm aware you're dominant. We've been living together for a while now, and I'm wearing your collar and your ring. Have you had long-term submissives before?"

"A few, but those relationships were more regimented, and I've never lived with anyone."

"The women at the charity event."

He nodded. "I don't need that level of control with you, and I crave more than just a physical relationship. I want everything."

"What do you mean?"

Stroking my back, Roman leaned in and kissed along my jawline. "I want you here. I love coming home and finding you somewhere in the house, either studying in a corner or making food. You're like finding the sun after years of cold, gray weather, and I have an obsessive desire to keep you close and safe. I'm a possessive bastard."

"You don't say." I hugged him to me. I loved his care and possessiveness. Until the Spade family enfolded me into their ranks, I wondered if anyone would ever love or care about me, and I'd decided not to chance it. But with Roman, the choice had been taken out of my hands.

He leaned down and took a nipple in his mouth, sucking deep and then biting down, making me arch back and moan.

He slid his hands up my thighs and brought his mouth to my ear. "You always taste like citrus and smell like fucking cinnamon candy. Christ, I could eat you up."

I moved along his hard length, the friction rubbing against my clit. Roman palmed my ass cheeks and I winced. "Ouch."

He grinned and squeezed harder. "That's what you get for not informing me they found Lionel and not inviting me to your Spade family BTK party."

I leaned in and bit his earlobe. "You're funny. I've never tortured anyone before, but I was so enraged."

He ran his hands along my spine and brushed my wet hair behind my shoulder. "Those yellow boots of yours. Fuck me, I didn't know if I wanted to laugh or throw you over my shoulder and drag you away. Put my cock inside your cunt, wife."

I stilled at his brisk, lewd command.

"Unless you prefer I bend you over the bench again and finish spanking you."

Nipping his neck, I slid my hand between us and wrapped my palm around his thick, pulsing shaft. Then I worked myself down onto his massive length, moaning as he pushed up inside me.

He let me ride him for a few seconds and then growled against my temple and clasped my waist, slamming me down on his cock. Roman thrust his hips upward, spearing me deep as he pulled me down on him. I gasped and threw my head back.

"That's it, take it all. You can do it, just relax and open for me." His words singed my mind, and red-hot lust coursed through me. He held both my wrists in one hand behind my back and found my clit with his thumb. When he leaned in and ran his teeth across my nipple, my orgasm rose.

"Oh, God. Roman, I want to come."

"Not yet. Keep your hands behind your back." He repositioned his thumb against my clit and reached down to stroke my ass before sliding his finger between my cheeks. I stilled and my eyes flew open.

"I'm going to take you here. Soon." His lips tipped up in a menacing smirk as he worked me over, and when he stroked my back hole and slid a finger inside, I cried out as an orgasm crashed through me with so much force, my back curved and my head flew back.

Roman kept at me until my climax receded, then grabbed my hips and brutally thrust up into me. I brought my hands around to steady myself on his shoulders as he slammed inside one last time and climaxed long and hard. When he finally came down, he cupped my backside with his hands and squeezed again, getting another whine from me. "Your cunt, this ass, and these lush, rosy tits are *mine*."

Then he grinned and kissed my mouth, running his lips up to my forehead. "And this beautiful brain."

I wrapped my arms around his neck and squeezed him to me. "Then you're mine too."

He nodded slowly. "I am, and you're probably going to regret that."

I slept late on Monday morning and vaguely remembered Roman kissing my neck before he left for work. I decided to give myself a lazy day, and deep pleasure coursed through me at not having homework, classes, or anything else hanging over my head. Milo was recovering in the suite above the garage, and I took some food and checked in with him.

"Are you sure you have everything you need?" I asked for the third time.

"Yes. You fed me breakfast, brought me something for lunch, and left snacks and more books than I'll read in a lifetime. I'm good."

"Okay. Can I ask you a few questions about getting shot?"

Milo sighed. "I knew this was coming."

"Is that a yes?" I asked, sitting on a kitchen barstool.

"Fine. Three questions."

"Ten," I pushed.

"Four," he countered.

"An even five."

"Alright, but first get me two pain relievers out of the bottle on the counter. I'm going to need them by the time we're done." I smiled and got the pain meds and a glass of water.

I finally left him to convalesce in peace, changed into workout clothes, and headed to Roman's gym. He spent at least an hour a day in here, either boxing, lifting weights, or working out with me before he'd sometimes tie me up with his jump ropes and play with me on the mats. He had an inventive mind, and he liked to use restraints. I shivered, thinking of our last session.

As I wound down on the treadmill, I glanced at my phone and noticed a text from a number I didn't recognize. My finger reflexively moved to delete it and block the number, but I paused when I noticed a recorded video attached. Squinting at the screen, something caught my attention. I decided to play it.

The video was wobbly and showed a familiar dark marble floor. I recognized the office conference room door when the picture panned up a little. Immediately, I heard one of the partners talking and had to put the phone up to my ear to hear what was being said. I recognized Ivan's voice first.

"Luna's father doesn't give a rat's ass about her, and she hates his guts."

"I'm aware. I still plan to fuck her."

"So, what? Now you're thinking that maybe instead of ruining her law career before it starts, you'll just destroy her life by fucking her while she's your intern."

My body locked when I recognized Roman's voice and Drakos's glib response. Xander replied next, but I barely heard what he said as pain and betrayal slammed through me.

"She doesn't deserve to have her life wrecked so you can get your revenge."

"Thank you for stating the obvious, but I'm not sure that's how revenge works."

"I agree with Xander. You framing her for stealing from this firm and cheating on a law school exam is juvenile and asinine.

My heart cracked painfully when I heard what Roman had planned for me all along, as Gideon continued lecturing Roman.

Her father may have been a major shareholder in Bitter Creek Ranch, but Luna wasn't. And now that you all know her, destroying her will make you feel exponentially worse... You need to fix this."

"I still plan to have her."

By the time the recording ended, I'd slid to the mat and sat curled in on myself. After a while, I stood and walked numbly into the bedroom, pulled a suitcase out, and started packing a few things. My mind felt bruised and traumatized. I'd been so happy a few hours ago, and yet now I wanted to find a place to hide and lick my wounds; I needed time and distance to digest what I'd just heard.

Did Roman still plan to frame me and ruin my life? Maybe afterward, he'd throw me out and divorce me. Was all this–our marriage and this life together–just another sick way to hurt me?

When I walked into the mortuary apartment an hour later, the place felt lifeless and still as I lugged my suitcase inside. That's what I'd thought about Roman's house the first time I was there. Then I remembered Luna had started taking Carl down to the funeral home during the day so he wouldn't be alone up here, and the space felt even more desolate.

I walked into my room and looked around. It seemed the same, except there were fewer books, and half my clothes were missing. Looking around the room, I realized I'd never fully moved into Roman's stark modern home. I probably knew on a fundamental level that the relationship wasn't real.

With my father being who he was, and him contributing to Roman's traumatic past, I was a fool to think he would ever care about me. And maybe I wasn't worth caring about. I just didn't know Roman had planned to set me up in the most brutal ways possible and wreck years of sacrifice and work.

So why string this out? Lionel was dead and we could all return to where we were before Klim started this mess. Except I knew that was a lie–at least for me. I hadn't felt this level of betrayal and hurt since my father shut that closet door.

I lay on the bed and stared up at the ceiling. Roman would look for me here first, and I needed to tell Sylvie and Fenn what I'd found out, then get away from Roman's reach. But I didn't move. He was still at work and I had time. Besides, I was just... tired. Turning to my side, my eyes blurred with unshed tears.

Chapter 33

Roman

Ivan wanted to spar, so we took off early to the No Name boxing gym. The place smelled like disinfectant and sweat, and it hummed with grunts and the clang of equipment.

As we faced off against each other, Ivan eyed me and shook his head in disgust. "You look fucking *cheerful*. Are you getting it regularly from the missus?"

I raised an eyebrow. "You jealous, Knox?"

"Hell, yes. You're a bastard, yet you end up with a gem like Luna when you deserve someone manipulative and shallow like Marla."

"That's low, even for you, asshole." Ivan's digs put me in the right headspace to spar with him, and by the time we called it, we both had a few bruised ribs.

When I walked inside the house an hour later, the stillness seeped into my bones. Dusk had fallen, and dark shadows danced on the walls. Shaking off a strange foreboding, I glanced around for signs of Luna, calling out to her. Only silence greeted me. I walked into the kitchen and checked the back patio but didn't spot her.

Over time, Luna had added plants and a few odd knickknacks that meant something only to us throughout our house. She'd also started using the stark, modern sculpture in the entryway that had cost me seven figures as a coat hook. My lip quirked when I noticed a black hoodie hanging on it.

Sometimes, she curled up on one of the loungers under a blanket with her headphones on, studying or reading. She had become one of my favorite views, but I couldn't shake the feeling that something was wrong. I checked the garage and saw Luna's car was gone. When I called her cell, it went straight to voicemail.

Then I dialed Milo. "Have you seen Luna today?"

"Yeah. Late this morning she brought me food and asked a million questions about getting shot. But I haven't seen her since. Everything okay?" he asked.

"I think so. She's probably with one of the damn Spade cousins."

Disconnecting, I pulled up the tracker locator and realized with rising dread it was in our bedroom. My fists clenched when I found her wedding band sitting next to the collar on my nightstand. *Fuck.* What had happened between this morning and now? We'd been slowly building a life together, and things had been so fucking good lately. She'd opened up to me, and she seemed happy and content here. So what made her run? The smell of her skin and the citrus body wash she used lingered in the air as I sucked in a long breath. She didn't know the depths of my ruthlessness or obsession if she thought I'd let her just walk away.

My naughty little wife also didn't know that I'd put tracking on her phone and car. Without an ounce of regret or guilt, I pulled up the app and saw she was at the apartment over the mortuary.

I considered texting her and telling her to stay put or face the consequences. It'd be the fair thing to do based on my mood. I pocketed her collar and ring and strode to my car. Fuck that. It seemed she still needed to learn she was *mine*. We'd do this the hard way then.

Chapter 34

Luna

My body hummed, and I smiled drowsily as sleep receded. Roman had pushed my shirt up and trailed his fingers along my torso. I lay on my side with him spooning me from behind, my hips instinctively pushing back so I could rub against his hard length.

When he palmed my stomach and pulled me into him, my eyes snapped open and my body locked as it all came rushing back. Then I yanked away, jumped off the bed, and turned to face him.

He lay on his side, his head propped casually in his palm, but the angry gleam in his eyes gave him away. "Hello, *wife*. Do you remember your promise regarding this?" He threw my collar and ring onto the bed between us.

I stared down at them, my mind reeling. Dull pain and anger seeped through me when I thought of that video again.

"Nothing to say, hmm?" He sat up, fury rolling off him as I instinctively backed up. "What the fuck are you doing here without your wedding ring?"

His words finally penetrated the haze in my brain. "Go screw yourself, you sadistic bastard. Every promise I made became null and void after I listened to you casually discuss with your partners how you're going to ruin my life." My voice broke as I picked up my phone from the nightstand.

His eyes went harder, but something flickered in them. "What the fuck are you talking about?"

I pulled up the video with shaky fingers, pressed play, and set the phone down on the bed next to the collar. Then I quickly stepped back. When Ivan's voice came on the speaker, Roman's face went blank as he listened to the recording without moving.

When it ended, neither of us moved for several heartbeats. I turned to run, but he leaned forward and his hand snaked out to catch my wrist. "No. You are going to stay and listen."

"And you can go fuck–" He yanked me to him, spun me around on the bed, and brought his weight between my thighs.

"Oh, I'll be fucking you–soon. But first, we'll talk and then you will promise me, and *mean it this time*, that you won't run if we have misunderstandings or problems in the future."

I stopped struggling but stayed stiff and turned my head away. "You planned to destroy me–before I ever walked into your office. Did you feel powerful and vindicated when you laughed and plotted behind my back with your partners?"

"Luna, look at me. I didn't–"

"Fuck. You. Did you fantasize about getting me kicked out of law school while you fucked me? Did you think it would hurt me more to make me care for you first?" Tears gathered in my eyes, but I tried to hold them back.

He froze atop me, then carefully laid his forehead against my temple. "My plans fell apart two, maybe three days after I met you, but I was too stubborn and full of hate to admit it."

"Just leave me alone, you've hurt me enough. You got your wish," I whispered brokenly.

"No. And I've fantasized about you plenty. About how to get my filthy hands on you, and tie you down and fuck you until you screamed my name. Now, *look at me*." He took my chin between his fingers and turned my head so his dark eyes bore into mine. "There's nowhere you can go that I won't find you. I'm obsessed with your sweetness and razor-sharp mind. You've become my addiction and salvation, and I don't give one single fuck that you're too good for me. I'm not letting you go, and my black heart is yours."

"Don't say that to me. You don't mean it." I struggled beneath him, and he rolled until I sat on top.

"When I finally read Ivan's full report and found out you tried to stop your father–and the price you paid–I started planning how to keep you. And you were right, I could've protected you without marrying you, but I saw a chance and I fucking took it. We belong together. I would burn down the world for you, and I'll eliminate anyone who tries to hurt you."

Anger and betrayal still burned through me, but I knew some of what he said at least, was true. We did get along together, and we were probably addicted to each other. When I didn't want to strangle him, he also made me happy. I sat straight and straddled his hips, glaring down at him. "Would you really have done that to me?"

"If you'd been anything like your father, then fuck yes. But I knew after spending two days with you I wouldn't go through with it."

"Why didn't you let me go then?"

"Because I still wanted to make your life hell and get under your skin."

That's exactly what he'd done the first few months. I shook my head and smacked his chest. "You're such an arrogant *asshole* sometimes."

"I know. Come here, I want to kiss you."

Staring into his eyes, I wondered if I could trust him. "No more secrets or lies."

"I promise, love. Now come here."

He flexed his hips and rubbed his hard cock against me. I wanted our clothes gone, and I rocked on his length, a moan slipping from me. "I hate wanting you this much," I choked out.

Roman pulled my shirt off, then yanked my bra down under my breasts, pinching and pulling on my hard nipples. Jackknifing up to a seated position, he took my stiff peak between his teeth, biting down just hard enough that I screamed at the brutal pleasure.

"Then I'll have to change your mind." He stripped me and himself in seconds flat and flipped me onto my back. Then he crouched down over my body, nestling his shoulders between my thighs and running his tongue along my slit in long, thorough licks. My head flew back, and I moaned in delicious agony.

"That's it, Sweetness. Let me in, take everything I give you." He shoved two fingers inside me and pumped hard. My hips jerked as I cried out in pleasure at the burn, twisting under his assault.

Roman sucked and flicked at me until my head thrashed and I shivered and pulsed around him., an orgasm threatening. He gazed at me from between my legs. "Come for me." Leaning back in, he continued to work my clit.

"Oh, sweet Jesus," I breathed and climaxed all over his face, grabbing his hair and grinding myself on him. When I came down, he got on his knees and thrust deep inside.

My body slid up the bed until he grabbed my hips and held on as he pounded into me. I jolted under his brutal assault, and my pussy contracted around him.

"You can either love me or hate me because if you do, I'll have either your head or your heart. There's no escaping us, Luna, we belong to each other. Accept it, accept *this*." He shoved inside me one last time, threw back his head, and spilled his semen deep inside.

Our harsh breathing mingled in the still room as we came down, and Roman set my hips back on the bed when he finally pulled out. Running his hand up my chest, he carefully circled my throat and kissed my lips. Then he pulled me to him and held me until we both drifted off.

In the middle of the night, I woke as Roman rolled me over onto my stomach and palmed my pussy, playing with my clit and reaching underneath me to pinch and tug on my nipples. My mind was foggy with sleep, but my body responded to him like it always did.

He leaned over and gathered my wild hair in his hand, then he pulled my head back and licked my ear. "I want into your sweet hot cunt again. Nod for me."

Moaning softly, I nodded unthinkingly. His legs held my thighs closed as he worked into me, causing a tight, almost painful fit. "Arch your back, take me deeper."

I obeyed and he growled low against my neck. "Fuck, your slick little pussy always takes my cock so well. Like you were made for me." He reached around and strummed at my clit, working his hips against me, his words and the tight fit triggering the beginning of an orgasm. Then he stilled.

"Whose pussy is this, my little cum slut?" he growled as I tried to move my hips against his.

When I didn't answer, his fist tightened in my hair. "Who?"

"It's yours," I cried out. "Now move, Goddamn it!"

He chuckled darkly, slamming into me, and when he reached around and fingered my back hole with his thumb, I went off like a rocket. A few strokes later, he pinned me against the bed and orgasmed deep inside.

As I came down, tears hit my cheeks, all the pent-up pain and anger coming to a head. He pulled out, lay back on the bed, and rolled me over on top of him. I draped across his body like a rag doll as his semen and my tears leaked onto him, but I couldn't find it in me to care. He tucked my head into the crook of his neck and kissed and licked my tears until I'd settled down a little.

Squeezing me softly, he stroked my hair. "I'm sorry you heard that conversation. It was a long time ago, and even then I knew I couldn't do that to you. You're mine, and you have been since you walked into The Firm. Tell me you forgive me, Sweetness."

My lonely heart wanted to believe him, but my mind warred with the past. "I'm tired of being hurt and used. You don't know how... worthless and disposable you made me feel."

He stilled, then rolled me to the side. "You're the most precious and indispensable person in my life. I'm an unscrupulous bastard, and someday I'll probably kill your father, but I want a life with you, and I'm selfish enough to take it."

I laid my palm on his cheek and searched his eyes in the darkness. "If you can't care about me because I have his blood running through my veins, please let me go."

When he brushed my hair back and kissed my mouth softly, I knew I was lost. "I'm not letting you go, and I don't give a fuck who your father is. We're better together, we're a fucking *family* together. I need you. Come back home and be with me. Please."

My body tightened at his words, then gradually relaxed against him. I wasn't ready to say similar words back to him. He'd wounded me, and the instinct to protect myself was strong. "Don't ever make me feel that way again, or I'll find a way to make you sorry you ever met me." I laid my head on his shoulder, then reached around and pinched his hard ass.

"If I ever do, you're welcome to try." He sat up and studied me, then held out his hand with the collar and tracking device in his palm, his face carefully blank. "These are yours–you can do whatever you want with them. I won't apologize for the tracker, but I should have told you what the collar meant when I put it on you." I slowly sat up next to him and looked down at the beautiful necklace.

When Roman first put the collar on me, I chafed at the lock, and when my friends told me what it symbolized, I wanted to punch him in his beautiful face. But now, I missed the soft weight of the collar, and I'd grown used to the subtle feel of it against my skin. Slowly, I reached up and gathered my hair in my hands, lifted it off my neck, and turned. "Put it on me," I murmured quietly.

A long, broken sigh escaped him, and Roman leaned over and gently draped the collar over my neck, then clicked the lock in place. "Let's go home, wife."

Brenna wasn't at her desk when I walked into the offices a few days later. In fact, her reception desk looked cleaned out and unused, like she'd never been there.

I walked through the doors and found Gideon. "Where's Brenna?"

"She no longer works here." He smiled benignly, but something hard shifted in his eyes.

"Did she quit?"

"No. She was fired and marched out of the building without references."

"What? Why?"

"Because she recorded a private, confidential conversation here and then disseminated it."

It hit me that Brenna had sent the recording. I rubbed my forehead as I considered her possible reasoning and the ramifications. "Gideon, it's no secret that Brenna and I weren't best buddies. But I think she sent it to protect me," I admitted reluctantly.

Gideon tilted his head and studied me. "She's been antagonistic toward you since you started here. We've all witnessed it."

I waved my hand. "Yes, at first. But things changed, and I don't want her penalized if she was only looking out for me."

He shook his head. "Even if that were the case, she should never have recorded the conversation. We deal in confidential, sensitive information, and she used extremely poor judgment."

"That's true, but I don't want her life ruined because she tried to help me. I'm going to call and talk to her." Setting my backpack on his desk, I started digging out my phone.

"May I request that you wait and speak to Roman first?"

It had been a few days since Roman tracked me down and brought me back home, but I still ached when I thought of listening to that recording. I studied Roman's door, avoiding Gideon's knowing gaze.

"Do you know what was in the recording she sent me?" I asked him quietly.

Gideon winced. "I recall the conversation. Please don't hold it against Roman and the partners. What happened at Bitter Creek was a travesty, and what we saw when we raided it was unconscionable."

I nodded jerkily. "How about this? You call and talk to her and if she was trying to protect me, you agree to pay her a month's worth of wages and a referral if the partners feel they can't hire her back."

He sighed but didn't argue. "I believe that's fair, but I have to inform the partners."

"Fine, but they don't get to veto it."

Gideon's mouth twitched. "Alright, we have an agreement."

That day, I also started working with Arthur Thorgeson on water law cases. I'd gotten to know him from holidays, family get-togethers, and several of Ezra's Monday night dinners. He'd become my uncle over the years. Arthur married into the Spade family, and he had a large, bulbous nose and wild tufts of white hair that stuck out above his ears. Artie looked like a full-size garden gnome in an expensive seersucker suit.

He grinned happily when I found him in one of the large, plush offices. "It doesn't surprise me these boys bribed you away, but I think it's a good move for both of us."

I shook my head. "They didn't bribe me. Klim changed the internship, Roman stole me, and then decided to keep me out of spite."

Artie shrugged. "Semantics. I know Klim, and he doesn't do anything without a good reason. In the end, I think it's a win-win for both of us." He cracked his knuckles. "Now, let's get to work."

Late in the day, Gideon knocked on my door as I contentedly researched a complex water law issue. Behind him, a stylish woman with a spiky pixie haircut and pristine makeup stood with a tape measure around her shoulders. I pulled off my headphones.

Gideon gestured to the woman. "This is Aida, our personal shopper. She's here to take your measurements."

"For what?" I asked.

"Clothing befitting The Firm, and other sundries."

I leaned back and studied him. "What do you mean, exactly, by clothing befitting The Firm?"

Gideon glanced down at my plain white button-down shirt and black pants. "You're a delight to have in the office, and I'm overjoyed you and Roman are together. But you're now an official part of our firm, and as such we have a certain... reputation to uphold. Bespoke clothing is part of that."

I eyed him skeptically. "Why are you the one introducing Aida to me instead of Roman?"

"He thought I'd have more luck," he admitted bluntly.

"Luck with what?" I asked. I noticed Aida's lip twitch, and she looked like she wanted to laugh.

"Luck with talking you into a new wardrobe."

"What's wrong with my clothes?" I asked.

Gideon raised an eyebrow and folded his arms. "Nothing is *wrong*, per se. But I believe you purposefully wear dark, drab colors to blend in and downplay your figure and looks. Am I right?"

"Is that what Roman thinks?" I asked, stung at his analysis and annoyed he was probably right.

Aida rolled her eyes and stepped forward. "Gideon, love. I adore you. But I have it from here." She patted his arm and waved her hand.

Gideon gave her a small, formal nod. "As you wish, my dear." He turned to me. "Remember one thing before you start in on Aida. Clothes aren't just for covering a body, they can also be used as a weapon and a statement."

After Gideon walked out, I eyed the woman. "Hello, Aida. I don't really need new clothes."

Her berry red lips tipped up, and she pulled her tape measure off her shoulders. "Very few people nowadays *need* new clothing. But Gideon's right."

I inclined my head. "Tell me the truth. What, exactly, did Roman tell you I needed?"

"Whatever I can talk you into. He also mentioned he's a 'jealous bastard' and besides lingerie and a few... select pieces, he prefers your professional style but just wants to upgrade the quality and cut."

Her answer appeased me, and I stood to shake her hand. "Alright, I can live with that. I'm Luna Cross, and I have a few questions."

She smirked charmingly and returned my handshake, then closed the door and locked it behind her. "Both Roman and Gideon warned me about your questions. Strip first so I can get accurate measurements, and I'll answer questions while I work. You're not an emaciated stick, and with your bone structure and those green eyes, it'll be a pleasure clothing you."

A few days later, clothes and shoes started arriving at the house. At first, it was fun to try on the clothes and see what Aida had picked out, but after the third enormous delivery, the novelty quickly wore off.

"I'm sending some things back, and there's no way I can wear all this," I informed her over the phone.

She laughed. "Even though you two haven't been married long, you seem to know each other well. Roman warned me this would be your reaction, but let me explain a few things."

"I'm listening."

"The partners are some of my richest clients, and Roman is *loaded*. You'll soon be a full-fledged attorney, and clothes and style are a big part of that. Lean into it."

"Aida, I understand and don't disagree. But I'm... overwhelmed by the sheer volume."

"Fine, I'll slow it down and if something doesn't fit or you truly don't like it, send it back. A few times a month, I'll pick up those items and drop off a few new things. We'll get into a rhythm. Trust me."

I stood in our closet a few weeks later, staring at racks of beautiful, expensive new clothes. Roman walked in, and I turned to him. "Do you remember when you bought me that shimmery white gown for a charity event a while back?"

Roman's mouth tipped up. "I do, and I'd still like to see you in it."

"And do you remember what I told you about buying me clothes?"

He smirked and walked over, wrapping his arms around me. "Why do I feel there's no right answer here?"

My lips quirked. "Because you're smart, but you never listen."

He bent down and sniffed my neck. "You were my intern, now you're my *wife*, and I do listen to you, especially when you're making those sexy little whimpers while I'm–"

I put my hand over his mouth. "If you start with the dirty talk, we'll never make it to Ezra's house for dinner. It also pains me to say this, but thank you for the clothes. Now I just need Aida to stop sending me things."

Ezra had invited us to a Monday night dinner. He didn't hold them every week anymore, but when he did, he expected me to be there. Today, he'd specifically asked that I bring Roman along.

I picked out an emerald-green maxi dress that had been delivered a few days ago. Along with the dress, a slew of delicious silky underwear and lingerie had also arrived.

Stripping off my robe, I slid into a lavender thong and matching sheer lace bra.

He watched me dress with hooded eyes. "We might have to be late," he murmured as his hot gaze trailed down my body.

I held up a silky lavender sash that had come with the lingerie and turned to him. "What's this for?"

He grinned wickedly. "It's a blindfold or tie to use while you're wearing that lingerie." Roman fingered the strap on my lavender thong. "Or nothing at all."

With that bit of information, I stuffed the cloth back into the drawer and held up my hands. "If you touch me, we'll be late."

"I can do quick and dirty." He ran his finger over the swell of my breast, then leaned in and followed its trail with his tongue. My head fell back, and he wedged his thigh between my legs. "Is that a yes, Sweetness? You look like a fucking wet dream, and I want to tie your arms, bend you over the bench, and fuck you like you're a porn star in a low-grade production."

I let out a low moan and rode his thigh while he reached into the drawer and pulled out the silk tie. We walked into Ezra's house a half hour late, and I still had Roman's semen seeping out of me.

"Sorry we're late," I called out as we rounded the doorway into his dining room. When I glanced over and saw who sat next to Ezra at the table, my breath whooshed out of me, and I stopped short.

Roman felt my body lock and grasped my hips, gently nudging me to the side so he could stand beside me.

I barely registered the others sitting around the table, or the uncharacteristic quiet in the room. The woman sitting next to Ezra looked older than I remembered, but she was still striking as she gazed haughtily at us. She styled her dark brown hair differently now, but the woman looked like an aged version of me. My *mother* sat next to Ezra at the table.

Chapter 35

Luna

Evelyn Cross, the woman who'd birthed me, gazed at me without emotion as I tried to process the strange sight of her sitting at Ezra's dining room table.

Roman took my hand and squeezed. "What the hell is she doing here, Ezra?" he growled.

It didn't surprise me he recognized her since we looked so much alike. His hard, warm presence helped ground me as I pushed back some of my dread.

Ezra stood. "She came to the mortuary a few days ago, looking for you. I asked her to leave, but she kept coming back. You can either kick her out now or listen to what she says, then make your own decisions." He looked around the table at my adopted cousins, who were all scowling viciously at her. "I arranged the meeting here so you'd have plenty of family around." I appreciated Ezra's words more than he'd ever know.

Evelyn stood, rounded the table, and carefully moved toward me. "I didn't know what Montgomery had done to you. At first, he said you wanted to spend your birthday with Sylvie. When I found out what really happened, it was too late."

Too late? I didn't know what that meant to her, but it was true for me. During the year following the attack, I believed this woman would come for me. I thought she would reach out and explain that maybe she didn't know, or that she chose me instead of the monster who was my father. I finally let go of that vain hope when my birthday, and then the holidays, came and went and I didn't hear a word from her. The ache of rejection and worthlessness lessened every year, and the Spade family—and now Roman—more than filled the void she'd left.

I'd been so young and lost, even before that hellish day. Roman squeezed my hand again, reminding me of his presence, and Sylvie came over to stand on my other side.

"I don't care," I answered quietly.

Evelyn stopped and lowered her hands. "What happened to you isn't my fault, Luna. I was a victim too, and I've lived with that man for almost thirty years, putting up with his vicious mood swings and—"

"Why are you here?" I interrupted. "You didn't come to apologize or try to make amends. Otherwise, you wouldn't be standing there blaming him."

She glanced at Roman, then looked down at our linked hands and let out a long, frustrated breath. My father might be a monster, but she'd chosen him, and his power and money, over her own child all those years ago. I thought that made her a monster too.

"Can we talk in private? I don't know these people, but I know their reputation." Her lip curled in faint disdain.

She hadn't changed. "Really? What is it you've heard?"

She seemed to remember where she stood and glanced around. "Well, your father complained about you living with them often enough."

"What did he say about them?" I asked mildly.

"That they're thugs and criminals."

"That's interesting coming from someone like Montgomery Cross. And you. A cryptic scribbled note on the back of a salon card doesn't compensate for years of neglect."

Her head jerked back. "You're still alive, and you look fine to me."

I studied her contemptuously. "I was *a child* when you threw me away like garbage, and you're not stupid. There's no way you could afford the three homes you have or all the clothes, cars, or vacations if your husband wasn't as crooked as an intestinal tract. He's a fucking *judge*, for God's sake, and you know where the money comes from. Why are you here?"

Pride and anger rippled through her. "How dare you compare me to him, or these people–"

I stepped forward and slapped her across the face. Her eyes narrowed to slits, but she didn't try to hit me back. "Shut. Up. One of 'these people' found me in my own blood and filth, dying in your fucking clothes closet. Then she and her family took me in, healed me, and showed me what a real family was. You're no better than him, and at least he isn't a hypocrite about what he is. Now, *what do you want*?" I asked again.

Her glassy eyes scoured my face, my handprint visible on her cheek. "I want your evidence against him. He's gotten worse over the years, and I need a way out that won't leave me destitute."

Sylvie snorted. "What's the matter, Evelyn? Or should I call you Mrs. Montgomery Cross? Weren't you smart enough to collect your own insurance? Luna was eleven years old. Obviously, she didn't get her intelligence from you."

Evelyn turned and sneered at her. "Hello, Sylvie dear. I hear you've become a mortician, of all things. Was that your dream job growing up, and what do you think your mother would say if she hadn't decided to hang herself?"

I wanted to scratch this bitch's face, but Sylvie just rolled her eyes. "My mother knew what I wanted to do, and she supported me. Even with manic depression, that woman was a better mother than you'll ever be. By the way, did you know your husband was screwing half your neighbors? He even hit on my mother, God rest her soul. She laughed in his face."

Evelyn's hands fisted. "I'm done talking to you." She turned to me and sucked in a breath. "Well?"

"Does he know you're in Las Vegas?" I asked.

"No. I told him I'm getting a little surgery done."

"What's in it for me?"

"What?" She had the gall to sound affronted.

I smiled coldly. "You heard me. Why should I help you unless there's something in it for me?" Glancing over at Roman, I wondered what he thought about all this.

"What do you want?" she asked carefully.

"My kneejerk reaction is to tell you to go screw yourself. But I'll talk to my husband and family, and get back to you. Give Ezra your phone number."

"He already has it," she snapped.

"Good, then leave."

My mother gazed at me with intense dislike. "Fine." She walked back over to her place at the table and grabbed her expensive designer purse. She sniffed as she passed me. "You didn't turn out at all like I hoped."

"Thank God for small favors," I retorted.

On the drive home after dinner, my mind raced as I thought about my parents, and what I really wanted.

Roman glanced at me. "What're you thinking?"

I turned to him. "My mother wants that information so she can blackmail my father into giving her more money in a divorce settlement. If she got a divorce based on his salary as a judge and not all his under-the-table business deals, bribes, and payouts, she'd never be able to afford the lifestyle to which she's grown accustomed."

"That's true. So what do you want from her?"

My mind raced through different answers, but I circled back to one thing. Turning to him, I studied his beautiful, severe features in the dark. "I want justice. For all of us."

The next morning, I texted Alexa and Fenn and asked them to meet us at the law offices later that day.

Fenn called less than a minute later. "What are you up to now, Lou?"

"Why would you ask if I'm up to something?" I countered.

"Because I know you."

"I'm ready to go after my father."

Fenn went quiet on the other end, then let out a long, happy sigh. "It's about fucking time. Okay, I'll be there." Fenn had been prodding me to let him take my father out for years. Up until now, I was too scared because I knew Montgomery Cross had a long reach, and his retaliation terrified me. But I knew it was time.

Alexa and I sat in the conference room that afternoon when Roman and Ivan walked in. Then Fenn sauntered in a few minutes later with blood splatters on his shirt and bruised knuckles.

I shook my head in mild disgust. "Fennick, it's barely past noon. You ask what dangerous thing I'm up to when you're the one who can't go a full day without fighting. What happened? Where have you been?"

He ignored my questions and grinned. "If I didn't let off a little steam now and then, I'd blow like a bad high school science experiment."

Ivan smirked and stroked his beard. "You should box with us at Colton's gym, it's good for working off excess energy."

Fenn winced and rubbed the back of his neck. "He banned me a while ago. Maybe if you put in a good word, he'd let me come back."

Roman glared at Fenn. "It'd be worth it to get you in the ring so I can beat the shit out of you for bringing Lionel Strack to Luna and Sylvie instead of me."

"Anytime, *cousin*." He grinned and turned to me. "Tell everyone why we're here."

I leaned forward. "I'm ready to go after my father, but I need help. My mother says she wants the account information I stole to use against my father–the same leverage Fenn used when he sent that man's arm back in a box."

Ivan's eyebrow rose. "What arm, and what man?"

"It belonged to the hitman my father sent after me when I was fourteen."

Ivan sat back. "What the fuck? How'd I miss *that* when I did your background check?"

"Probably the same way you missed finding Lionel," Alexa muttered out of the corner of her mouth.

Ivan raised his eyebrow at Alexa. "What was that, Peaches?"

Alexa blushed and glared at him. "Don't call me that, *cabrón*."

Roman leaned forward and interrupted their budding argument. "If she gives that information to her mother, Luna loses her own leverage, and chances are her father *will* come after her again."

"Then don't give it to her," Fenn answered. "She's a bitch who deserves to rot."

"But what if we use her to flush him out?" I asked.

"What're you thinking?" Ivan asked me.

I leaned forward. "We pit them against each other and take them both down."

Over the holidays, we celebrated with a few Spade family dinners and a poker brunch party at the mortuary. All the partners showed up, and even Xander came for a little while, but he didn't stay to play poker.

Ivan beat Alexa in a stunning upset. In a tense final hand, she laid down three queens, and I thought she'd easily beat him. But she looked a little sick when he stroked his beard, leaned forward, and laid down three aces.

I suddenly suspected those two were playing for more than just the large pile of chips in the center of the table, and I knew in my bones Ivan had somehow cheated.

He stared at her like she was his first meal after a long fast as he laid his cards down. "Three aces beats three queens, Peaches."

Alexa's eyes flared, and she pushed her chair back and stood. Ivan leaned back and stretched his arms behind his head, his posture deceptively casual as he watched her with predatory hunger. She glared at him silently, then turned and strode out.

"See you tomorrow," he called, grinning as she held up her middle finger in response.

Sylvie turned to me and asked quietly, "What was the final bet?"

I shook my head. "More than just money I suspect. There's definitely something going on with those two."

She nodded and stared, unseeing, at the door. "Those three are sneaky fuckers. Ivan hides it better than Roman and Drakos, but he's got that same possessive, sadistic streak in him. You're right, something's happening between them."

I snickered. "You're a damn hypocrite, and not as sly as you'd like to think. What's with you and Drakos?"

She scowled and stood. "What? Nothing. I don't hate him, but if he were on fire and I had water, I'd drink it."

"You know what's interesting?"

She looked at me suspiciously. "What?"

"I never asked you if you hated him. Your answer gives you away."

"Oh, shut up." She turned and started clearing off the tables, obviously wanting to end the conversation. My two best friends were involved with two of the partners. I had no idea how I felt about that.

Roman and I exchanged gifts in bed. He gave me a trip to Bali, and I bought him a Cherry Box subscription for a monthly sex toy box. I also told him that within reason, I'd try out the merchandise with him. I started to worry when, later that morning, I saw him peruse their website with a cheerful gleam in his eyes.

We took a few days off during the holiday break, but I was anxious to start interning with Arthur, and Roman had work piling up, so we went into the office together every day before my last semester started.

Gideon had hired a temp agency to fill the receptionist spot until they could find a permanent receptionist. The search hadn't been going well. The first receptionist was a young man who asked me to lunch on his first day. Roman found out, and the man didn't come back the next day.

When I asked Roman about it, he shrugged. "Your wedding ring and collar are prominent enough that he's either clueless or just didn't care. Neither trait is desirable in an employee."

The receptionist today looked like Miss Trunchbull from *Matilda*, complete with the mean scowl and hairy mole.

Wanting to give her the benefit of the doubt, I raised my hand and smiled when we walked into the reception area. "Good morning. I'm Luna–"

She turned her office chair to face Roman and talked right over me. "You have three messages and a Fed Ex package. I emailed you regarding the messages and set the package on your chair." Then she turned back to her computer and started typing. She was gone before lunch.

Alexa, Sylvie, and I met for dinner at Luigi's at the end of our holiday break. We ordered, got our drinks, and settled in.

Alexa got right to the point. "We have an idea about your father and how to smoke him out." We discussed what she and Ivan had been working on for the next hour while plowing through pasta and wine. When I looked up from the decimated plates on the table, Ivan and Roman walked in together. When Alexa looked up and saw Ivan, she flushed and went quiet. That's when I started to worry.

The next morning as I made coffee, I turned to Roman. "What's going on with Alexa and Ivan? After declaring her undying dislike for men since I've known her, Sylvie says she's practically *living* with him."

He took my coffee cup and put it on the counter, then pulled me to him and wrapped his hands around my hips. "It's their business. You need to let it go."

But I didn't let it go. She seemed withdrawn, and I was concerned. Alexa stopped answering my calls and texts after telling me she didn't know what I was talking about, and everything was "just fine." So, I went back to badgering Roman.

He eventually lost his patience one evening out by the pool as we sat in the loungers.

"I told you if you asked me again, I got to pick your punishment." He grinned and stood, pulling his belt out of his belt loops and grabbing my wrists. He flipped me around and deftly tied my forearms behind my back.

"What are you doing?" I squirmed as he wrestled me into place on the lounger.

"Giving you something else to think about." He pulled my leggings and thong off, pushed my upper body onto the lounger, and palmed my ass. Then he spread my thighs as far apart as they would go and spanked my pussy with his large, rough palm.

"Ouch, Goddamn it, you fucking caveman!" I ruined my outrage by laughing breathlessly and trying to wiggle away.

Leaning over me, he murmured in my hair. "I warned you, Sweetness, but you kept at it. I think you're craving a hard pussy spanking." He reached in and cupped my wet slit, running his fingers through the moisture there. His next smacks targeted my inner thighs until I was a panting hot mess underneath him. He understood what aroused me, and I knew he needed to tie me up and control my pleasure sometimes. We were a match made in hell. My thoughts spun away as my body absorbed the erotic stings and dark pleasure.

I moaned as he worked two fingers inside me, pumping hard while I panted beneath him. Arching my back, I pushed myself against his fingers. "Fuck, that feels so good."

"Your soaked, swollen pussy tells me you don't mind being tied up, pussy-spanked, and finger fucked. I'll remember that."

"Please, I want to come," I whimpered. He hadn't touched my clit, and I knew it was on purpose.

"You'll come when I want you to come—with my cock buried so deep inside, you won't be able to walk tomorrow without feeling the wreckage." He smacked my thighs, then ran his palms over the sting.

His hands disappeared, and I heard him unzip his pants and shed his clothes. Then he pulled my hips up. "Spread your knees wider, my sweet little cock slut." He slapped my ass, and I cried out. Then he drove inside me as he held my hips immobile, working his cock deep, just like he'd promised.

My pussy was so tender and sensitive, I shivered when he stroked me as he took me hard and deep from behind. Groaning, he wrapped his hands on my shoulders as he pounded into me. Moments later, when he finally reached around and stroked my clit, I came, screaming so loud he wrapped his other palm across my mouth. He orgasmed seconds behind me.

It took a few minutes to settle down, and he undid the belt he'd cinched around my forearms and grabbed a towel. After cleaning up, he held me while we watched dusk turn into night. A cool breeze picked up, and he grabbed a plush cashmere blanket and draped it across us.

A few stars appeared in the darkening sky as he kissed the top of my head. "I know you're worried, but they need to work it out. Alexa will find you and Sylvie when she's ready to talk. But if you want to keep bringing it up, I have a few other ideas." I could hear the grin in his voice, and my pussy clenched.

Chapter 36

Luna

I didn't throw up this time. My mother came to Las Vegas again, and we'd agreed to meet her at Ezra's office the next morning. The night before, I suffered another nightmare. Roman woke me up as I gasped and struggled against him. Then he sat with me on his lap, trailing his fingers along my skin until I calmed.

"I've got you, love. Neither of those fuckers are going to hurt you," he murmured into my hair. I turned my face into his neck and breathed him in. Only my father appeared this time, and thankfully my dinner stayed down.

When we arrived a few minutes late that morning, coffee and a plate of scones were on the desk. Ezra was always the consummate gentleman, and he believed in manners, even when his guests didn't deserve them.

"Luna, are you going to help me or not?" my mother asked impatiently seconds after we arrived.

I ignored her and walked over to hug Ezra. "You and Sylvie should come to dinner tonight."

He smiled. "She's working this morning, but I'm sure she'd love that. The apartment is lonely without you and Alexa there."

"Thanks for allowing us to use your office."

Ezra squeezed my arm. "No problem. I'd step out and give you some privacy, but I don't trust a woman who leaves her child for dead and doesn't contact her until she wants something. Pretend I'm not here."

Evelyn sniffed but didn't respond. I turned to her and crossed my arms. "Why are you here?" Seeing my own green eyes in her cold, annoyed face was so odd. A wave of gratitude swept through me toward Ezra and the Spade family for taking me in and loving and nurturing me. If they hadn't, I probably would have turned out as frigid and unhappy as this woman.

"I need that information. He's getting worse, and I'm afraid of him."

"Has he hurt you?" I asked.

Evelyn looked away, and I saw her swallow heavily. "He's hit me, and he threatens me almost every day."

The silence in the room felt heavy and thick. Ezra stood, poured coffee, and handed the cups to Roman and me. He had a slight tremor in his hands, and as I reached out to take the cup, a few drops splashed over Evelyn's white linen sheath.

She jerked back and glared at Ezra. "Damn it! You're too old to play the gracious host anymore."

Ezra grimaced at the small brown stains. "My apologies, I have a stain removal stick in the bathroom that may work."

As he ushered her to his restroom, he looked back over his shoulder and gave me a slight nod.

While they worked on removing coffee stains, I quickly rummaged through her five-thousand-dollar designer handbag, pulled out her phone, and handed it to Roman. He then stepped out of the room. When Ezra and Evelyn came back, I listened to the woman lie through her teeth.

"If you give me a copy of those account records, I can use it as leverage to get a better settlement. He won't know where I got them, so you should be perfectly safe."

I told her what I expected in return. While we talked, I knew Ivan and Roman were in Sylvie's office a couple of doors down, adding a program to Evelyn's phone so we could eavesdrop on her conversations. They also planned to pull data from it if they could.

Roman returned a few minutes later with his own phone in hand, as if he'd just gotten off a call. But Evelyn had picked up her handbag and set it on her lap. As Evelyn got ready to leave, she put her bag on her shoulder.

I folded my arms and addressed her. "I'll let you know when I decide. Have you given him divorce papers yet?"

She turned to me. "No, but as soon as I have some insurance, my attorney plans to have him served."

While she faced me, Roman stepped up behind her and deftly slipped the phone back into her bag. Seconds later, she said goodbye and walked out.

We sat in Ivan's office an hour later, listening to Evelyn make several phone calls from her hotel room. It'd been scary getting her phone back in her bag, and I was still coming down from the adrenaline high.

As we listened to her make the first call, I heard a man's voice on the line. At first, I thought it was my father.

"Hello, darling. How did your fishing expedition go?" he asked.

"I think they bought it. I'm in my hotel room now. She wants his records on that horrid boys' ranch Montgomery was involved in, and whatever else I can scrounge up about his business dealings in return for the account numbers."

"Are you going to provide those?" the man asked.

Evelyn hummed thoughtfully. "I don't have much to give them. Since Luna stole that information, Montgomery has been much more careful with his records. I've looked around, but his account passwords are the only thing I've found that might be useful."

"Offer her a small share of your settlement. She doesn't have to know you plan to take *all* the money," the man suggested.

My mother agreed. "It would be better not to implicate Montgomery anyway, since we don't want the police looking too closely into his finances."

"Give her the secret email account I set up for you, and tell her to send those account numbers in exchange for... say, a million dollars. Start there. If my niece is as smart as I remember, she'll ask for more."

Evelyn giggled, sounding so carefree and young it was creepy. "Just think, Alistair, in a month, maybe two, we should be on some tropical island, or maybe Europe somewhere, living rich and carefree without him, the police, or some government regulator breathing down your neck." They continued planning and scheming as I sat down hard in a chair.

When they hung up, Alexa raised a brow and turned to me. "Isn't Alistair your uncle's name?" she asked.

"Yes," I answered faintly, my mind struggling to compute this strange twist.

She grimaced. "Holy shit. Your family might be even more dysfunctional than mine."

Roman shook his head. "Jesus, what a mess. She's having an affair with Montgomery's brother, which puts you in even more danger. Your father isn't going to give up that money easily, especially if he finds out it's his own brother who's fucking his wife."

Evelyn made two more phone calls, one to her divorce attorney, and the last to a day spa to schedule an appointment.

I stood and paced. "Their divorce will make that *Housewives* show look like child's play."

Ivan picked up an expensive-looking pen and started twirling it through his fingers as he stared at Alexa. I turned to them. "If my mother kept those passwords on her phone somewhere, can you guys find them?"

Ivan quit twirling the pen. "Yeah. I downloaded her data while I had her phone. When she gets home, I can probably access her laptop too."

I resumed pacing. "If we find his account passwords, can we drain his balances?"

Ivan watched me carefully. "If he finds out she's been coming to see you, he's going to suspect you're involved."

Roman straightened off the desk. "This could make him come after you again."

I didn't bother to deny it. "I hope so, then I can watch them burn each other to the ground."

On my first day back to school, Roman and I argued. He insisted on sending Milo with me, but I didn't want a bodyguard anymore.

"Lionel is dead, and I don't want to live with someone tailing me for the rest of my natural-born life. When we make a move on my father, then he can be my shadow again."

"And I want your natural-born life to be more than just a few more days, *wife*. You're the one who wanted to stir the hornet's nest with your father, and do you think Silas and Jerome Strack don't believe we're the reason Lionel is missing?"

I filled my coffee thermos and grabbed an apple from the fridge. "They know who my adopted family and husband are. Come on, they can't be *that* stupid. I also have your collar and tracker on, and you've bugged my phone, my car, and probably my backpack."

Roman stared at me. "How'd you know about the other trackers?"

The man didn't even bother to deny it. I rolled my eyes. "Because I'm not stupid, and you're a tad overprotective."

Milo snorted and then tried to cover it up with a cough.

Roman studied me. "You have two options, mouthy girl. I can send *two* bodyguards with you who will walk beside you to every class and sit there with you–in class–or we can compromise and Milo will shadow you and be reasonably discreet. But he'll drive you in the SUV, and you won't go anywhere alone for the foreseeable future."

I glanced over at Milo, who leaned against the kitchen counter drinking coffee and watching us with an amused smirk. He'd recovered well, and he looked much better–except for his smirk.

My molars ground together, but I knew Roman wasn't bluffing. "Fine. I see your point but don't expect me to be happy about it. And you're still a bossy asshole."

Roman grinned and stalked toward me. "I would never presume, and I'm fine with being a bossy asshole if it keeps you alive. Milo, make yourself scarce for an hour. Arguing with my wife makes my dick hard, and since she doesn't have to be there for a while, I want to–"

"Oh, my God! Don't finish that sentence," I cried, blushing furiously. Roman didn't stop coming, so I turned and ran into the living room then sprinted down the hall.

Roman

Later that morning, I walked into *Euphoria* to meet with Fennick and Kilian Spade. The Spades were a powerful, violent, strangely close-knit family, and if I needed someone in my corner besides my partners, they weren't a bad choice. That didn't mean they didn't get under my skin.

Samuel stood next to me, and Fenn pounded him on the back as they walked in. "How's Misty?" he asked.

"She's recovering. Luna and Sylvie come by regularly to help keep her from going crazy while she heals."

Fenn grinned. "They probably bring the crazy with them."

Samuel's lip quirked. "It's a good crazy. Misty and Sasha are going to give them pole dancing lessons when Misty heals." Fenn laughed, and I grunted in surprise. Luna hadn't mentioned it.

Kilian shook his head. "That'll be interesting, and not something I *ever* want to see."

Samuel showed us to Fiona's empty office, and Fenn turned to me as soon as the door closed. "What's this about?" Our business interests often competed, so I understood his question.

I gestured to the chairs, and we all sat. "Don't worry. Today isn't the day I inquire about the Spade family trying to buy out the strip club a block away to compete with Euphoria. Or the Spades starting a marijuana grow facility in the same block as Ivan and Drakos's lofts."

Fenn leaned back and laced his hands behind his head. "That's a relief. If Drakos doesn't want industrial neighbors, maybe he shouldn't live in the middle of an industrial neighborhood. And I won't bring up Ivan putting surveillance cameras at the mortuary and cheating his ass off at cards to get his hands on Alexa." Fenn lost his grin and leaned forward. "Or you drugging Luna and coercing her into marrying your sorry ass. Sylvie talking me down is the only reason you're not buried out in the fucking desert somewhere."

Kilian sighed. "Fennick, will you wait until we hear what this is about before you start a war?"

I mentally counted to ten, trying to bring my temper under control. Fennick could drive Mother Theresa herself to take a swing at him. "Luna is *mine*, I don't care about the rest. This meeting is about Luna's parents and the shit storm that's about to erupt. Luna's mother is fucking her uncle, and she's going to bring Montgomery Cross here sooner or later. We need to be prepared."

Fenn grimaced. "The thought of that cold bitch fucking anyone makes my skin crawl, and I have no idea how her two demon-spawn parents created someone like Luna. Whatever your plan is, I want in."

I nodded and laid it out. As we sat and talked, I couldn't help wondering how I'd ended up aligned with the Spade family. Necessity certainly made strange bedfellows.

Kilian shook his head as we finished up our meeting. "Luna just can't catch a break."

Leaning forward, I gazed at him. "She doesn't need to catch a fucking break anymore, she's got me now." He studied me for a few seconds, then smiled.

Chapter 37

Luna

Less than a month after my mother left the second time, she returned with my uncle in tow. They cornered me outside the law school as I walked out with Milo. Her red face and disheveled clothes made me take a step back.

"You fucking bitch! Do you know what you've done?" she screeched as Milo blocked her from getting to me.

"I'll call the campus police and have you arrested if you don't control yourself, lady," Milo warned.

"Fuck you!" she yelled, pointing her finger at us.

"Evelyn, step back. This isn't what we talked about," Alistair muttered as he tugged on her arm.

"I won't step back," she hissed. "You're his daughter, alright. You're the only other person who knew about those accounts. How did you get his passwords? Did your criminal friends hack into my phone or his computer?"

My eyes went round, and I stared at them. "What are you talking about?"

Alistair studied me, and I could see the resemblance to my father. His styled, light brown hair, posture, and clothing screamed good breeding and a country club membership. His eyes also held that same cold, reptilian gaze. Unease slid through me.

"What happened to the money, Luna?" he asked quietly.

I shook my head, my eyes wide in disbelief. "I don't know, and why are *you* here? Are you two... together?" My voice held a note of shock. I wondered briefly if I was overacting, but I would have been shocked if I hadn't already known about them.

"I'm just helping her get away from him. You, of all people, know what he's capable of."

Turning to my mother, I gazed at her earnestly. "I sent you the list of his account numbers, but it's over ten years old and I was eleven when I copied it. Are you sure he even has those accounts?"

"Yes," she hissed, glaring at me with frustration. "And the passwords to those accounts were changed yesterday. Montgomery came after me this morning when he found out they'd been emptied and he couldn't get in." Her voice hitched, and I knew she'd finally been the one on the receiving end of his brutal temper. "If the housekeeper hadn't been there, I don't know what would have happened." My stomach lurched because I had a good idea.

Milo pushed her back and pulled me away from them. "So you came to confront Luna, probably leading that bastard right to her, even if she doesn't know what the hell is going on." He shook his head in disgust. Neither of them looked guilty or ashamed.

My eyes slid to my mother. "That email account you gave me to send the bank account numbers to. Does Alistair have access to it? And the passwords. Could he have gotten those as well?" Then I turned to Alistair. "I don't remember you very well, Uncle, but I do recall you being audited by the IRS, and your company paying some hefty penalties. I doubt you would have any problem cheating my parents out of their blood money."

Evelyn stared at me and opened her mouth as if to deny my allegations, but I witnessed doubt and suspicion slowly seep in.

Alistair scoffed. "What are you insinuating?"

But when he turned to Evelyn, he saw the suspicion in her eyes. I stepped back as they silently stared at each other.

Milo took my arm. "Don't contact Luna again or she'll be filing a restraining order against you." We turned and walked away, leaving them on the steps staring at each other.

On the drive home, I asked Milo to stop by the mortuary to check on Ezra and Sylvie. I had a bad feeling in the pit of my stomach.

He shook his head. "You can call them, but it's too dangerous."

"What did you mean when you told Evelyn she led my father right to me?" I asked.

Milo glanced at me. "Just what I said. I bet your father doesn't trust anyone, and I wouldn't be surprised if he's already aware your mother is having an affair."

The feeling in my stomach grew. "Milo, knowing what you know about my father, if you were him, what would you do?"

He glanced at me. "You and your questions. If I were him, I'd follow her and try to get the money back."

"How?"

"Torture, threats, coercion. Maybe find someone she's attached to–although I doubt that woman loves anyone but herself–and threaten them."

My blood went cold, and I dug my phone out of my backpack and speed-dialed Fenn.

"Hey, Lou? What's up?"

"Where are you?"

"I'm eating lunch. Where are you?"

"Driving with Milo. My mother and Alistair Cross were waiting for me outside the law school. I think Montgomery followed her here, and I'm worried about Ezra and Sylvie."

He hummed. "I'll send someone to check on them, but any-one who tangles with Sylvie is asking to get their balls sucked out of their scrotum." I could hear laughter in his voice.

"Fenn, this isn't funny."

Suddenly, Milo's arm shot out in front of me. "Hang on," he warned. I looked up in time to see the van in front of us suddenly stopped in the middle of a three-lane thoroughfare. Its back door flew open, revealing two men with guns.

"Fuck. This isn't good." Milo swerved sharply to the right, throwing me violently to the side. I heard two pings and realized the men were shooting at us. The SUV bumped up onto the curb, taking out a couple of landscape shrubs. Milo maneuvered around the van and swerved back onto the road.

He glanced in the rearview mirror and swore. Ducking, he pushed my head down. "Stay low!"

Shots thudded against the back end of the SUV, the sounds ringing through the cab. The back window shattered, and two round holes spidered across the front windshield.

Fenn yelled at me through my phone. "Luna, I heard gun-shots. What the fuck is going on?"

"Someone's shooting at us! A gray van stopped in the middle of the road, and they started shooting. I think a white Mercedes is with them."

"Where the fuck are you?"

I looked around and punched the speaker button on my phone. "Milo got around them. We're on Tropicana, just past Eastern. Oh shit, we're coming to a red light!" I screamed as Milo ran the light and swerved sharply, barely missing two cars and a work truck carrying landscape supplies. The van behind us clipped the truck but didn't slow down much, and the Mercedes wound through the stopped cars.

Fenn swore, and I could hear his car starting up. "Come to the mortuary. Take a hard right on Pecos, and drive to the empty lot in the back of the cemetery–we'll probably be there before you. Call Sylvie and warn her you're coming in hot and with a tail."

He hung up without a goodbye, and I speed-dialed Sylvie.

She answered on the first ring. "Hey, bitch. Are you calling to do lunch? I just got done with a consult–"

I interrupted her. "We're coming to the back cemetery parking lot with a tail. We'll be there in about three minutes unless whoever is shooting at us gets lucky. Fenn said he'd be there before us." I took a deep breath, trying to ram down the terror bubbling in my chest. "Sylvie, get Ezra and get out, I don't want you two hurt. There's a gray van with armed men behind us."

"Someone is shooting at you? Fuck! Tell Milo to drive faster! We'll be fine, just keep your head down and don't let them get too far up on your side." I briefly wondered how many car chases she'd been in. Glancing back behind Milo, I saw the van inching up beside us.

I pointed behind him and yelled, "Milo, they're coming–" He yanked the wheel hard to the left, pushing the gray van over the short concrete curb into oncoming traffic. A box truck hit it head-on, the vehicles smashing into each other, and the sound punching through the air. A chain reaction of screeching breaks and fender benders piled up behind them. We kept going, and the white Mercedes changed lanes and continued following us.

"Sylvie, I need to go. Stay safe." I stared, wide-eyed, as Milo barely made the right turn onto Pecos Road, our tires screeching loudly. The Mercedes overshot, but quickly whipped into the Burger King parking lot on the corner. We'd bought ourselves a little time, but not much.

"Milo, take the second right to get to the back parking lot. It's vacant. Fenn said he and his men would beat us there."

He swore, slowing down for a vintage baby blue Cadillac driving ten miles under the speed limit in front of us. He passed the car and got a loud honk.

"You need to call Roman and tell him what's happening," he muttered.

My heart thudded loudly in my chest, and my hands shook as I hit Roman's number. How had things gone from a boring school day to *this*? He didn't answer, so I left a voice message.

"Hi honey, this is your favorite wife. We've had a busy Monday. Evelyn and Alistair ambushed us outside the law school, but that's not all. Several men with guns in a van tried to shoot us off the road. We got rid of the van, but Montgomery Cross and another man are in a white—Milo, turn right here!" I interrupted myself. "Anyway. Fenn is meeting us at the back cemetery parking lot to intercept them. I... I love you. I wanted you to know that, you know, just in case. Okay, bye."

Milo shook his head when I ended the call. "Is that the first time you told him you love him?"

My silence answered for me.

"I'm a sixty-year-old retired FBI agent with more romance and game than you."

"Oh, shut it, and Roman doesn't have a romantic bone in his body so we're a good pair." I noticed Fenn's vehicle and pointed. "There! There's Fenn in the gray minivan." We pulled into the empty back parking lot. The space was only ever used for random storage and landscape equipment.

"Fennick Spade drives a *minivan*?" Milo asked skeptically.

"Yes. He says it's the best all-purpose vehicle he's ever owned. It's probably better not to ask what he means by all-purpose."

We pulled up next to Fenn. "How far behind?" he asked.

"Maybe thirty seconds," Milo answered.

"Park in the middle of the lot." Then Fenn rolled up his window and backed his vehicle to the side of the entrance.

When the Mercedes approached the parking lot, the driver zeroed in on Milo and me sitting in the large SUV in the middle of the lot. As they drove through the entrance, Fennick gunned his minivan and plowed it into the white Mercedes' passenger side where my father sat. The stunned surprise on his face almost made me laugh.

Before the driver could recover, Kilian stepped out and put two bullets in his skull, then turned his gun on my father. It happened so fast and with such precision that I knew they'd done this before.

Less than an hour later, Montgomery Cross–a prominent federal district court judge–sat in the same chair in Ezra's office that my mother had occupied about a month ago. He'd been stripped down to his blue silk boxers and tied to the chair. Kilian had also given Montgomery and his driver's phones to Declan to create a false trail. My father still had a haughty, aloof look on his face, like he thought he'd be walking away unharmed and just needed to bide his time.

Ezra sat at the edge of his desk, looking down at the man. "Hello, Monty. How's your bid for a Ninth Circuit Court of Appeals judgeship going?"

Montgomery smiled coldly. He hated being called Monty. "Hello, Ezra. It's going well. How's your mortuary business and your sprawling, hooligan family?"

"We're fine, and my family is better now that you won't be sending any more nasty surprises our way. Do you happen to know who the men standing behind you are?"

Montgomery awkwardly twisted his head around to look at Roman and Drakos. He already knew Fenn and Kilian. Shrugging, he turned back around. "I believe one of these thugs is my estranged daughter's new husband."

I shook my head at him calling us estranged. Since he'd tried to kill me–twice–I thought of us as more like mortal enemies.

Ezra's lip twitched. "That's partially correct. Let me introduce you to Roman Fowler and Drakos Creed. They're law partners in a rather... famous firm here in Las Vegas. The other partners couldn't make this impromptu meeting, but they'll be here later. I'll let Roman and Drakos fully introduce themselves."

Roman stepped beside my father and looked down at him. "Hello, Monty. I'm the thug who married your daughter. Do you know who else I am?"

Montgomery stared up at him disdainfully. "No. Should I?"

Putting his foot on the side of the chair, Roman slowly pushed it over and sent it crashing on its side. My father's eyes went wide, and when the chair hit the floor, the side of his head cracked against the marble tile floor.

Roman squatted next to him. "I'm also one of your former guests at Bitter Creek Ranch Academy. You remember that hell hole, don't you, Monty? The facility you and your partners touted as one of the most effective reform academies in the United States?"

Montgomery's eyes went wide, and for the first time, I saw fear in his eyes.

"That's right, you spineless, psychotic prick. My partners and I are all former inmates. And your old employees gave us several ideas about what to do with you before we let you die."

Roman stood and looked down at the man. "Did you know it's your brother who's fucking your wife?"

Montgomery went still, then turned his head to look up at Roman. "You lie. Oh, I know she's having an affair, but my brother would never do that."

Drakos straightened off the wall and stepped forward. "We intercepted a phone call a while back." He pulled out his phone and played the recording. We listened to my mother and Alistair discuss how to steal from Montgomery, and he blanched when he heard his brother call his wife darling. When the recording ended, my father looked shell-shocked for a moment. Then he started bargaining.

"I have money. I can transfer it to your accounts in mere hours." No one answered him, and his voice rose. "I'm a federal district court judge, for Christ's sake. Do you think they won't come looking for me? There'll be a manhunt like you've never seen."

Roman smiled coldly. "We're not worried. You're going to send a suicide text to your wife, describing how you couldn't go on when you found out she and your brother were having an affair behind your back, and they planned to run away together."

Montgomery started panting and begging. "Let me go, and I swear I won't tell anyone about this. I've got money in accounts all over the world. You'll be rich beyond anything you could earn as an attorney or even a judge," Montgomery pleaded in a shaky, scared voice. I stared down at him, and some of my bone-deep fear of him dissipated. He looked old and scared, laying there on the floor.

Roman stood back and casually kicked the man in the guts. "That's for eleven-year-old Luna. You're finally figuring out who has you, and what's going to happen to you over the next few hours before you die broken and alone in your own blood and waste. Sylvie has a special casket picked out just for you. It's soundproofed, and you'll be buried alive out in the cemetery where you chased down your own daughter earlier today."

Drakos clucked his tongue. "Cold, calculated revenge is a terrifying thing, isn't it? That gives me an idea, let's keep him in the body fridge here for an hour before we begin playing with him. I remember how hot and cold those fucking cells got at the Ranch."

A wet stain slowly spread against my father's boxers. Drakos sniffed disdainfully as he watched the man pee himself. "Those tables always turn at some point, you spineless fucker."

"Don't do this. I'll give you anything you want." He turned to me. "Luna, don't let them do this. I'm your father, for fuck's sake!"

My body jolted when he addressed me directly, but I fisted my hands and walked over to stoop by him. "Do you remember that day?" I asked quietly. He looked up at me blankly, not understanding my question. "The day I told you I knew what you were doing, and asked you to stop taking money for verdicts and favors. Do you remember what you did to me?"

He swallowed, finally understanding. "I was enraged... out of control. You were my child, acting so righteous and making *threats*. I didn't mean for it to go that far." Tears gathered in his eyes, but I knew they were for himself and not me.

I studied his face–and the fear there–but felt nothing for this evil, pathetic man. "I begged you to stop, to listen. I screamed and blacked out when you dragged me by my broken arm to your closet, and I pleaded for *days* to be let out." My voice cracked, but I kept on. "Then I pleaded with God to let me die, to let the pain and the thirst take me because I was *eleven fucking years old*."

His pleading expression gave way to fear and frustration. "Are you going to let them torture and kill your own *father* out of petty revenge? It will eat away at you."

I stared at him. "You don't know me. I won't feel an ounce of regret about your death, and this isn't about revenge. It's about justice. I'm going home now, knowing they'll do what needs to be done." Roman would understand I couldn't be a part of what came next. But I fully condoned it. Squeezing his hand, I walked out of the office.

Chapter 38

Roman

Ivan and Xander arrived at the mortuary not long after Luna left with Milo. We planned to use some of Sylvie's instruments while we worked Montgomery over, and Drakos grinned thoughtfully as he examined a wicked-looking scalpel with Sylvie Spade's name engraved on it.

I idly wondered how many living people had found themselves in this room tied to a gurney besides Lionel and Monty. The Spade family had some unusual hobbies.

"I can't lie, Cross. This is going to be fun. You're a piece of shit and a fucking blight who *still* thinks he's better than anyone else. But this world will be safer without you."

"You're all nothing but bottom-feeding trash," Montgomery spewed as he tried to thrash on the table. "My men will come after you."

Ivan shook his head. "Your men are dead or incarcerated, you stupid fucktwit. Now it's your turn." He hooked forceps into Montgomery's mouth, pried his teeth open, and stuffed wads of cotton inside as the man spewed garbled insults. Then he slapped a few pieces of duct tape across it. "Now, who wants to go first?"

"Fuck, yes. I will." Drakos raised his hand and grabbed a stool, then sat and rolled it to the foot of the gurney. He studied Montgomery's feet for a moment and grimaced. "You have *foot fungus*, asshole. I planned to rip your toenails off, but this is disgusting."

Ivan leaned over to look at the man's feet, then wrinkled his nose. "Goddamn, you weren't kidding. Use rubber gloves if you're set on it. I'd wear a face shield too."

Drakos sighed dramatically and gloved up. He put a face shield on and grabbed some plyers and a metal bowl. Then he started methodically ripping off Montgomery's toenails as he sang "Everybody Hurts" by *R.E.M.* I'd forgotten Drakos had such a good singing voice. He sometimes used to hum or sing under his breath at the Ranch.

He paused every once in a while to savor Montgomery's pain as the man screamed in agony behind the duct tape, wreathing on the gurney. Drakos threw the last toenail into a bloody steel bowl, then pulled off the stained gloves and threw them in the basin as well.

I stepped to the side of the table and looked down at Montgomery's face. "My turn." I picked up a heavy, industrial-grade fire extinguisher. "You broke Luna's arm–so I'm going to return the favor." I smashed it hard against Montgomery's tibia and heard a distinct crunch. Montgomery sobbed and choked around the cotton jammed in his mouth, tears and mucus running down the sides of his face. He didn't look disdainful or haughty now.

Ivan picked up a cordless nail gun lying on the back counter. "Who keeps a goddamned nail gun in their embalming room?" he asked rhetorically.

Drakos grinned manically. "Sylvie Fucking Spade. That's who."

For the first time, Xander moved, straightening off the wall and holding out his hand. "May I?" Ivan nodded and handed the nail gun over.

Xander walked over and stared down, unblinking, at the man on the table. "I heard what you did to Peter." Montgomery's terrified, pain-filled eyes seemed confused, but Xander explained. "The day you came to Bitter Creek with your investor friends. I was in the cell beside his. He'd tried to run again, and you said you were there to 'teach him a lesson.' I know what you did."

Montgomery's face went gray, and he started shaking his head frantically.

Xander leaned over and murmured in his ear, "*Te videbo in infero.*"

I struggled to translate the Latin phrase, and then it clicked. Xander told Montgomery he'd see him in Hell. If Xander thought he was going to Hell, the rest of us were fucked.

He pressed the nail gun against Montgomery's crotch and pulled the trigger. Then he moved the nail gun down a few inches and pulled it again. Montgomery's head flew back, and the tendons in his neck bulged as a muffled, high-pitched screech tore out of him. He hadn't fully recovered before Xander circled the table and pushed the gun against the backs of Montgomery's hands, the nails gouging into the metal table. Then Xander laid the nail gun down and backed up.

Drakos patted him on the back, his expression grave for once. "Brutal but brilliant, brother. I think Peter would have approved. We've got the rest." Xander stared at Montgomery Cross, bleeding and struggling on the table, then he nodded and walked out. I had a hazy recollection of Peter; he was one of the boys who hadn't made it.

Ivan came forward with a scalpel. "And now it's my turn. I'm going to gut you like a fish and use your intestines to decorate the inside of your casket. This is going to hurt."

A few days later, my cell phone rang as I sat in my office, finishing up some last-minute work before heading home to Luna. I looked forward to going home now since it had gone from a cold mausoleum where I slept and ate an occasional meal, to a warm place full of light, laughter, and reminders of hers scattered around. Diego's name flashed on my screen.

"Rodriguez. What's going on?"

"Hey, motherfucker," Diego chuckled. "I just heard you're having a renewal of vows at the Wild West Wedding Chapel next week. I better be invited."

Gazing out my office window, I grinned as I took in the Las Vegas skyline in the dusky light. "You're invited, and Heath Cassidy is performing the ceremony. He took a liking to Luna when she couldn't get enough of his whorehouse memorabilia. Roy and Rick are *not* invited, though, just so we're clear. I don't want them sitting in the back, fantasizing about double penetrating my wife."

He laughed. "Fair enough, but you can't stop people from having a few thoughts when your wife looks that fine."

I sighed. "She asked Heath a million and one questions, and he offered to teach her to shoot."

"He only does that when he *really* likes someone."

"I know. How are things at the bar and shop?" The Area Fifty-Three biker bar was located near Bonanza and Maryland Parkway in North Las Vegas and was usually packed with bikers, hotheads, and clueless tourists. Diego and Ivan were partners and owned the bar together. It was in a rougher part of town and an MC club hangout.

"Well, neither has burned down yet. I'm turning business away at the shop, and Fifty-Three is always jammed with fuckin' rubberneckers who have death wishes. There's been a lot of activity about Luna's father, though. A few members have been pulled in for questioning."

I leaned back in my chair. "I'm not surprised, we've been questioned too. Luna gave her statement to an officer, but she hasn't seen her dad in years." It was better for Diego and his crew to have plausible deniability.

"I also heard through the drug trafficking grapevine that the drug syndicate cracked down on the Stracks, and Silas is going crazy again because his other son is missing now."

Xander stepped into my doorway, and I waved him inside. He'd let his hair down and untucked his shirt. I looked down to check and see if he still had his shoes on. "We're aware," I told Diego. "If you hear of the Stracks making a move, I'd appreciate a heads up."

"You got it. I'll see you next week at the Wild West Wedding Chapel. Lucky fucker."

I set my phone down. "Did you hear that? A few of Diego's men got dragged in and questioned."

Xander nodded. "It's fine, since they don't know anything. Have you told Luna about the vow renewal next week?"

"No. I'll tell her tonight."

He cocked his head and studied me. "For such a controlling man, you've done a good job of almost ruining things with the one woman who matters."

"What do you mean, asshole?"

He crossed his arms. "How you met, what you planned to do to her, how you drugged and tricked her into marrying you. Have you even told her how you feel?"

Scowling, I stood and shrugged into my jacket. "That's none of your damn business."

"You're my brother, Roman. So I decided it's my business. Don't be a coward, and don't let those fuckers take anything else from you. Tell her how you feel and lock it down."

Xander rarely talked this much, so I knew he thought it was important. I paused at his serious tone, thought about what he'd said, and nodded. "I will. Now get out your ass of my way so I can go home to my wife." He grinned and stepped aside.

Chapter 39

Luna

When I entered the quiet house, a light from a side table lamp cast soft shadows through the room. I searched for signs of Roman as I walked into the kitchen. A bottle of whiskey sat on the counter, and I inhaled its faint smoky tang. Heading to the back patio, I found him sitting in a lounger beside the lit stone firepit, its warmth warding off the desert chill.

He smiled and patted the cushion. "Hello, wife. Come here."

"Hello, husband. It's good to be home." I crawled up the over-sized lounger and snuggled into his warmth. His scent and the feel of his muscular arms around me felt more like home than anything I'd ever experienced, and I just breathed him in for a moment.

"Diego called today," he murmured.

"What'd he have to say?"

He filled me in on Diego's phone call. I'd told the police what I knew when they interviewed me, leaving out what would implicate us and that my father had been tortured and buried alive. Minor details.

He pulled me closer and held up his phone. "Do you remember calling my phone and leaving a voicemail that day?"

My face went warm, and I shifted uncomfortably. Things had been hectic lately, and we'd talked mostly about my father and covering our tracks. I figured he'd maybe listened to my voicemail, deleted it, and thought no more about it. But his arm tightened around me, and his eyes didn't leave my face.

I cleared my throat. "When we were being chased, Milo told me to call you and let you know what was happening."

"Do you remember what you said?"

Exhaling a long breath, I laid my head on his shoulder and stopped pretending I didn't know exactly what he was asking. "Yes. I told you I love you."

His fingers gently stroked up and down my arm, as we sat quietly for a few moments, then he leaned over and kissed my hair. "When I listened to your message, I'd never been more terrified or happy in my entire life. I didn't know a person could feel those two emotions at once."

A wave of adrenaline surged through me, and my heart started pounding. Over the last month, I vacillated between hope and despair, knowing I'd fallen in love with this beautiful, scarred, possessive man who also happened to be my husband, but wondering if he could ever love me back.

"Why were you happy?"

He turned my face to him, searching my eyes in the dim firelight. "Because you love me, and I love you. I've known for a while, but I wanted to give you time to grow into it. I hoped like hell you would, but I was afraid it could never happen after the way I maneuvered you into marrying me. And because of my... quirks." He stared down at the collar on my neck, his fingers caressing me there.

I cupped his face and smiled. "I love you too, *because* of who and what you are. We're quite a pair, and you didn't just *maneuver* me into marrying you. I vaguely recall drugs, unlawful detention, and coercion being involved."

He slid his hand lower and cupped my breast before running his thumb across my hard nipple. "I plead the fifth. Now open for me so I can kiss–then fuck–my favorite wife."

I reached around to grab his perfect ass. "Who said you aren't a big romantic at heart?"

"You're my heart, Sweetness, and I want to spend the rest of our godforsaken lives together. I love you."

My vision went blurry, and a tear escaped as I buried my face in his neck. "I've never felt like this. Thank you for loving me, and giving me a home. Now let's try not to torture and kill anyone else–and maybe stay out of trouble for five minutes."

He grinned and pushed a strand of hair behind my ear. "If it's to protect you, I make no promises."

Luna

White roses and greenery adorned the archway leading to the small wedding chapel, where Roman and I would soon exchange our vows. I hoped I'd remember this ceremony better than the last one. Sylvie, Alexa, and I stood outside the chapel doors with the surprise wedding gift I'd gotten for Roman, and Ezra waited just inside. Ezra had teared up when I asked him to walk me down the aisle. I didn't understand why he'd seemed surprised since he and his family were the reason I'd turned out okay.

Roman didn't tell me he planned this ceremony until a week ago, but somehow we'd pulled together a nice little celebration. The Wild West Wedding Chapel was a little kitschy, but I loved its charm and history.

"What do you think of Heath?" I asked Sylvie and Alexa as we waited for Ezra to give us the signal.

Alexa shrugged. "He might be a cowboy, but he still reminds me of them." Sylvie and I knew she was referring to the partners.

Sylvie nodded and turned to me. "They're pushy, arrogant assholes—all except Xander. But I can't argue that you love Roman for some ungodly reason. If you didn't, I would've found a way to strap his ass to my embalming table and teach him a lesson for everything he put you through."

An excited yip sounded next to me, interrupting Sylvie's tirade. I looked down at the little ball of chocolate lab fur straining on her leash. The puppy, who I'd temporarily named Hazel, was so adorable, and after the story Klim had told me about Roman's dog, I thought she'd be the perfect wedding gift.

When we heard the music start to play, Ezra cracked the door, smiled at us, and held out his arm for me. "It's time, ladies." Alexa and Sylvie held open the doors, and I led the little puppy inside. I saw Roman's eyes flare with delight and shock when he saw who trailed beside us, sniffing everything as she went. He grinned and shook his head.

Ezra patted my arm approvingly. "I think he likes his gift."

"Damn it. Do I have to be nice to him now?" Sylvie whined quietly as I handed her Hazel's leash.

Alexa smirked. "I know. I'm starting to like the asshole too."

I wore the beautiful, shimmery white dress Roman bought me months ago when I was his intern, and it seemed perfect for today. Before I moved to Roman's side, Sylvie squeezed my hand. "I love this for you—my sweet, beautiful, adopted sister. You don't know it, but when we befriended each other all those years ago, you saved me, too. I'm so happy for you."

My eyes started to water, and I turned and gave her and Alexa hugs, then walked over to Roman's side. Drakos, Ivan, and Xander stood next to Roman, and when Sylvie and Hazel passed by Drakos, the little terror sniffed his expensive leather shoe, squatted on the tip, and peed. Drakos growled and pulled his foot back. Sylvie burst out laughing and cooed at Hazel. "You're such a good, sweet little girl."

I shook my head and scooped the little menace up, then turned to Roman and held her out. "I've been calling her Hazel, but you can name her whatever you want."

Roman kissed my cheek, then took the small puppy in his arms and laid her on his chest, not caring about dog hair or pee dribbles. The little girl snuggled in like she knew he was her home, and I understood how she felt.

Then Roman pulled me to stand in front of Heath. "I love you, Sweetness. Thank you for the gift. Now, let's do this before Hazel decides to pee on me too." I laughed and leaned in to kiss them both.

Afterword

Thank you for reading *Barristers & Bones!* If you liked this book, please leave a review on Amazon and other book review sites. <u>Even a simple star rating helps</u>. Your reviews and feedback are critical in helping authors share our novels and grow our reader bases.

Do you want a chance to win free signed books, special sneak peek previews of new releases, and bonus features? Sign up for my newsletter at jlbrannick.com.

Check out my other books, including the Palm Springs Poolside Series.

The law school in Las Vegas is fantastic, internships are voluntary, and the mentorship program is phenomenal. I've also taken artistic license to create the *House of Spades* world, but I contend Las Vegas is like the Wild West.

The research for this book probably put me on a few watchlists. If any of you are reading this, *see?* It all really was for a novel. Mostly. Thank you to my favorite local mortician, who wishes to remain anonymous, for answering strange—and strangely specific—questions. You were very patient and didn't grimace (much) at all!

To my family. You are my heart and foundation. I appreciate your support, humor, and patience.

Thank you also to my beta readers and editors, Shelby Nesbitt, Gennifer Ulman, and Smart Mouth Editing, Inc. Gennifer, the scrotum scene is for you!

To my cover designer, Maggie Jackson, at Smart Mouth Publishing LLC.

Follow me on social media and subscribe to my newsletter for the latest news, free giveaways, exclusive bonuses, and new releases!

www.ingramcontent.com/pod-product-compliance
Lightning Source LLC
Chambersburg PA
CBHW022008310726
48972CB00006B/1574